1 A 8/19

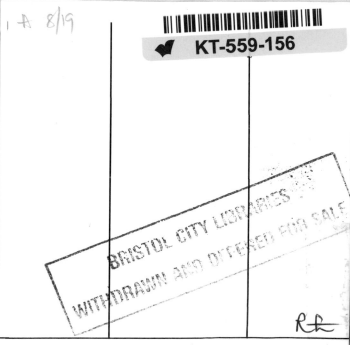

KT-559-156

R.L.

Please return/renew this item by the last date shown
on this label, or on your self-service receipt.

To renew this item, visit **www.librarieswest.org.uk**
or contact your library

Your borrower number and PIN are required.

LibrariesWest

4 4 0060030 9

Discover more at millsandboon.co.uk

ONE NIGHT
IN PROVENCE

BARBARA WALLACE

ONE NIGHT WITH
THE COWBOY

BRENDA HARLEN

MILLS & BOON

First Published in Great Britain 2019
by Mills & Boon, an imprint of HarperCollinsPublishers,
1 London Bridge Street, London, SE1 9GF

One Night In Provence © 2019 Barbara Wallace
One Night with the Cowboy © 2019 Brenda Harlen

ISBN: 978-0-263-27256-7

0819

MIX
Paper from
responsible sources
FSC **FSC™ C007454**
www.fsc.org

This book is produced from independently certified FSC™
paper to ensure responsible forest management.

For more information visit: www.harpercollins.co.uk/green

Printed and bound in Spain
by CPI, Barcelona

ONE NIGHT
IN PROVENCE

BARBARA WALLACE

For Jenna, Shirley, and Donna (the real ones).
I couldn't have gotten through this without you.

And, as always, for my hero, Pete. I love you.

CHAPTER ONE

Early August

Is the place as gorgeous as it looked in the brochure? Wait, don't tell me. I don't want to know. Tell me it's horrible.

SUNSHINE WARMED JENNA'S face as she read her friend's text. Setting down her champagne, she quickly snapped a photo, knowing the camera phone could never do justice to the Provençal sea of gold and lavender. Her phone dinged in response almost immediately.

I hate you.

Jenna snorted. She shouldn't laugh. Poor Shirley was back in Nantucket with shingles instead of sitting here in the sunshine with her.

She quickly typed a response.

Would it make you feel better if I told you everyone looks like a swimsuit model? I'm the pastiest person here.

That wasn't exactly true. There were definitely some gorgeous people floating around, but there were plenty of pale tourists like Jenna as well. What was a little white lie, though, if thinking her best friend felt out of place made Shirley feel a little better?

I'm not going to have nearly as much fun without you with me.

That *was* true. Shirley was her wing person, both at the nursing home where they worked and off duty. In fact, it was Shirley who'd heard about the Merchant charity auction and convinced Jenna to bid on this Provençal vacation. Without her, Jenna wouldn't be sitting on the terrace of a centuries-old French castle drinking champagne for breakfast.

Better double down on your efforts, then. Otherwise, Beatrice will come back to haunt you. She expected you to have as much fun as possible.

I plan to!

No way was she risking the posthumous wrath of her favorite patient.

Unfortunately, I've lost my translator.

Shirley was the one who could speak French. An ex-boyfriend had given her an immersion software course one Christmas with the promise of a French vacation.

Besides, there's only so much trouble a person can get into by themselves.

A trio of bouncing dots on her screen indicated that Shirley was typing a reply.

Go find a sexy Frenchman to help you. I can think of plenty of trouble you can get into with one of those.

Jenna laughed out loud, causing the couple at the next table to look over. She waved her phone at them to show she wasn't some random crazy person before replying.

R U kidding? With my luck it'll be some poser.

You think everyone is a poser.

With good reason. Nantucket attracted them like a magnet. Thirty K millionaires, she and Shirley liked to call them. Guys with rented boats and empty bank accounts who spent their summer weekends pretending they were part of the beautiful people with the hopes of scoring with as many women as possible.

The South of France isn't the White Whale Tavern.

It's probably worse. I'd rather be haunted by Beatrice, thank you.

Shirley responded by sending a GIF of a dancing ghost.

If you do find a Frenchman, let me know. If I'm going to be covered in sores, I need some kind of vicarious thrill.

Don't hold your breath.

I never do.

After a few more exchanges, Shirley signed off to go back to sleep, it being early morning in New England. Jenna signaled the server for a second glass of champagne. Because when in France…

On the other side of the terrace railing, the landscape rolled out like a sea of purple, green and yellow. A picture postcard come to life, only better.

Ten days in a French castle at the height of lavender season. That's how Merchant Hotels had described the dream package Jenna bid on at the auction. The accompanying brochures made the trip sound magical. Now that she was here, she realized the pictures didn't begin to do the magic justice.

She raised her glass in honor of the woman who'd made the trip possible. "Thanks for the adventure, Beatrice. I'll make the most of it."

Lifting the glass just a bit higher, she snapped a picture and sent the shot to Shirley. Then she switched seats so she could get a photograph of her drinking with the fields behind her. If she was going to rub salt in Shirley's wounds, then she might as well rub a lot of salt.

Unfortunately, she was the only millennial alive who couldn't shoot a decent selfie. She either looked like she was squinting at the sky or like she had two extra chins. After four aborted attempts, she gave up and tossed the phone on the table.

A shadow crossed her table. "*Excusez-moi de vous déranger,*" said a deep voice, "but would you care for some assistance?"

Ho. Ly. Cow. Shirley would be choking on her champagne right now. Jenna nearly did. She was looking at quite possibly the most gorgeous man she'd ever seen. He stood at the ready in a double-breasted suit similar to what the other hotel managers wear wearing, looking like someone plucked him from a hotel brochure. In fact, Château de Beauchamp should put him in the brochure; they'd probably triple their reservation rate. Who knew jaws that chiseled existed in real life?

Granted, he was a tad on the lean side, but then who needed muscles when you could wear a suit with style and had eyes the color of the fields outside?

And…she was staring. As though she'd never seen a handsome man before.

Not this handsome, a voice whispered in her head.

He knew he was handsome, too. She could tell from the way he smiled, his teeth all white and perfect.

"Your camera," he said in heavily-accented English. "I couldn't help noticing your frustration. I would be glad to take your photograph, if you'd like. You are trying to take a photo in front of the lavender, are you not?"

From the way he focused all his attention on her, you would think there was nothing else he would rather do than help her with her vacation shots. Her stomach fluttered, and she had to remind herself this was France's— or rather the Merchant Hotel chain's—version of five-star service.

"Thank you," she said. "I'm afraid I don't have the selfie trick down yet."

"That is a good thing, is it not? Means you're busy looking at things other than yourself."

Smooth, the way he threw in the compliment. "I'm trying to break that habit on this trip. My friend Shirley was unable to come, so I want to document everything so I can show her when I get home."

"Well, you won't find a better backdrop in all of Provence than this one right here," he replied. "Why don't you stand by the rail? The view is its most breathtaking up close."

Jenna would call him biased, except that he might be right. She'd never seen so much color in one place. Maybe it was an effect brought on by the champagne, but everything seemed more vivid here. The lavender's purple deeper, the sunflowers' gold more brilliant. Even the mountains, with their shadows, looked like they were bathed in blue and green.

"You're American," her photographer noted. "Is this your first visit to Château de Beauchamp?"

"Yes, it is." First time to the château. First time to France. First time outside the United States since spring break in college. "I couldn't resist the idea of staying in a real-life castle. Especially one that's a thousand years old. America wasn't even a gleam in Columbus's eye then."

"I hate to disappoint you, but you've been shortchanged by a few hundred years."

"What do you mean?"

He joined her at the railing. As he eased his way around the chair, Jenna noted the fluid grace with which he moved. Like water rounding a bend.

"This isn't the original castle," he told her.

"But the brochure said the Château de Beauchamp had stood watch over the valley since the eleventh century. Were they making that up?" If the hotel misled her, she was going to be really ticked off.

"*A* Château de Beauchamp has stood guard," he

replied. "Just not this one. The original fell into ruin sometime in the sixteenth century. If you look beyond that clump of trees to the right, you'll see the remains of the tower."

A gold signet ring on his pinkie finger glittered in the sun as he pointed. Squinting, Jenna made out the peaks of toppled stone.

"The d'Usay family built this as a replacement. They called it the *Château Neuf*."

"So I'm staying in a five-hundred-year-old castle instead of a thousand-year-old one."

"I trust you're not too disappointed?"

"I'll survive."

"I hope so. It would be a shame if you were left unsatisfied."

Damn, if the double entendre didn't send a quiver through her. If it was a double entendre. The jet lag had thrown her instincts off.

"Have you taken the tour?" he asked.

"Not yet." A castle tour was one of the suggested itinerary items listed in her information package, but Jenna had yet to book anything. She'd told Shirley it was because she wanted to be spontaneous, but really it was because she'd been too busy before departure. "I thought I'd take a day and soak in the atmosphere first."

"You should, if only to appreciate the atmosphere in which you are soaking. Did you know, for example, that the wine cellar doubled as a meeting locale for *les Compagnies du Soleil* during the White Terror?"

"The white what?"

"When members of the region took revenge on those who supported the revolution. That would be *our* revolution, by the way," he added. A dimple in his left cheek punctuated his cheeky grin.

"You mean they were rebelling against the rebellion?" she asked.

"We prefer to think of it as an attempt to preserve tradition. And perhaps their heads."

"No, they definitely wouldn't want to lose those." She wondered how many women had lost their heads over this guy. She'd met men like him before. Players, albeit not as suave.

Or as handsome, the voice reminded her.

Men like him were the worst, because they tricked you. Most poseurs were so obvious you knew not to take them seriously. This kind of guy, however... This was the kind of guy who sucked you in with their smoothness, leading you to believe he were sincerely interested in more than sex. Next thing you knew, you were spending your life like a puppet, dancing a jig every time he jerked your string.

This guy looked like someone who pulled a lot of strings.

He leaned an elbow against the rail, allowing his eyes to lock with Jenna's. "Speak for yourself, mademoiselle. Sometimes losing your head can be rather fun."

"Not in my experience," Jenna replied.

"Perhaps you haven't had the right experience."

If she were in Nantucket, this would be the point where she told him to take a hike. Instead, whether it was the jet lag, the champagne on an empty stomach or the heady French atmosphere, she found herself leaning into his gaze. The hue was far deeper and richer than she realized. More blue-violet than purple, making them even more unique. And captivating...

"How did they make out? The rebels against the rebellion. Did they keep their heads?" she asked him.

"You'll have to take the tour to find out." The dimple reappeared. "Unless you would like a more personal tour."

Despite knowing better, the offer went straight to the base of her spine.

"French history just happens to be a personal passion of mine," he told her. "Particularly the d'Usay family."

Wait? Was he offering her an actual tour? "Won't you get in trouble? With the hotel?" she added when he gave her a quizzical look. There was personalized service, and then there was personalized service. "I wouldn't want to take you away from the other guests."

An amused smile tugged the corner of his mouth. "I'm sure the other guests will survive."

Jenna debated the offer, turning her phone end over end as she thought. What the heck—it was only a walk around the hotel, not a marriage proposal. Besides, unlike most guys on the make, this one was actually entertaining. If he got annoying, she could always beg off by blaming jet lag. "In that case, I would love a tour."

"Wonderful. My name is Philippe, by the way."

"Jenna Brown."

"*Enchanté*, Jenna Brown."

Amazing how an accent could turn the plainest of New England names exotic and sensual. Particularly when the words were accompanied by a sweep of admiring eyes. Again, she found herself throwing out Nantucket rules. Instead of being insulted, she felt goose bumps trail in its wake.

He motioned toward the door. "Shall we?"

Jenna scooped up her wine on the way past her table. Let the adventure begin.

"An auction, you say?"

"A fund-raising auction," Jenna replied. "People bid on different experiences, each to be held at a Merchant hotel. One hundred percent of the profits went to build a clinic for recovering drug addicts on Cape Cod. Our area has a terrible opioid addiction issue."

They were descending a spiral stone staircase, having discovered the door to the western tower was locked. Philippe might have been flirting when he offered a tour, but, to her surprise, he took his tour guide duties quite seriously. Jenna found herself treated to a master class in regional history and the colorful role the d'Usay family played in it.

At some point, the conversation had turned to her, though, and now she was explaining about the inheritance that brought her to France.

"Sounds like a very noble cause," Philippe remarked.

"It is, although I have to confess that when my friend Shirley convinced me to go, helping the opioid crisis wasn't my primary motive. I went looking for adventure."

"Is that so?" He stopped midstep.

The spark in his eyes set the goose bumps skittering again. Tempted as she was to pretend otherwise—because why not pretend on vacation?—it was time to burst his bubble. In case he thought her a rich American on holiday. "The vacation," she clarified. "I'm a nurse in a nursing home back in Massachusetts. One of my patients left me an inheritance with orders that I use the money to have an adventure."

"Interesting terms for an inheritance." If he was disappointed by her lack of wealth, the reaction didn't show on his face. She'd studied closely to notice a change. His eyes remained intently focused on her.

"Not if you knew Beatrice. She was like Auntie Mame on steroids. Wore red lipstick and a silk kimono right up to the end." She smiled at the memory. "The two of us would watch travel documentaries, and she would mock me for not having seen enough of the world. 'If you're not careful, you grow old and boring,' she used to tell me."

"That doesn't sound very sweet."

"It was all in good fun. I made the mistake of telling her I'd never been farther than Mexico on spring break. She insisted she was going to leave the nursing home and the two of us would take one last adventure together."

Feeling a lump rising in her throat, she looked away so he wouldn't see the moisture teasing her eyes. "Adding the stipulation to the inheritance was her way of making sure one of us did."

"How fortunate for us you decided to have your adventure here."

"My friend Shirley was supposed to come, too, but unfortunately she got sick at the last minute."

"Well, if you find you need company…"

The practiced way the words came off his tongue said she wasn't the first to hear them. Didn't stop her insides from growing warm, however.

"It's okay. I'm a pro at having fun on my own."

Sidestepping the offer for the moment, she pointed to a giant portrait hanging on the wall across from the bottom step. "What can you tell me about this painting?"

The middle-aged couple in 1930s period clothing looked to be overseeing the tower traffic. There was something very striking about the portrait. The couple looked intimidating, but in a regal way. From their place on the wall, their eyes could judge everyone who went up and down the stairs.

"That is Antoinette and Simon d'Usay." Philippe stopped and leaned against the stairway's stone rail. "They were the last of the d'Usays to actually live in the castle. After World War I, they built Château d'Usay."

"On the other side of the lavender fields." Jenna had read about the smaller château, which was still three times as large as anything she'd seen, in the guidebook. Seeing it, and its rolling purple fields, was one of the trip highlights she'd most been looking forward to.

"You won't be disappointed," he replied when she told him. "Château d'Usay remains the largest producer of lavender in the region. Many of the top perfumes in the country rely on d'Usay blossoms for their scents."

There was pride in his voice. She wondered if all the locals felt this way or if he had a particular affinity for the d'Usay family because of their rich history.

She thought of her own family and its history of codependency and bad decisions. There definitely weren't residents of Somerville waxing proudly about the Brown family's contribution to society.

"So much history attached to one family," she mused. "In a way, it's a shame they decided to sell the castle."

"Buildings this age are very expensive to maintain," he replied. "Mold, rot, water damage—they take their toll. Better to let a corporation keep the building in existence rather than let it crumble from neglect like other abandoned French relics."

He had a point. Even if the castle weren't centuries old, the size alone would make upkeep a fortune. Slowly, she made her way down the rest of the staircase until she stopped in front of the painting. The couple looked familiar. A byproduct of spending weeks studying hotel literature and web guides, she'd bet. "Does the family still live in the region?"

"If you call a single person a family. There is only one direct descendent left."

"Really." She'd expected him to say that half the valley was related to them or something. Glancing over, she noticed Philippe studying the painting with a frown.

"Life hasn't been good to the d'Usays over the last decade," he said. "Only two of Simon and Antoinette's children lived to adulthood, and only one of them had children. A son, Marcel. He died in the late twentieth century."

"How sad. For a family to survive a thousand years only to fade away."

"Happens to all families, eventually." His frown sharpened momentarily, only to disappear just as quickly. Once again he was the charming flirt from the terrace. "So let us talk about more pleasant topics. Such as dinner. Would you care to join me this evening?"

So smooth. Such polish. Jenna had no doubt he would pull out all the stops and that dinner would be a romantic, seductive affair. Designed to melt her heart and inhibitions.

"There aren't rules about fraternizing with guests?" she asked, pretty sure that he wouldn't care if there were.

Sure enough. That amused smile from earlier returned to his face, and he shrugged. "I won't tell if you won't."

She met his gaze again. Dear Lord, but his eyes sucked you in. She'd bet he made every woman he met feel like the only woman in the world. Until the next woman crossed his path, that was.

"I appreciate the offer, but…" Shirley was going to kill her. "I think I'm going to stay in and order from room service tonight. Alone," she added, for extra emphasis.

He took the rejection like a pro. "Another time, then. We can have what you Americans call a rain check."

"Sure." Like that would happen. "Thank you for the tour."

"It was my pleasure." She gasped as he caught her hand and raised it to his lips. *"Au revoir*, Jenna Brown," he said, planting a soft kiss on her knuckles. "I look forward to our paths crossing again."

"Au revoir," Jenna replied. She stood on the stairs and watched as he strolled away in search of someone else to charm. The first, and likely the only, sexy Frenchman of the trip.

Oh well, she thought, rubbing her knuckles, *easy come, easy go.*

Philippe waited until the American disappeared around the corner before heading to the front desk. The petite brown-haired woman—girl, really—straightened with recognition. "Is there something I can do for you?" she asked. Philippe didn't miss the eagerness sparkling in her eyes, or the way she flipped her hair over her shoulder when she spoke.

"Oui," he replied. "I was wondering if you might do me a favor… The American, Mademoiselle Brown…"

"Whatever he asks, Nicole, the answer is no."

Yves St. Dumond, the hotel manager, suddenly appeared in the office doorway. A large man with thickset features and silver hair, he placed a beefy hand on Nicole's shoulder. "This hotel is not your personal playground, Philippe. If you want to pick up women, go someplace else."

"I'm hurt." Philippe pressed a hand to his chest. "Haven't you known me long enough to know that if I wanted to seduce a guest, I wouldn't need to bother your staff?" To prove a point, he winked at Nicole, who, on cue, blushed.

"Then what is it you need?"

A distraction. Something—or someone—to keep him from falling into a week-long dark hole.

"It's August," he replied.

Yves's expression immediately softened. *"Je suis désolé. I wasn't thinking. I lost track of the date."*

"So did I. Almost." In the end, the calendar reminded him, like it always did.

The consistency was almost humorous. Every year he vowed that this would be the year he broke the pattern, but apparently he was a glutton for punishment, because he insisted on returning for harvest every year. How could he not? Harvest remained a tradition in his family—even if he was a family of one. It was the least he could do for his family. His penance for being the last of the d'Usays.

He forced a smile. "Don't worry. I'll be out of your hair soon enough." He just had to survive a few weeks. Come September, the yearning for whatever it was he yearned for would cease and he'd return to his apartment in Arles.

"In the meantime, why are you interested in Mademoiselle Brown? She's certainly not your usual type."

"No, she is not." Philippe preferred shallow women who had expensive tastes and short attention spans. Women like him. Jenna Brown with her copper hair and shorts with tiny whales was as far from his type as he could imagine.

Perhaps that was why he'd noticed her the moment he stepped onto the hotel terrace. Sitting there, getting frustrated with her inability to take a self-portrait. He found that particular lack of skill extremely attractive.

Add what was obviously a sharp mind and dry wit… Yes, she was exactly the distraction he needed. "Nevertheless, I found her very stimulating and would enjoy spending more time with her."

"Meaning you've already spent time with her. Why didn't you simply ask her to dinner? Wait a moment…" Yves's eyes widened. "Don't tell me she turned you down."

"I believe it is called a rain check," Philippe replied.

Something else that stirred his interest. There had been obvious attraction in her green eyes, and yet she'd still said no. He couldn't remember the last time a woman rebuffed his advances. What his looks didn't accomplish, his name usually did.

And there was what might be the most attractive thing of all about Mademoiselle Brown: she had no clue as to who he was. Their interaction had been based solely on his charm and her interest in their conversation. He found it amazingly refreshing.

"Which brings me back to why I need Nicole's assistance," he said. "She's going to help me cash in my rain check."

A frisson of anticipation passed through him. He couldn't wait to see Jenna Brown's face when their paths crossed again.

CHAPTER TWO

JENNA HAD A HEADACHE. Too much sun and strong floral aroma had left a knot behind her eyes. She needed a glass of water and some pain relievers. Hopefully the word *aspirin* was the same in French?

Day two of her adventure wasn't off to a very auspicious start.

She never did eat dinner. She'd fallen into a deep sleep shortly after she returned to her room and woke up before dawn starved and eager to start her adventure. Since Philippe had sounded so enthusiastic about the excursion to Château d'Usay, she took his advice and signed up. Part of her wondered if she'd see him at the front desk when she went downstairs, but the only person she saw was a sweet girl named Nicole who grinned every time Jenna gave her name. She wondered if Philippe had found a dinner companion after they parted ways? Immediately, she pictured a leggy French heiress and felt a prick of annoyance in her stomach. More because she was thinking about Philippe than because of the woman she imagined. It wasn't like her to dwell on a random stranger. Philippe with his mesmerizing eyes should be no exception.

She had to give him props, though. The tour was as

interesting as he'd promised. They began in the green-house, where she and other visitors learned about the various varieties and uses for lavender. The d'Usays, they were told, grew *lavande fine*, or "true" lavender rather than the more popular *lavandin*.

"The *lavandin* actually produces more oil per flower," the guide told them. "The family has a separate property a few kilometers away, which provides the bulk of their harvest. Here at Château d'Usay, however, they continue to grow *lavande fine* as they always have."

The family certainly liked to maintain its tradition, didn't it? Jenna crouched to take a picture of the spiny purple flower up close. The deep purple blossoms reminded her of Philippe's eyes.

After a visit to the fields, where they were given a lesson on Provençal climate and agriculture, as well as ample photo opportunities, their group made their way across a limestone pavilion to the château itself, the final stop before they visited the lavender store. It was in the fields that the knot had morphed into a full-blown headache. Making matters worse, today's tour guide had a high-pitched voice that turned into a high pitched squeak whenever she feigned enthusiasm. She must have chirped the phrase, "In the world!" at least a dozen times, her voice piping upward each time.

The group made their way up the front steps, where they found themselves in a large marble entranceway dominated by a large staircase. Several audible sighs could be heard as the temperature dropped several degrees.

Their guide pointed to a portrait guarding the entrance. Simon and Antoinette d'Usay, captured many years after the painting in the castle. Although both had gray hair and were noticeably heavier, their eyes were still sharp and intimidating. "This is Simon and Antoinette d'Usay, who built the château after the First World War. It's considered one of the finest examples of French Renaissance Revival architecture in the world. I'm sorry, sir, the staircase is off-limits."

She was talking to one of the older tourists, who had moved too close to the velvet rope blocking the stairs. "Those lead to the family's private rooms."

"Does the Comte d'Usay still live here?" someone asked.

"We do not use titles in France. They were eliminated with the revolution. To answer your question, however, Monsieur d'Usay lives most of the year in Arles. Although he does visit from time to time. Now, follow me through these doors. The next room we'll see is the main salon, or as the family called it, *le Salon des Fleurs*."

Jenna hung in the back of the line as the guide led the group through the double doors. No way she was going to handle that voice for the entire tour without taking an aspirin. There had to be something for sale at the store. Surely, she wasn't the only person to take the tour and suffer from lavender overload.

Her sandals made a tiny squeaking noise on the tile as she turned around.

"Running away, Mademoiselle Brown?" a familiar voice asked.

Philippe? Her ears had to be playing tricks on her. Why would he be touring the mansion? When she looked to her left, however, there he was. Walking down the stairs in a pair of faded jeans and a white linen shirt that gaped ever so nicely. As opposed to her mouth, which simply gaped. *What on earth?*

He grinned, the dimple in full bloom. "Didn't I tell you our paths would cross again?"

"Yes, but how did…?" *Wait a second.* Jenna rewound her thoughts. He was coming *down the stairs. Where the family stayed.*

"No way," she said. "You can't be…"

"Can't be what?" Stepping off the bottom step, he side-stepped the velvet barrier to join her at the room's center. "You aren't wearing your little whales today," he said.

Took her a moment to realize he was referring to her shorts. After noting yesterday that none of the other women at the resort wore shorts, she'd ditched them in favor of a Lilly Pulitzer shift and platform sandals. The pink tropical print still marked her as an American tourist, but at least she was slightly more stylish.

"No," she replied.

"You look lovely."

"Thank you. What were you doing upstairs?"

"What do you think?"

"You work here?" But even as she asked, she knew the answer. He was dressed too casually, and his eyes sparkled too brightly for an employee.

"How could I possible work here and at the hotel?" he asked before leaning in and adding, "That is what you thought yesterday, is it not?"

"You were wearing a hotel uniform."

"Was I?"

Yes. The same dark suit as the concierge and desk manager. Granted, his was more finely tailored, and he hadn't been wearing a name tag, but…

She looked over her shoulder at the portrait on the wall, before looking back to Philippe. He bore the same regal carriage as Simon and Antoinette.

"Philippe d'Usay, at your service." He swept his arm wide and bowed. "Welcome to Château d'Usay."

Shoot. Her. Now. "Why didn't you say anything? If I'd known, I would never have…"

"Been such relaxed and enjoyable company?" he supplied. "Precisely why I didn't correct your mistake. You have to understand, everyone in Avignon knows who I am. I found it refreshing to meet someone who did not."

How nice for him that she could be a novelty. She wasn't sure what was worse—her mistaking him for an employee or his deception. "Must have been very entertaining, having to give me that tour."

"It was."

And what if she'd said yes to his dinner invitation? How long would he have carried on the masquerade? Through the meal? Later? "Well, bully for you."

"Jenna, wait. I'm not explaining myself well. You think I was playing a game."

"Weren't you?" Her eyes traveled to where he'd caught her hand as she tried to turn away. The gold signet ring on his little finger gleamed against his tanned skin. Ten to one that was a d'Usay family crest engraved on it. She felt like such an idiot.

"Not the way you think. I did not intentionally mean to mislead you."

Jenna raised a brow.

"All right, it was intentional, but it wasn't malicious. I told you, everyone in the valley knows who I am. When I realized you didn't recognize me, it was a chance for me to be simply Philippe, without all the baggage that comes with being a d'Usay."

Sure, and Jenna had a Roman bridge she wanted to

sell him. The man wasn't even trying to look apologetic. His eyes twinkled with amusement.

"You don't really expect me to believe that line, do you?" she asked.

The dimples appeared. "It was worth a shot."

Of all the… She should be annoyed by the deception. She should be insulted. In fact, she should be a lot of things. Smiling was not one of them. But darn if she couldn't help catching his good humor.

"Didn't anyone ever tell you it's not nice to lie?" she said.

"Would you have believed me if I told the truth?"

That he used to own the castle? No, she would have told him to get lost, because no one owned castles.

"I rest my case," he said after she answered. "And then you and I would not have had the opportunity to spend time together. So in the end, my lie of omission was a good thing."

"I'm not sure I'd use the word *good*," Jenna replied. It was meant to be a grumble, but the corners of her mouth insisted on curving upward.

"But not entirely bad, either, no?"

Much as she hated to admit it, he was right. "No, not entirely bad."

"*Merci, ma chère.*" He smiled down through his lashes, the purple a dash darker than before.

That's when Jenna realized they were still holding hands. Lightly, but Philippe's grip had enough firmness to cause a flutter of awareness. Warmth spread to her cheeks.

"Could I…?" She dropped her gaze down to their hands.

"But of course." He released her, stuffing his hands into

his back pockets. Her palm suddenly feeling naked, Jenna had to settle for running a hand over the back of her hair.

"Now, tell me," he said. "What is it that has you running out of my house in the middle of your tour?"

Her headache. In her surprise, she'd nearly forgotten the reason she was sneaking away from the tour in the first place. "I wasn't running," she told him. "I was heading to the gift shop in search of water and aspirin. No offense, but your lavender gave me a headache."

"None taken," he replied. "The aroma can be overpowering if you are not used to it. But there's no need to go all the way to the gift shop. Come with me."

"Where are we going?" She glanced over her shoulder. Philippe was guiding her past the stairs to a corridor, the end of which was also blocked by a velvet rope.

"To the kitchen to get you a glass of water," he said.

"But…my tour."

"Will carry on without you," he said. "I will make sure you meet up with them in time to return to the hotel."

She glanced over her shoulder. The group must have moved to another room; she could no longer hear the guide's chirp. "Aspirin and water. No more."

"Absolutely, *ma chère*," he replied. "You have my word."

Said the man who'd already misled her once. Apparently Jenna had left her common sense in America, because she followed him anyway.

The kitchen was out of a French countryside fantasy. Big and airy, with an abundance of copper pots and pans. There was a battered butcher-block table and gleaming stainless steel appliances. The stove alone, Jenna decided, would eat up her entire kitchen back home.

The air smelled of fresh bread and lemons. A wonderful change from the floral notes she'd been breathing all morning. "Were you baking?" she asked.

"That would be the *fougasse*. My housekeeper, Henrietta, makes a point of baking it whenever I visit the house. Would you care for some?"

"Depends. What is it?"

"Only a slice of heaven wrapped in a golden crust," he said with a laugh. "Sit down and I will get you your aspirin. Henrietta keeps a bottle in the cupboard."

Jenna did as she was told, settling herself on the bench while Philippe opened and closed cabinet doors. A part of her still couldn't quite believe he owned the château, despite his obvious comfort with the surroundings.

"Do you come here often?" she asked. The corniness of her question struck her, and she nearly rolled her eyes at her own lameness. "I meant the house. The guide mentioned that you don't live here full-time."

"She is correct. I have an apartment in Arles, near our executive offices."

"I'm surprised."

"Success! It was with the spices." He held up a bottle of white tablets. Taking the bottle, Jenna saw the label read *aspirine*.

"Why are you surprised?" he asked.

"Considering how poetic you were about the countryside yesterday, I would have thought you'd spend as much time here as possible."

"I also appreciate a fine Beaujolais, but I would get bored drinking it every evening. I much prefer the variety of the city. One can only sit around and listen to the drone of the bees for so long."

He returned with a glass of ice water and an earthenware platter on which Jenna saw a flatbread sculpted to look like an ear of wheat. Sitting next to her, he immediately tore off a chunk and offered it to her. "I promise, you will not be disappointed."

"And if I am?"

"Then you have no soul."

Jenna tasted the bread. The warm crust broke away to reveal a soft inside that tasted of rosemary and orange.

"See? I told you," he said, tearing off a piece for himself. "No one makes *fougasse* like Henrietta."

For a few moments, they ate in silence. Whether it was the aspirin or the change in aromas or both, Jenna could feel her headache receding. Food helped, too, just as Philippe suggested. Every so often she stole a look sideways to watch him. He didn't eat the bread; he experienced it. His eyes would close and a contented smile would curl his lips upward as he savored each bite. The sight was almost as pleasurable as tasting the bread.

A thought struck her. "Why were you certain we'd see each other again? When you were on the stairs, you said you knew we'd meet again."

He was in mid-savor when she asked her question, so he pried open one eye. "What can I say? I believe in fate. And…" A hint of pink crept into his cheeks. "I may have asked the front desk to call me when you signed up for the hotel excursion."

"What?" No wonder the girl at the desk kept smiling at her. She was in on the joke.

"I did not want to take a chance on missing your visit. Tours come and go all day long."

"So you asked for advance information."

"I prefer to think of it as arranging for fate to be on my side."

Jenna narrowed her eyes. "You could have called my room and asked me."

"But that would have spoiled the surprise. And you were surprised, no?"

"Hmm." She continued to stare at him with narrowed eyes. Honest to God, she'd never heard of someone doing such a thing. Asking a clerk to tip him off. Certainly no one interested in her had ever gone to such lengths. "You're incorrigible. You know that, right?"

"Oui."

He leaned closer, the gap in his shirt treating her to a glimpse of the smooth skin beneath. "And you are flattered. I can see it in your eyes."

Jenna was flattered—immensely—but she wasn't about to let him know. "How do you know it's not amusement at your arrogance?"

"Amusement doesn't make a woman's skin flush."

Flashing a smug smile, he sat back in his chair. "I am sorry about your headache. That was not part of my plan. Is it better?"

"Getting there."

"Good. I'm glad. I forget how pungent the smell of lavender can be. When we were children, my brother Felix and I complained incessantly about the aroma." While speaking, he reached for her glass. The ice clinked as he lifted it high for a drink.

"You have a brother? Yesterday on the tour you said you were…" Jenna paused.

"The last of the line? I am. My brother died of cancer several years ago."

He spoke with nonchalance, but Jenna caught a

shadow in his eyes as he raised the glass to his lips for another drink.

"I'm sorry."

"So am I. He was a good man." He fell silent for a moment as a shadow darkened his features. Only for a moment, though. Jenna would have missed it altogether had she not been watching closely. "Let us talk about something more pleasant, shall we?"

He'd made a similar request yesterday. It was obvious he didn't like dwelling on his family. "What would you like to talk about?" she asked.

"How about dinner? Clearly, since fate has reunited us, we are destined to enjoy a meal together."

"You mean fate and a front desk clerk."

"A technicality. I knew we were destined to share each other's company as soon as I saw you on the terrace."

He was smooth. Charming, too. Much as she hated to admit it, Jenna enjoyed his company. He kept her on her toes. Dinner could be fun, as long as she kept her wits about her.

"Well, a girl does have to eat," she told him. "I might as well have some company."

He grinned like he'd won the lottery. "*Ma chère*, a woman needs to do more than eat. You need to experience French cuisine. Tonight, I shall make sure you have an experience you'll never forget."

"We'll see about that," Jenna replied. "I don't impress easily."

"Is that so? In that case…" He leaned in again, the purple in his eyes taking on a dangerously mischievous glint that made Jenna's insides flutter in spite of herself. "I look forward to meeting your challenge."

* * *

You know I was kidding about having a fling, right? All I meant was don't be your usual picky self.

I'm not having a fling; I'm having dinner.

Despite what Philippe d'Usay might think, her "French experience" was beginning and ending with dinner.

I don't do flings, remember?

You don't do anything.

That's not true. I do plenty.

Since when?

Since...

Jenna paused before hitting the backspace button. So it had been a while. Big deal. She was taking a dating hiatus. All the sweet talk and pretend interest in commitment that ended after a few weeks? Who needed it. She was trying to break her family pattern, not contribute to it.

Excuse me for being selective.

She leaned back against the headboard. Shirley's thoughts didn't need a phone for her to hear them. Her friend had given her the tough-love speech a half dozen times over the past couple years. *You're too picky. You never give anyone a chance. You rule guys out before you ever get a chance to know them.*

Maybe, Jenna thought, she was picky because she wanted more than a guy who claimed to want a relationship only to bail when he got bored. Of all people, Shirley should understand why.

Her phone buzzed. Shirley had replied.

This guy must be something if you are giving him the time of day.

He's okay.

Actually, he was everything Jenna claimed to detest. A guy like Philippe wasn't interested in depth. She wondered if he even knew what the word meant. And yet as bad an idea as the man was, he intrigued her in a way she hadn't felt in a long, long time.

After their conversation in the kitchen, Philippe had walked her through his back garden to the gift shop.

"Until tonight," he'd said, kissing her hand. Affected as all get-out, it still managed to set her entire arm aflame. The entire bus ride home, she found herself reliving the moment. If a kiss to the hand could set off her inner fireworks, she'd wondered, what would a real kiss do? Or...?

Her phone buzzed.

Just okay?

Maybe a little more than okay.

If her friend could only see him.

In that case, you know what they say. What happens in France...

Ha-ha.

All I'm saying is keep an open mind. A little fun never hurt anyone. Remember, Beatrice wanted you to have an adventure.

Somehow she didn't think Beatrice meant falling into bed with a sexy stranger.

Since when are you so invested in my sex life, anyway?

Since I'm home with shingles and no one wants to come near me. One of us ought to have a good time.

Jenna shook her head.

Sorry, babe. You're simply going to have to use your imagination.

Killjoy.

Yep. I've got to go get ready. TTYL.

She exited the application before Shirley could respond with Do what I'd do or some other nonsensical words of encouragement.

Tossing the phone on the bed beside her, Jenna stared at the black silk dress currently hanging on the door of her armoire. It was a simple wrap dress, modest by most standards. It was also the only fancy item she'd packed, since she hadn't actually planned on any dating or dining alone in super-fancy restaurants. Was it fancy enough for wherever Philippe intended to take her? He'd said he'd pick her up at eight, but he hadn't said where they were going.

All of a sudden, Jenna felt nervous. She was being silly. What did she care whether her wardrobe was appropriate? Wasn't as though any of the people in the restaurant would see her again. And it wasn't as if she was trying to impress Philippe. Then again, she didn't want to embarrass herself, either.

"Clothes, schmothes," Beatrice had said once. "Like anyone cares." At the time, she'd been insisting on wearing her silk robe—just her silk robe—to the dining room. "I'll have you know I ate naked once when I was in Bali."

Good old Beatrice, feisty and independent until the end. She didn't care what people thought. Married thirty years to her partner in crime, she'd told Jenna. Until he wasn't a partner anymore. Then she moved on. "No sense wasting your time on something that's not working," she'd said. What she would think of Philippe, Jenna could only imagine.

Never trust a man who's prettier than you, she immediately thought in Beatrice's raspy voice.

It was a good rule. Especially since Philippe was prettier than everyone.

Philippe entered the hotel early. Usually he didn't pay attention to time, as the women he called on always kept him waiting. Instinct told him Jenna was the kind of woman who appreciated promptness. He chose not to think about the fact that he'd spent the last thirty minutes dressed and watching the clock.

He smoothed the front of his dinner jacket. Funny, but he was actually anxious about the evening going well. He'd spent the entire afternoon planning the perfect dinner, which was one afternoon more than he'd spent planning any of his previous dates. Why bother when a table at the hottest club or restaurant would suffice? Tonight, however, required more. Mademoiselle Brown had a cynical streak, meaning she wouldn't be easily impressed. That required he put an effort into the evening.

Which was good. Planning kept him from brooding, and he despised brooding. There was nothing he could do about the tragedies life dealt him. He hated that he was forever dodging a shadow of sadness. It was far better to distract oneself with living.

Or a beautiful woman.

Simon and Antoinette greeted him on his way to the elevator. He stopped to say hello, as he always did when visiting. They greeted him with their usual haughty stares.

Did his ancestors approve of how he was running their empire? He'd like to think he was doing a good job, but he was also aware that he was never meant to be the one running D'Usay International. Felix was the one who'd been groomed to walk in their father's footsteps, and they both left very large shoes. Philippe did the best he could, but there were times when he wondered if they would approve of the changes he'd made. The expansion. The move beyond French flowers. Were they staring down in disdain or relieved their empire would continue even when the company no longer had a d'Usay in charge?

He supposed he wouldn't know until it was all over for him.

And there he went, thinking maudlin thoughts when he had a beautiful woman waiting upstairs.

Considering what Jenna had worn on their previous two meetings, he expected to see her wearing something bright and touristy. The woman who opened the door, however, was gloriously sophisticated. His eyes skimmed her length appreciatively. The black cocktail dress was classically elegant, modest but revealing in all the right places. Arousal curled through him. *"Tu es belle."*

She smiled appreciatively. "I'm going to assume it was a compliment."

"It was. I said you look beautiful."

To her credit, she took the compliment in stride, without the faux modesty he'd come to expect from his dates. "Thank you."

"No, thank *you*." He held out his arm. "Shall we?"

"Where are we going?"

So suspicious. He would definitely need to work if he wanted tonight to end successfully. The challenge was exactly what he needed.

He patted her hand. "Wait and see, Mademoiselle Brown," he replied. "I promise you will not be disappointed."

CHAPTER THREE

"Is all this for us?"

Philippe swelled with satisfaction as he watched Jenna walk across the terrace. Her reaction was everything he'd hoped for and more. He watched as she circled the candlelit table with wide-eyed astonishment.

"Would you prefer a table on the main terrace?" He had requested a private table on the northeast terrace overlooking the garden. The cloudless night was perfect for dining outside, the full moon and lanterns casting a silvery light over everything.

"This is… I mean, I wasn't expecting…" She paused her exploration to look up at him. "You shouldn't have gone to all this trouble," she said.

"You said this was a fantasy vacation. I figured why not give you a fantastical dinner?"

"Fantastical dinner?" she repeated.

Even from a distance, Philippe could see the wariness in her eyes. Questioning his expectations. And why shouldn't she? His intentions were fairly obvious. Also obvious was that Jenna Brown wasn't a woman easily swept off her feet. But then, he'd suspected as much, which was why he'd gone to all this effort.

Apparently his work wasn't finished.

"An experience that would make your late friend proud," he replied. "And your texting friend jealous."

"Mission accomplished. On both points. This is..." She swung her arm around. "Wow."

"You approve. I'm glad."

He watched as she moved to the terrace rail, her skirt flowing around her knees. Most of his dates preferred to bare as much flesh as possible. Miles of it, actually, all toned and tanned to perfection. He never would have guessed how erotic—and arousing—pale modesty could be.

"The garden looks beautiful from here," she said. "You don't get an appreciation of the layout when you're on ground level."

He joined her. Normally, he would take advantage of the moment to encircle her waist from behind. Instead, he stood to her left, his hand resting on the railing a millimeter from hers. Below them, the garden spread out in perfect geometric symmetry. Concentric squares marked in the center by a giant fountain. The stone paths that bordered each square looked whiter than usual thanks to a series of strategically placed spotlights.

"French gardens are designed to be enjoyed both up close and from a distance. So that when people look down from their upper stories, they will experience the garden's beauty as a whole."

"Do you think your ancestors stood here once upon a time, or is this part of the newer construction?" she asked, leaning forward.

"They might have." He was fibbing slightly. The private terraces *were* part of the new construction, but the room leading to them was original, and she sounded too enchanted to disappoint.

And her eyes... He took in her profile, admiring how the green sparkled in the moonlight. "The garden was designed to resemble the original as closely as possible."

"Really?" She turned, and Philippe sucked in his breath when confronted with the fullness of her wide-eyed wonder. The woman respected tradition. Bravo to her.

"I provided the photographs," he told her.

"It's gorgeous. This is the first time I've seen the fountain under lights. I wanted to explore last night, but I was too jet-lagged to do anything, including eat."

"Should I worry about you falling asleep during dinner?"

"That depends," she said.

"On?"

She grinned. "How entertaining you are during the meal."

Challenge accepted. "Do not worry. I can be very entertaining." The muscles in his hand twitched as he fought the urge to mark a trail along her arm. Too forward, and he would scare her off.

That didn't mean he couldn't let his eyes complete the innuendo. Her eyes responded in kind, the pupils growing wide. He watched as she swallowed away the rest of her physical response. Rather, she tried to. It remained in the depths of her gaze. The air between them pulsed. Once. Twice.

Jenna broke the silence. "What is that scent?" she asked. "It's not lavender."

"Jasmine," he answered. "The aroma is stronger in the evenings. Do you see those white flowers?"

Reluctantly, he raised his arm—taking it away from the warmth of her proximity—to point out the bushes lining one of the inner squares. "Our Grasse property has a large jasmine crop. We'll harvest the blossoms in a few weeks and sell them to the perfumeries for use in their fragrances."

She nodded as though digesting a great truth. "Would it be sacrilegious if I said I like the scent more than lavender?" she asked him.

"Only if you say the words loudly." No surprise, given her headache earlier. Jasmine had a far lighter scent.

Light scents would definitely suit her more, he decided. As surreptitiously as possible, he leaned to inhale the air near the crook of her neck. Notes of citrus caught his nostrils. Clean and crisp.

"You don't wear perfume," he noted. A foreign concept in his world.

"Got out of the habit, I'm afraid. Strong smells sometimes bother my patients, so I find it easier to avoid them altogether."

"Shame. I'm of the belief that a woman should always wear perfume. The right scent can transform a woman from ordinary to something mysterious and seductive that is indelible to the mind. Eye color, the curve of her cheek—those may fade from memory, but the smell of her perfume? That is something the brain never forgets."

"Says the man who makes his money selling flowers to perfume companies."

She had him there. "Perhaps I am a tad biased."

"Just a tad," she said with a sideways glance.

It was the perfect night for dining outside. The trill

of a piano floated in on the breeze to join the crickets in a summer duet. Philippe absorbed the sound as he took in Jenna's profile. "What is it?" he asked when a smile broke across her features.

"Nothing." The pink that immediately filled her cheeks was adorable. "I was looking at the garden and it dawned on me that you're a farmer. That's harder to imagine than you working for the hotel."

"You can't picture me digging in the dirt?"

"In a word? No."

Philippe laughed. "Don't worry. Neither can I. For the sake of everyone involved, I leave the actual agriculture to those with far greener thumbs. Otherwise we run the risk of destroying half the region."

"Surely you don't have that black a thumb."

"Don't be so sure. My brother, Felix, once made me swear that I would never interfere with that side of the business. He didn't appreciate how I managed to kill a lemon tree he'd bought me."

Your apartment is where plants go to die was what he'd actually said. Nearly set off his vital monitor for laughing, too. His nurse scowled at them for being rambunctious.

"I take it he…"

"Had a green thumb?" he asked, to save her from stumbling over tense. "Very much so. He loved the farms, especially the lavender fields. He'd come out every summer to help with the harvests. He lived for this time of year."

"What about you? Do you live for this time of year as well?"

Did he live for a season that reminded him of the family he lost? An honest answer would kill the mo-

ment. Now was not the time to think of life's injustices.
Not when there was champagne chilling and a beautiful woman to share it with. "Come," he said, taking her
hand. "Before the champagne grows flat."

The bottle sat in a silver ice bucket waiting to be
poured. While they'd been talking, he'd heard the *pop!*
as a waiter carefully uncorked the bottle and then disappeared. Philippe filled the glasses and handed one
to Jenna. "To bucket lists and fantastical memories,"
he said before washing away his less fantastical ones.

"I killed an air fern once."

He coughed as the last swallow caught in his throat.
"*Pardon?*"

"It's a plant that only needs watering every couple
weeks. Very low maintenance. I killed it. I also killed
a terrarium. And I'm pretty sure I'm the reason my
poinsettia bit the dust last Christmas as well. To this
day I cringe when one of my patients offers me a plant.
Might as well just give the thing a death sentence and
be done with it."

Her effort to lighten the mood succeeded. The
shadow retreated farther. "So you're saying we're both
horticulturally challenged?"

"I was going to say we're plant angels of death, but
your phrase sounds better."

Indeed. But hers made him smile. Doubly so, because he suspected she was being outrageous for his
sake. "A second toast then," he said. "To sparing nature
from our deadly touch."

"To giving plants a fighting chance," she replied.

Philippe clinked his glass to hers and downed the
contents. "So Jenna Brown saves lives and kills plants.
What else does she do?"

"Do?"

"Tell me about yourself." To his surprise he was genuinely interested in her answer. "Your family. Do they live in Nantucket as well?"

"No. They're in Boston."

There was tightness in her voice. He'd touched a nerve. "I'm sorry. It is an unpleasant subject."

"Yes and no," she replied with a sigh. "My parents... Let's just say they have a complicated relationship and leave it at that."

Very well. He knew when not to push. "And your job? You enjoy being a nurse in...?" Where was it she told him she worked? "A nursing home?"

A switch flipped inside her. "Absolutely. I love my patients. Some of them are like family."

A family that eventually died on her. While her living family was estranged. Philippe didn't understand. "It doesn't bother you, spending all your time around death?" He marveled at her answer. How could anyone love watching people die?

"Death is a part of life. I'm glad I can be there at the end to help them leave this world with dignity."

No, Philippe thought, death was a thief, taking good people before their time. "All the more reason to pack as much life as possible into our time on earth. Since death is inevitable."

"You sound very French."

"I'm only quoting you, and we are a fatalistic people."

"Is that what you are?"

"Hardly," he replied. "I'm much more of a hedonist."

"Pleasure above things?"

"Why not? Good wine. Beautiful women." He met

her eyes as he said the last part, earning a small blush. "Life should be embraced with both hands, should it not?"

"Beatrice used to say stuff like that."

"The woman who left you the money."

Her smile softened. "She would have liked you. I remember one night we were watching a documentary about some ancient Greek city known for excessive living…"

"Sybaris," he interrupted.

She looked at him in surprise. "Yes, that's the one."

"A lucky guess. I remember the lecture from university."

"You have a very good memory."

"It was a very interesting subject," he said with a shrug.

"Anyway, when the show ended, Beatrice looked at me and said, 'Those Greeks had the right idea.'"

"My kind of woman."

"She must have dozed off during the part where the city was destroyed."

"Yes, but at least they enjoyed themselves on the way out." Reaching for the champagne, he filled both their glasses. "*Vie amoureuse*, as they say."

"She definitely would have liked you."

"Of course. I am a very likable person. You do not agree?" he asked at her enigmatic smile.

"Oh, I agree." He watched while she traced the rim of her glass. "You're extremely likable."

"And you find that a problem." A statement, not a question. He'd begun to notice a pattern with his American. Whenever she began to relax and enjoy herself, the wariness would rear its head to cool the enjoyment off. Such as now. Instead of laughing at his silly joke, she responded seriously.

"You do not trust me." Again, he presented the words as fact.

"You're a millionaire," she countered. "Where I come from, millionaires don't usually take women like me out to dinner."

"They don't believe in dating beautiful women?"

"They don't pull out all the stops unless they have an agenda."

Before he could reply, they were interrupted by a service. "*Pissaladière*," the man announced before lifting the cover to reveal an onion tart, crust browned to perfection.

"I hope you don't mind," he said, "but I took the liberty of selecting the menu. Various Provençal dishes I think you would enjoy."

"Case in point," she replied.

"If your point is that I am trying to impress you, then I plead guilty as charged."

"Impress me with the goal of coming back to my room."

"Again guilty." Did she expect him to deny human nature? Most women he knew would be swept off their feet by a moonlight dinner. Half of them would be in his arms before the tart arrived. With her, his efforts brought suspicion, despite his openness. It was almost as if she were afraid to enjoy herself.

He would need to rethink his approach.

"You always have the power to say no," he reminded her.

"So long as we both realize that." She smiled as she replied, but her eyes were serious.

"*Ma chère*, I never go anywhere I'm not invited. Although I hope you will save your rejection until after the tart."

He placed a slice on her plate and waited while she took a bite. When her eyes closed, he knew he'd scored his first point. No one could resist well-done French cuisine.

"Amazing," she replied.

"And that is only the beginning. By the time tonight is over, you'll have discovered that most things in Provence are amazing. And irresistible."

Philippe was right about the food. By the time dessert rolled around—melon pastry drizzled with lavender honey—Jenna was in love with French cooking. That included the French champagne. Philippe insisted on keeping both their glasses full at all times.

She wasn't stupid; she knew what he was doing. But everything tasted so amazing. With every bite—and sip—her guard slipped a little more. Before she knew it, she had literally kicked off her shoes and was enjoying herself.

They kept their dinner conversation light. He talked of Paris and local attractions. She told stories about Beatrice and some of her more colorful patients. By mutual agreement, they both avoided probing personal questions. Jenna would have liked to ask more about his brother. It was in those rare moments of personal revelation that she thought there might be more to him than mere charm. Asking questions, however, only opened the door to him asking more questions about her family. A topic best left unmentioned. Since nothing killed an evening faster than dysfunctional drama.

Sometimes there was something to be said for staying superficial.

The rattle of ice broke her thoughts. Philippe was pouring the last of the champagne into her glass. "Whoa there, cowboy. I don't think I should have any more." Her inhibitions had slipped enough.

"If you're certain."

"What, no insistence?"

"Not from me. I prefer my invitations be delivered with a clear head."

Spoken with the confidence of a man who had never wanted for an invitation. She shifted in her seat. "Thank you for dinner. It was delicious."

"You speak as if the evening is over."

Maybe because now was a good time for it to end. "It's getting late," she said.

"Nonsense, the night is young. I thought we might walk off dinner in the garden."

"And then what?"

"Then I will walk you to your door. I have no expectations, Jenna."

Bull. He had expectations; he was just telling her the final decision was up to her. Still, maybe it was the champagne getting to her, but a moonlight stroll amid the jasmine did sound lovely.

"You'll have to give me a moment to put on my shoes," she told him. "I kicked them off around the second course."

Before she could blink, he was on his knees with her discarded heels in his hand. "Allow me."

Gently cupping her heel, he guided her foot into her shoe. "We wouldn't want the crushed gravel hurting your feet," he said as he slipped the heel strap in place.

His fingertips lingered a moment on the back of her ankle before he switched his attention to her other foot. This time, his fingers brushed upward ever so slightly. The sensation traveled the length of her leg. He gazed upward, and even through lowered lashes, Jenna could see the heat in his eyes.

"Now you are ready to walk."

They walked slowly and separately along the gravel paths. The air smelled sweeter in the garden. It was warmer, too. In fact, now that they were on the ground, everything seemed more. The moonlight. The soft ripple of the fountain. Jenna swore could even feel the brush of the air on her skin every time Philippe's arm moved. Without lifting a finger, he somehow managed to feel impossible close.

Then again, he *had* lifted a finger when they were on the terrace. If she concentrated, she could still feel his hands on the back of her ankle.

Philippe pointed to a line of bushes closest to the fountain. "There's your jasmine," he said. While the petals on other flowers in the garden had folded closed for the night, the jasmine's tiny white blossoms were open wide. "They bloom at night," Philippe told her. "There's a horticultural reason for it, but I won't bore you. Better to simply enjoy them as they are."

Tonight, Jenna had to agree. Plucking a flower from its stem, she twirled the blossom between her fingers and imagined the subtle scent drifting upward. Maybe she'd go back to wearing perfume after all. Then when she wanted to remember this trip, she need only inhale.

"You said you grow these in Grasse?" she asked.

"We grow everything in Grasse," he replied. "Roses

in the spring. Jasmine and lavender in the summer. You can tell the time of year by how the air smells."

He lifted her hand to smell the flower she was holding, touching her for the first time since the walk began. "Jasmine suits you," he said.

"What makes you say that?"

"Because it is sweet but subtle. Rose is too floral and lavender too heavy. Jasmine, however, entices without overpowering. It doesn't need to advertise its beauty. Rather, it is perfect in its simplicity."

"Are you saying I'm simple?"

"*Ma chère*, you are far from simple. But you are perfect. And enticing."

While he was speaking, he slipped the flower from her and traced it along her cheek. Jenna's eyes fluttered shut. "You're trying to seduce me," she whispered.

The blossom brushed her lower lip. "Is it working?"

More than it should, and it frightened her. Opening her eyes, she found herself staring into his, their color darkened to fine wine by the night sky. So dark she could almost imagine the light reflecting in them was from the stars. It left her feeling off balance.

Intoxicated.

"Philippe..."

"Shh." He pressed the flower to her lips. "Don't say no. Not yet."

Jenna didn't want to say no. That was the problem. What she wanted was for Philippe to kiss her until she couldn't breathe. The moment was right there. All she needed to do was whisper one word, and he would sweep her away.

Only to wake up in the morning hating herself. Try as she might, she couldn't do it. As magical as the moment felt, it was all surface magic, designed to seduce. She'd grown up witnessing the damage romantic illusion could do. She saw how a few well-played promises could lure a woman into believing they meant more. No matter how badly she was tempted, Jenna refused to let the moment sweep her away.

Ignoring her racing pulse, she stepped back. It wasn't a huge step, but it was enough that the temperature around her cooled. "I think we'd better call it a night."

"Are you certain?" His expression was dangerously understanding.

"Yes, very."

"Very well. I will walk you to your door."

"The elevator will suffice." Truth be told, she didn't trust herself not to weaken if they made it anywhere near her bedroom. Already, she could feel the prickles of remorse nipping at her insides. That was the curse of leading with your head.

They resumed their walk in silence, the awareness from before replaced by a different kind of tension. "I'm sorry if you're disappointed," she caught herself saying, despite having nothing to apologize for.

He replied with a shrug. "*C'est la vie.* I told you before, I only go where I am invited."

"Dinner truly was lovely."

"I am glad you enjoyed yourself. Perhaps tomorrow I can impress you again. I thought you might like to tour the Pont du Gard and have a picnic by the river."

"Tomorrow?" Was he asking her out a second time? Even after she…?

"My ego is not so fragile that I would walk away from an interesting woman simply because she ended the evening early," he replied. "I have been in need of…

company…this week, and you are exactly the breath of fresh air I was looking for. So, tomorrow. Shall I pick you up in the morning? The bridge is best enjoyed before the crowds."

"I—I had signed up for a bus tour." She meant the response as an excuse, but the words lacked conviction. Philippe made for a far better guide than any professionally run tour.

Plus, the prospect of seeing him again made her spine tingle. "Will nine o'clock work?" she asked him.

"Perfectly." His face brightened with satisfaction. "I shall see you then. And who knows? Perhaps tomorrow night you will reconsider issuing an invitation."

"Don't bet on it," she replied.

"Oh, but I like to gamble." Shivers passed through her at the way his voice dropped. "And now," he continued, "I will say good-night."

"But…we're not at the elevator."

"I know, but I thought it best we stop here."

"Why?" She looked around. They had stopped at the edge of the gardens, at a point where the pathway intersected with a concrete sidewalk. The door to the hotel was a few feet away, guarded by a pair of olive trees.

Fingers curled around the shell of her ear. "Because, *ma chère*, I plan to kiss you good-night, and I prefer privacy."

Jenna's mouth ran dry. "Oh."

The kiss was gentle to start, as though he were waiting for her to kiss him back. Which Jenna quickly did, their lips sliding into a natural rhythm. The kisses grew deeper, and soon she found herself pressed tight against him, her hands clutching his shoulders.

No one had ever kissed her like this. With such passion and patience. He didn't grope or try to rush things to the next level. He just held her and tasted her as deeply as he could.

Until suddenly, abruptly, he broke away, leaving them both struggling to breathe again.

"Good night, Jenna," he whispered. "Sleep well."

After a kiss like that? Jenna wasn't sure that was possible.

Philippe couldn't remember the last time a woman rejected him and he went home smiling. Never? More proof that Jenna Brown was what he needed this week.

He inhaled, letting the jasmine and lavender fill him. Every season, the pungency caught him off guard. One would think, after a lifetime of harvests, he would remember. Hadn't he told Jenna one never forgets a perfume?

His brother loved the smell, as did his parents. Usually, the scent filled him with melancholy, but not tonight. Tonight, for the first time in a long time, the floral scent accompanied more pleasant thoughts.

Should he feel guilty, pursuing Jenna so ardently? After all, he was everything she oh-so-cynically accused him of being.

Then again, she was a grown woman, intelligent and strong enough to know whether she wanted to sleep with a man.

He ran a thumb across his lips. How enjoyable it would be if she invited him into her bed. He certainly looked forward to convincing her she should.

CHAPTER FOUR

"WHY DIDN'T YOU tell me you were afraid of heights?" Philippe asked.

"I'm not afraid of heights. It's narrow, circular stairs I don't like." One hundred forty very narrow stairs that were expected to accommodate both up and down traffic. Every few steps, Jenna found herself having to hug the railing in order to allow a descending tourist to pass.

"Relax." Philippe's voice sounded in her ear. "I'm standing right behind you. You're not going to get knocked over."

"You better hope not, because I'm pulling you down with me to break my fall," she told him.

They were in Nîmes, climbing the famed Tour Magne, a thousand-year-old tower that promised panoramic views of the city. It had been four days since their dinner on the terrace. Four days of romantic outings followed by Jenna sending Philippe home to sleep in his own bed despite wanting to do the opposite. No matter how enticing Philippe's kisses, a voice told her to hold back.

He was too perfect; that was the problem. Charming. Witty. Sexy. Always knowing what to say. And none of it dipping below the surface. Except for that one slip of a moment on the terrace, he kept his true self at bay, as much a stranger as the day they met—albeit a very enticing stranger.

At the top of the stairs, they passed through a doorway and onto a stone observation deck. "See?" Philippe said. "I told you the view was worth it."

He was right. All around them spread the city of Nîmes. Despite the dark clouds rolling in over the mountains, the view was spectacular. In the distance, Jenna could see the walls of the arena of Nîmes, the famous Roman amphitheatre, while if she looked down, she could see the walls and waterways of the public gardens. They made their way to a spot along the wall and stood one in front of the other, Philippe's arms holding her in place. "I see what you mean now about the gardens being designed so you can view them from above," she said.

"The tower wasn't originally this tall. After Rome conquered the area, Augustus doubled the height for protection purposes."

Of course, he knew such a fact. "Is there any piece of local history you don't know?"

"Not really."

"I feel spoiled, having my own walking, talking guidebook," she told him. One whose eyes lit up when sharing interesting facts. She wished they weren't standing back to front so she could see his eyes right now.

"We aim to please." His arms came around either side of her to rest on the top of the battlement.

Maybe standing back to front wasn't so bad after all.

She snuggled into his space while he pointed out landmarks and shared historical anecdotes.

"You should have been a history professor," she said after a while. She could imagine how popular he would be with university students. The waiting list for his class would be a mile long.

"Believe it or not, there was a time when I wanted to do just that."

"What made you change your mind?"

"The business needed me. My parents were gone. Felix's illness made it hard for him to keep on top of everything. Since I've a knack for numbers…"

"You stepped up to help."

"I had to. What good is D'Usay International without a d'Usay at the helm? Some of these companies have been dealing with our family for nearly a century."

"Tradition is important to you, isn't it? Forget I asked." The answer was obvious, given his passion for history.

A man who valued the past but lived for today. Quite the contradiction.

"When you belong to a family with deep roots, you cannot help but respect tradition. The d'Usay name has been an integral part of Provence's history."

With him being the last of them. "The pressure is on for you to boost the family numbers."

"Or let the name die out."

"You don't plan to have children?"

"Good Lord, no. Not on purpose, anyway."

"Really?" She was surprised. For someone who believed in honoring the past as much as he did, you'd think he'd want to preserve that history into the future for as long as he could.

"Children and relationships require commitment," he replied. "In case you haven't guessed, I prefer to stay as entanglement-free as possible."

Hopping from one good time to the next. Didn't that

sound familiar? "You're not afraid you'll get bored? Even pleasure seeking has its limits."

"Not if you do it right," he teased.

Releasing her from his arms, he came around to face her. The wind had ruffled his curls, adding emphasis to his devil-may-care remarks. "Not everyone in the world is meant to settle down, *ma chère*."

"But what about your family legacy?" The history he so respected. How could he, on one hand, talk so reverently about his ancestors, and on the other, talk about never settling down?

"Families die out." As he spoke, a cloud passed in front of the sun, casting his face in shadows. "If the d'Usays were meant to continue, there'd be more family around than only me."

But if he had children... Jenna kept her thoughts to herself and instead stared out at the city below. Terracotta roofs and white marble dotted with evergreen spires. It wasn't Philippe's fault he'd picked at an emotional scab. What did it matter to her if he spent the rest of his life jet-setting around the world? In fact, more power to him for being honest than misleading women with false hopes.

"You're frowning." Philippe's fingers played with the hair by her ear. "You're disappointed with me."

"Quite the opposite, actually. I was thinking of someone who should have taken a page from your book. Might have saved a whole lot of pain."

"Someone broke your heart?" His hand combed through her hair before coming to rest on her shoulder. "The man is a fool."

His sentiment made her smile. "Not my heart," she

told him. "My mother's. My dad never should have married her. Unfortunately, he wasn't as forthright as you."

"I'm sorry."

"It is what it is. I figured out a long time ago I'm not responsible for my parents' mistakes." Not even if she was one of them. "You learn to deal."

Unless you were her mother, that was.

Jenna could feel Philippe's eyes on her as he waited for her to go on. She didn't want to. Talking about her family, even in the most vague of terms, depressed her, and she didn't want to spoil the afternoon.

"Anyway, you're right. Relationships take commitment, and if that's not your thing, more power to you for realizing before someone gets hurt."

"Precisely. Thank you for understanding."

Jenna shrugged. "I take it I'm one of the few?"

"There are women who consider my resolution a challenge," he said, "and therefore feel the need to take up the gauntlet, so to speak."

She could only imagine what the gauntlet entailed. "Let me guess. You don't let these women down gently."

"Sometimes bluntness is the only way to get the point across."

"What about you?" Philippe asked.

"What about me?"

"Are you looking for marriage and children?"

"Not with you, if that's what you're worried about," she replied. "But eventually, I suppose. If the right person comes along, and if his heart doesn't have vascular ADD."

"Vascular what?"

"It's a term Shirley and I came up with to describe

guys who can't stay committed longer than a month before falling in love with someone else."

"Ah, I see. Well, I can promise you, I do not have vascular ADD. My heart doesn't wish to commit, period."

Leaning closer, he added in a low voice, "You realize you are making the perfect argument for our enjoying each other's company for the remainder of the week. Because we are both on the same page."

His logic was hard to follow with his breath tickling her neck. "Are we? On the same page?"

"I like to think so. Don't you?"

Jenna shouldn't have turned to meet his eyes. The promise in his voice already conjured up way too many delicious connotations. Falling into the purple, she felt her resolve fraying. It would be so easy to tumble and get lost, she thought. But, oh, how tempting.

"But if I say yes, then who's to say I'll see you again?" she asked. Surely part of his attraction was the challenge.

"You are far too interesting for me to lose interest in one night. I find myself wanting to know every bit of you. Inside…" He traced his index finger across her collarbone. "And out."

Jenna started to melt, the way she always did when he turned seductive. "You make a strong argument."

He caught her face. The feel of his palms on her skin reached all the way to her toes. "I can make a stronger one, if you'd like."

Oh dear. Jenna's mouth ran dry.

Thunder rumbled in the distance. "It's going to storm," she managed to say.

The sky above them was quickly darkening. The tourists who'd been enjoying the view around them began filing their way down the stairs.

Philippe stopped her when she started to follow. "We have time," he told her.

"For what? Getting struck by lightning?"

"We will be fine. I want to take advantage of the privacy to finish explaining myself."

"I really don't think…"

He kissed her. *Oh.* That *explanation.*

Jenna fell into the kiss.

They got caught in the rain. A drenching downpour of a storm that left them soaked to the skin before they could sprint to the car. Hardly the romantic moment Philippe had planned for.

It was his fault, of course. He got caught up in the kiss and completely forgot about the advancing storm. Jenna's kisses had the strangest effect on him. The taste of her went straight to his head the way champagne used to when he was a boy. Only she tasted much sweeter.

He could only imagine what taking her to bed would be like.

From the passenger seat, Jenna flashed him a valiant smile. She was soaked. Water dripped from her curls and ran down the sides of her face, and her once brightly colored outfit stuck to her skin. Although he'd turned the air temperature as warm as he dared, goose bumps still covered her arms and legs. She looked miserable. Beautiful, but miserable.

He spied the road sign ahead and made an executive decision.

"I don't remember taking this turn on the drive in," she said.

"We didn't. I'm going to my apartment in Arles instead."

Right on cue, the wariness flashed across her face. "To dry off and get something to eat. Unless you'd rather stay in those wet clothes for an extra thirty minutes."

"Not really," she replied. There was a moment, though, when he saw her considering the option. Fortunately for them both, common sense won out.

"Then it's settled. We'll find you some dry clothes and I'll order us some dinner from Chez Marguerite." The café on the corner was one of his favorite haunts. His living room looked out on the amphitheater. He could set up a small table so they could enjoy the view.

Amazing, how much he enjoyed entertaining her. Yes, part of his enthusiasm was driven by a desire to seduce. He'd never met a woman so determined to keep him at arm's length. Well, not quite arm's length, or they wouldn't be soaked to the skin. But, the last day or so, his desire had taken on another layer. He *liked* her. She challenged him intellectually, something his usual dates never did, and when he spoke about history, she listened. Actively listened, not the lip service he so often received. Surprised him to admit it, but if their time together never progressed beyond a few kisses and good company, he would still consider the week a success.

Of course, their time together could be far richer if they explored each other as well as the region. If only she would let herself go.

It was still raining buckets when they pulled up in front of his building. "So much for drying in the car," Jenna said as they raced up the front steps. "I think my sneakers are going to squish for days."

"We will throw everything in the dryer. It'll be dry in no time." He tossed his keys on the table by the front door, next to a stack of mail. The house was hot and muggy after being locked up for several days, making his wet clothes feel ten times heavier.

Jenna, meanwhile, stood by the door, hugging her frame. Her arms glistened with rainwater. So did her face. Her lips. It was all he could do not to kiss the moisture from her skin.

"Come with me," he said, reaching for her hand.

"Where are we going?"

"To get you out of those wet clothes." She was far too tempting in them.

He led her upstairs to his en suite. Thankfully, the housekeeper had cleaned up before taking the week off. Grabbing his robe from behind the bathroom door, he handed it to her.

"This should keep you warm while your clothes are drying. There are fresh towels in the bathroom as well, if you'd like to take a shower to warm up. Or I could draw you a bath…"

He liked how her brows knit together as he pointed out the tub. "It looks big enough to swim in," she said.

"It's meant for two people. But in this case, I'm merely offering an opportunity to get warm," he quickly added. "I will be downstairs ordering dinner."

"Thanks, but the towel and the robe are fine. I don't think I need to go swimming in your tub right now."

"The choice is up to you. You can always change your mind later." Because he couldn't help himself, he combed the wet hair from her face. "You can have anything you want this evening. All you have to do is ask."

Philippe was whistling in a room on the second floor when Jenna stepped out of the bedroom. Clutching her wet clothes, she padded her way toward the sound. His "apartment," as he called it, was really a narrow antique house with the main living quarters on the upper floors. Philippe's bedroom occupied the bulk of the third floor.

It was gorgeous. Elegant and masculine, much like the man himself. The entire time she was undressing, Jenna had been painfully aware that she stood feet away from the bed he slept in. When she wrapped his robe around her body, his scent had enveloped her, too. All of it reminding her that all she need to do was ask.

She found him at the far end of the second floor in what had to be the living room. Again, the decor reeked of wealthy masculinity. Leather furniture. High-end electronics. The perfect bachelor apartment.

While she'd been upstairs, he'd managed to find dry clothes of his own—a pair of striped linen pants and a shirt that hung loose. He was moving a small table from the corner to in front of the terrace window, the exertion causing his shirtsleeves to tighten around bulging biceps.

Jenna coughed the sudden frog from her throat. "What would you like me to do with these?"

"I'll take them downstairs." He looked her up and down with a grin. "You wear that robe well."

"I feel like a character from those science fiction movies." The long garment pooled around her feet, and the sleeves wouldn't stay rolled.

"You'll have your own clothes soon enough. I poured us some wine. It's by the fireplace."

Sure enough, two glasses of red wine sat on the fireplace mantel. "You've been busy," she called after him. How long had she lingered in his bedroom?

There was a photograph on the mantel as well. One of those formal family shots like the ones on display at the hotel, only this one was more recent. In it, a middle-aged man stood behind a sofa, his hand on the shoulder of a beautiful dark-haired woman. A young boy of about eight sat next to her, while she held a baby on her lap.

Philippe's family.

She spied another frame by a lamp. Of two men in bathing suits this time. They stood on the beach, the older one with his arm hooked around the younger boy's shoulders. Despite the fact both men wore sunglasses, Jenna recognized Philippe's grin immediately. He'd clearly been a charmer since birth.

"That was in St. Tropez." Philippe returned from the kitchen with plates in his hands. "My parents insisted on a family holiday before Felix returned to the university."

"You look like you're having a good time."

"That was the last time we were all together. My father flew to Milan in the morning. He was struck by a car leaving his hotel a few days later."

No wonder he displayed the photo. Carefully, she set the frame back on the mantel. Meanwhile, Philippe was busying himself by setting the table, carefully arranging the two plates as though hosting a formal dinner. "I thought you might prefer a view while eating. Ideally, I would have preferred to enjoy the fading sun, but it is still better than the dining room."

"You don't like talking about family, do you?"

"*Pardon?*"

She'd been around enough difficult conversations, not to mention ducking more than a few herself, to recognize avoidance tactics when she saw them. Philippe's sad family history was none of her business, but the sadness in his voice when he mentioned his father's death called to her. Just like when he mentioned his brother the other evening, she saw a glimmer of what lurked beneath his perfect surface, and the sight had her wanting more. To quote someone in the room, she wanted to know him inside and out.

"Whenever the topic comes up, you change the subject. It's happened three times now."

"Has it?" He shifted one of the plates an inch to the left. "Interesting you should notice, seeing as how you do the same thing."

Touché. "That's different," Jenna replied.

"How so?"

"Your family is worth talking about."

Her comment, which came out before she could censor herself, hung in the silence, waiting for elaboration. There was no way Philippe would let her move on until she did. Not after she'd challenged his reluctance to share. Taking a long drink of wine for fortification, she thought of how to best explain.

"My mom stopped living the day my dad moved out," she started.

"I'm confused. I thought your mother was alive."

"She is, but there's a difference between being alive and living."

"I see."

"She wakes up, she works, she does all the things she's supposed to do, but…" Jenna's hand tightened on the goblet. As was the case whenever she talked about her mother, she felt the frustration squeezing at her throat. "It's like she hit pause the day he moved out and has been on hold ever since. Waiting for my father to come home." Never moving forward. Never giving up hope. "Twenty freaking years."

"And your father? Does he know?"

"Oh, he knows all right, and he *loves* it. Encourages it, actually. Every few years, he pops up, like a bad penny. Usually around the time his current relationship is on the rocks, and he needs an ego stroking. Last I heard, he was shacking up with some girl half his age. To be honest, I lose track."

"He has a lot of relationships."

"He is a jerk," Jenna replied. "He uses women, makes promises he has no intention of keeping and is out the door as soon as something better comes along." Thinking of him left a bad taste in her mouth. "Pretty sure the only reason he stuck it out with my mother for as long as he did was because Grandpa threatened to kill him."

"Must have been very hard for you growing up."

Jenna swallowed the mouthful of rosé she'd gulped. "I caught on to his bogus promises in the sixth grade. Mom, though..." She shook her head. A lifetime wasted waiting on a man who didn't love anyone but himself. "See why I'm not keen on talking about my family? At least your family accomplished things. Your father loved your mother. My mother sat on the sofa waiting." She stared into her glass.

"Maybe she waited because she didn't know what else to do?"

"Clearly." She let out a harsh breath. "I'd understand if my father were some kind of prize, but he isn't."

The sofa sagged as Philippe joined her. A moment later, his arm wrapped around her shoulders, pulling her close.

Leaning on him was dangerously natural.

"My mother sketched," he said.

"I beg your pardon?" His comment didn't make much sense given their conversation.

"After my father's accident, my mother took up drawing. Day in, day out, she sketched things. Fruit. Furniture. Page after page of unrecognizable objects. You might say it was a compulsion."

"Why?"

"Felix asked the same question. She told him it was to make the day go by faster. She didn't know what else to do with herself. Felix took over my father's job. Her job had been to take care of my father."

"And you," Jenna replied. "Weren't you only a teenager?"

"Yes, but I also had the life of a teenager. I didn't need my mother the way I once did."

His fingers combed through her hair as he talked. "Perhaps your mother waits because she doesn't know how to draw."

Jenna didn't know what to say. When she first mentioned the photograph, she hadn't expected the conversation to turn into a bearing of souls. But, here they were, sharing.

Lifting her head, she looked at Philippe and was taken aback by the seriousness of his expression. How beautiful he looked when stripped of all pretenses. It was a face she imagined the world seldom got to see, and she was honored he showed himself to her.

A wall shifted inside her. She'd been attracted to Philippe since first glance, but the attraction was deeper now. Underpinned by a layer of connection that came from two people sharing their hidden selves.

Suddenly, she wanted to be closer. In a few days, she would be back in Nantucket, and she wanted this night, this closeness, to be the memory she carried home.

"Philippe?" she whispered. "Do you remember when you said I could have anything I wanted?"

She caught him by the chin, forcing him to meet her gaze. Watching the violet slowly turn to indigo as he realized what she was saying. "I'm asking."

Jenna woke to an empty bed and the sound of Philippe on the phone speaking in rapid French. When he saw her sitting up, he winked and pointed to a tray on the dresser where a carafe of coffee and two mugs sat. After shaking the sleep from her curls, Jenna padded over to pour a cup.

"Dits Pierre d'embaucher quelques mains supplémentaires s'il est en désavantage numérique. Nous ne pouvons pas tomber en retard sur l'horaire. Dior s'attend à tout pour être envoyées par la huitième," she heard Philippe say.

He could be discussing plumbing fixtures for all she knew, but it didn't matter. The language sounded beautiful dripping off his tongue. Setting herself on the end of the bed, she watched how the muscles played across his bare back each time he gestured with his arms. Memories of different, soft French words came back to her. Words of encouragement and pleasure. The muscles in his arms flexed, reminding her how they'd held her close.

"Je suis désolé, ma chérie," Philippe said when his conversation was finished. "I am sorry. They are behind schedule in delivering the lavender to the distillery. The oil isn't perfect unless the flowers are at their freshest. We already have enough competition with Egypt undercutting us on price. The least we can do is deliver on time." He set the phone aside and joined her on the

bed. "I told them I would go back and cut the branches myself."

"Would you?" she asked.

"It would not be the first time. And good morning." Leaning in, he gave her a lingering kiss before slipping the coffee from her hands and helping himself to a sip. "Did you sleep well?"

"Very."

"Good. I am glad. I apologize for not letting you sleep in, but as it turns out, it's for the best that you're awake. I wasn't joking about heading back to supervise the harvest."

So much for her keeping him interested. Having finally succeeded in seducing her, he was saying goodbye. No more reason to play tour guide. "You want to head back to the valley."

"I'm afraid I don't have a choice. My absence is part of the reason they have slowed down, so I need to make an appearance. Which is why it is good that you're awake. Now we have time to see a bit of Arles after breakfast."

"You're still playing tour guide?"

He cocked his head. Their night had left his hair wavy and askew, making him more beautiful than ever. "Unless you'd rather take a swim in my tub," he teased.

Was he serious? There wasn't going to be a quick goodbye? No morning drop-off at the hotel with a kiss before he drove out of her life?

"You're frowning again," he said, brushing a thumb across her lips. "You didn't believe me yesterday, did you?"

"I…"

"I told you yesterday. You are far too interesting to

let go after one night. You don't leave for five more days, correct? The way I see things, that means we have five more days to enjoy each other's company. That is, if you enjoyed last night." His knuckle caught her chin. "Did you? Enjoy it?"

Jenna nodded. She was getting lost in his stare again. Those magnetic violet eyes were going to be the death of her.

He smiled. "So did I, *ma chérie*. So did I."

CHAPTER FIVE

AS FAR AS Philippe was concerned, it wasn't unusual for him to have a lover stay around the morning after. He'd even been known to enjoy a romantic weekend or two. But he'd never found himself eager to spend an entire week with someone, let alone two. While he'd begun this venture looking for a few days' distraction, he hadn't anticipated being so thoroughly entertained.

They ended up in the tub after all, the notion of seeing Jenna glistening wet again too enticing to pass up. Later, they lingered over coffee and croissants as they waited for the market to open. There he helped her pick out French perfume. He'd been right that first evening. Jasmine did suit her.

The entire time, he could tell, she was waiting for him to say goodbye. Therefore, it was no surprise to see her eyes widen when he drove past the hotel entrance and headed straight to Château d'Usay.

"You would rather go to your room?" he asked.

"Eventually," she replied. "Seeing as how that's where my clothes are."

He thought of telling her not to worry about something she wouldn't need, but thought better. "We'll go together once I finish my meeting. Do you mind waiting?"

"No. If you don't mind me giving myself a private tour. I missed a few rooms when I was here earlier in the week."

That was when it hit him how much time they'd spent together. Five days had never passed so quickly. Suddenly five more didn't seem like enough.

The meeting lasted longer than he intended. In an effort to keep costs low, Pierre, his manager, had hired fewer workers, a mistake, as it turned out. Now they were going to be forced to pay for extra help at the height of harvest season and recalculate their production schedule.

As a result, two hours passed before he returned to the house.

"Jenna, are you here?" The quiet upon entering made him nervous. She might have gotten bored and gone back to the hotel on her own.

"In the room next to the salon," she called out.

His great-grandfather's library. He found her curled up in the desk chair studying the photos that lined the bookshelves behind her. For a moment, he simply stood in the doorway. The desk was near the back window where it got the afternoon sun. Flecks of dust floated in the beam like tiny little lights. It was like looking at an angel.

"My mother used to call this room a dust-collecting nuisance," he said, finally announcing his presence.

She looked up, and the smile she greeted him with took his breath away. *"Tu es belle,"* he caught himself saying.

"I really need to brush up on my French," she replied. The blush on her cheeks said she guessed at the meaning, if not the literal translation.

Interesting that she would blush at his compliments now.

Strolling to the desk, he saw that one of the photographs rested on her lap. It was his parents by the Eiffel Tower. "I believe that was taken on their honeymoon."

"They look very happy."

"*Oui.* They loved each other very much. They were always laughing and enjoying themselves." Until his father died and his mother stopped laughing, that is. He took the photo out of her hands. "In many ways, she is like your mother. Part of her died with him. Perhaps that is why she didn't put up a fight when she got sick."

"How did she die?" Jenna's question was soft and hesitant.

"Meningitis. It was very quick. One day she had a terrible headache and a stiff neck. A few days later, she was gone."

A thickness filled the air, not unlike the thickness in his throat. Jenna reached across the space and touched his arm. No words. Just a touch. Philippe felt more comfort than he had in years.

"When I think of how quickly she died, I tell myself it is a good reminder that we should pack as much living into our days as possible."

"You do a good job," she replied.

"Since I'm the only one left, I have to live for three. Did you finish your tour?"

"Pretty much." She put the photo back in its spot. "You definitely have a lot of family history to unpack. Between the castle and here, I'm realizing your family didn't just live for centuries—they were involved in every major historical event in France. I envy you. My family's more of a mishmash of mistakes. The part I know of, anyway."

Philippe wanted to say that not everyone knew their family's roots as intricately as he did, but he held back. Jenna tended to share very little of herself. He wanted to see if she'd share more.

She did. "I never met my dad's family," she told him. "I asked once, during one of my parents' reunions, but all he said was that he didn't talk to them. The grandparents I do know? Total pieces of work. Grandma did nothing but complain when they visited. About Grandpa. About how pathetic my mom is."

"Didn't your grandfather say something?"

"He was too busy complaining about my grandmother." She smiled. "Made for some fun Christmas dinners. Especially when my uncles and their wives came around."

"I can imagine." Actually, he couldn't. What she described sounded like a horribly toxic environment. How on earth had it produced such a preppy little angel? No wonder her friend Beatrice gave her an adventure. If ever a woman was in need of fun memories, it was Jenna. Made him more determined than ever to make sure the remainder of her trip was as memorable as possible.

"There is one thing your family did right," he said.

She came around to his side of the desk to sit on the edge. "Really? What's that?"

"They created you."

Pink crept into her cheeks. She doubted him, but he meant the compliment. For all the issues her parents had, or in spite of them, they'd raised someone special.

"Flattery will get you everywhere, Monsieur d'Usay," she told him.

"Is that so? I'm glad to hear it." He dipped his head for a kiss. "What do you say we continue this tour upstairs? There are a few rooms you haven't seen."

"And what rooms would those be?" As she asked the question, she hooked her fingers through his belt loop and pulled him toward her. For a woman who only a day earlier had been dodging his advances, the brazenness was an amazing turn. Snagging her belt loops in return, he tugged her to her feet. "To begin? My bedroom."

Sunrise had never looked so beautiful. Jenna watched as inch by inch, the fields outside her hotel room turned from blue to gold and purple. If she could only stop time from moving forward. Not forever. Only for a few more days.

She was going to miss Provence. The smells, the sounds, the people. She felt at home here in a way she couldn't explain. The feeling went beyond the man in her bed. The region itself spoke to her.

Philippe's arms slipped around her waist, wrapping her in warmth. "What are you doing awake so early?" He pressed his lips to her temple. "Come back to bed."

"I have to leave for the airport in a few hours," she replied.

"Six hours. We have plenty of time yet."

Six hours didn't sound like plenty of time to her. She couldn't believe her trip was almost over. The final few days had passed in a blur of sunny days and tooshort nights. Tomorrow she would be back in Nantucket, going to bed. Alone.

"I wish this week didn't have to end," she said.

"Mmm…" Philippe was too busy peppering her jaw and neck with kisses. "Then cancel your flight. Stay a few more days."

If only she could. "I can't. I have to be back at work day after tomorrow."

"I'll get you a new job."

"While I appreciate the…er…offer…" Philippe's lips had moved to the curve of her shoulder. "I think I need to stick to the original plan." Even if it were possible, a few more days would only be postponing the inevitable. Besides, she was already perilously close to letting the affair cross into emotional territory. Sharing secrets in the dark, it was easy to forget this was a vacation fling. Every time Philippe shared some moment from his life, Jenna could feel herself slipping deeper under his spell.

Far better she leave as scheduled. Before she made a fool out of herself and actually fell in love with the man.

"If that is the case, then I insist you come back to bed," Philippe said. "So I can leave you with a proper memory for the flight home."

Who was Jenna to argue with creating another memory?

"Have I thanked you for such an amazing week?" she asked as he led her away from the window.

They reached the bed, and he sat down on the edge, trapping her between his knees. Jenna gasped as his fingers brushed the backs of her legs. "Last night while we were dancing on the terrace, but you can thank me again, if you'd like."

"I'm never going to forget this trip for as long as I live," she said. *God bless Beatrice.*

"Should I take that to mean you had a proper adventure?"

"Let's see… Roman ruins, champagne under the stars, a sexy French lover. Most definitely. I have been well and truly spoiled."

A expression she couldn't recognize softened his features. "You deserve to be spoiled, *ma chérie*. I am glad you chose Provence for your adventure."

"Me too." Smiling back the lump in her throat, she combed her fingers through his dark waves. "It was the trip of a lifetime. I'll never forget it."

"And I shall remember you, Jenna Brown. Very fondly."

For a little while, maybe. Jenna wouldn't fool herself into thinking she would dwell in his memory forever. A few weeks from now, another woman would be in his bed, while she went on with her life. It was how holiday affairs worked.

Until she stepped through those airport doors, though, Philippe was still hers. And he'd promised her another memory.

She climbed onto his lap.

Philippe watched the crowded checkpoint until he could no longer see Jenna's copper-colored head. That was that. The week was over. A heaviness settled in his stomach. He would miss his little American. Too bad she'd never know how much he appreciated her passing through his life or how she'd managed to return pleasure to harvest week. There were times, usually when they were lying together in the dark, when he was struck by how well they blended together. Like the notes of a perfume. Strong enough that he almost—almost— suggested he fly to Nantucket to see her again. Thankfully he came to his senses. What had drawn him to

Jenna was her difference from the other women in his world. But that difference was also why he shouldn't see her again. Beneath her cynical exterior was a woman who believed in love and forever. The kind of woman men fell in love with.

The kind of woman he avoided.

In the end, it was best he leave Jenna Brown and her enticing smile here at the airport and go back to his routine.

He wished her a wonderful life. She deserved it.

September

Jenna sat on the linoleum floor watching the second hand sweep across the clock. One minute. Two minutes.

Her breathing matched the steady pace. In one second, out the next. In, out. In, out. She wanted to close her eyes but was too afraid she'd lose count of the time.

Twenty seconds. Thirty seconds.

Ninety-nine percent accurate, the package said. She didn't really need a package. She already knew the answer. Two weeks of procrastinating had her pretty certain. Still, nothing was one hundred percent—not even the test, apparently.

Forty-five seconds.

Her heart was racing. The slow breathing wasn't helping. In fact, trying to breathe slowly caused a tightening in her chest. A knot the size of her fist blocked the air from flowing comfortably.

Fifty-five seconds.

She looked down at the stick in her hand. A bright blue plus sign peered up at her through the result window.

Pregnant.

* * *

"Do you have any plans to actually eat that?"

"Huh?" Jenna looked up from her plate to find her friend watching her intently. They were sitting at their favorite restaurant having lunch. Peak tourist season was over, meaning they could enjoy an ocean-view table. On the other side of the glass, the harbor was quiet. At this point in the year, island traffic slowed except for the weekends.

Shirley pointed to Jenna's plate. "Your salmon," she said. "You've been stabbing it for the past five minutes. Is there a reason why you're mutilating it?"

"Teaching it a lesson?" Jenna offered before setting down her fork. "Sorry. I got lost in thought."

"No kidding. You barely reacted when I mentioned Joe asked me to go to New York City with him for the weekend." Joseph Kwan being the lawyer Shirley had recently started dating.

"He did?"

"See? I knew you weren't listening. And yes, he did. We're going Columbus Day weekend."

"That's fantastic," Jenna replied. Good for Shirley for making a meaningful connection. "Just be careful. Don't do anything stupid."

Retrieving her fork, she started poking at her fish again. "Are you sure you're okay?" Shirley asked. "You've been acting weird since you returned from France. You're not hung up on that guy you met, are you?"

"Philippe. His name was Philippe, and the two of us were clear from the start that once the holiday ended, so did we."

Seven weeks had passed since Jenna came back from

France, long enough for the memories of her trip to recede. Some memories, anyway.

Some would stick with her forever.

What was Philippe doing now? It was evening in France. Was he with a woman?

Who was she kidding? Of course he was with a woman. Someone beautiful and sophisticated.

Looking down, she saw her knuckles had turned white from squeezing the fork.

"I don't mean to be distracted," she told Shirley, setting the fork down again. "I've got a bunch of stuff on my mind, is all." Three little sticks, all with the same double blue lines.

"Anything I can do to help? It's not family stuff, is it?"

"Kind of. The thing is…" She stopped herself. Philippe deserved to be the first to know. She'd been avoiding calling him for a week, telling herself it was because she didn't know the right words. What would he say? Would he be happy?

"The thing is what?" Shirley asked.

"Something I need to handle on my own," Jenna replied. And soon. The time for procrastinating was over. There were decisions to be made.

Her stomach started churning. On her plate, the once attractive piece of fish had become a pile of pink chunks smothered in apricot sauce. Jenna grabbed her water to keep the sour taste from rising in her throat.

"I'm sorry," she apologized to her friend. "I'm not feeling well. Do you mind if I bail?"

"Sure. Let's flag down the waitress."

"No. You stay and finish your meal. No sense in

both of us ruining our lunch." Besides, she needed to be alone to formulate her thoughts.

"If you're sure," Shirley said. When it came to food, she was easily convinced. "Call me later and let me know how you're feeling?"

"Sure."

It would be the second call Jenna made.

The first would be to France, to let Philippe know that the d'Usay family line wasn't going to die out after all.

She had her phone out before she stepped through her front door, only to catch herself before hitting the dial button. What would he say when she told him? Would he believe her or, would he think it a trick? He was a well-known millionaire; it wasn't inconceivable to think a woman might try and score a payday.

Jenna took a deep breath. In the end, it didn't matter if he thought she was trying to trick him, did it? She was pregnant, and he was the father.

She dialed.

"*Allo*?" The sound of his voice swept over her, taking her breath away. She'd forgotten how smooth and melodic it was.

"*Allo*?" he repeated.

"Hel…" She found her voice. "Hello, Philippe? This is Jenna. Jenna Brown. From Nantucket."

"Jenna?" Was it her imagination or did he sound happy to hear her voice? It was hard to tell because of the background noise. He was in a restaurant or at a party or somewhere. She could hear the voices and the sound of cutlery.

Oh God, he was on a date. "Is…is this a bad time?"

"No, no. Is something wrong?"

"Well," she said, wincing, "that depends on your definition of wrong. I'm pregnant."

Silent greeted her announcement. She might have thought they were disconnected except for the crowd noise. "Philippe? Did you hear…?"

"Are you certain?"

Jenna's heart sank. Stupid her. Apparently a small part of her had held out hope that he'd be excited about the news. "I took the test three times. I'm going to take a blood test this week to make sure." The test was more of a formality than confirmation at this point.

"That is a good idea," Philippe said. "To be certain, I mean. You'll call me when you get the results?"

"Of course. As soon as I know them."

"*Merci.* I would appreciate that."

He might as well have been asking her to call about a flower order, for all the emotion in his voice. *He doesn't want his dinner companion to know his business.* Again her stomach sank, and again she kicked herself for being disappointed. "I know this is probably the last thing you were expecting," she said. "I'm still trying to wrap my head around the news myself. It was as big a surprise to me, I assure you."

"I—I'm sure."

"Anyway, I thought you should know."

"*Oui. Merci.* That is, thank you for telling me. You will call when you have the results?"

Jenna nodded. "As soon as I have them," she said into the phone.

"Good. *Merci.* I'll talk to you soon, then."

Hopefully that call would go better. This call was so

awkward it hurt. It more ways than one. "I should probably let you get back to your meal," she said.

"How did you…?"

"I can hear the silverware."

"Ah."

Silence filled the line again. Jenna wished she could
see his face to know what he was thinking. The flatness of his voice left no clue.

"Good night, then," she said.

"Jenna…"

Her thumb froze. "Yes?"

"Nothing. Good night."

The dial tone kept her from saying any more.

Well, it was done, she thought, as she let the phone
slip from her ear. He knew.

Philippe hung up the phone and returned to his seat in
the restaurant. The crowd, which had been loud and
boisterous before Jenna's call, had faded as though
someone pushed the entire setting into the background.

A baby. His baby.

"Is something wrong? You look like you saw a
ghost."

Shaking himself from his fog, he smiled at his dinner
companion. "No ghost, Xavier, just unexpected news."

"Good news, I hope," his friend replied.

"I—" He wasn't sure. "I think so."

He was still trying to absorb the phone call. For the
last few years, Philippe had told himself he would be
the end of the d'Usay line. That there would be no wife,
no child, *no heir* to carry on the family tradition.

Now, thanks to Jenna, that was no longer the case.
There was going to be another d'Usay after all. The con-

cept filled him with an emotion he couldn't describe. All of a sudden he felt…happy.

At the opposite end of the table, his lawyer Xavier Cousteau was carving up his steak. "How strong are you when it comes to family law?" he asked him.

"Not very. I studied it in law school, but my knowledge doesn't go much further," Xavier replied. "Why?"

"I'm going to need a person who can help me establish a trust." A trust. A support plan. His mind was ticking off steps. "Can you find me someone?"

"*Oui.* Of course. But why?"

"Because, my friend…" Philippe paused while he signaled the server. When the man approached, he asked for two glasses of malt whisky.

"Philippe?" Xavier prodded.

"Because," Philippe replied, "it's time for me to start thinking about the future."

CHAPTER SIX

October

MORNING SICKNESS WAS the worst. For the past week, her stomach revolted every morning at five thirty. The only thing that quelled the nausea was a sweet cheese croissant from the bakery next to her apartment. Leaning over the sink in the break room, Jenna inhaled the pastry in two bites like she was trying to hide a dirty little secret.

"You're definitely part French," she told her stomach. Eight weeks in, her abdomen was still flat. For now. If she kept scarfing down pastry, she was going to gain twenty-five pounds in the first trimester alone.

Shirley poked her head through the door just as Jenna was washing her hands. "Mr. Mylanski was complaining of discomfort. I went ahead and gave him his morphine."

Poor old man's pain was getting worse. "Thanks." She'd check in on him before she left to make sure he was sleeping.

"No problem. I saw you duck in here and figured you needed a second. Morning sickness strike again?"

"Uh-huh. Guess this means the pregnancy is a reality," she joked. "I was armed today, though. I bought an extra croissant. I should be fine until end of shift."

"Have you heard any more from…?"

The pastry grew heavy in her stomach. "Not since our last conversation."

She and Philippe had spoken twice. Once when she took the home pregnancy tests and again when the blood test made the pregnancy official. Both times he treated her like a business call, his tone flat and emotionless. One hundred and eighty degrees from the man she knew in France.

Could she blame him? Hadn't she stood on the Tour Magne and listened to him say he didn't want children?

In case you haven't guessed, I prefer to stay as entanglement-free as possible, he'd said.

He was in shock. When she called to report the blood test, he'd replied by saying, "I don't understand. We used protection."

"Nothing is one hundred percent," she'd reminded him. "And neither were we. Remember?"

The morning she departed France, when they'd been eager to make one last memory.

They made one, all right.

His silence had told her he remembered, and was kicking himself for getting carried away.

"What do you want to do?" had been the second thing he asked.

"I—I don't know," had been her reply. At the time she'd been as shocked as he was.

But, as her mind—and body—got used to the idea, she came to a conclusion. She wanted the baby, whether Philippe wanted to play a role in its life or not.

"You'll come first, too, I promise you that." She

patted her stomach. "If your father doesn't want to be around, that's his loss. We'll live our lives just fine without him." The little life growing inside her belly would be the start of her new family legacy.

The floor was quiet when she stepped out of the break room. Always was this time of morning. Most of the patients were still asleep. Jenna stifled a yawn. Thirty minutes and she could get some sleep. Between working nights and the new pregnancy hormones, she was wiped. Lord help her when she reached the last trimester. Especially since she'd be carrying an extra two hundred pounds of pastry weight.

She was sitting at the nursing station, focused on logging patient notes, when the elevator door dinged. The morning shift had started to arrive. "Give me five minutes and I'll be ready to catch you up," she said, eyes focused on the computer screen.

A shadow crossed her desk. "Hello, Jenna."

It was Philippe.

Eight weeks hadn't changed much. Other than a few wrinkles in his dark suit, he looked as breathtakingly handsome as he had when they met.

Jenna's pulse stuttered. "What are you doing here?" In Nantucket. At the crack of dawn.

"It's good to see you, too." He smiled, but it lacked the sparkle she remembered. "Your custodian let me in. I think he thought I was here to see a patient."

"That's because family members are allowed twenty-four hours a day." Jenna didn't care how he'd gained entrance. She was way more interested in how he'd found her. "How did you know where I would be?"

"There's only one nursing home on your island. It

wasn't too difficult," he replied. "And you mentioned how you often work overnights. How are you feeling?"

Really? He thought they would simply chat like nothing was wrong? "You don't speak to me for almost a week and then show up at my place of work unannounced. How do you think I feel?"

"I meant…" His eyes dropped to her midsection. "You look tired."

"Happens when you've worked all night." She left out the morning sickness.

"Of course," he replied. "I should have realized."

Meanwhile, he looked amazing.

God, but this was awkward. What happened to the easiness they shared in Provence? *Oh, right.* Her hand pressed to her stomach.

Philippe cleared his throat. "I'm sorry for…"

He was interrupted by a loud moan coming from one of the rooms. Mrs. Symonds. The elderly woman always moaned for several minutes upon waking.

"Morning, Mrs. Symonds," she heard Shirley say in a cheerful voice. "I'm going to visit you in about five minutes to give you your morning pill."

Her friend's shoes squeaked on the linoleum as she rounded the corner and stopped short. "Well, isn't this a surprise," she said.

Philippe tilted his head. *"Pardon?"*

"This is my friend Shirley," Jenna said. "Shirley, this is Philippe d'Usay."

He reached for her hand, shaking it politely, not kissing it as he had done Jenna's the day they met. "You are the woman with the shingles. I trust you have healed?"

Shirley looked as surprised as Jenna felt. The last

thing she expected was for Philippe to remember those kinds of details.

"Right as rain," she replied before shifting gears and moving into protective mode. Eyes narrowed, arms crossed in front of her chest, she assessed Philippe up and down like he was a stray dog. "Funny, but Jenna didn't mention you were coming to the island."

"I didn't know he was coming," Jenna responded. "It was a surprise."

"Really? How interesting."

"Tell me about it." To Philippe, she added, "I'll be wrapping up my shift in a few minutes. We can talk after that."

"Very good." He nodded. "I will wait for you outside."

As soon as he disappeared behind the elevator doors, Jenna's composure vanished.

"Are you going to be all right?" Shirley poured her a glass of water.

"I... I don't know." She honestly hadn't thought she'd ever see him again. Now that she had, her insides were a jumbled mess. "I suppose he wants to finish our discussion in person."

"Mighty nice of him, seeing as how he has fifty percent of the responsibility. This is a good sign, though, his showing up. Means he's stepping up."

"Maybe." Jenna was too mixed up to theorize. Whatever the reason, she'd have to wait until after her shift to find out.

Who knows? Maybe her nerves would have dissipated by then.

Along with the strange ache in her chest that arrived the same moment Philippe did.

* * *

Philippe took a seat on a bench just outside the nursing room door. The autumn air was brisk and damp; the sun hadn't been up long enough to burn away the fog. Employees walked past, barely giving him a moment's notice. How many of them knew Jenna? All of them? He imagined her being a popular coworker.

His head ached. He'd never been good at sleeping on planes, and this last flight was no exception. Too anxious about seeing Jenna, he'd tossed and turned the entire trip. A decent cup of coffee would help. Whatever the black liquid was that he purchased at the local airport did not count.

They'd had the most marvelous coffee that morning after in Arles. He smiled remembering how they'd strolled to the corner café for café au lait. Jenna's hair had been damp from the bath, her face freshly scrubbed and shining. Neither of them could stop grinning. You'd have thought they were a pair of virgin newlyweds the morning after their wedding night.

What did Jenna think of their week together now? Was it still a fond memory, or did she regret meeting him? His chest grew tight at the thought.

As if his thoughts conjured her, the door slid open and Jenna stepped outside. He was struck, just as he had been upstairs, by the fact his memory hadn't embellished the uniqueness of her beauty.

In France, she'd favored bright colors and comfortable, modest clothing. The American version was no different. Her uniform was a bright purple over which she wore a heavy knit cardigan. Together they hid her shape. No matter, his brain filled in the gaps.

Instinctively, he stood to kiss her hello, catching himself. If he'd only had this kind of restraint their last morning together...

He settled for an apology. "I'm sorry for showing up unannounced. I should have called and let you know I was coming."

"Yes, you should have. In fact, you should have called, period." Arms crossed over her chest, she glared at him with fiery green eyes. This was not, Philippe reminded himself, the time to be aroused by her feistiness. Before he could do or say anything, he needed to rectify the mistake he made by not communicating with her this past week.

"You are right. I've been in the UK on business and wanted to wait to talk in person. Still, that is no excuse."

"No, it isn't."

He could see he had some ground to make up. "Well, I am here now, and I want to deal with this."

"*This* is a baby."

"*Oui*, I know it is a baby." *His* baby. No matter how many times he repeated the phrase, the words continued to sound surreal. "Forgive me, I'm still in shock. I never expected to have a child."

She continued to glare, but her features softened slightly. "I suppose I've had a little more time to get used to the idea."

"A little," he replied.

The awkwardness between them was killing him. On the flight over, he'd mentally rewritten what he wanted to say until he had the perfect speech. Those words had vanished. All he could think about was how lovely she looked in the early-morning light. "Is there somewhere we can go to talk? I could use a drink."

"At seven thirty in the morning? Good luck." For

the first time in their reunion, Jenna cracked a smile. "You'll have to settle for coffee."

"Coffee will do." Anything that let him clear his head.

They walked, in awkward silence, to a coffee shop a few blocks away. Looking around, Philippe took in Jenna's world. Nantucket was not Provence. The air tasted salty. The landscape was more rugged. There was a sense of pragmatism to the surroundings, he'd noticed, even with the most elegant of homes.

Despite it being a workday, the coffee shop was fairly empty. Only a handful of people waited in line to order. "Things quiet down here once summer is over," Jenna told him. "Plus, the only people around at this hour are locals heading to work. We can sit out on the deck and we won't be disturbed."

He let her lead the way to discover the small wooden structure overlooked a marsh pond filled with squawking birds. On a sunny day, the view was probably quite beautiful.

"You never answered my question about how you were feeling," he said once they'd settled in at one of the white plastic tables. She had refused his offer of coffee in favor of a sweet cheese pastry and a cup of warm water with honey and lemon. "You aren't suffering any kind of complications or anything?"

"Nothing sweet cheese croissants won't cure. Morning sickness," she clarified when he frowned. "Of course, it's still early in the pregnancy."

"You intend to…see the pregnancy through, then." *Mon Dieu*, but that sounded crass.

"Yes."

He allowed himself to exhale. "Good. I was hoping you would say that."

"You are?"

Given what he'd said in the past, he could understand her surprise. He was as surprised as she, really. Children—family—had never been in his plans. He'd always figured that when he grew too old to work, he would pass D'Usay International on to some deserving person and let the name live on through the company. The more he thought about having a child, however...

"Once the news sank in, and I got used to the idea..." He paused while he sipped his coffee. "I like that I will have an heir."

"You know that whether you like the idea or not doesn't really matter, right?"

"I know," he replied. "Which is why I'm glad you want this child as well."

"I see." She sat back in her chair, studying him. Philippe's skin warmed under the scrutiny. "Does that mean you're planning to be a part of this baby's life?"

"I take my responsibilities seriously. I intend to make sure he—or she—wants for nothing. I've already talked to my attorney, and he is making all the necessary arrangements."

"Financial arrangements, you mean."

"Yes. I want to make sure my child, and its mother, are well provided for," he said.

Jenna was frowning.

"What is wrong?"

"Nothing," she replied. "Go on."

He hated when women used that word. *Nothing never meant nothing.* She was upset with him, probably still angry for his being out of touch this past week. There was little he could say that would go over well until her irritation cooled. "Perhaps we should wait and have this discussion when we've both had some rest," he said. When they weren't tired and peevish. "Tonight, over dinner?" Good food, the right atmosphere. Yes, dinner was definitely a better plan.

Jenna shook her head. "I can't. I have to work."

"Not until later on. We can eat early, and then I can drive you to the nursing home."

"I…"

Acting completely on impulse, he reached across the table to clutch her hand. The first thing he noticed was how cool and damp her skin was. It reminded him of that afternoon in Arles when they'd gotten soaked to the skin. He covered hers with his second hand to warm her. "Please, Jenna. I want to do this right."

Her eyes darkened. Was she thinking of that day as well? "All right, dinner." She pulled her hand free. "But I'll drive myself."

"Very well." Why her answer bothered him, he wasn't sure, but no sooner had she mentioned driving herself than he felt a wave of frustration. "I'm staying at the Merchant Seafarer."

Naturally Philippe would stay at the Seafarer, the hotel where the adventure began. As she walked into the lobby, Jenna recalled how excited she and Shirley had been when they attended the fund-raiser. The sumptuous hotel wasn't someplace they regularly hung out, it being far too pricey for anything but special occasions.

"I guess dinner with your daddy counts as a special occasion, too," she said as she settled in amid the seascapes and whaling artifacts to wait for Philippe. Apparently talking to her stomach was going to be a thing.

The fire in the giant fireplace gave the room an old-fashioned warmth. Under different circumstances, the setting would be romantic with its candlelight and black ocean views. Two months ago, she and Philippe would have been exchanging simmering smiles from across a table. Tonight they would be discussing financial arrangements for their child.

The thought made her stomach churn. Why did his emphasis on money bother her so? Seriously, what else did she expect? The man had made his feelings about children quite clear that afternoon on the Tour Magne. As far as he was concerned, she was carrying an unexpected liability. She should be grateful he wanted to shoulder responsibility at all, and that times had changed enough that he didn't feel the need to do "the right thing."

What was it about the women in her family and accidental pregnancies, anyway? First there was her grandmother—unless her mother had been the healthiest five-month preemie ever born—then her mother, and now her. Talk about a family legacy.

"How about when you grow up, you break family tradition," she said to the baby. "Find someone who loves you back, and *then* have the baby."

When she put it like that, she sounded like she was in love with Philippe. She wasn't.

At all.

Not a bit.

At precisely six o'clock, the elevator doors opened and Philippe emerged, accompanied by a blond man who looked vaguely familiar. When he saw her sitting by the fire, he smiled. Jenna hated how her insides swooped in response. Months later and she was still reacting to him physically. Had to be hormones.

He greeted her with a kiss on the cheek. "You look beautiful."

No, she didn't. She'd worn the most staid outfit she owned. Black slacks and a bulky gray turtleneck. She looked like she was attending a funeral.

"This is Kit Merchant," he continued, turning to his companion.

That was why the stranger looked familiar. The hotel owner had sponsored the charity auction.

"Kit and I spent a summer sailing in St. Tropez back before I took over D'Usay International. It was a fortunate coincidence that he was here this week as well."

"I understand you recently stayed at the Château de Beauchamp," Kit said after the introductions. "I hope your trip was everything you imagined."

"And then some." To Jenna's surprise, the answer rolled right off her tongue without embarrassment or awkwardness. The trip had been wonderful. It was only her carelessness that she regretted.

"Congratulations, by the way," she added. "I read in the paper that the clinic is just about complete."

"Yes, and not a minute too soon, what with cold weather coming. Beating an addiction is hard enough without the added pressure of finding a safe place to stay. This clinic will help a lot of people."

"That's wonderful."

"I wish I could do more. The islands have as big a problem as the rest of the Cape."

"It's a good start."

"You're right, and if we're lucky, we'll help spare a family the torture of losing a loved one to the streets."

As he finished, his eyes took on a faraway look. This wasn't mere generosity on his part; it was personal. At the auction, someone said Kit lost a friend to an overdose. Clearly the story was true.

"And," he added, "thanks to Philippe, we'll be able to provide some of the extras we had to strike from the budget."

Philippe had made a donation?

"It was the least I could do," the Frenchman replied. "Matt was a good guy."

"It's still greatly appreciated," Kit said. "If there's anything I can do in return, let me know. It was good seeing you again, my friend. Ms. Brown, I hope you won't be a stranger."

"That was very generous of you to make a donation," Jenna said once Kit departed.

Again Philippe shrugged. "The three of us, Kit, Matt, and I, enjoyed some good times together. Matt was a hell of a sailor as well. I had heard rumors he was battling something, but I didn't know how bad things had gotten."

And he knew as well as anyone how it felt to lose someone close to you. In her annoyance over his comments this morning, she'd forgotten that part of him. "Opioid addiction is insidious. It can take hold before you realize, and breaking free is a hard battle. I have seen more than one nurse fall prey after an injury at work. Goes to show, addiction can affect anyone, no matter the background."

"Let us pray then that neither of us ever have to watch a friend battle the disease." Philippe squeezed her hand. The soft understanding in his eyes made Jenna's heart clench. *This* was the Philippe she remembered from her trip. The one who made her feel understood.

"And that Kit's clinic makes a difference," she said.

"*Oui.* Let us hope."

Neither of them made a motion to let go. From the corner of her eye, Jenna caught his arm lifting upward, to tangle in her curls the way he loved to do before kissing her. Her pulse quickened. Was he going to kiss her now?

The hand pulled back, and just like that, the moment vanished. "Ready for dinner?" he asked.

The heaviness in her stomach was annoyance, not disappointment. "Sure," she said. Might as well get the financial arrangements settled.

Kit had arranged for them to have a table by the corner window, tucked away from the other diners. An ice bucket was already in place, the bottle chilled and ready to be opened. Just like that first night on the terrace, she thought wryly. How appropriate.

"Sparkling cider," Philippe told her. "I've never had it myself, but I thought it bad form to drink in front of you."

"I wouldn't have minded."

"I would have. Besides, how can we toast unless you have a glass as well?"

"What do we possibly have to toast?" she asked.

"Many things," he replied. "The *bébé* for one."

"I'll give you that." The baby was definitely worthy of a toast.

As they touched the rims of their glasses, their eyes connected. Two months hadn't diminished the magnetism of Philippe's eyes. They were as deep and vivid as ever. Maybe because there were no lavender fields to invite comparison. Only cold dark water and gray October sky. Jenna loved color. In France, brightness had been everywhere.

Or was her memory being misled by the eyes across the table? The fields would be barren now. Bright never lasted.

"Did you finish your harvest on time?" she asked him.

"Pardon?"

"You were worried the harvesters would fall behind schedule when I left France. Did they get everything cut and distilled on time?" Her question had caught him off guard. She asked because she wasn't ready to talk finances yet, and the farm was the first topic that came to mind.

"We did," he answered. "In the end, it was a good harvest. The jasmine did particularly well. We managed to produce a surplus of jasmine oil."

"Congratulations." She was wearing the jasmine perfume he'd bought her and wondered if he'd noticed when he kissed her hello. Although whether he did or not didn't really matter.

"What comes now?"

"Are you referring to the company? Or for…"

"The company." She still wasn't ready for baby finances.

"We start working on securing contracts for the next year or so and focus on the crops growing in our other locales." He took a sip of cider. "That is why I was in the UK. Colliers of London is interested in our lilies."

"The soap company?"

Philippe nodded. "They are one of the few large companies left who prefer natural to synthetic materials."

"Does that mean we should toast congratulations?"

"It's too premature for toasts, I'm afraid," he said. "We're still in the negotiation phase."

"That makes sense. You don't want to celebrate until you are absolutely sure."

"Exactly."

Having milked the topic as much as possible, they fell silent. Jenna filled the space by pretending to study the menu. Peering over the edge, she saw Philippe running his fingers up and down the stem of his glass. It was the first time she'd ever seen him do anything that could be considered fidgeting. "About this morning," he began. "I am sorry I didn't warn you of my arrival. I didn't mean to put you off balance."

"Thank you." Even though they'd covered his regret this morning, she appreciated the direct apology. As an olive branch of her own, she teased, "I thought maybe it was your passive-aggressive way of getting back for putting you off balance with my call."

He smiled. "I'll never tell."

Once again, they grew silent, the elephant in the room making civil conversation impossible until it was acknowledged. "I'm sorry," she said. "I know the situation—"

"Don't." He cut her off. "It was my eagerness that got us here."

"We were both eager, if you recall."

"Indeed I do." The candlelight flickered in the dark of his eyes, and for a second they were back in France. Jenna's cheeks warmed the way they did whenever she pictured them together. Remembering how Philippe's touches flipped a switch inside her, causing everything else to fade away.

"Regardless of how…" The sound of his voice brought reality back. "It's important you know I have every intention of meeting my responsibilities as a parent."

So much for avoiding the elephant. "You said as much this morning," she replied. He'd even used the same word. *Responsibility.* She felt a sting in her midsection, although she wasn't sure why. *Responsibility* was a perfectly good word. An accurate word. "You… you said you talked to your lawyer?"

"I asked him to establish a trust in the child's name with you as trustee. Whatever happens to me or D'Usay International, the child won't suffer."

"You envision something happening?"

"I believe in planning for contingencies. Nothing lasts forever, especially in a world where technology is quickly replacing tradition. For all I know, D'Usay International will fade long before I do. I want to make sure my son's future is secure."

The word *son* didn't escape her. "You're hoping for a boy. To carry on the d'Usay name."

"Are you surprised?"

"Not really." Given his attachment to family history, she expected nothing less.

"I'm glad you understand," he said, reaching for his glass. "Seeing the name continued is important to me. In fact…"

Their conversation was cut short by the arrival of the waitress to read the evening specials. A tall blonde, she had breasts as perfect as naval oranges and wore a pencil skirt so narrow that Jenna was surprised she could walk.

Launching into a detailed description of the catch of the day, the woman kept her attention squarely on Philippe. Jenna might not have existed. To his credit, Philippe kept his charm dialed back to seven out of ten, smiling with charm, but not overtly so as he listened.

"I hope I'm not cramping your style," she said once the waitress walked away. Slowly, Jenna might add, and with a whole lot of hip action.

God, that sounded jealous and petty. She drowned the thought with a gulp of ice water.

Philippe gave her an odd look. "Are you talking about the waitress?"

"She's very pretty, and obviously interested." Her second sentence came out moderately less shrewish.

"I'm here to discuss our child, not to pick up waitresses. Would think you'd give me a little credit."

"I'm sorry. I didn't mean to insult you. It's just that I know I don't…never mind." The fact she didn't have any claim on his dating life didn't require saying.

How many women had shared his bed since her departure? She didn't want know and yet at the same time had a perverse curiosity. She had a feeling the answer would depress her.

"You were about to say something before the waitress arrived," she said. "We were talking about the baby having your last name."

"Right." Suddenly he was back to twisting the glass stem. "I was about to say that I'd like the child to carry my name whether it is a boy or a girl."

"Okay."

"Unfortunately, my lawyer informs me I don't have

control over the matter. Since we are not married, you are free to give the child your last name if you prefer, even if I acknowledge paternity."

Was this why he was fidgeting with the glass? Because he thought she might refuse his request? "I don't really know the law regarding baby names, but I just said I was okay with the child having your name."

"But you could change your mind."

"Are you suggesting I would renege on a promise like that?" Now she was the one insulted. "I know how important your family legacy is to you. What do you think I'm going to do, threaten to name the baby Brown as some kind of bargaining chip?"

Philippe looked down at his place setting. "Xavier…"

"Xavier what?"

"Hasn't had the pleasure of knowing you as well as I do," he replied. "As a result, he's being overprotective."

Underneath the table, Jenna balled her hand into a fist. She tried to see the situation from Philippe's perspective. All the attorney knew was that she was a pregnant American. He was paid to be mistrustful.

Philippe, on the other hand. They'd shared a bed. Bared their souls. "I would never be that petty or vindictive."

"I know."

His right hand disappeared from the tabletop. A second later, Jenna felt his grip surrounding her fingers. "I know," he repeated softly. There was nothing but sincerity in his expression.

The warmth from his touch spread up her arm and into her chest. "So, what kind of legal assurances does Xavier want?"

"Well…" He took a deep breath. "Xavier outlined a

couple of possibilities. One is to make my last name a stipulation of the trust."

"In other words, sign something that says I don't get access to the funds unless the baby carries your name."

"Exactly."

Sounded crass when said out loud, as if the money was the sole factor. She never wanted their child to think he or she was a cash cow.

"And the other option?" she asked. "You said there were a couple."

"Yes, we…"

Jenna had forgotten they were holding hands beneath the table until his grasp grew tighter. Philippe's expression had grown serious, too, making the hair on the back of her neck start to prickle.

"We could get married," he said.

CHAPTER SEVEN

JENNA'S JAW DROPPED. Marry him? That was the next suggestion? Mr. Marriage and Family Require Too Much of a Commitment?

"Don't dismiss the idea out of hand," he said, gripping her hand tighter. "If you are my wife, the child carries my name."

"So would I," she pointed out. Surely the attorney had noted that she came with the deal.

"Only for a short while. We need only stay married long enough for the baby to be born. Then we can dissolve our agreement."

"Not dissolve, divorce," she corrected. Semantics, maybe, but the word mattered. Marriage wasn't the same as an agreement to grow flowers.

"Very well, we will divorce once the baby is born."

Jenna took a deep breath. "Tell your lawyer I'll sign any kind of stipulation he wants," she said.

Philippe frowned. In his confusion, Jenna pulled her hand free but kept it under the table. She didn't want him to see how much she was trembling. How could he make such a suggestion? Was he not listening when she talked about her parents?

"I do not understand," he said. "I am offering…"

"To do the right thing. Yes, I know." That added to the suggestion's sting. Philippe believed he was doing the right thing.

"My father did the right thing, too. So did my grandfather. And, while I appreciate your dedication to family traditions, I'd prefer not to repeat mine." Mentally, she gave herself a pat on the back for speaking calmly.

He shook his head. "But this would be different," he said.

"How? I'm pregnant, you're suggesting marriage." Where was there a difference? "Seems the same to me."

"Except that both of us would be entering the marriage with the same expectations."

In other words, their marriage would be different because there was no expectation of it being real. Jenna had to give him credit. He was honest.

What surprised her was to hear him press the issue. Was it an ego thing—shock that someone would say no—or was it because he wanted the baby born in wedlock? Either way, there was one very key ingredient missing. No way she was marrying anyone who didn't love her. She, and her baby, deserved better.

"Doesn't matter. The answer is still no."

"Are you sure?"

"Positive. Have your lawyer draw up whatever papers he wants." She looked to her glass, not wanting to see the relief that was no doubt in his eyes.

Or for him to see the disappointment that was in hers.

That could have gone better. Philippe ordered a brandy before settling into the shadows of a leather bench seat. Jenna and he had said their goodbyes a few minutes earlier. A very polite hug outside the front doors, barcly long enough for him to register the lines of her body, before she slipped into her waiting car. As soon as her taillights disappeared into the night, he'd headed for the hotel bar.

Fortunately, the place was deserted except for the bartender, who was more interested in the American football game on the television set. His disinterest allowed Philippe the privacy to recount the night's events.

Had he thought honestly Jenna would consider his proposal? He knew her story—part of it, at least. But their situation was different, was it not? Besides, he wasn't offering permanence; she could leave whenever she wanted.

But apparently she preferred to sign a legal document instead. Fine. He should be relieved the situation would be resolved so civilly. He'd dodged a bullet, as it were. There were plenty of women in his past that wouldn't have been so understanding.

"You lost your friend."

It was the waitress from the restaurant. She set his brandy on the table before angling her head toward the bartender. "He's more interested in seeing if New England scores on this drive, so I volunteered to bring your order. I'm surprised to see you alone."

"She had to go to work," Philippe replied.

"Too bad. Would you like some company?"

He studied the woman over his drink. She was quite lovely, and from the gleam in her eye, she was the kind of woman who wasn't looking for anything beyond a good night. Just his type.

The image of cinnamon curls splayed across his pillow popped into his head.

"Perhaps another time. I have a lot on my mind tonight," he told the waitress.

The waitress shrugged, disappointed, but not too. "Signal if you need anything."

She swayed back to the bar, leaving Philippe alone to sip his drink.

And wonder why he hadn't accepted a woman's invitation since Jenna left France.

Jenna had just enough time to change into her uniform and report for her shift. When she stepped off the elevator, Shirley was waiting for her at the nurses' station.

"We've got five minutes," her friend said. "How'd it go?"

"Dinner? Fine. I had the chicken *amandine*. We toasted the baby's good health. Oh, and he proposed."

"He what?"

"Keep your voice down!" Jenna whispered harshly. "I don't need the whole floor knowing." She looked out on to the floor to see if anyone was listening, but their colleagues had their heads hunched over the computers, updating patient information. "He suggested that we get married."

Once she finished explaining the whole story, her friend sank into a nearby chair. "Wow, he doesn't mess around, does he? From the way you described him, I never would have pegged him for the traditional type. Did you…?"

"He only proposed out of obligation."

"You sound disappointed," Shirley said.

"Don't be ridiculous." Why would she be disappointed? Wasn't as though she was in love with Philippe d'Usay. What they shared in France—the connection, the intimacy—were emotions of the moment. Trying to extend them was a pipe dream. She wasn't about to compound reckless behavior with more reckless behavior.

"I have absolutely zero interest in marrying Philippe. Why would I want to be my mother?"

"Trapped in a never-ending codependent relationship with a narcissist?" Shirley asked.

"I meant tying myself to someone who doesn't love me."

"Only in this case the tie would be temporary and you don't love him. Right?" Shirley held up a hand. "Relax, I'm yanking your chain. You totally made the right call."

"Thank you."

A glance at the clock said the shift was about to start. Jenna headed into the tiny room behind the nurses' station to lock up her pocketbook. As she shoved it into one of the lockers that lined the back wall, she heard her phone start to buzz. Whoever it was would have to wait. Patients came first.

"I hate to start the shift on a down note," said Donna, one of the nurses on the eleven-to-seven shift, "but Mr. Mylanski isn't doing so good." She relayed the older man's vitals. "You might want to call his family and give them the heads-up."

The news cast a pall on the atmosphere. Shirley swore. "I thought he'd have a little longer. Poor guy. I'll call his daughter."

"And, on the opposite end of the spectrum," their colleague continued, "Lola has been restless all night." Lola being one of their patients with dementia. "She keeps sneaking out of her room and climbing into other patients' beds."

"I'll keep an eye on her," Jenna volunteered. Chasing after Lola would keep her too busy to think about Philippe. At least for a few hours.

Eight long hours later, an exhausted Jenna stepped out into the early-morning sunshine. "I don't know about you, but I could use breakfast," she said to Shirley. "I forgot my sweet cheese croissant and baby's annoyed. Wanna join me? My treat." Mr. Mylanski had passed an hour before, and she figured her friend could use the distraction.

Shirley shook her head. "Thanks, but I'm going to go home and take a hot bath."

"You sure?" Wasn't like Shirley to give up free food. The phone in Jenna's bag was buzzing again. She wasn't in the mood to take the call now anymore than she was any of the other times during her shift. "Did you miss the part where I said my treat?"

"Positive," Shirley replied. "Besides, I think you already have plans." She nodded to the parking lot, where Philippe was walking their way.

"What's he doing here?" Jenna asked.

"Beats me. You'll have to ask him," Shirley replied.

He'd gone casual, in jeans and a black sweater that emphasized his shoulders and muscular arms. When he saw Jenna he smiled.

Jenna's stomach swooped, and it wasn't morning sickness.

"*Bonjour*, ladies," he greeted. "The time difference had me up early, so I thought I would bring you breakfast." In his hand he carried a tray of cups and a white paper sack. He handed one of the cups to Shirley. "This is for you. I am afraid I don't know how you prefer it."

"Free works," Shirley replied, "but if you have sugar, I won't say no."

"Sugar packets are in the bag, along with one of those sweet cheese pastries you said helped with the morning sickness." He looked back and forth between her and Jenna. Shirley had dark circles from the night's stress; Jenna guessed she looked the same. "Is everything all right?" he asked.

"We lost a patient last night," Jenna explained.

"I'm sorry."

"Thank you. He was a sweet old man," Shirley said. "I'll miss him."

"At least his family made it in time to say goodbye," Jenna said.

"Yes, that is good. No one should die alone." Philippe frowned, leaving her to wonder if he was referring to more than Mr. Mylanski.

"Is this a bad time?" he asked.

"Not for me," Shirley replied. "I've got a date with a hot tub."

"Jenna?"

Jenna eyed the white paper sack he held. Baby really needed to eat. She couldn't believe he'd remembered she said the baby craved sweet cheese croissants.

"There's a park a short way from the coffee shop we visited yesterday. If you don't mind eating on a bench, we can go there. This hour of the day we'll have privacy."

"A park bench is fine. Lead the way."

Jenna waited until they'd walked a few paces before accepting the drink. Warm water with honey and lemon. Same order as the day before. She tried not to be touched that he remembered.

"I didn't think I'd see you today," she said.

"Why not?"

"Because…" Because they'd said everything they had to say last night. With his business complete, what reason would he have to stay? "Is this about the paperwork you wanted me to sign?"

"Xavier is fast, but not that fast," he replied.

"Then…?"

"Perhaps I wanted to enjoy your company. We are having a child together. Shouldn't we be friendly? What is that buzzing sound?"

Jenna sighed. "It's my phone." The vibration could be heard coming from her pocketbook.

"Do you need to answer?"

"Definitely not." It was way too early for drama, just like last night had been too late. "They'll leave a message." Or call back again, more likely. "I'm not talking to anyone until I've had my pastry."

"Present company excluded, I hope."

"Only because you brought the pastry," she replied. "Although there's no guarantee I won't be too busy soothing my stomach to talk with you, either."

Because of the hour, the park was empty except for a lone dog walker. In the center, there was a bench overlooking the walking paths. Using his handkerchief, Philippe wiped away the moisture and fallen leaves and they took a seat.

The moment was surprisingly peaceful. After a long, crazy night, it was pleasant to simply sit and listen to the sounds of the birds waking in the bushes. Philippe had stretched his arm along the back of the bench, a warm, protective barrier against Jenna's shoulders.

"Reminds me of the morning we had breakfast at Marguerite's," he remarked.

"Except the weather was warmer and we were on a busy street corner surrounded by people instead of sitting under an oak tree," Jenna said once she'd washed down the last of her croissant. "Other than that, though."

"Completely the same."

They both chuckled. Jenna knew exactly what Philippe meant.

That morning had felt peaceful, too. The silence between them easy.

He nodded and sipped his coffee. "I'm sorry about your patient."

"Thanks. He'd only been with us a couple months, but we all liked him. I feel bad for his family. No one likes losing a loved one."

"No, they do not."

Jenna winced. Fatigue was making her insensitive. She touched his knee in apology, earning a slight smile in return.

"You said his family was there, correct? He did not die alone?"

He wouldn't have died alone regardless—Shirley would have made a point of sitting with him—but something in the way Philippe was double-checking about Mr. Mylanski's family said the point mattered to him.

"All but one son," she told him. "He lives in Boston and couldn't get across until this morning."

"Too late," he murmured. "He must feel terrible."

He looked out over the grass, his profile as open as Jenna had ever seen, excepting that afternoon in his apartment. "I wasn't with either of my parents when they died. No one told me until after the fact. With Felix... I tried, but I couldn't get there in time. I was in Italy, and by the time I saw the hospital had called and arranged a flight... He died all alone."

In that moment, his comments from before made sense. Mr. Mylanski's death must have triggered his guilt. Armchair analysis wasn't what he needed right now, though. She sat back and waited for him to continue.

"I thought I had more time. I wanted to make this one last deal before... So he'd know he was leaving the business in good hands. If I had known the end was close, I would have..."

"Canceled your trip?" she asked. "Do you think that's what your brother would have wanted? For you to let the business languish while you sat vigil twenty-four-seven?"

Tucking a leg beneath her, she turned to face him, her hand squeezing his knee. "You were doing what your brother wanted you to do—you were taking care of the business."

"How do you know what he wanted?" he asked.

Oh, why did his eyes have to be so sad? "I don't know for certain," she told him. "But you told me your brother loved the business."

"More than loved. He was born to run D'Usay International."

"And did he want you to be as dedicated to the company as he was?" Philippe nodded. "Then he would have wanted you to be spending your time making the business grow..."

She cupped his cheek and looked him straight in the

eye as she told him the same words she'd told others over her career. Only this time, they felt far more important. "You tried your best, Philippe. That's all you could do. Your brother knows that."

"*Merci*," he whispered, eyes shining. He leaned briefly into her touch before kissing her palm and backing away. "Listen to me. You lost a patient and I'm making the moment about myself."

"Don't apologize. I like when you open up." Knowing he trusted her enough to reveal even the slightest vulnerability touched her more than any compliment. "You don't have to be charming and witty all the time."

"But I am so good at being charming and witty." His eyes sparkled for a moment before returning to the dark violet they were before. "You make it easy," he said. "To share the thoughts in my head. I don't know why, but you do."

"Not at first," Jenna reminded him. "Remember I had to push?"

"And now look at me. You've created a morbid monster."

"Morbid? Maybe. Monster? Far from it."

His eyes locked with hers. Piece by piece, the noise around them died away until all Jenna could hear was the pulse fluttering in her throat. She wasn't even sure she was breathing.

"Thank you for listening." Philippe was whispering. Was he afraid to break the silence, too?

"Anytime," she whispered back.

His gaze dropped to her mouth, his eyes dark and heavy-lidded. Jenna's gaze hitched. She knew that look. She felt her body start to lean toward his, the way metal moved toward a magnet.

"I want to see you tonight," he whispered. "Will you have dinner with me?"

"I don't know." When he looked at her like that, she had trouble thinking clearly. Was this entire conversation to break down her defenses and revisit what they shared in Provence, or was he attempting to be friendly with the mother of his child? She was too confused to know.

"I've never been to Nantucket," he was saying. "I'd like to see your island."

Her island. He knew the right phrases to melt her resistance. Pulling her eyes away she studied the dents in her drink lid, hoping the answers lay in the white plastic.

"All right." The answer came out automatically. "I'll show you around Nantucket. You might as well know about where your child is going to grow up."

Out of the corner of her eye, she thought she saw Philippe shooting her a look. Apparently he hadn't considered the baby would live on Nantucket.

"But first, I need to go to bed. To sleep," she quickly added. "We can take your tour later this afternoon."

"Very good. I will call you to work out a time." His expression brightened, and Jenna immediately felt her insides take a tumble. Damn if he couldn't obliterate her resolve with a single smile. "I'm looking forward to it."

Heaven help her, so was she.

CHAPTER EIGHT

PHILIPPE STARED AT the string of messages in his in-box. Xavier was on him to go over the contracts for the upcoming year. There were changes in the terms that the lawyer wanted to review with him. The growers in Belgium were making noises about a potential work stoppage over wages. If they succeeded, it would start a chain reaction eastward to Asia. Dozens of little fires demanded his attention, and here he was thinking of ways to extend his stay in Nantucket.

Truth be told, he could have departed that morning, but when his alarm went off, he found himself unwilling to leave. Normally he couldn't wait to be on his way home. Then again, normally he grew tired of a woman's company by this point in their relationship as well. Instead, he looked forward to seeing Jenna as much that afternoon as he had that first day in France. Every time he tried to work, his brain went to her sitting on the bench in the sunshine. He'd thought of her all night, too, her soft, pale skin invading his dreams.

Of course her dominating his thoughts could be easily explained. She was carrying his child. It was only natural that she—and her well-being—should be on his mind.

Only it isn't her well-being you're thinking about, it's her.

Once again, Jenna Brown was proving the exception to his rules.

Like the strange ability she had to make him share his feelings.

Until today, he'd never told a soul how guilty he felt at not being by Felix's bedside when he died. His only chance to actually say goodbye, and he'd failed.

Strangely enough though, he felt better for talking. Jenna hadn't said anything profound, but she'd still managed to comfort him. Small wonder he nearly kissed her.

Leaning back in his chair, he relived those moments on the bench, rewriting them so that he tasted her kiss. Been too long, he thought. Far too long. He missed her.

Shortly before three thirty, Philippe pulled up in front of Jenna's address. Immediately, he knew which side of the duplex was hers. The one with the tricolor corn hanging on the door wreath and potted cabbages lining the porch steps.

As he stepped out of his car, he spied Jenna through a first-floor window talking on the phone. Whoever was on the other end was making her tense. She was pacing in and out of view and rubbing the back of her neck.

She was still tense when she answered his knock, her pink lips drawn in a tight line. "Is everything all right?" he asked.

"I need to learn not to answer the phone on the way out," she replied. "Someone always needs something when you're rushing to get ready."

Her face held the same taut expression as this morning when she'd refused to answer the phone in her bag.

His guess? Whoever she'd been avoiding had finally connected with her, and she wasn't happy.

"If you have business, I don't mind waiting," he told her.

"Not necessary. I'm done with them." She stepped outside and shut the door. Not before Philippe caught a glimpse of a brightly painted entrance way, however. "Besides, we only have a couple hours of daylight. If you want to sightsee, we shouldn't dawdle."

"Good point," he replied. Although was her rush really about daylight?

"I'm looking forward to seeing your island," he said as they walked down her steps.

"I wish you wouldn't call it my island. I don't even own the house I live in."

"You live here though, no? Experience all the seasons? Then it is your island," he added once she'd nodded her answer. He opened the passenger door and waited while she slid in and buckled her seat belt. "And I am looking forward to taking a tour."

"As long as you don't expect a detailed history lesson along with it."

"I believe we've already established your historical illiteracy." His teasing comment barely elicited a smile. The phone call had definitely dampened her mood. At least he hoped it was the phone call. "Where to first?"

"Main Street."

They spent the next hour or so walking the winding cobblestoned streets. Little by little Jenna's mood seemed to lift, and soon she was pointing out landmarks and sharing anecdotes with a smile. True to her warning, she didn't provide much enlightenment in the way of local history, but she did provide a glimpse into her life, which Philippe found just as enlightening. Listening to her wax enthusiastically about the fried clams and lobster rolls served at the various restaurants, he learned that her dining tastes were simple and unpretentious. Her anecdote about the pets on parade during the local Christmas walk told him she had a fondness for animals. And her soft gaze at a little boy buying a stuffed black dog from one of the stores said she was looking forward to having their child. It was, perhaps, better than any history lesson.

They moved from Main Street to the south. "From what I'm told, this street used to be called Prison Street," Jenna told him.

"Why is that?"

"Going out on a limb, I'd say because there was a prison." He cast her a look. "Seriously. They're restoring the old jail about a half mile down. No doubt that's what inspired the name."

"Logical." Saltbox houses from the eighteenth century lined both sides of the road. Philippe found their brown and gray shuttered shapes quaint. One particular house had a tall tower in its backyard, a strangely modern-looking structure. "Is that an observatory?" he asked.

"Yep. On weekends they open it up so you can see the stars."

"Odd that would be stuck in a row of antique homes."

"Not really. The woman who lived in that particular house was an astronomer. One of the first female astronomers in the country, in fact."

"You don't say." Philippe craned his neck to look upward. "Too bad it is not yet dark—we could go look at the stars ourselves."

"Closed for the season," she told him. "Plus, I already climbed one narrow tower with you. I'm not climbing a second."

"Chicken." The remark earned him a nudge from her shoulder—the first contact of the evening. Instantly Philippe wanted to touch her in return, but he held back, stuffing his hands in his back pockets instead.

"I didn't appreciate how much of your island closes up during the winter," he said.

"Only the parts that cater to the tourists and summer residents. There are plenty of year-round businesses to keep the economy flowing in the off-season."

"Nevertheless, so many people leave when the weather turns cold. It must get very cold and lonely."

"Cold, definitely. Nantucket nor'easters can be pretty brutal."

Philippe wasn't sure what a nor'easter was, but he understood the word *brutal*. If he counted correctly, Jenna would be well into her second trimester during those brutal months. When ice and snow could make a person lose their balance.

A wave of unease washed over him. "Perhaps you should consider staying off the island during those months, and go somewhere a little less stormy."

"No need." She waved off his concern. "I've been here a couple of years now, and it's not so bad. You learn to deal with the weather."

"You weren't pregnant those winters."

"No, but… Oh, I get what you're saying now." She stopped walking so she could face him. "I hate to break it to you, but people have babies on Nantucket all the time, winter included."

But they weren't having *his* baby. Philippe was only

concerned with her. "What if you slip on ice and fall during one of these nor'easters you talked about?"

"I could slip and fall anywhere," she replied. "Conditions don't have to be icy for a person to lose their balance. I'll be fine." She started walking again.

Fine. Philippe had heard that word before. He didn't want Jenna to be fine. He wanted her—and their baby— safe.

"It isn't as if you will need to work during the pregnancy," he called after her. "You would be free to go and do whatever you wanted." Except fall.

"Philippe." Again she stopped, only this time when she turned, she had her arms crossed. "Are you planning to make my getting off the island one of the trust stipulations?"

"No."

"Then back off, okay? I'm a grown woman. I don't need you mother-henning me into moving."

"I'm not trying to make you move," he said. "I'm simply trying to keep the baby safe."

"Well, you'll have to trust me."

"I'll try." The knot in his chest made it difficult.

"Try hard." Spinning on her heel, she resumed walking, her pace quick enough that he had to pick up speed to catch up.

"Do you mind if I ask you a question?" he asked after a quarter mile of silence. He didn't want to contribute to the chill between them any more than he already had, but he was curious. "What made you choose here to live? A single woman like yourself, I would think Boston would be far more appealing."

To his relief, she took the question for the peace offering he meant it to be. "I lived in Boston for a year or two after graduation. Decided I'd rather be three hours away."

He was about to ask why when her pocketbook began buzzing. The woman had the loudest vibration setting he had ever heard. "Your phone is ringing."

"I'm sorry. I probably should answer. Only because the nursing home might be looking for shift coverage." Unzipping her bag, she reached in and pulled out her cell phone. "I'll let them know…never mind." Her expression fell. "It's not the home after all."

She dropped the phone into her bag unanswered.

"You still could have talked with them," Philippe said.

"Could have, but I don't want to," she replied. He noticed the way the muscles in her jaw twitched from it being clenched. Her tension had returned. Was it the same caller as before? The one she had spent the morning avoiding as well? He was trying his best not to pry, but watching Jenna turn from smiling to angry in the blink of an eye had him suddenly quite upset with the person as well—whoever that person might be.

A thought struck him. "You are not being bothered by someone, are you? A former lover, perhaps?"

"Good Lord, no." Her laugh had a mocking tone. "More like the opposite."

"A current lover." He was definitely angry.

"Try my mother."

Ah, the woman who couldn't move on from Jenna's father. Why didn't she want to speak with her? He ventured a semi guess. "You are mad at her?"

"Frustrated," Jenna replied. "It's just more of the same, and I've got enough on my plate without piling on more drama. Honest to God, sometimes I don't understand what's going on in her head. Do you know what I mean?"

"I take it she is making decisions you don't approve of."

"I'm not really in a position to judge other people's behavior, am I?" She pressed a palm to her stomach. "But, yeah, I think… Check that. She is making a big mistake."

"Are you sure? Perhaps you don't know the whole story." Much like how he felt right now. He was playing devil's advocate because saying *I'm sorry* seemed trite and he didn't know what else to say.

"Oh, I know the whole story, all right," Jenna replied. "This isn't the first time we've been through this drama."

This time he did apologize, for the stress the call was obviously causing. Both Jenna's jaw and her fist were clenched. Such tension couldn't be good for the baby. He looked around for a place where they could sit and talk in earnest, saw mostly trees and weathered picket fences. There was, however, a small historical center across the street from the observatory that had a tall set of steps leading to its porch. He motioned for Jenna to follow him over. If anyone balked, he'd pay the membership fee.

"Why?" she asked.

"So you can relax," he said. "Your shoulders look ready to snap."

"Sorry. I just get so…"

"Frustrated. You said as much." He waited until she'd taken a seat on one of the steps before positioning himself behind her and placing his hands on her shoulders. Naturally, as soon as he touched her, the muscles tightened even more. Philippe kneaded the tension. Over the years, countless women had told him he had talented hands. Now was a good time to put the compliments to the test.

"Perhaps you would feel better if you told me what was going on," he told her.

"I can't," she replied. "It's too… God, that feels good."

He pressed his thumbs against muscle. "Your shoulders are in knots."

"That's because every time I think about it, I want to scream. How can someone, in this day and age, be as clueless as my mother? I know what's going to happen, too. I'm going to have to pick up the pieces."

Pieces of her mother? "I'm sorry," he said. "I'm confused."

"I know you are. I don't mean to be cryptic." Heaving a deep sigh, she closed her eyes. Philippe would have liked to say it was because she enjoyed the massage, but the look on her face suggested it was out of embarrassment.

"My father's back."

Saying the words out loud only made her feel more frustrated. She felt Philippe's hands still for a moment before continuing their ministrations. Under other circumstances, the massage would feel heavenly.

"Your parents are having an affair."

"Yep." And not for the first time, either. "Dad's current relationship is on the rocks—that can happen when you sleep with the new inventory manager at work—and he needed a friendly shoulder. Naturally…"

"He turned to your mother."

And like always, her mother was ready, willing and able to give him all the compassion he desired. "They've been 'involved' for a couple weeks," she told him.

"Perhaps this time they will…"

"No, they won't." While she appreciated his attempt to be positive, she'd seen this situation too many times before. Her father coming back all smiles and sweetness, telling her mother everything she wanted to hear. "This is the same thing he always does," she said. "They'll be together two, three weeks, until someone else catches his eye. Mom's his emotional comfort food."

"And your mother, she lets him treat her this way?" Jenna could tell he found the idea as unfathomable as she did.

"Every single time. Dad can be quite the charmer when he wants to be."

Like someone else Jenna knew. Although unlike her father, Philippe managed expectations. You knew what you were—or weren't—getting with Philippe. Her father promised love and forever.

She allowed her head to fall forward as Philippe's fingers slid upward along either side of her spine toward her neck. "Naturally my mom's over the moon. She spent ten minutes talking about the two dozen roses he sent to her office."

"Roses are the lazy man's flower."

Jenna couldn't help but smile. Of course he'd say something like that.

"I wish you could have heard her on the phone. Going on and on about how this time was different. That she always knew they'd get back together."

*"He's changed, Jenna. He realizes now what's impor-
tant, and that's a home with someone who loves him."*

*"He had that, Mom, with what's-her-name. He
cheated on her."*

*"Because he was so unhappy. He hasn't truly been
happy since we divorced."*

"She must love your father very much to keep for-
giving him."

"Love? Try worship. All he has to do is crook his
finger, and she comes running. It's sad."

"Surely he loves her somewhat as well." Jenna looked
up to see his serious expression looking down at her.
"He keeps returning to her. Comfort food or no."

"If he loved her, he'd let her move on," she replied.
For a man who eschewed emotional commitment, he
sounded oddly romantic. She blamed it on his having
grown up with parents who loved one another.

"The worst part is the fallout *after* he moves on.
Last time she went to bed and cried for a week." She
sighed. "I just wish she'd show some pride and tell him
to get lost."

"She can't. She loves him. What is that old phrase?
You can't control what the heart wants?"

"The heart can want whatever it likes," she replied.
"Doesn't mean you stop listening to your head."

Her mother was never going to change. Jenna was
going to spend the rest of her life watching her have her
heart broken. "It's like watching someone driving a car
you know is going to explode. You warn them and warn
them, and they insist on driving anyway."

"All you can do is hope they aren't too badly burned."

She lifted her head so she could look at Philippe.
"Very wise words, Monsieur d'Usay."

"I have my moments." Returning her smile, he returned to working on her shoulders. His fingers were magical—although Jenna already knew that. This was different from lovemaking, however. His hands were doing more than massaging. They were bringing calm with every tense muscle he smoothed away.

"You are right about one thing," she heard him say as he pressed the base of her neck. "People would be far better off if they led with their head."

"There would certainly be a lot less heartache in this world if they did," Jenna agreed.

"Unfortunately, not everyone is as wise as we are. Do you feel better?"

"Yeah, I do." She wouldn't have thought it possible. Normally she would keep her mother's drama to herself. At most, she shared with Shirley, but since her friend tended to get angry on her behalf, Jenna usually left those conversations as ratcheted up as when she began. Talking with Philippe was different. Whenever they spoke honestly, it was as though they were on the same page in terms of emotion. They understood one another. There was a connection.

Careful, Jenna. These kinds of thoughts were what had led her into Philippe's bed.

Not to mention sounding dangerously close to something her mother would say.

"Are you sure?" Philippe asked. "Your shoulders tensed again."

"From hunger." She twisted out of his touch. So she could face him—no other reason. "How about I treat you to some true New England clam chowder? We'll see if your bouillabaisse can compete."

"And if I'm not impressed, do I get to pick dessert?"

With those dimples of his, she'd swear the man could make the simplest question sound like an innuendo. "Sure," she replied. "As long as it's ice cream. Baby needs lots of calcium."

Not to mention that, innuendo or not, she had zero intentions of letting the evening be anything more than platonic. She'd already decided as much before, but she was doubly resolved after their conversation. Taking her own advice, she was listening to her head.

And not to whatever it was she could feel swirling around her heart.

A short while later, they were driving south, stomachs warm and full. "How do you say 'I told you so' in French?" Jenna asked.

"Je te l'avais dit."

"Then *je te l'avais dit*," she replied. Someone had eaten their soup like it was their last meal. "Better than bouillabaisse, no?"

"Apples and oranges, *ma chérie*, but since thinking so makes you smile, I won't argue."

"Can't argue with someone who's right," she shot back with a laugh.

The day wasn't supposed to be this lovely. It was like they were back in France, free and easy, again. Leaning against the passenger door, Jenna studied Philippe's profile. His hair was mussed from walking in the wind, the brown waves making him look every inch the carefree playboy. She knew better, though. She knew that beneath the facade dwelled a very complex man who mourned his family and respected the past. She loved when he dropped his mask around her. Those moments were a gift that made her feel incredibly special. In those times, it was easy to pretend theirs was a bond unlike his other relationships.

"You want to turn by that street sign," she told him.

They were headed to Madaket. Taking in the unobstructed sunset from the beach was something every visitor to the island had to experience. "The view will rival your lavender fields," she told him.

"Never, but again I am willing to indulge. As I said, I like your smile."

Jenna's cheeks warmed. "I'm looking forward to seeing the sunset myself. Believe it or not, I haven't been out this way in ages."

"Is that so? Why not?"

Sunsets were a date activity or for tourists, neither of which applied to her. "Just haven't."

She wasn't surprised to see only one other car in the beach parking lot. "Midweek in the off-season doesn't attract a lot of sunset fans," she told him. "In the summer, this lot is much fuller."

"Our lucky night, then."

"How so?"

"We'll have privacy. I like having time alone with you."

"We've been alone all day."

"I know. I've enjoyed it." He pulled the car into a front-row space, behind the log fence that divided beach from lot. They could see the beach grass blowing in the wind. Beyond it was the silvery-brown sand and beyond that still farther, the black Atlantic with its choppy whitecaps.

"In fact..." There was the soft click of his seat belt and then Philippe was leaning just close enough for

Jenna to smell his body wash and the woodsy under-
tones of his aftershave. "I enjoyed it very much."

Jenna's eyes fell to his lips. She knew what he was
doing. He was offering her the chance to cross the line,
same way she did this morning.

Her mouth and throat were suddenly dry. "The best
view is on the beach," she told him.

"Are you sure, *ma chérie*? The view is quite beautiful from this vantage point." He gestured toward the
ocean, but his eyes stayed on her.

"Positive. For starters, the sun sets in the west." She
pointed over her shoulder. "The only thing you'll get
from this view is a gray sky."

"The only thing?" The dimple in his cheek was as
pronounced as ever. He definitely didn't play fair.

"By the way, you'll want to take off your shoes. The
sand is very soft."

Soft and cold. Jenna forgot how quickly the grains
lost their warmth when the shade moved in. She shivered as her foot sank ankle-deep into the cool damp-
ness.

"You are going to want this as well." Philippe draped
his leather jacket over her shoulders. Completely un-
necessary since she was wearing a light jacket of her
own, but if he wanted to play gentleman, who was she
to argue? Especially when the jacket felt like having
his arms around her. She pulled the leather tight and
breathed in his scent.

"I will say, this is far different from Beau Rivage,"
Philippe remarked. "The sand is softer, and it's very
peaceful."

"One of the things I love about this beach is how far
removed it feels from the rest of Nantucket. It's almost

like walking on a different island. Look." She pointed ahead at a trio of objects lolling on the beach. "Gray seals," she said. "There's probably more swimming around in the water just past the breakers."

"Those three look like giant gray rocks from here," Philippe remarked.

"I'm sure they appreciate the comparison. We shouldn't get too much closer. I don't want to spook them."

"Then we'll stay here." To her surprise, he sat down on the sand. "A little cold, but we will survive. If you prefer, you can sit on the jacket."

Jenna considered the supple leather wrapped around her shoulders. Much as she hated to lose the comforting scent, she'd sat on evening sand enough to know she preferred a warm bottom to extra-warm shoulders. Reluctantly, she slipped it off and spread it on the ground.

She needn't have worried, because no sooner did she take her seat than Philippe pulled her close. "To block the wind," he whispered as his arms wrapped her in a hug. "Nothing more."

Unless she chose different. Disappointment swirled in her stomach even as she appreciated the gesture. He was truly staying on his side of the line and ceding her the power. Same as he had their entire relationship. Respecting her wishes and never pushing for more.

Did he have any idea what his chivalry did to her? How giving her the space she needed to use her head actually fueled her attraction?

Handsome, charming and respectful? What woman wouldn't fall?

"What is the beach in Nice like?" She needed to focus on something other than her thoughts. "You said it was different?"

"Much. Like I said, the sand is softer here, and the water much darker. Where I spent my time, there was more development. I like how much of your coastline is open space. This is especially peaceful."

"Mmm. A few more weeks and dark this time of day." Jenna didn't know if he meant to or not, but his voice had turned soft and rhythmic, like the waves meeting the shoreline. His jaw rested against her temple, each modulated word he spoke teasing her skin. It was a struggle to keep her eyes open.

"When I first moved here, I loved how you could go to the beach any time you wanted," she told him. "Not like Boston Harbor, where going to the ocean meant visiting the piers."

"My parents loved the beach," Philippe said. "We used to go every summer as a reward for working the harvest." Jenna remembered the photo he kept on his mantel in France. She knew it was a keepsake from a happier time, but she hadn't realized it also represented the end of a tradition. Thinking of him holding on to the memory, she felt an ache in her chest.

"God, how I hated the harvest," she heard him say. He chuckled.

"You did?" Shifting in the sand, she looked to see if he was joking.

"All those hours in the sun? Who would enjoy it?" he replied. "Soon as I was old enough, my father trained me to pick the jasmine. My smaller hands would be gentle like the women we hired," he explained. "How I would curse him for sticking me with the old women. All day long telling me stories about the house and the village. I thought I would scream."

"But you love history."

"Now, yes. Wasn't until I attended university that I realized how much of those stories I had absorbed and how much I appreciated them."

"I had no idea." In her mind's eye, she imagined a young Philippe, gritting his teeth as the women chattered around him, all the time hanging on every word in spite of himself.

"Ironic, isn't it? How the things we hated as children become the things we cling to as adults."

"Like the harvest."

"*Oui*, like the harvest," he replied in a faraway voice. Jenna wondered if he was in fields of his memory. His expression always turned bittersweet when he talked of his childhood. You could feel his loss weighing down the stories.

It left her wanting to brush the weight away with her fingers.

"Is that why you come back for the harvest?" she asked, already knowing the answer. A better question would be why he chose lavender over the fields of his childhood.

"I have to," he said. "My father, his father, his grandfather... Felix...they all worked that field. They all left part of themselves there. Every August, I feel them calling to me, and I feel too guilty not to go."

"Guilty?"

"For being the one who survived. I was the one who cared the least."

"That's not true." Jenna scrambled to her knees. With her knees pressing his jacket into the sand, she reached out and captured his face in her hands. "I've seen how seriously you take your business. I've listened to you on the phone. I watched you in the fields with the farmers. You care about that company. And when your child is born, you're going to teach her to love it, too, right down to her picking jasmine."

"Jenna, I…" It was all right if the words fell away. The moisture glistening in his eyes said it for him. Jenna brushed her thumb across his cheek. Turning his head, he nuzzled her palm before offering a smile.

"You really believe the baby will be a girl, don't you?" he asked.

"The way she demands carbohydrates? I know she is."

"Our very own Antoinette. I would like that."

While his right hand continued to hold hers, his left slipped free to splay across her abdomen. Jenna caught her breath. It was such a natural, paternal gesture, and it made her heart sing. "Part of me still can't believe it's real."

"I've got four pregnancy tests that says it is," Jenna teased. She had to make light of the moment; his touch was weaving its way into her skin. Gazing into his eyes, it was all too easy to picture a future where his hand rested on her expanded belly as the baby kicked.

"I know" was his reply. "I never doubted you for a second."

"The sun is starting to set."

The two of them turned their attention westward, where the sun was slowly disappearing behind the horizon. Only half could be seen. The remaining light painted streaks across the sky. Reds, oranges and purples blended between clouds. Jenna heard a splash, then two more as the seals headed into the Atlantic.

"Isn't it beautiful?" she said with a sigh. "Told you it was worth a drive."

"Yes," said Philippe. "Although I would have traveled anywhere if it meant holding you like this."

Jenna's heart skipped.

Little by little, the sun sank and the colors receded into black. They sat in silence, their breathing the only sounds they made. It was as if they were the only two people in the world.

"Jenna..." He didn't say anything else. Didn't have to. Jenna knew what he was asking. She took in his darkening silhouette and remembered how it felt to be in his arms. *Once more*, she thought. He wanted her, and she ached for him. She leaned in.

And kissed him.

In a flash, they were pressed hip to hip. Philippe's hands tangled in her curls as he rained kisses along her jaw and down her neck. "I've missed you, I've missed you," he murmured against her skin.

She'd missed him, too, with an intensity she hadn't realized until this moment. The ease with which she slipped under his spell frightened her, and yet it felt as natural as breathing. Which was why, when Philippe rose to his feet and held out his hand, she knew she would go with him to his hotel.

Philippe had the most vivid dream. In it, Jenna and he stood on the balcony of his apartment. Only instead of his street, the balcony looked out on an enormous field filled with crows. It must have been early morning, right after sunrise. The light was slowly spreading across the field. He stood behind her with his arms wrapped around her waist, his hands pressed to her swollen belly. Every so often the baby would kick, and he would start with amazement.

"She's a bossy one," Jenna said to him.

"Like her mother," he started to reply. But before he could finish the sentence, Jenna changed, her body turning into liquid. She flowed out of his arms and under the balcony railing.

He awoke with a start to a darkened hotel room.

"Everything all right?" Jenna's sleepy voice came to him from across the king-size bed. "You jumped in your sleep."

"Only a dream. Did I wake you?"

She made some kind of sleep noise. "My back was cold."

Immediately he rolled to his side so she could spoon against his chest. "Better?"

"Mmm…"

He lay in bed listening to the sound of her breathing. Sleep wasn't going to come back easily for him. The dream left him too tense.

Of course, he didn't need to be a psychoanalyst to parse the dream's meaning. He'd been battling a gnawing sense of anxiety since he and Jenna argued about her staying on Nantucket in the ice and snow.

If only she would return to France with him, then he wouldn't have to worry. He would be around to prevent anything happening to the baby. The two of them could experience the pregnancy together. And, if tonight was any indication, they could enjoy the physical side of their arrangement as well. Clearly their attraction hadn't waned. Unusual, but then Jenna was unusual, as evidenced by the fact he hadn't found a woman as interesting or attractive to him since her departure.

"Come back to France with me." The words poured out of him. "I would make sure you had the most wonderful pregnancy. You and the baby could have every-thing you wanted."

Feeling her stiffen, he pulled her closer. He'd caught her off guard.

"That must have been some dream," she said after a moment.

"I want to keep the baby safe," he told her. This was his child. The continuation of his family.

When she didn't respond, he wondered if she'd fallen asleep. "Jenna?"

"Can we talk about this in the morning?" she asked. "When you're thinking a little more clearly?"

"Of course." She had a point. The words *had* spilled out of him without much thought. There would be plenty of time for them to talk in the morning, after he'd put some distance between himself and the dream.

In the meantime, she was in his arms. He burrowed his head into the crook of her neck and willed himself to sleep.

CHAPTER NINE

"I DON'T KNOW. I just don't know where they put the cat."

"You made him sit with Lola?" Shirley remarked. Her friend was at the nursing station logging patient care information into the computer. "Are you trying to test his patience?"

As she wheeled the thermometer cart into the corner, Jenna cast a look into the activity area to where Philippe and Lola sat at one of the tables. The older woman was chattering nonsensically while nervously arranging scraps of paper into patterns. Every so often, Philippe would nod in agreement or offer a comment. "I'm sure the cat is fine," she heard him say in a voice you'd use with a young child.

Jenna's heart stuck in her throat. Patient, gentle. He was going to be a wonderful father.

"I didn't put him with anyone," she said. "He arrived for breakfast early, and Lola latched on to him. I think she might have a little crush."

"She wouldn't be the only one," Shirley replied.

"I simply appreciate the way he is treating her. It bodes well for when the baby arrives."

"I meant the other patients on the floor. He charmed a few of them the other night when he delivered you to work. How long is he planning to hang around, anyway?"

"I don't know. He hasn't said." She left out how they'd spent her evenings off the past two nights sharing a bed. Those memories were hers alone. Besides, Shirley would read too much into things.

"But *where* is the cat?" Lola persisted. "It doesn't make sense. He was watching TV and now he's gone."

"I'm sure he'll show up," Philippe assured her. "Cats are very resilient. Maybe he went to get himself a mouse for breakfast."

"A mouse for breakfast!" Lola laughed like he'd told a joke and went back to arranging her squares. "A mouse for breakfast," she repeated, shaking her head. "That's funny."

"Lola," Jenna called over. "How about we get you cleaned up for your breakfast?"

"A mouse for breakfast," Lola called back, shaking her head again. Philippe shot them a grin.

"I don't think you're going to break them apart any time soon," Shirley said. "At least not until Lola gets her oatmeal." She leaned back in her chair. "Are you all right? You look more pale than usual."

"Apparently the pastry didn't work this morning. I'm still nauseous."

"Maybe you should tell Monsieur d'Usay to stop wining and dining you."

"He's not wining me. Alcohol is bad for the baby." Shirley had a point, though. She had been burning the midnight oil a little too much. The baby was telling her she needed to rest. When her shift ended, she'd tell Philippe she needed to take a night off and sleep. He wouldn't mind. After all, he was all about making sure baby was safe.

"You know…" She double-checked to see if Philippe was still distracted. "He asked me to go to France with him the other night."

"No way! He's persistent, I'll give him that."

"I don't think he was serious."

"Why not?"

"Because he…" *Didn't follow through in the morning.* "I think it was more of a passing comment."

"Some passing comment. What did you say?"

"Nothing. Like I said, he really wasn't serious."

"But if he was serious…? You already told him no, right?"

"Of course." Jenna suddenly needed something to do with her hands. Picking up a pen, she began twisting the plastic cap between her fingers. "I've already made that clear, which is why I know he wasn't serious."

When was the shift change, anyway? Her stomach was churning.

Shirley give her a sideways glance before picking up a set of folders and tapping them on the desk. "Speaking of bad marriages, what does your mom think of all this?"

"You mean about the baby?"

"And the proposal."

"The proposal…" Feeling a little more in control of the subject now that Shirley was being pesky about it, Jenna set down the pen. "Is none of her business. As for the baby? She's over the moon. She keeps talking about how she and my dad are going to spoil their grandbaby rotten."

"Her and your dad, huh? They're still hot and heavy, then?"

"Oh yeah, till death do them part," Jenna replied.

"Hey, maybe the sixth time is the charm," her friend said. "You never know, right?"

"You sound like Philippe."

"Philippe knows about your parents? You don't talk about your parents to anybody."

"Philippe's different." Shirley arched a brow, forcing Jenna to grab the pen again. "I mean, crazy or not, they are the baby's maternal grandparents. The man should know what he's getting into."

"*Pardon*, ladies. I don't want to interrupt, but the two of us are going in search of a cat."

She looked up to find Philippe and Lola had left the activity room to join them at the nurses' station. The old woman was holding Philippe's hand.

"I don't know where she is," Lola said.

"I think she might be in your room," Shirley told her. "With your breakfast tray."

"Then her room shall be the first place we check," Philippe replied. Leaning over the counter, he used his free hand to tuck a curl behind Jenna's ear.

"Do not let your parents worry you so much, *ma chérie*. They are going to do what they want. Foolish or not."

He'd given her the same advice last night. "I'm trying," she told him.

"I know, but their affair still bothers you. I can tell from your frown." His fingers brushed her cheek before dropping away. A whisper of a touch that had her nearly leaning forward for more. "We will talk about it more during breakfast, all right? First I must find a cat."

"*Bonne chance.*" As she watched him walk away, Lola shuffling by his side, she thought her heart might split her chest in two.

"Oh my God."

"What?" Yanking her attention away from Philippe, Jenna saw Shirley staring with her mouth open. "What?" she repeated.

"The look on your face. You're falling for him."

"Don't be ridiculous. I was smiling at how sweet he's being with Lola."

"Uh-huh. Sure. You keep telling yourself that."

"I will," Jenna replied. Same way she would ignore the way her heart was taking up extra space in her chest with its fullness. She was not falling for Philippe. She couldn't. Because if she was falling, then she would have to take back every criticism she ever mentally hurled in her mother's direction. After all, how could she criticize someone when she was no better?

From somewhere down the hall, Lola laughed. Jenna's heart skipped a couple beats.

Oh man, she was in trouble. She wasn't falling for Philippe.

She'd already fallen.

"I finally managed to convince her that the cat was outside on holiday. Luckily, she saw a squirrel through the window and decided from the tail that I was correct."

"Are you sure it wasn't the arrival of her breakfast tray that convinced her?"

"Possibly, but I prefer to take credit."

Philippe shot her a grin before disappearing into her kitchen. A second later she heard the sound of mugs being taken out of a cupboard.

She'd been so exhausted after her shift that she asked Philippe if they could skip their breakfast in the park. With predictable protectiveness, he'd immediately brought her home and tucked her into bed so she could sleep. To her surprise, when she woke up – nearly ten hours later! — he was still there, sitting at her dining room table, typing away on his laptop. The scene looked so incredibly right, her knees nearly buckled.

Things were so much easier when they were together in France without strings or messy emotions. When did her expectations change?

Maybe they didn't, she realized, thinking of that afternoon in Arles when they first made love. Maybe she simply didn't want to acknowledge what that connection signified.

It wasn't the baby that complicated their situation— it was her heart.

"Now what are we going to do?" Like it had all afternoon, her stomach responded with a twinge.

"Let me be the first to say that I do not like the smell of this tea."

She jumped a little at the sound of Philippe's voice. He came in from the kitchen carrying a pair of steaming mugs. "It has the base notes of a barn."

"One of the nurses at work recommended it. Says it has lots of vitamin K."

"So does romaine lettuce, but I wouldn't make a tea out of it. I made you a cup of chamomile as well in case you change your mind."

"After a sales job like that, why would I want to drink anything else?" His thoughtfulness was killing her. It'd be a lot easier to stay emotionally detached if he didn't insist on treating her like a princess.

She took a sip of tea and immediately put the mug back on the coffee table. "You're right," she said as she choked back a gag. "Barnyard."

"I told you so. Interestingly, we've had a request from Collier's for nettle leaf. They want to use it in a shampoo. I will suggest they buy a top note to go with it. And to avoid drinking it. Are you feeling better?"

"I'm not sick. Just out of sorts." She wondered if the growing realization that she was falling for the man sitting in the upholstered chair across from her was the reason. "I'm not feeling anything that isn't normal for this stage of the pregnancy." Damn. She shouldn't have said that.

You could practically see the alarm bells going off in his head. "What do you mean? What are you feeling?"

"Relax. I need to put my feet up for a little while, that's all. That's why I called in for the night." She was glossing over details, but if he got overprotective about a potential fall on the ice, she could only imagine how he'd react to hearing she felt crampy, even though she knew it was a perfectly normal feeling.

Thankfully he appeared to accept her excuse. "I've kept you up late these past couple nights," he said.

"I wasn't exactly begging to go to sleep." Bits and pieces of memories flashed through her brain, warming her cheeks. She looked over to see Philippe studying her with an amused look.

"You didn't blush on our first date," he said.

"I didn't?"

He shook his head. "No. Every one of my compliments, you took in stride. I remember being impressed that you knew your worth."

"More, I knew a line when I heard one."

"But now that we are lovers…"

Jenna blushed over the fact she could feel herself blushing. "There's an intimacy when you sleep with someone," she replied. "The compliments have more weight." She dared not say more.

"I'm glad you believe me sincere now."

Sincere about what? That he thought her beautiful? That he wanted the best for their child? "You've never been anything but honest with me."

"You make it impossible not to be. I knew when I met you that you would be judging every compliment that came out of my mouth."

Jenna laughed. "You didn't do yourself any favors by pretending to work for the hotel."

"I never pretended anything—I lied by omission. There is a difference."

"A very small one," she said. "When our daughter asks, I'm going to make sure she watches out for men like you."

"I hope so. Men like me are not to be trusted."

Sometimes they were, thought Jenna, and that made them more dangerous. She reached for her chamomile tea.

Philippe was studying his hands all of a sudden, his thumb massaging the center of his palm. It reminded Jenna of how he'd played with the wineglass the night he proposed. He was working up to something.

"There's a labor issue brewing at one of my properties. A potential work stoppage. I have to fly back to the corporate offices to oversee negotiations."

"You're leaving." Jenna's insides crumpled. *Fool.* This shouldn't be a surprise. Philippe's leaving was inevitable. She couldn't expect him to stay around Nantucket waiting on her forever. "When do you leave?"

"I fly out in the morning," he replied. "I'm sorry."

"Don't be," Jenna said. "You have a business to run. You can't stick around Nantucket doing nothing forever." Tomorrow, when he was gone, she would give herself points for keeping the disappointment out of her voice.

"If only I could. I enjoyed spending time with you again. I wish I could stay longer."

She had enjoyed spending time with him, too. "Seeing as how I didn't expect you to come to Nantucket at all, I'll take these last few days as a bonus."

So this was it. He would fly home and their affair would truly and completely be over. It was a good thing. Distance would ease the hold he had on her emotions.

A lump rose in her throat.

"You could come with me," he said suddenly.

"Back to France?"

"Why not? When negotiations are finished, we can visit Paris. You've never been to Paris, have you?"

Jenna shook her head.

"Then I could show you the city. We could have a second French holiday, so to speak."

What a wonderful, horrible idea. To what end? Wouldn't that be like pulling the bandage off slowly? Her stomach twisted at the thought.

"*Ma chérie?*" She must have frowned, because Philippe was across the space and at her side in a heartbeat, the concern etched on his face making the lump worse. Why couldn't he be aloof and uncaring? Why did he have to tease her with kindness and eyes that reflected emotions that weren't there? This whole situation would be so much easier.

"I—I can't take time from work. I need to save the time for when the baby comes."

"Oh." There was disappointment in his voice. "Forgive me. I didn't stop to think."

"Plus, you have no idea how long these negotiations will go. I could end up just being in the way."

"I doubt that."

"Even so, I think that maybe we should… We should say good…" She pressed a fist to her stomach.

"Jenna?"

Something wasn't right. That last cramp was stronger. Sharper.

Oh God, no. Please no.

She bolted from the room.

"Jenna?"

Philippe started down the hall after her. She rushed into the bathroom, slamming the door behind her. Morning sickness, he decided… That's what made her run so quickly. He didn't want to think about what else could make her turn so pale.

He knocked on the bathroom door. "Is everything all right?"

"Can I have a minute?" was the muffled reply.

Definitely morning sickness. Heading back to the living room, he sat back down in his chair. Jenna's teacups sat on the table untouched. He picked up the nettle tea and inhaled.

"No wonder she's nauseous," he said.

Perhaps the nausea was also the reason why she was acting so strangely. He could have sworn that before she bolted from the room Jenna was about to say something about goodbye.

He would ask her to explain when she returned. They were enjoying each other's company too much to simply end things. He would be able to return to Nantucket in a few weeks, once his business was completed. In fact, he would no doubt be back several times over the course of her pregnancy. They still had financial and legal issues to hammer out, and naturally he would want to track how her pregnancy was going. As far as he was concerned, they could enjoy each other's company indefinitely. There was no reason for her to make their goodbye sound so permanent.

Why was she, then?

Back in France, when they were first doing their dance of attraction, she used to back away whenever the chemistry became too intense. Hide behind a wall of mistrust. There was no need to mistrust him now, though. And yet here it felt as though she was throwing up another wall.

Why did he feel he was missing something? Something important. An answer that was just out of reach?

The afghan she'd been using lay on the floor where it fell when she left the room. He bent over to pick it up. As he folded the soft pink material, he smelled the faint scent of jasmine. Closing his eyes, he inhaled deeply. Beautiful. No one wore jasmine like Jenna. The flower belonged to her. He wondered if he'd ever be able to smell the summer nights again without thinking of her.

In the distance, he heard a door followed by the sound of Jenna's footsteps as she walked into the room.

"Philippe?"

The tremor in her voice knocked him from his reverie. Opening his eyes, he found Jenna hovering in the doorway, her face paler than he'd ever seen. Even her lips were white.

His stomach dropped.

"I think we need to go to the hospital," she told him.

CHAPTER TEN

MAYBE A WIZARD put a curse on his family during the Middle Ages, or had the powers above decided the d'Usay family had spent enough time on the planet and therefore anyone attached to the name needed to go? Or had he simply done something horrible in a previous life and therefore needed to suffer punishment in this one?

Jenna was bleeding. "Not a lot," she said, but her voice had been tight and lacked conviction.

Bleeding meant miscarriage.

Philippe broke the speed laws driving them to the emergency room. There, he was forced aside while an overly chipper nurse shooed him from the room.

"We need to get her changed and then do an exam," the nurse told him. "We'll come get you as soon as we're done."

Now, with the tests and exams finished, he returned to find Jenna lying alone in the dim light. It was mid-morning, or so the clock on the wall told him. He sat by her side and held her hand while the monitor beeped out her vital signs with soft regularity.

She looked like a pale angel. Soft and delicate. The hospital gown didn't suit her— the colors were too muted. She was brighter than that.

Felix had not looked like an angel in his hospital bed. The last few weeks, his brother had looked like Nosferatu, all tight white skin and teeth.

Mama, however. She would have looked like an angel. He knew without having been there, because Mama had always insisted on looking her best.

She would have been jealous of how beautiful Jenna looked.

Jenna wasn't dying, he reminded himself.

But their child might be.

He brushed a curl from her forehead, forcing a smile when she turned her head to look at him with large, frightened eyes. "The doctor come back yet?"

"Not yet. She's on her way, the nurse outside said." His voice was surprisingly calm, considering his insides felt ready to shatter. How he hated this feeling. The hollow feeling that felt as though someone cut your insides from your heart to your stomach.

The shadow he'd spent so many years trying avoid gripped his shoulder and held on fast. This was why you didn't get involved. This was why you avoided falling in love. Because people you loved died, leaving you cold and hollow inside. Leaving you alone.

What had made him think he could escape the pain?

Jenna's lower lip trembled. "I'm scared," she said. They both were. "I've been lying here listing all the logical reasons for spotting, but it doesn't help. All I keep thinking is what if…"

"Shh. Don't say it." If they swallowed the word, perhaps it would disappear. Pressing his forehead to hers, he whispered the refrain again as if reciting a prayer. "Don't say it." His hands squeezed hers as tightly as possible, their viselike grips grounding one another.

In his mind's eye, Philippe saw all the events he might never see—first steps, dances, smiles—and he prayed he was overreacting.

A knock on the door interrupted them. Looking up, he saw a woman no bigger than a girl with a gray top-knot. "I am Dr. Bhattacharya," she said, her voice soft and singsong. "How are we feeling?"

Horrible, Philippe started to say.

"Nervous," Jenna replied.

"Not surprising. I have good news, though. Your exams came back with no signs of irregularities. The cervix is intact, the uterus looks in good shape and the bleeding seems to have stopped as well."

"Oh thank God." Jenna let out a sigh of relief that Philippe could feel reverberating through her body. He wasn't quite as ready to relax. There was more that the doctor was leaving out.

"Your blood work did show that your progesterone level is low. There's a good chance that's what caused the bleeding. I'm going to prescribe a progesterone shot to see if we can boost your levels and keep this from happening again."

"But everything's going to be all right," Jenna said. "I'm not miscarrying."

"Obviously, with bleeding in early pregnancy, there's always a chance of miscarriage," Dr. Bhattacharya said. "I'm going to recommend that your ob-gyn monitors you closely just in case. But, looking at all the tests, I'm feeling good about the progesterone solving the problem."

Relief tore through him. Was it possible to lose one's breath from happiness, because he felt like all the air had rushed from his lungs in a single *whoosh*.

Thank you, he said silently. To whom, he didn't know. All he knew was they'd been given a reprieve.

"There is one more test," Dr. Bhattacharya said. She smiled at them both. "We'd like to do an ultrasound to check the baby's heartbeat."

"C-can we hear it at this point?" Jenna looked at him with excitement in her eyes. "It's not too early?"

"Shouldn't be," the doctor replied.

A few minutes later, a machine had rolled in and Dr. Bhattacharya was tracing Jenna's stomach with a wand and describing what she saw. Philippe was speechless. There, on the monitor, was his child. Tiny and hard to visualize, but more beautiful than anything he could imagine. That was, until...

"Here you go," Dr. Bhattacharya said.

Jenna gasped. "Oh my God," she whispered. "That's our baby."

It sounded like soft rapid hoof beats. Their child's heart beat strong and sure. She was a fighter.

Like her mother. Philippe gazed at the woman beside him, awe in his heart. "*C'est beau*," he said. "Perfect."

"...you or the baby are at risk."

The doctor's words ripped him from the moment. "What did you say about risk?"

"She was talking about precautions in general," Jenna said.

"I was saying that her doctor will want to monitor her closely throughout her pregnancy to make sure neither she or the baby are at risk."

"You're saying there still could be a problem then?" Worse, Jenna could be in danger as well?

"It's just a precaution, Philippe. I'm sure they monitor pregnancies all the time."

"We do," Dr. Bhattacharya said. "We don't want to take anything for granted."

"No," Philippe replied. "You don't." Hadn't he, though? He sat back and studied the hand in his. In all his worry, he'd assumed Jenna would be all right.

What would he have done if he lost her? What would his world be like?

Dark, that's what it would be. A world devoid of color and warmth.

He couldn't let that happen. The d'Usay bad luck stopped here. Stopped now. Philippe wasn't going to lose Jenna or his child. There was only one solution: keep them close and do everything in his control to keep them safe. Starting now.

"I don't know about you, but I could use a few dozen hours of sleep." Jenna sank her head against the headrest of Philippe's rental car. Exhausted didn't begin to cover how tired she felt. "Soon as I get back to the house, I'm going to scarf down some food and take a nap."

"You will not scarf. You will have a healthy breakfast. If there is a possibility of risk, it will not be because of poor diet."

"Yes, Mother." She smiled as she said it. "Seriously, you don't have to warn me twice. I'm aiming for a picture-perfect pregnancy from here on in. The next time I visit the hospital in a rush, I want it to be because my water broke."

She ran a hand over her stomach. While she'd wanted the baby, she hadn't known how deeply that desire went until she saw the blood. Then she knew with every fiber of her being. "You hear that, baby? No more scaring your father and me, or you'll be grounded."

"Then we are in agreement. We both want to do everything possible to keep you and the baby safe."

"You are preaching to the choir. Although I feel better having talked to Dr. Bhattacharya. She knows her stuff, don't you think?"

Philippe shrugged. "She was competent."

"Well, I liked her," she replied. Philippe had been in this weird, hard-to-please mode since they left the hospital, where everything on the island bothered him. She was cutting him some slack because of the stress they'd been under.

Sunshine was beginning to breach the horizon, its orange and yellow colors mixing with fading gray. "How long were we at the hospital, anyway? The clock was behind my head and I couldn't see my... Oh my God, your flight. What time do you need to catch it?"

"Do not worry about the flight—I will reschedule."

"Thank you." In the midst of the chaos, she'd forgotten Philippe was planning to leave her. The two of them had been about to say goodbye, in fact, when the cramping hit.

Dragging out their goodbyes for another few hours might be postponing the inevitable, but Jenna was grateful anyway. "I hope it won't cause too many problems."

"They will have to deal. You and the baby come first."

Jenna was so exhausted from the ordeal that she closed her eyes and pretended the words meant more than they did.

"You really are tired," she heard Philippe say. "Once

you have a few hours sleep, you can pack and we'll head to my hotel."

She pried open an eye. "Pack? For what?"

"The flight. Don't worry about packing a lot. Just the essentials will do for now. I'll have someone handle the rest."

"Whoa, back up there, cowboy." She opened her other eye and turned so she had a full view of his profile. "Where is it you think I'm going?"

"To Arles, of course."

"What?" She shook her head. "No, I said last night that I couldn't go to France with you, remember?"

"Yes, but…things are different now."

They'd reached her driveway. Unbuckling his seat belt, Philippe turned so he too was studying her. He had one elbow propped on the wheel and the other on the seat back. If he leaned forward, he could pin her in place, Jenna noted. "We both agreed we were going to do everything possible to keep the baby healthy," he said.

"Healthy, yes, but I was talking about more fruits and vegetables, not flying across the world for a vacation."

"Not vacation," he replied. "To live."

Jenna looked at him and counted to three. "I'm going to pretend you didn't say that."

She got out of the car, and he followed her across the front lawn. "The situation is different now," he said. "I realized just how much was at stake. How much I…that is, we…stand to lose."

"Don't you see?" He reached out and caught her arm. "If you come to France with me, I can make sure you have the finest doctors money can buy."

"French doctors," she replied.

"French, British, German. The best in the world. Whatever you need."

"I don't need French doctors! What I need is for you…" She stopped herself and took a deep breath. "We have perfectly adequate doctors in Nantucket."

"My child deserves more than adequate care."

"Then I'll go to Boston if I need to. Or are you going to tell me they aren't good enough, either?"

Yanking her arm free, she stomped up the front steps. The front door was open. They'd left in such a rush, she'd forgotten to turn the latch. Great, the way things were going, there was probably a robber pilfering through her jewelry.

Philippe was two steps behind her. "*Ma chérie*, please."

"It was a scare, Philippe. Pregnant women have scares all the time, and they go on to have perfectly fine pregnancies. They don't pick up and move halfway around the world."

"People die all the time, too," he shot back.

"No one is going to die."

The entire conversation was ludicrous; she didn't know why she was even entertaining it. She headed into the kitchen, where she found the bowl of fresh fruit Philippe had brought the day before. Part of their country dinner he'd planned to make. Bread, fruit and cheese. She grabbed an orange and a knife and began slicing with vehemence.

The worst part of this stupid conversation? It wasn't that he had decided she needed to live in France, or that the basis for his decision had nothing to do with her, but rather his fear of losing the baby. No, the worst part was that she felt like an afterthought, and she hated herself for it.

A shadow fell across the doorway. "I didn't mean to upset you. When we were in the hospital, I realized— I mean, *truly* realized—how much … I don't want to lose her.… I don't want to lose…"

"I know. I don't, either. When I first saw the spotting, I thought…" Jenna's hands started to shake. The knife clattered to the counter as she pressed a trembling fist to her mouth. She would not sob. She would not…

"Shh." Philippe's hands gripped her shoulders, turning her to his chest. "It's all right."

She buried her face in his collar, letting his voice chase the tremors away. His arms were the balm she needed. The anchor. "I don't know what I would have done without you at the hospital," she said. His presence had kept her sane. She'd needed him.

She loved him.

A long, shuddering breath escaped her lips. She'd been dancing around the feeling with euphemisms for days, but now there was no escaping the truth. She loved Philippe d'Usay. She loved his child.

And he didn't love her.

Sniffing, she pulled back. "You're going to need a clean shirt," she said. The collar was wet where she'd buried her face.

"I have plenty of shirts." He kissed the top of her head. "Why don't you sit down and rest and I will bring you a proper breakfast. I will impress you with my culinary skills," he said, guiding her to a kitchen chair.

She let out a watery laugh. "You already impress me."

"*Mon Dieu*, it's a miracle. And here I have yet to

crack an egg. How far we've come from that day on the terrace when you thought me a threat to your virtue."

"I considered you a playboy who went through women like water," she countered.

"'Like water' is an exaggeration. I like to think I am more selective than that."

Jenna noticed he didn't say *was*.

Perhaps she was being childish by playing games with semantics, but words counted. For as long as she could remember, she'd promised herself that when she fell in love, she would pick someone kind, considerate and devoted. Most importantly, however, she would fall for someone as far removed from her father as possible. Leave it to her to fall for a kind, considerate playboy. Words reminded her, during moments like this, that while Philippe was a part of her life, he was not committed to her.

"Fried or scrambled?"

"Scrambled."

"Excellent choice. My fried eggs are horrible. You know," he said, kicking the refrigerator door shut, "when you come to France, we can do this every morning."

She looked up from the orange rind she was playing with. "What's that? Cry over fruit?"

"Eat scrambled eggs."

"We have scrambled eggs in New England."

His face darkened, and he turned around. A second later, she heard the crack of an egg against the bowl. "I have lost every person in my life who has ever mattered to me. I can't lose any more."

The naked vulnerability in his voice punched her right in the heart. She wasn't trying to hurt him.

Couldn't he see that? She was trying to protect herself. "This baby means everything to me, too," she told him.

The baby she carried was part of Philippe which made her as precious to Jenna as her own life. "I would never let anything happen to her."

"I know, but…"

"But what?"

He turned around. "You'll be halfway around the world. There's only so much flying back and forth that I can do. There are too many people depending on me to be in France."

"I understand."

"But I want to be there. I want to be a part of everything. I want to hear the baby's heartbeat, see the ultrasound." His face grew wistful. "Watch her smile for the first time. Share her first Christmas."

In other words, he wanted to be a father. A true, hands-on father.

He knelt in front of her, hands grasping the sides of her chair. "That is why I want you to come to France," he said. "So we can share these moments together."

"Be a family," Jenna whispered. Philippe painted a beautiful picture, prettier than any Provençal landscape. There was only one piece missing from his scenario.

She stared at the buttons on his shirt, thinking how smooth and starched he looked despite a night in the emergency room. She tried to image the same starchiness holding an infant as she cried and dribbled formula. He probably wouldn't show a wrinkle. To the outside world, Philippe d'Usay would never look less than perfect.

"Tell me something." Slowly, she lifted her eyes.

"In this family picture, where are the baby and I when you have a date?"

At least he had the courtesy to look shocked at the question. "*Pardon*?"

"Would we be upstairs out of sight, or are we going to be super cosmopolitan about the whole thing and double-date and stuff?" With that, she pushed herself out of the chair and headed into the living room. Her teacups from the night before were still on the coffee table, half-full. Picking up the nettle tea, she gave it a sniff, smiling sadly at the barnyard smell.

"What are you talking about?" Philippe asked.

"You and your 'selective' lifestyle," she replied. "A family—a real family—is based on mutual commitment and love. You've made it very clear you don't believe in either."

"Perhaps I've changed."

Jenna nearly dropped the cup. "Changed how?"

"What if I told you I'm just as afraid of losing you as I am the baby?" Taking the cup from her hands, he set it on the table. "There's three parts to a family, Jenna. The baby, the father and the mother." As he spoke, he traced a shape on her palm with his finger. "I cannot imagine my family without you as the third part. Our world would be very dark without you, Jenna Brown. My world would be dark. *Je t'aime*."

She didn't know what to say. His world would be dark? How she'd longed to hear words like that come out of his mouth. Her heart leaped with happiness.

Her head, however... She stepped back just as Philippe leaned in for a kiss. He ended up stumbling slightly and stubbing his shin on the coffee table.

"Leopards don't change their spots, Philippe," she told him.

Lines of confusion marked his forehead. "What does that mean?"

"It means…" That it took having his back against the wall for him to declare his feelings.

Turning her back to him, she crossed from the sofa to the window. It was light enough now that she could see her backyard. The foliage had turned, she noted. The leaves on her maple had become a kaleidoscope of yellow and orange. New England foliage was beautiful until you had to rake it up.

She played with the hem of her gingham curtain. "It means that you had a horrible scare tonight, and I think that you will say anything to make sure you have as full a role as possible in this baby's life."

Silence. The air grew thick. She could feel Philippe's eyes at the back of her head. Pictured how they widened before darkening with offense.

"Is that how you really feel?" he asked.

Jenna continued to look out the window.

"Your silence says everything. If you don't believe me, I don't know what I can say to convince you." There were footsteps as he walked across the room. Moving away, not closer. "You should get some rest," he said.

"Where are you going?"

"To my hotel. I… I need to change my travel arrangements, and we obviously could use the space. Hopefully these negotiations will not take long, and I can return soon."

"Don't."

She turned around. Philippe stood in the doorway,

wearing a hopeful expression. It was clear he thought she wanted him to stay. "Don't keep flying in and out."

His face fell. "You're cutting me out?"

"No." She didn't want to keep him from being a part of the baby's life—she simply wanted to protect her heart. "I'll let you know when there are important appointments so you can attend. But I can't have you coming and going without warning. It's too…"

"Much like your father?" he asked.

His comment brought her up short. "I was going to say disruptive. What on earth does my father have to do with anything?"

"The way he pops in and out of your mother's life."

"You think I'm comparing our situation to theirs?"

Philippe folded his arms. "I don't know, *ma chérie*. Are you?"

"You're out of your mind."

"Am I? Since the day we met, I have had to fight to gain your trust."

"That's not true," Jenna said.

"Oh, but it is. You held yourself back from day one. Always wary, always waiting for me to prove I was a cad. I needed to take two steps forward for you to take one. And now I lay my soul bare and you don't believe me. So tell me, Jenna, who are you comparing me to, if not your father?"

Jenna glared at him. Thanks to their argument, she never got her eggs—a promise Philippe failed to keep—and now she had a raging headache. The last thing she needed was his attempt at armchair psychology. And on top of it, to paint himself as the victim? Give her a break.

"First off," she said, stabbing the air with her index

finger, "you didn't 'lay your soul bare.' You decided I was moving to France for the baby's sake."

"And yours," he shot back. "Were you not listening? I told you how much you mean to me."

"Only as an afterthought. You wouldn't have mentioned your feelings at all if I hadn't pressed the issue."

"That is not true."

"Isn't it?" she asked. "You weren't exactly professing undying love."

"Do not presume to know my thoughts."

"Then don't presume to know mine!" Her shout hung between them. Philippe ran a hand through his hair.

"What are you afraid of, Jenna? We could have something good. A true family."

Until you broke your promise and left us alone.

Left her alone.

The world would be a lot better if people used their heads instead of their hearts.

Wasn't that what Philippe said the other afternoon? Well, she was using her head.

"I think you better leave," she told him.

"Jenna…" He took a step forward. Jenna held her breath. Her resolve wasn't as strong as she made it out to be. One kiss, one impassioned *please* and it would shatter. *Convince me I'm wrong*, she pleaded with him silently. *Change my mind.*

"I'll let you know my travel itinerary as soon as I know it." Turning on his heel, he walked away. Leaving Jenna alone.

"At least my father says goodbye when he leaves," she whispered.

CHAPTER ELEVEN

HE'D DONE THE right thing, Philippe told himself. Walking away. If he had stayed, he would have lost his temper. A leopard didn't change his spots, indeed.

Heaving a groan, he threw himself facedown on his hotel bed. Why was she being so stubborn? He was offering her a wonderful life. A home, a family. *Mon Dieu*, he'd told her he loved her!

And what had she done? Spat it back into his face. Suggested he was lying to get his way.

Only after your back was against the wall.

Argh! He flipped over onto his back. When they left the hospital, he'd been consumed with worry. Making sure Jenna and the baby came home were foremost in his mind. He intended to tell her his feelings, but then they started arguing about France and the conversation got away from him. But he did tell her eventually. *Je t'aime.* I love you. Even a woman who didn't speak French had to know what he meant. And if she didn't understand, hadn't he implied his feelings enough? After all, he'd told her he couldn't lose another person whom he loved. Wasn't the meaning obvious?

She hadn't said she loved him back.

A hole opened in his chest, the pain ripping through

him. Reminding him he was, again, alone with no one to love him in return.

Jenna, with her wary wall, had a point. In fact, he knew she was right. He should have listened to his own advice and walked away as soon as Jenna started slipping under his skin. Instead, like a fool, he kept coming back for more.

Perhaps if he had, his chest wouldn't feel so battered and empty. Turns out he didn't need someone to die to feel alone.

The biggest irony of all? After years of protecting his heart from pain, he was destroyed by a woman who played the game better.

Jenna sighed and began counting the syringe kits for the third time. No one ever mentioned the downside of keeping your pride. Dignity might let you walk with your head held high, but it also left you with a six-foot-two hole in your heart.

"At least I've got you," she said to her belly. Baby, at least, seemed to be doing better. There hadn't been any more spotting or cramping, which was good. In fact, she noticed today her pants were too snug.

"You look a million miles away." Shirley joined her behind the counter, a stack of admission papers in her hand. "Everything okay?"

Far from it. Everything was blown to smithereens.

"I had to use an elastic band to button my pants this morning," she said out loud.

"Because of the baby or the breakfast treats?"

"That's not funny."

Her friend held up a hand. "Sorry. Didn't realize that was a sticking point now."

No, Jenna was the one who was sorry. Shirley didn't know that talk of pastry poked at the hole in her heart.

At least she was at work. She refused to waste her time crying over what might have been. Give the sting a couple days to fade and she'd be fine. Alone, but fine.

"Oh, for crying out loud." She started counting the syringe kits *again*. "I've forgotten how to count to ten. Stupid baby brain."

Shirley gave her a look but fortunately decided to keep any comments to herself. "We've got a new patient arriving this afternoon," she said. "Coming over from the hospital to go on hospice."

"And so goes the circle of life," Jenna replied. "We live, we die and in between we struggle not to make fools of ourselves."

"Wow, thanks for the wisdom, Miss Sunshine."

"Sorry. I don't mean to be witchy. I'm just tired." Despite being exhausted, she hadn't slept very much. Another reason why she was unable to count the kits.

Shirley slid the kits to her side of the desk. "What happened?" When Jenna finished explaining, her friend practically pushed her into a chair. "Oh, Jenna. I'm so sorry! What are you doing at work on your feet, you idiot?"

"I'm fine," Jenna replied, slapping her friend's hands away. "Work won't hurt me. Besides, I need to keep my mind occupied."

"And how's that working out for you?" Shirley asked. She pointed to the saline bags that were still uncounted.

"How do you think?"

"I can't believe he walked out like that—and that you let him."

"What was I supposed to do? Beg him to stay?"

Their final goodbye wouldn't stop haunting her. Every time she closed her eyes, she saw the look on Philippe's face when he said goodbye. The light in his eyes faded away, leaving them dark and shuttered. "If he wanted to stay, he would have."

"Oh, sure—totally," Shirley drawled. "I know I would stay if I told someone I loved them and they threw it back in my face."

Not her, too. Philippe painting her as the bad person she understood. Didn't like, but understood. Shirley was supposed to be on her side, though. "He didn't say he loved me. He said he needed me to make a family."

"He didn't say anything else?"

"Something in French that was probably supposed to be romantic, I'm not sure."

"Do you remember what it was?"

"Does it really matter?" He was gone. Probably caught the first flight he could get.

"No, but I'm curious," Shirley said. "I never got to try out my French immersion software, and I want to see if it stuck."

Jenna shook her head. She really wasn't planning to get into a word-for-word recap. It hurt too much. "Jet something."

"Was it *je t'aime*?"

"I think so."

"You idiot!" Her friend smacked her on the shoulder with a force that sent her chair rolling backward. "That's 'I love you' in French."

He'd said the words? Jenna's heart started to skip until common sense shut it down. "It doesn't matter. People say 'I love you' all the time and don't mean it."

"Some of them do."

"Yeah, well, he also meant it when he said he had no intention of ever marrying or having a family, and there is a lot more evidence to support that claim."

"True," Shirley replied. "I mean, he only flew halfway across the world so he could bring you breakfast and hang out with your dementia patients." She waved to Lola, who was straightening magazines in the entertainment room. "Oh, and spent the night in the emergency room holding your hand."

"Because the baby is important to him. She—it—means the continuation of his family line. What?" Shirley had rolled her eyes.

"You just said he had no intention of ever having a family. Clearly he does if that baby matters."

"The baby's name." But even as she snapped the response, Jenna knew that wasn't true. The baby mattered very much, so much he'd wanted her to go to France so he could keep an eye on her pregnancy.

Because he wanted a family. Something he claimed to never want. Was it possible she was wrong? Or did wishful thinking have her hearing what she wanted?

"Did you know that Philippe accused me of having daddy issues?"

"Seriously?"

"Yeah. He said I didn't trust him because I lumped him in with my father, or something to that effect."

Her friend started counting the syringe kits.

"Don't tell me you agree with him," Jenna said.

"Well, you don't really trust men," Shirley replied. "Whenever we go out, you shoot down most of the guys who talk to you."

"With good reason."

"I'm not saying you don't have reason. I'm just saying you don't trust many of the guys you meet."

"Because I've seen the damage the wrong guy can do."

"You mean guys like your dad," Shirley replied.

"I…" She didn't want to have this conversation anymore. "I'm going to go down to the front desk to see if Nelo knows anything more about our new patient," she said.

Shirley took the hint. "Suit yourself. There are eleven kits. You're welcome."

Daddy issues. She did not compare every man to her father. Jenna marched around the workstation to the elevator. Before she could push the button, however, the doors slid open to reveal the very man they'd been discussing.

Jenna's heart stopped. What was he doing here? "I—I thought you were going home."

He was dressed for business in a dark suit and cashmere coat. The same outfit he wore his first morning on the island, only this time he had the benefit of a fresh shower and shave. Thankfully sunglasses covered his eyes, meaning she didn't have to see his shuttered gaze again.

"I am." The flatness in his voice made her cringe. "I should have departed earlier, but …" He shook his head. "Never mind."

He had a gift bag in his had. "I wanted to drop this off before I left," he said, handing it to her.

Jenna didn't know what to say; she was too focused on the idea of him leaving. Taking the bag, she looked at it and saw the gift label read "For Lola."

"You're bringing a present for Lola?"

"Something I promised last time I was here. I didn't want her to think I forgot."

It was more likely Lola had forgotten the conversation and the promise. "She's in the entertainment room if you want to give her the present yourself," she said.

"Thank you, but I cannot stay. I have a conference call in an hour. I thought…" Once again, he shook his head. "Tell Lola I said goodbye."

Still no goodbye for her.

"Philippe, please." She stopped him from boarding the elevator again. "I… I'm sorry."

"Are you really?" he asked.

"Yes. I don't want us to part with unsettled business."

"But you still want to part." When she went to speak, he held up a hand. "You don't have to elaborate. I accept your apology."

"Thank you." She waited for the relief to arrive and free the tension from her shoulders, but it didn't come.

"When do you leave?" she asked him.

"I have a flight out of Boston this afternoon. I leave the island at ten."

Five hours from now. He'd be gone for real this time. No miraculous appearance off the elevator. Her heart sank even as she reminded herself the decision to stay behind had been hers.

"The…um…that is… I spoke to my ob-gyn yesterday. She suggested I have an ultrasound next month. I will let you know when it's scheduled, in case you decide you want to attend."

"You know I will."

Jenna nodded. Was this to be their new normal? Awkward, cordial conversation about tests and appointment dates? A lump the size of a boulder rose in her throat. "I guess I should let you go, then," she said. "I don't want you to miss your call."

"Merci."

"Philippe, wait!" Once again, she stopped him from stepping on the elevator. "Can I at least get a good-bye?" she asked, hating herself a little for the request, but needing the closure more.

A look crossed his face, and then he nodded. *"Oui.* Of course."

He combed his fingers into her hair, the way he did when they made love, and lifted her face to his. Jenna looked into his eyes, hoping for one more look into their deep violet depths, but the sunglasses kept them hidden. She pictured them anyway, the image seared into her memory.

Dipping his head, he kissed her softly. Sweetly. Too sweet for her tastes. Clutching his shoulders, she deepened the kiss, workplace professionalism be damned.

"Je t'aime, ma chérie," he whispered when they parted.

"I…" *Say it,* her heart urged. *Tell him.*

The words stuck in her throat. No longer able to look him in the eye, she focused on the base of his throat. "I'm sorry," she whispered.

His Adam's apple bobbed up and down. "So am I."

Ignoring the look on Shirley's face, Jenna turned around and walked past the nurses' station to the entertainment room.

"For me?" Lola's eyes lit up with surprise when Jenna handed her the bag. "What is it?"

"I don't know. You'll have to open it to find out." It was hard to speak while holding back tears, but she managed.

Lola tossed the bright blue tissue paper on the floor and let out a laugh. "That's why I couldn't find him! He was in the bag!" She pulled out a stuffed gray and white cat.

"I was just thinking about Beatrice," Shirley said as they were leaving work a short while later.

Jenna was only half listening. Her mind was still at the elevator hearing Philippe whisper *I love you*. The reply had been right there in her throat. All she had to do was say it aloud. Why couldn't she? Why couldn't she trust that Philippe's whispers meant something? Meant forever.

"What made you think about her?" she asked.

Her friend shrugged as she burrowed through her pocketbook. "I don't know. You and Philippe and how her inheritance was the reason you met him in the first place. Makes me wonder what she'd say about this whole mess."

"Probably something like 'don't worry about what anybody else thinks,'" Jenna replied.

"Maybe." Pulling out her car keys, the blonde pressed the auto-lock button. A few feet away, her SUV's lights flashed. "She ever talk to you about her husband?"

"Her partner in crime? All the time. Called him the love of her life."

The conversation was making Jenna's tears threaten again. Bad enough she had to fight them back every time Lola showed her that stuffed cat.

"Did you know she once told me that marrying him was the greatest adventure of her life?" Shirley said.

Jenna nodded. Beatrice had shared the same memory with her several times. "What's your point?"

"No point," her friend replied. "I think it's interesting, though, that she considered marriage her greatest adventure, and then left you money to have an adventure of your own. Makes you wonder what she really wanted you to do."

"I doubt she expected me to meet Philippe." Beatrice was awesome, but she wasn't psychic.

Shirley opened her driver's door. "True. On the other hand, it does make you wonder if she thought you should take a chance on something more than a trip to France."

Suddenly Jenna got the point of the conversation. "Subtle."

"Don't blame me," her friend replied. "Blame Beatrice. Call me later if you feel like talking."

Jenna's phone began to buzz the second she shrugged off her coat. Kicking herself because her first thought was about Philippe, she checked the call screen. Not Philippe. Or Shirley, either. It was her mother.

The two of them hadn't talked for a couple of days. The last thing Jenna was in the mood to hear about was her parents' extramarital affair with one another.

She could only ignore the inevitable for so long, though. Sooner or later, she would need to talk to the woman.

"Hi, Mom," she said as she lay down on the sofa. "What's new?"

A gut-wrenching cough answered her greeting. "Sorry," her mother croaked.

Awesome. They could be miserable together. Jenna waited until her mother caught her breath before talking. "You sound horrible."

"I feel worse. This will teach me for waiting on my flu shot. How are you feeling?"

"Just got home from work." No sense telling her about the hospital visit. There was nothing the woman could do at this point. And she definitely wasn't going to tell her about Philippe.

Instead she forced herself to ask her next question. "Dad taking good care of you? Bringing you hot tea, crackers and all that?"

Even if her mother hadn't paused, Jenna would have guessed her response. "You know your father. He doesn't do well with sickness," she said. "Plus he needs to keep his distance so he doesn't get sick, too. Things are crazy busy at work for him. Lots of business dinners…"

"His new inventory manager attending these dinners, too?" she asked.

"Your father works with all sorts of people, Jenna."

In other words, yes. Looked like this reunion would be shorter than usual. Maybe it was because she was emotionally drained, but she couldn't stomach the excuses anymore. "Why do you take him back? He does this to you every single time."

"I love him," her mom said simply.

"But he doesn't love you."

"That's not true. He tells me he loves me all the time."

"Then turns around and leaves you home sick while he goes out to dinner." *And dumps you as soon as he finds a replacement.* "Actions speak louder than words, Mom. When's the last time he did something nice for you, or anyone, for that matter?"

"You don't understand. Your father has a lot of people demanding things of him. The last thing he needs is me distracting him with a lot of whiny demands. I'm lucky he spends as much time with me as he does."

It was the same load of bogus excuses her mother gave every time. "All I'm saying is that maybe there's someone out there that's better than Dad. Someone who… I don't know…sticks around."

Someone who wants to build a family, a voice said in her head.

On the other end of the line, her mother sniffed— and it wasn't from the flu. "I didn't call to hear a lecture about relationships from my single-mother daughter. Your father and I are back together, and that's that."

"Fine," Jenna said. She didn't want to have this conversation, either. Her mother was going to stay in her bubble of delusion forever, and there was nothing Jenna could do. Some things never changed.

Pleading a headache, she told her mother she'd call her back and let the phone drop on the floor.

"Your grandmother's in love with a loser," she told the baby. "How on earth a woman can be so blind to the obvious is beyond me. I mean, the guy's taking his girlfriend out while she's home with the flu. All I did was complain about feeling tired and your daddy made me two different kinds of tea."

Actions speak louder than words…

Her father would never bring her mother pastry or hang out at a nursing home hunting for an invisible cat. God knew he'd never fly across the world for her.

Or move heaven and earth to keep her safe.

How on earth could Philippe have thought she was comparing him to her father? There was no contest. Her father was a bastard. Philippe…

Loved her.

The awareness of it hit her like a ton of bricks. Philippe loved her. All this time she'd been afraid of falling in love with a man who didn't love her, and he was saying it every day. With every pastry, every neck rub. She'd simply been too blind—or too scared—to see the truth.

But Philippe wasn't scared. Philippe, who in his own words had lost everyone he ever loved, was brave enough to love her.

She pressed her hand to her stomach. "What have I done, baby?"

Ten past ten. Philippe checked his watch against the clock behind the concierge desk. The times were identical. If he didn't leave soon, he would miss his flight to Boston.

Maybe two more minutes.

Why bother? He already delayed his departure a day on the chance Jenna would knock on his door. Now he was stretching out his ultimatum. It was time to accept that Jenna wasn't coming. He didn't know what made him foolish enough to think that she might. Hope was a very stupid emotion.

No more.

From now on, whatever love was left in his heart belonged to his child. For as long as she was in his life. A bitter, gloomy thought, he knew. It appeared the brooding he'd spent his life fighting had won the battle. Why not? He was tired of the struggle. His heart didn't feel like pretending it wasn't broken.

The doorman approached with his keys. "Your rental

car is parked out front, Mr. d'Usay. I put your bag in the trunk."

"I hope you enjoyed your stay at the Merchant Seafarer," he added when Philippe handed him a tip.

"You have an excellent hotel." Thankfully the man didn't ask if he'd had a pleasant stay, saving Philippe from having to make up a suitable answer. "Could you leave a message for Mr. Merchant letting him know I will email him soon?"

"Absolutely, sir. Have a good trip."

Nodding his goodbye, Philippe made his way through the front door. True to the doorman's word, his car was parked and running a few feet down the curb.

He was reaching for the door handle when he heard the sharp blare of a car horn, followed by another. Three, in fact, in rapid succession. Looking up, he saw a red sedan barreling up the hotel driveway.

It was Jenna. She stopped the car next to his.

"What are you doing?" he hollered as she leaped from the driver's seat. Driving like a maniac. Didn't she know she could have an accident?

"We were afraid we'd be too late," she said.

Too late for... His jaw dropped in disbelief. Was she saying what he thought she was saying? He was afraid to guess; all his other assumptions had been wrong.

But it was there. In eyes warmer and greener than he'd ever seen. Like the color of plants in the spring.

"*Iloveyou*," she said, the words rushing out as one. "I love you, Philippe d'Usay."

"Are you sure?" He was almost afraid to believe what he was hearing.

"Yes. I think I have loved you from the moment we

met, but I was too scared—too stupid—to let myself feel it."

Listening to her words, it felt as though the sun burst through the clouds. The fullness in his heart chased away the darkness. "I love you, too."

"I know." She gave him a watery smile. "And I am so very sorry I didn't believe you. I was wrong the other day. I didn't understand..."

Oh dear God. The French. He was such an idiot. "I should have told you in English."

"No, that's not it. I didn't understand what love looked like. I thought love was something people talked about, but it's not. It's something you do."

With a shaking hand, she took his and pressed it to her stomach. "I want to show this baby what love really is. I want us to be a family. The next generation of d'Usays." She gazed up through damp lashes. "If you'll have me."

They were the most beautiful words he'd ever heard. "Oh, *ma chérie*, you've had me since the day on the terrace. I love you. I will always love you."

"Then that's all I need to hear."

Philippe too. Wrapping her in his arms, he held her tight. Heart to heart. He would never let her go.

"Take me home," she whispered in his ear.

A wonderful request, but he needed to make sure of her answer. "Which home is that?" he asked.

Her face beamed with love. "Wherever you are, my love. Wherever you are."

CHAPTER TWELVE

July

If you send me one more photo, I will kill you.

Just trying to show you what you're missing. Hurry up and get here. Your bedroom is waiting.

Forget the bedroom. I want a big bottle of French wine. You and I are seriously overdue for a celebration. You owe me for cutting me out of the wedding.

JENNA LAUGHED. SHIRLEY had been on her about the wedding since she broke the news. Upset that she didn't get to be maid of honor.

You're coming to the reception. Isn't that enough?

The wedding, by mutual choice, had been a private affair. Since she'd been six months along at the time, Jenna hadn't wanted an elaborate event. Of course, as Philippe pointed out, if she'd married him the first half dozen times he proposed, she would have been earlier in her pregnancy. But Jenna had held out for Valentine's

Day. There was something poetic about pledging your heart on the most romantic day of the year. She, who had always viewed hearts and flowers with cynicism.

But, while the ceremony had been intimate, Philippe's position required some kind of public celebration, and so they were having a formal reception that weekend at the château. Shirley, who was finally getting her trip to France, had landed in Paris that morning.

Hey, did I mention Philippe has some really cute employees?

Shut your mouth. Joe's already paranoid I'll meet a sexy Frenchman and run away.

Hey, it happens. Maybe we can send him a few photos. Make him jealous enough to propose.

Listen to you…all romantic. What happened to the cynical girl I know and love?

She went to France. And decided to take a chance on love.

All thanks to Beatrice. Her thoughts traveled back a year, to when the old woman was still alive. One night she hadn't been able to sleep, so Jenna sat with her looking at old photographs. Picture after picture of Beatrice and her husband on their many trips.

"You had an amazing time together," Jenna had told her.

The woman had set down the album and taken Jenna's hand. "We live, we die, but in between we have to live," she'd said. "I got to live a lot. You should, too."

Jenna was glad she'd taken Beatrice's advice.

She took in the fields below. Once again, nature had created a magnificent tapestry of purple, green and yellow. It would be harvest time shortly. The air was already heavy with the sweet smell of lavender. Had it really been a year since the first time she saw these fields? The time had flown by.

"Someone missed you," Philippe announced.

He stepped onto the terrace, looking very domestic with a cloth towel draped over one shoulder and a sleeping baby on the other. Jenna's breath caught as it always did when she saw him.

"You're sexy when you change diapers," she told him. "Did you know that?"

"I know that is a shameless ploy to try and make me change more." He leaned in and kissed the spot behind her ear. "Did you reach Shirley?"

"Uh-huh. She's on her way."

"And your mother?"

"About thirty minutes ahead of Shirley." Her parents' reconciliation had managed to last three months before imploding. As usual, her mom was handling the breakup poorly. But she had agreed to attend the reception, so maybe things were looking up. Maybe the Brown habit of finding love in France would rub off on her. A girl could hope, anyway.

"It will be very interesting having this place filled with people again," Philippe said. "There hasn't been a proper party since my parents died. It feels good."

Yeah, thought Jenna, it did. She rested her head on her husband's shoulder. "Do you think your family would have liked me?"

"Are you kidding? *Chérie*, they would have loved

you more than I do, if that's possible. And they would have adored our little prince."

As if on cue, Felix Antoine d'Usay began to whimper. "I told you he missed his mother," Philippe said. "Here you go, my son."

He placed the squirming child in her arms, pausing to adjust the sun hat that covered Felix's head. "And you thought we were having a girl."

"So I predicted wrong and gave you a son to carry forth the d'Usay name. Are you complaining?"

"Absolutely not." His kissed her, and together they smiled down at the child in her arms. Jenna had never been happier.

It was going to be a wonderful adventure.

* * * * *

ONE NIGHT WITH THE COWBOY

BRENDA HARLEN

This book is dedicated to my dad.
Daniel Stickles
5 December 1931–25 September 2018
My first hero. Forever in my heart.

Prologue

Brielle Channing slid out of bed in the darkness before dawn, dressing quickly in a plain T-shirt, a pair of well-worn jeans and her favorite cowboy boots. She didn't need any light to make her way down the stairs, out the back door and toward the stables—she'd traveled the familiar route more times than she could count.

She saddled up Domino, the black gelding with white markings, and tried not to think about the fact that this would be their last ride before Brie piled her bags into the back of her father's truck and headed to the airport. She would miss her equine companion as much as she'd miss her parents and sister and brothers, but the hardest goodbye would be the one she said this morning, by the stand of ponderosa pines on top of the rocky ridge that formed part of the northern boundary of the Crooked Creek Ranch.

By the time she led Domino out of the barn, the sun had begun to rise, painting streaks of orange, pink and purple across the early morning sky. She lifted herself into the saddle, then let her horse take the lead, bending low over Domino's back as the gelding galloped across the field, hooves biting chunks out of the tired, dry soil. The wind whipped through Brie's hair and made her eyes sting, but she kept them open and focused to absorb all the sights and scents and sounds of the world around her—as if to lock them into her memory forever.

The sky was more light than dark now, and she could see the outline of the simple cabin that had been built as a shelter for cowboys caught by unexpected severe weather. The first time she'd given herself to Caleb Gilmore had been in that cabin, and the primitive shelter had become their private refuge from everything that wanted to tear them apart.

She was thinking about Caleb as she dismounted and led Domino to the narrow stream to drink. The boy she'd known for most of her life had always been serious and intense, and when he'd focused that intensity in her direction, she hadn't stood a chance.

Not that she'd resisted. Not even for a minute. Because she'd loved Caleb Gilmore with every beat of her heart—and loving him had nearly destroyed her family.

The thundering hooves of Indigo, his prized stallion, crashed through her reverie moments before horse and rider came into view. As always, the sight of him made her body quiver and her heart sigh. Though barely twenty, he was already so much more man than boy: over six feet tall with a solid build that attested to years of work on his family's cattle ranch. He controlled the powerful animal beneath him with a light hand on the reins and subtle signals from the strong thighs that gripped its flank. Indigo pulled up and Caleb slid off the stallion's back, releasing the reins so the animal could dip its head to drink from the stream beside Domino.

Though Caleb's face was shaded by the brim of his hat, Brie felt the intensity of his gaze on her. After a long minute, he finally said, "I hear you've decided on Columbia."

She nodded. "It's a really good school," she said, because it was true, though not even a fraction of the whole truth.

"So's UC Berkeley," he pointed out, naming the college she'd originally planned to attend.

She nodded again.

"But California wasn't far enough from Haven," he guessed.

"I just think it's best, for everyone, if we put some distance between us," she said.

He shook his head. "Do you really believe that?" he challenged. "Because I can guarantee it's *not* best for me, and I don't think it's what you want, either."

She'd known this wouldn't be easy, but she hadn't imagined it could be this hard. After everything they'd been through over the past few weeks, her heart should be numb. But it wasn't—it was torn open and bleeding, and she knew that going away from here, away from Caleb, was the only way to make the hurting stop.

She had to swallow before she could speak. "I've always wanted to get out of this town," she told him, her voice breaking just a little. "And you've never wanted to be anywhere else."

"You didn't always want to get out of this town," he contradicted. "There was a time when you wanted to be my wife and help me build our home on the Circle G."

"That was before I knew that the idea of a Blake married to a Gilmore would give my grandfather a heart attack."

"Your grandfather is a grumpy old man whose heart is kicking along just fine with his new pacemaker. And you're a Channing, not a Blake."

"My mother was a Blake," she reminded him, as she retrieved a manila envelope from her saddlebag. "And her blood runs through my veins."

He had no choice but to take the envelope she thrust

into his hands. "There's nothing I can say that will change your mind, is there?"

She shook her head. "This is a great opportunity for me."

"And when you're finished with school—what will you do then?" he asked. "Will you come home?"

She looked away. "I don't know."

"Yeah, you do," he said, his tone resigned as he hoisted himself into the saddle again. "Good luck in New York, Brie."

Then he rode away, Indigo's hooves trampling the already broken pieces of her heart.

Chapter One

Seven years later

"We're going to Las Vegas!"

The words stole the air from Brie's lungs, like the first big drop of the Cyclone at Coney Island. But unlike the thrill of plunging eighty-five feet at sixty miles an hour, there was no exhilarating rise that followed—only an uncomfortable queasy feeling.

Judging by Lily's excited squeals, she had an altogether different reaction to the announcement.

"Okay." Grace clapped her hands together and grinned. "Stop squealing and start packing—we fly out at eight forty-five tomorrow morning."

"Tomorrow?" Brie echoed, when she'd managed to find her voice. "But—"

"Don't you dare say you can't go," Grace interjected. "We talked about this months ago, and we all agreed that we would take a long weekend to celebrate my twenty-fifth birthday."

"Of course I'm going to celebrate with you," she assured her friend. "I just thought you'd want something a little more...or maybe a little less. And Vegas in August is going to be sticky and gross."

"Worse than New York?" Lily asked dubiously.

"Trust me," Brie said.

"I realize you've probably been there a thousand times," Grace said. "But I never have and that's where I want to go. Plus, the plane tickets and hotel are already paid for by my parents as their birthday present to me."

Although Brie had grown up less than 450 miles from Las Vegas, she'd only ever made one trip to Sin City. One unforgettable trip more than seven years earlier, and though the heartache had begun to fade, she knew she could never forget the man—or their reasons for making that trip.

"Now I'm off to the obligatory birthday dinner with the family at Per Se," Grace continued, already heading toward the stairs. "Make sure you pack your party clothes—I want to celebrate my quarter-century milestone in a big way."

Lily pushed off the sofa. "I knew there was a reason I bought that sexy red dress at Bergdorf's last weekend."

"I thought you bought it because you couldn't resist a sale," Brie noted dryly.

Her friend grinned. "That, too."

Lily disappeared into her bedroom to begin packing, and Brie decided to do the same, albeit with less enthusiasm. Because going to Nevada naturally made her think about Haven, where she'd grown up and where most of her family still lived, and thinking about Haven brought back memories of Caleb, the first—and only—boy she'd ever loved. And even after seven years, those memories made her heart yearn.

When she left Haven, she didn't think she'd ever go back. And for the first four years, she hadn't. Then her grandmother died, and she'd needed to grieve with her family. Two years after that, she'd returned for a much happier occasion: the wedding of her brother Spencer to Kenzie Atkins, Brie's best friend throughout high school. The next spring, she'd gone back for the birth of her sister

Regan's twin baby girls—and again for Piper and Poppy's baptism.

Each successive trip had been a little easier than the one before. Of course it helped that she didn't need to worry about running into Caleb, because her parents had built a big house closer to town a few years earlier and he rarely ventured far from the Circle G.

She pulled her suitcase out from under her bed now and set it on top of the mattress—and vaguely wondered if she could fake being sick to avoid the trip. She immediately felt guilty for even contemplating such a ruse, but the way her stomach tied itself into knots at the prospect of returning to Las Vegas, she might not have to fake anything.

But she would do this for Grace. She would do anything for either of the two women who'd been her best friends since her first week in New York, when they'd met as freshmen residents of Hartley Hall.

There was a light tap on the partially open door, then Lily poked her head into her room. "Can I come in?"

"Of course," Brie invited.

Her friend looked at the still empty suitcase, then at her. "You absolutely hate the idea of going to Las Vegas, don't you?"

Brie opened a drawer and began rifling through the contents. "There are a lot of other places I would have preferred to visit, but I can understand why Grace wants to go. Everyone should experience Sin City at least once."

"I'm not particularly close to my family—as you know," Lily admitted. "But even I go home at least three times a year."

"My parents come to New York periodically."

"*They* come *here*," her friend agreed. "How often do you go there?"

In the past year, more than she'd wanted to, but Brie knew that response would only raise more questions. "I don't enjoy traveling as much as they do," she suggested as an explanation instead.

"Says the woman who visited ten countries in Europe on her summer vacation last year," Lily noted.

"That was a once-in-a-lifetime opportunity."

Her friend lowered herself onto the mattress, leaning against the headboard with one leg tucked up beneath the other. "Las Vegas is 432 miles from Haven," she pointed out.

A detail of which Brie was well aware, but not one that she'd expect an East Coast native to know.

Her surprise must have shown on her face, because Lily shrugged and explained, "I looked it up."

Brie continued packing.

"Are you ever going to tell us what happened to make you leave Nevada and never want to return?" her friend asked gently.

"What can I say? I love New York."

"I know that's true, but I also know it's not the whole truth."

Brie sighed. "Maybe I should have told you—and Grace—a long time ago, but I was feeling too raw and vulnerable at first. And then, as time passed, I realized that my heartbreak wasn't nearly as big a deal as it seemed."

"It must have been a bigger deal than you're pretending now," Lily said. "Or the thought of going to Nevada wouldn't have you strangling that dress the way you are."

She immediately unclenched her hands and shook out the garment, then folded it neatly into her suitcase. "It wasn't a big deal," she insisted. "I simply fell in love with the wrong guy."

"Why was he wrong?" her friend wondered.

"Our families were the Montagues and Capulets of Haven," she explained. "And while the whole star-crossed lovers thing seemed incredibly romantic at the time, it didn't end well.

"No big surprise there, of course, but I chose to walk away with a broken heart rather than put a dagger through it."

"Are you still in love with him?"

"It was seven years ago," she reminded Lily.

"Which doesn't actually answer the question," her friend noted.

"I'm not still in love with him," she said, because she needed to believe it was true.

After more than seven years, she didn't want to admit—even to herself—that Caleb Gilmore still owned the biggest piece of her heart.

Caleb Gilmore had been back to Las Vegas a handful of times since his impulsive trip with Brielle Channing seven years earlier. But each subsequent journey inevitably brought back memories of the first time.

And of Brie.

Of course, it was rare for a single day to pass without him thinking about her, because in Haven, there were reminders every way he turned. Driving past the high school, he couldn't help but think about the first time they'd danced together. Riding up to Eagle Rock to herd a lost calf, he was reminded of their first kiss. And returning to Las Vegas brought back memories of the promises they'd made to each other so long ago. Promises that had obviously meant more to him than to her, since she'd broken every one of them within a few weeks of their return to Haven.

This time, he'd made the trip at the request of his childhood friend Joe Bishop, to serve as best man at Joe's wedding. They'd arrived late the night before and checked into The Destiny—a newer luxury hotel on the strip that

Joe had chosen because he was certain he was about to meet his destiny.

"Do you have the ring?" the groom-to-be asked, for the tenth time in as many minutes.

Caleb nodded. "I've got it," he confirmed, as he'd done each time before.

"It was my grandmother's," his friend said. "She wore it every day for almost sixty years."

And now he was ready to put that ring on the finger of a woman he'd known for less than *six hours*.

"You know this is crazy, right?" Caleb felt compelled to ask his friend.

"I know you think so," Joe acknowledged. "But me and Delia have been chatting and gaming online for almost seven months, and I knew I loved her even before I saw her. Now that we've finally met, I have no doubt that she's the woman I'm destined to be with for the rest of my life."

"The rest of your life is a long time," he warned.

"I hope so," his friend said sincerely. "But if you're not comfortable standing up for me, I can—"

"No," Caleb interjected. "I want to do this. Because even if I do think this is more than a little impulsive, it's obvious that Delia is just as smitten with you as you are with her."

"Then why are you scowling?" Joe asked him.

He shook his head. "If I tell you, you're going to think *I'm* crazy."

"Tell me anyway," his friend said.

Caleb slipped his arms into his jacket, then buttoned the front, tugged on the cuffs. "I caught a glimpse of a woman in the hotel lobby downstairs," he finally admitted. "And I thought—for a minute—that it was Brie."

"Brielle *Channing*?"

He nodded.

Joe considered the admission for a moment before responding. "Let me see if I've got this right. *I'm* crazy for falling in love with a woman I met online seven months ago, but it's okay that *you're* still in love with the woman who walked away from you more than seven *years* ago?"

"I'm not still in love with her," Caleb denied.

"Then forget about her," Joe advised. "Because what happens in Vegas—"

"Stays in Vegas," he finished, the marketing slogan being truer than even his buddy realized.

The groom-to-be grinned. "That's right, my friend. And after the ceremony, I will be escorting my bride to the honeymoon suite, which means that this room is all yours."

"I'll keep that in mind," Caleb said. Although the idea of spending the night with a random stranger held absolutely no appeal, admitting as much to his friend would only result in more questions about Brie—and he definitely didn't want to go there.

"Good." Joe adjusted his tie in the mirror. "Do you have—"

"Yes," he interrupted. "I have the ring."

"Okay."

Caleb glanced at his watch and decided they had some time before they needed to head down to the chapel. The thick carpet of the luxury room muffled his footsteps as he crossed to the bar to retrieve two bottles of beer from the fridge.

"Do you have any idea what they charge for those?" the anxious groom asked, his preoccupation with his grandmother's ring momentarily forgotten.

"No," he admitted, as he uncapped both bottles and handed one to Joe. "But undoubtedly less than the champagne, and I thought you'd prefer to toast your marriage this way."

"Can't argue with that," his buddy decided.

"To you and Delia," Caleb said, lifting his bottle in the air. "May you have a long and happy life together."

"And to my best friend," Joe said, raising his drink. "I hope that someday you find your perfect match and feel as lucky as I do right now. In the meantime—" he grinned again "—I hope you at least get lucky."

They tapped their bottles together and drank, then Joe went to escort his bride while Caleb headed to the chapel.

On his way, he passed one of the hotel's three pools and lingered for a minute to admire the crystal clear water sparkling in the afternoon sun—and the numerous shapely female bodies in and around it.

He felt an unwelcome tug in the vicinity of his chest when he saw her there: the same woman he'd caught a glimpse of earlier. The woman he'd believed—for the space of one endless, aching heartbeat—was Brielle.

Of course, it wasn't her. There were more than fifty hotels on the strip, and the odds that she might be vacationing in Las Vegas and staying at this particular hotel on the same weekend that he was here were…incalculable.

Whoever the woman was, she wasn't Brie, and he had to stop imagining otherwise.

Brie stepped out of the water and reached for one of the thick, fluffy towels provided by the hotel.

Then her gaze lifted to his face, noted the light brown hair that showed hints of gold in the sun, the tanned skin and square jaw, the hazel eyes framed by thick lashes—eyes that seemed to be staring right into hers even through the dark lenses of the sunglasses perched on her nose.

Her breath caught in her throat and her heart actually skipped a beat before it resumed its rhythm, albeit a little harder and faster than before.

"It *is* you," he said, in a low voice that was achingly familiar.

She ignored the racing of her heart and reminded herself that she wasn't a teenager anymore. She was a twenty-five-year-old woman who could handle an unexpected encounter with a former lover without falling to pieces.

Buoyed by this quick internal pep talk, she managed to respond casually, easily. "Hello, Caleb."

Though she couldn't take her eyes off him, she was aware that both of her friends were avidly watching the interaction. She felt the weight of their stares—and their unspoken questions.

"I wasn't sure it was really you at first." He settled on the edge of her lounger, so that he could look her in the eye—despite the fact that hers were still shaded.

She was grateful for the protection, because Caleb had always been able to see too much of what she was feeling. And his sudden and unexpected appearance here had brought to the surface too many feelings that she'd thought were long forgotten—or at least deeply buried.

"I saw you waiting for the elevator earlier," he continued, "but by the time I crossed the lobby, the doors had closed, and I decided that it couldn't have been you, anyway."

She didn't know what to say to that—or if she was even capable of forming a coherent sentence. So many thoughts and questions were swirling through her mind, so many emotions battling for dominance inside her heart.

Her friends came to her rescue now, with Lily shoving her hand toward him. "I'm Lily—one of Brielle's roommates in New York."

Deeply ingrained manners forced him to shift his attention and accept the proffered hand. And Grace's, too, when she followed the initial introduction with her own.

By then, Brie had recovered sufficiently from the shock of the unexpected encounter that she was able to string enough words together to say, "Caleb and I grew up together in Haven."

"So the two of you are...old friends?" Grace guessed.

Caleb looked at Brie again, waiting for her to answer.

"Yes," she agreed. "Old friends."

He gave the slightest shake of his head then, as if he was disappointed by her response.

"We're a little more than that," he said, and though he was answering Grace's question, his eyes never left Brie's face.

"How much more?" Lily asked curiously.

He settled a hand on Brie's knee, the casual gesture of a man accustomed to touching a woman.

Her breath caught in her throat as the contact caused her blood to heat and race through her veins, the effect of his touch exactly the same as it had been so many years before.

The barest hint of a smile tugged at the corners of his mouth as he registered her body's instinctive response to the contact before she drew her leg away. Then he shifted his attention to her friends and finally responded to Lily's question.

"Actually, Brielle is my wife."

Chapter Two

"*Ex*-wife," Brielle said through gritted teeth.

But her short-lived marriage was a detail she'd never shared with anyone outside of her immediate family, so it was no wonder her friends were looking at her with nearly identical expressions of shock and disbelief right now.

However, it was Caleb's focused gaze that unnerved her. "We've got a lot of catching up to do," he said.

"So do we, apparently," Grace murmured.

"I can't believe you never told us you were married." Lily sounded not just stunned but hurt.

And justifiably so, Brie acknowledged, as the two women had been not only her best friends but her surrogate family for the past seven years.

"It was a long time ago," Brie told them. "And over almost before it began."

"It was a long time ago," Caleb agreed. "But over... well, I'd have to disagree with you on that, darlin'."

"I'm not your *darlin'*," she protested.

"Well, this might finally explain why she hardly ever goes out," Lily remarked to Grace.

"And why she rarely goes out with the same guy more than once," Grace added.

"That's not true," Brie said to her friends. "And I'd appreciate it if you didn't analyze the intimate details of my love life in front of a stranger."

"Our point is that there are no intimate details," Grace said.

"And how can you refer to your husband as a stranger?" Lily chided.

"Ex-husband," she said again. "And he's a stranger to both of you."

"Any friend of yours is a friend of ours," Grace said, and turned to smile at Caleb. "So how far back do you and Brie go?"

"We went to school together, though I was a couple years ahead."

"You were high school sweethearts?" Lily guessed.

"Secret high school sweethearts," he clarified.

One of Grace's perfectly arched brows lifted. "Why the secrecy?"

"There's some…history between our families," he explained. "And we knew they wouldn't approve of our friendship—or our dating."

"The Montagues and the Capulets," Lily murmured, obviously recalling what Brie had told her when they were packing for this trip.

"Or the Hatfields and the McCoys," he suggested.

"Tell us more," Grace urged.

"I wish I could," Caleb said, rising to his feet again. "But Brie will have to fill in the rest of the details, because I've got a wedding to get to."

She'd thought nothing could surprise her as much as seeing him standing in front of her, but the way Brie's stomach dropped in response to his words proved otherwise. "You…you're…getting married?"

He sent her a look that she couldn't begin to decipher. "I'm not the groom. I'm the best man."

"Oh," she said, and exhaled the breath she hadn't realized she was holding.

"We're definitely going to find out from Brie if that's true," Grace teased.

Caleb grinned, appreciating her friend's flirtatious humor.

It was the same familiar cocky grin that had always made Brielle's heart pound and her knees weak. And it was frustrating to discover that, seven years later, its effect on her was undiminished.

"Joe Bishop's getting married," he said to her now.

She knew Joe, because he'd been friends with Caleb for as long as she'd known him, prompting her to ask, "Is the bride anyone I know?"

"The bride isn't anyone *he* knows," Caleb remarked dryly. "They met online seven months ago and in-person—" he glanced at the watch on his wrist "—about nine hours ago."

"I never thought Joe was the impulsive type."

"A lot of things can change in seven years," he said, holding her gaze. "Then again, some things never do."

"I'm *so* glad you wanted to come to Vegas." Lily's comment to Grace cut through the heavy silence.

"I just wanted to get drunk and lose some money at the tables," Grace replied. "This live show is so much better than anything I could have anticipated."

"Show's over, ladies," Caleb said apologetically. "I've got Joe's grandmother's ring, so I can't be late."

"Maybe we could just consider this an intermission?" Lily said hopefully.

He chuckled at that, but his expression grew serious when he turned to Brie again. "Will you meet me for a drink later?"

She shook her head. "I can't. We're here to celebrate Grace's birthday and—"

"Just one drink. Six o'clock?" He glanced at her friends, as if to enlist their cooperation. "I'm sure Grace and Lily can manage to occupy themselves for an hour or so."

"It doesn't matter whether they can or can't," Brie said. "I'm here with my friends and we've got plans for dinner."

"Plans but no reservations," Grace piped up helpfully. "So we're not on any particular schedule. And if we're not still here after the happy couple say their 'I do's,' we'll be in room 1268."

He nodded to Brie. "I'll find you there later, then."

Of course, she watched him walk away. She couldn't help herself. And she couldn't deny that he looked as good now as he'd looked the last time she saw him, seven years earlier. Maybe even better.

She suspected that her friends were watching him walk away, too, because it was only when he'd disappeared through the doors and back into the hotel that they turned to her.

"Oh. My. God." It was Lily who spoke first. "I can't believe you were married."

"And didn't tell us," Grace added.

"Because it was for a very short while a very long time ago," she said again.

"I don't care how short it was or how long ago," Grace said. "That's not the kind of secret you keep from your best friends."

"So maybe we're not her best friends," Lily suggested, sounding hurt.

"You know you are," Brie assured them sincerely.

"And yet, you didn't tell us about your hunky husband," Grace remarked. "Not a single word."

"Actually, she said a few words," Lily noted. "But only after you told us about this trip. And there was definitely no mention of a wedding or a husband."

Brie sighed, resigned to the imminent interrogation—and maybe a little relieved that she'd finally have the opportunity to unburden herself of the secrets she'd held on to for so long. But aware that her emotions were already running high, she'd prefer not to do so in public. "Can we continue this conversation upstairs?"

"Stalling for seven years wasn't long enough?" Lily challenged.

"I'm not trying to stall," Brie denied.

But she wouldn't have minded a few minutes under the spray of the shower to clear her head and organize her thoughts. Except that after unlocking the door to their suite, Grace pointed to a chair, a wordless command to her to sit.

Her dark-haired, dark-eyed friend with the take-charge personality had always been the unspoken leader of their little group. The other two women sometimes teased her for being bossy, but they were mostly content to follow her lead.

And because Brie accepted that she owed her friends an explanation, she sat. Lily and Grace settled side by side on the sofa, facing her.

"So…you were married," Grace prompted, when Brie remained silent.

"I was married," she confirmed.

"Before you moved to New York?" Lily asked, seeking clarification.

She answered with a slow nod.

"Which means you were barely eighteen."

Brie nodded again. "I was eighteen and—" her voice wavered and her eyes filled with tears "—pregnant."

The silence that followed her announcement was so complete, she could almost hear her friends' jaws drop.

Grace recovered first and asked, "You had a baby?"

Now Brie shook her head and pressed a hand to her chest, as if to assuage the ache that had never quite gone away. "No, I… I lost the baby."

"Oh, sweetie." Grace breached the distance to embrace her.

If anyone had asked, Brie would have said that she'd finished crying for her unborn baby years earlier—but the tears that spilled onto her cheeks now proved otherwise.

"Oh, crap." That remark came from Lily, because any outpouring of emotion inevitably brought on her own tears of empathy. "We didn't know…we didn't mean… Oh, Brie, we're so sorry. Oh, please don't cry." She shoved a box of tissues into Brie's lap, after plucking a couple out for her own use.

She managed a watery smile. "You did so mean to push and pry—it's what you do."

"Well, okay," Lily conceded. "But we didn't mean to make you cry."

"Although tears can be therapeutic," Grace said soothingly. "So you shouldn't be afraid to let them out."

"I don't think I can stop them now," Brie admitted. It was as if she'd built a dam around her emotions and that dam had suddenly given way, allowing seven years of repressed feelings and grief to flood over her.

She told her friends everything: from the first terrifying suspicion that she was pregnant, to Caleb holding her hands while they waited for the result of the home pregnancy test, followed by his impulsive proposal and their impromptu trip to Vegas, all without telling anyone in either of their families about their plans. And then the fallout, when they finally got back to Haven and shared the news about their wedding and the baby with their parents and grandparents.

"Your grandfather actually had a heart attack when he found out you'd married a Gilmore?" Lily asked.

"I don't know if the announcement of our wedding directly caused the cardiac arrest, but yes, he had surgery the next day." She plucked another tissue from the box as her eyes overflowed again. "Four days after that, I had a miscarriage. And since the baby was why we got married, losing the baby meant there was no reason for us to stay married, so I went to see a lawyer and had divorce papers drawn up."

"I'm sorry," Grace said again, clearly at a bit of a loss for words.

"You don't have to apologize. I should have told you both everything a long time ago."

"We would have been there for you, if we'd known," Lily said gently.

"Even without knowing, you were there for me," Brie assured her friends. "When I first went to New York, I didn't want to talk about it. I couldn't. The hurt was too raw. Not even Regan or Kenzie knew all the details of what happened. And then…well, the more time that went by, the more I didn't want to remember everything that happened."

"Is this really the first time you've seen Caleb since you moved away?" Grace asked.

"It is," she confirmed.

"That's why you always avoided going home," Lily realized.

"And why you weren't thrilled about coming to Vegas," Grace guessed.

"Well, I never actually believed I'd run into him here," Brie said.

"And I never would have suggested coming here if I'd known," Grace said, almost apologetically.

"It's fine," Brie said, wishing it was so. "And it was inevitable that our paths would cross sooner or later. Now at least that first awkward meeting is done—and it wasn't even all that awkward."

Her friends exchanged a glance.

Brie frowned. "Or was it more awkward than I realized?"

Lily gave a slow shake of her head. "No. At least, *awkward* isn't the word I would have used to describe it."

"I'd suggest *sizzling* as a more appropriate descriptor," Grace added.

"Well, it is one hundred and six degrees outside," Brie remarked.

"And about a thousand degrees hotter between you and your sexy ex," Lily noted.

She couldn't dispute the accuracy of her friend's description. Because even though almost half of the more than eight million people who lived in New York City were male, she'd never met a man who turned her on as much as Caleb Gilmore. "He did look good, didn't he?"

"I never understood the cowboy mystique," Grace confided. "*Now* I do."

"Of course, it doesn't matter how ruggedly handsome he is," Lily hastened to add. "We hate him for breaking your heart."

Brie managed a smile, touched by the unswerving loyalty of her friends. "When I left Haven, I broke his, too," she admitted.

"He shouldn't have let you go," Lily said.

But Grace shook her head. "He had to let her go."

"Why?" Lily demanded.

"Because he loved her," Grace said simply. "And he knew that she didn't want to stay."

"I couldn't stay," Brie told them. "There were too many memories—and too much heartache—in Haven."

"But you loved him, too," Grace noted.

"When I was a teenager," she agreed. "And maybe for a long time after."

"And maybe still," Lily said, obviously choosing not to believe her friend's previous denials.

"I'm *not* still in love with him," she said again.

"Are you sure?" Lily pressed. "Because all the evidence suggests that you still have some pretty deep feelings for your cowboy."

"What evidence?" she challenged.

"The fact that you didn't mention his name to either of us—even once—in the seven years that we've known you."

"That's somehow proof that I'm still hung up on him?" Brie challenged skeptically.

"Actually, I think I agree with Lily on this one," Grace said. "If Caleb didn't matter to you, you wouldn't have been so careful to avoid talking about him."

"Or maybe I just didn't want to talk about him," she suggested as an alternative. "Maybe I didn't want to think about the fact that I'd been in love and had my heart broken."

"We've all had our hearts broken," Grace pointed out.

"Yours probably more than most," Lily interjected.

Grace shrugged, because it was true. "I do seem to fall in and out of love frequently and easily. But sharing the joys and heartaches with friends is part of the journey—and the healing process."

"You're right," Brie said. "And I do feel better now that I've told you about my ill-fated marriage, but I don't want to talk about Caleb anymore."

"We'll table the discussion for later," Lily agreed. "Because you don't have a lot of time left to get ready before he's going to be knocking on the door."

"I wouldn't have to worry about that if someone hadn't given him our room number," Brie remarked, with a pointed look at Grace.

Her friend shrugged. "What can I say? Apparently I've got a weak spot for handsome cowboys."

"So maybe *you* should go for a drink with my ex-husband," Brie suggested.

"I wasn't invited," Grace pointed out.

"I'm still not sure why I was," she admitted.

"Don't worry about his reasons," Lily suggested. "This is your opportunity to prove to your ex—and to yourself —

that you're one hundred percent totally and completely over him."

"If you're sure that you are," Grace said.

"I am," she insisted.

But as she stood under the spray of the shower and thought about the evening ahead, Brie couldn't deny that seeing him again made her suspect she wasn't as totally and completely over Caleb Gilmore as she wanted to believe.

Seven years after she'd walked out of his life, Brielle Channing still had the power to take his breath away—a fact that was proved to Caleb when he spotted her by the pool earlier that afternoon.

He'd given himself a minute to draw air back into his lungs and think about what he was going to say so that he didn't stutter and stumble over his words, and he'd thought that first meeting had gone rather well. But seeing her had sent his whole world into a tailspin.

Although he'd made it to the chapel to witness the exchange of wedding vows, Joe had to elbow him in the ribs—twice—to prompt him to hand over the ring when requested by the officiant. Because the whole time he was standing beside his friend, he was thinking about Brie.

His first love. His wife. The woman he'd always believed would be the mother of his children.

The only woman he'd ever loved.

Yeah, he knew it was pathetic. And no way in hell would he ever admit it aloud to anyone else, but it was a truth he couldn't deny to himself. For Caleb, it had always been Brie. She wasn't just "the one"—she was his everything.

But she'd walked away from him, forcing him to acknowledge that she didn't feel the same way. To accept that the love they'd shared was gone, the vows they'd exchanged were broken, the lives once joined together were now torn apart.

And he'd moved on. Or at least continued to live his life, working beside his father and brother, grandfather, uncle and cousins at the Circle G. He'd even built the house that he'd once imagined he would share with Brie, but he lived in it alone, and the three extra bedrooms planned for their children remained empty and silent.

Not forever, of course. Just because he'd lost Brie didn't mean he'd given up hope on finding another woman to fill his heart and share his home. The only problem was, every other woman he met wasn't quite right—because no other woman was Brie.

His brother believed that Caleb loved the memory of Brielle more than he'd ever loved her. Liam had encouraged him to see her again, insisting that he wouldn't be able to move on with his life until he'd put his past with Brie behind him. Caleb didn't think his brother was any kind of an expert, but since Liam had recently gotten engaged to Macy Clayton—a single mother of year-old triplets—Caleb was forced to acknowledge that his brother might know a little bit more about relationships than he did.

So tonight, he was going to have a drink with Brie—and finally confess the secret he'd held close to his chest for seven years.

Chapter Three

Caleb knocked on the door numbered 1268 and mentally braced himself to see her again. This time, it wouldn't be a surprise. This time, he would be prepared.

Except that nothing could have prepared him for the stunningly sexy woman in the little black dress and sky-scraper heels who suddenly appeared before him.

He felt breathless and a little dizzy, as if he'd been sucker punched. Then she smiled, a follow-up jab that nearly brought him to his knees.

"You're punctual," she noted.

"And you're—" his gaze skimmed over her, from the sleek fall of pale blond hair that fell past her shoulders, to the deep vee at the front of her dress and the short skirt that hugged her hips and thighs, down long bare legs that went on and on to the narrow feet tied into strappy sandals that added four inches to her height "—wow."

Her smile widened as she stepped back to allow him entry to the suite. "I left my denim and flannel in Nevada when I moved away. And because Lily helped me pack, I didn't have anything more appropriate for a drink with an old friend."

"I'm not complaining," he assured her. But while the dress and shoes were nice, he suspected that he would have had the same reaction if she'd been dressed in a pair of jeans and an old shirt. Because Brielle had always been sexy, regardless of what she was wearing—and especially when she was wearing nothing at all.

Which was definitely *not* something he should be thinking about right now.

He cleared his throat and attempted to shove the tantalizing image to the back of his mind. "Now I'm really glad I didn't take the time to change after the wedding," he said, keeping his tone light.

"You look good in a suit," she told him.

"I feel naked without my hat," he admitted.

She chuckled softly. "I'll bet you're missing your boots, too."

"I am," he confirmed. "But Joe put his foot down with respect to my footwear."

"The things we do for our friends," she mused.

"Speaking of—where are Grace and Lily?"

"They went down to the casino." She slid a key card into her handbag.

"You didn't want to join them?"

"I was reminded that I had other plans," Brie admitted.

He glanced around the suite and briefly considered suggesting that they stay in and order up drinks. But while that option would afford them more privacy, the proximity of the bedroom might be too much of a distraction—at least for him.

"Do you want to go to The Gilded Lion or The Reservoir?" he asked instead, opening the door for her to exit.

"I assume I can get a glass of wine at either, so I'll let you decide," she said, moving past him.

"It looked like you were drinking something fancier than wine at the pool earlier," he noted.

"Several things fancier," she acknowledged, as he closed the door behind them and checked to ensure that it had latched. "That's why I'm sticking with wine tonight."

He punched the button to summon the elevator. "Let's try The Gilded Lion," he suggested. "And maybe get something to nibble on along with the wine. I haven't had a chance to eat anything all day myself."

"Sounds good to me," she said.

They rode down to the main level in silence and were quickly seated in a cozy booth by the hostess of the lounge.

After perusing the drink menu, Brie opted for a Napa Valley Merlot; Caleb ordered a draft beer and an appetizer sampler.

"How was the wedding?" Brie asked, after their drinks had been delivered.

"Short and sweet. And…nice," he admitted. "I had some reservations, but Joe and Delia seem really happy together."

"I still can't believe it. I never imagined Joe Bishop as the marrying kind."

"Seven years ago, he wasn't," Caleb agreed. "But most of our mutual friends are married or in committed relationships, some even with kids, and Joe decided he wanted the same thing."

"But why the quick ceremony in Vegas?"

"I guess not every bride dreams of a big fancy event," he remarked.

But they both knew that Brie had done so, because they'd spent hours talking about the wedding they planned to have one day. Of course, that had been a long time ago—before she'd gotten pregnant, when they'd let themselves believe that their families would celebrate their love rather than object to the nuptials.

Back then, she'd envisioned riding to the ceremony in a horse-drawn carriage and walking down the aisle in a designer dress with a bouquet of pink roses. Instead, she'd traveled more than four hundred miles in an old pickup truck to exchange vows in front of a fake Elvis wearing tattered blue suede shoes.

"And a positive pregnancy test can change a girl's dreams," she noted.

He wondered if her casual tone was an accurate reflection of her feelings or merely a balm to cover old wounds. "I'm sorry you didn't get the wedding you wanted," he said to her now.

"It wasn't your fault, Caleb. And it's ancient history, anyway."

Which was his cue to speak up. "Actually, it's—"

"So why did Joe and Delia decide to elope?" she interjected to ask again.

He suspected that she wasn't as interested in the details of a wedding between a groom she'd lost touch with a long time ago and a bride she'd never met as she was in not hearing what he wanted to say. And though he couldn't let her walk away from him again without knowing the truth he'd kept hidden for too long, he allowed her to steer the direction of the conversation, at least for now.

"Delia lost her father a few years back, and she didn't want a traditional wedding without him there to walk her down the aisle," he explained.

"What about Joe's family?" she asked. "What do they think about the elopement?"

"Well, his mom gave him his grandmother's ring, so I have to assume she knew what he was planning and didn't have any objections."

"An engagement is different than a wedding," she pointed out, perusing the appetizer platter that had been set on the table and selecting a deep-fried ravioli.

He swallowed a mouthful of beer before venturing to ask, "Do you think your parents would have been okay if we'd announced an engagement before we got married?"

"It doesn't really matter at this point, does it?"

"Maybe it matters to me."

She dipped the ravioli in marinara sauce and popped it into her mouth. "Well, my grandfather might have had his heart attack before we ever exchanged vows," she said, when she'd finished chewing. "And then we wouldn't have needed to get a divorce."

Though her tone was deliberately light, he sensed the lingering hurt beneath her words. "Yeah, that's what I wanted to talk to you about," he said.

Her brows drew together as she lifted her glass to her lips and sipped her wine. "My grandfather?"

He shook his head. "The divorce."

She set the glass down again and traced a fingertip slowly around its base. "I've spent enough time today dredging up our past—can we talk about something else instead?"

"We *need* to talk about this," he told her.

"Tell me about the Circle G," she said, ignoring his entreaty.

"Really?" he asked dubiously. "You want to know what's going on at my family's cattle ranch?"

"I want to hear what *you've* been doing over the past seven years," she said. "I know, from conversations with my sister, that your brother's been busy with The Stagecoach Inn, Katelyn's law practice is booming and Sky's still tending bar at Diggers', but I haven't heard much about you."

"Have you asked?" he wondered.

"That would be a good way to start the gossip mill churning, wouldn't it?"

"The gossip mill never stops," he pointed out.

"Well, I have no desire to add grist to the mill."

"I heard you were back for the baptism of Regan's twins," he remarked.

"Proof the gossip never stops. But yes," she said, and smiled then, obviously thinking about her infant nieces. "I'm not just Piper and Poppy's aunt, I'm also their godmother."

He wished he could ask her if she ever thought about

the baby they'd lost, and all the ways their lives would have been different if their baby had lived. But he bit back the question, instinctively understanding that, even after seven years, bringing up the subject would rip a scab off a still-raw wound for both of them.

Instead, he snagged a cheese ball from the plate and washed it down with a mouthful of beer while Brie nibbled on an onion ring.

She wiped her fingers on a napkin when a chirp sounded. "Grace said she'd text to let me know the dinner plan," she explained, retrieving her cell from her purse.

He nodded as she unlocked the screen to read the message.

"Apparently there's been a slight change of plans," she remarked.

"What's happening?" he asked.

"They got tickets to the seven o'clock show of Cirque du Soleil."

He glanced at his watch. "You have to go now?"

She shook her head. "No, they only got two tickets."

"Your friends didn't get one for you?"

"Grace said there were only two available, but Grace has a habit of thinking she knows what's best for her friends without consulting them."

It took him a moment to read between the lines. "You think she didn't try to get you a ticket?"

"She feels pretty strongly that I need to spend some time with you, to achieve relationship closure in order to move on with my life."

Which was similar to what his brother had said, so maybe there was some validity to the argument. "Is that what you want—to move on with your life?" he asked.

"It's been seven years," she reminded him. "I think I need to move on with my life. We both do."

"How do you know I haven't?" he challenged.

"Maybe you have. But the fact that you're here with me now would suggest otherwise."

He nodded in acknowledgment of her point. "I guess I just always thought—*hoped*—that you'd eventually come back to Haven and we'd work things out."

"There's nothing left to work out," she said gently.

"Do you really believe that?"

"It's been seven years," she said again.

"Which doesn't answer my question," he noted.

He was right, of course, but Brie hadn't expected him to pick up on her effort to sidestep his query. In her admittedly limited experience, men weren't usually very intuitive. But Caleb had always been more attuned to her thoughts and feelings than anyone else she'd ever known.

And because she still didn't know how to answer his question, she tried to buy herself another few seconds by lifting her glass to her lips again—only to discover that it was empty.

As if on cue, the waitress appeared. "Can I get you another glass of wine?"

"Just the bill, please," Caleb said, before Brie had a chance to nod her head.

"Of course," the server agreed, and hurried away.

"Maybe I did want another glass of wine," Brie said.

"You can have one with dinner," he told her.

"We still have half a plate of appetizers right here," she pointed out.

"I need real food," he said.

"This tastes real to me," she said, selecting another onion ring.

"Does it taste like steak?"

She dropped the onion ring back onto the plate.

He grinned. "Let's take a walk, darlin'."

Since her plans for a girls' dinner had fallen by the wayside, she decided there was no harm in sharing a meal with an old friend—even if that old friend was also her ex-husband. So after Caleb signed the check, they headed out to the strip.

But he didn't seem to be in any hurry to find a restaurant, and he held her hand as they weaved through the crowds.

"So I don't lose you," he explained, when he linked their fingers together.

And because it felt both natural and comfortable to hold his hand, she didn't protest. Or point out that they'd lost one another a lot of years before.

They talked while they walked—casual conversation about mutual acquaintances and family members. The initial awkwardness had passed and being with him felt easy and familiar again. It also made Brie remember all the good times they'd shared, and that enticed her imagination to wander down the dangerously tempting path of "what if."

They lucked out and managed to snag a table at Prime—a steak and seafood restaurant inside the Courtland Hotel. Caleb put his hand on her back as they followed the hostess, and even through the fabric of her dress, Brie felt the heat of his touch branding her skin and making her knees weak.

The small square table was covered with a white linen cloth and set with gleaming silver and sparkling crystal. Comfy armchairs were positioned on adjacent sides of the table, contributing to the intimacy of the atmosphere. Caleb pulled one of the chairs away from the table for her, and as Brie lowered herself into the leather seat, she found herself thinking that this suddenly felt a lot like a date with a capital D.

When they'd been dating, and trying to hide the fact from their respective families, they'd never shared a meal in a fancy restaurant. Because even grabbing a bite at Diggers' had stretched their budgets—and set tongues wagging. Instead, they'd usually chosen to spend their meager dollars at Jo's, where they could hang out as friends without anyone blinking an eye.

Brie had never felt as if she was missing out, though. And she'd especially enjoyed the times that they'd taken their pizza up to the old cabin at Crooked Creek and eaten it cold after making love.

She dragged her attention back to the present when she was handed a leather folder. The hostess then recited the drink and dinner specials and promised that their server would be over in just a minute.

"This is few steps up from Diggers'," Caleb remarked when they were alone, the comment suggesting that his thoughts had wandered down a path similar to her own.

"It's very nice," she agreed, opening her menu to peruse the offerings.

"Of course, you must dine in fancy restaurants all the time in New York."

"I go out to eat more than I probably should," she acknowledged. "But rarely to fancy restaurants. In fact, one of my favorite places reminds me a lot of Diggers'—right down to the burly bartender."

"I wouldn't describe Sky as burly," he said, his eyes twinkling with humor as they met hers. "Though she can definitely be surly, at times."

"I was referring to Duke, not Sky," she chided. The former was the owner of the bar and grill; the latter was his sister, an employee at the bar.

"Oh." He nodded. "That does make more sense."

Brie was smiling when the server, who introduced himself as Eric, delivered a basket of warm bread and a pot of whipped butter to the table.

Caleb ordered a bottle of Argentinean Malbec and Eric uncorked it at the table, then poured a first glass for the customer's approval. He swirled the liquid in the bowl, passed it under his nose and finally sipped before nodding. The server then poured a second glass for Brie.

"When did you become a wine connoisseur?" she asked, when they were alone again.

"I'm hardly a connoisseur," Caleb said. "But I paid attention when Macy was explaining the tasting procedure to my brother."

"Macy's the manager of the inn, right?"

"And now Liam's fiancée."

"Your brother proposed to a single mom of triplets?"

He nodded. "And if you think that's surprising, you should see him dote on those kids."

Except they both knew that wasn't likely to ever happen.

On the rare occasions that Brie went back to Haven, she'd done everything she could to avoid running into Caleb. She'd been apprehensive about seeing him: uncertain about what to say, wary about how she might feel. And for more than seven years, her efforts to elude him had been successful.

Though she hadn't been thrilled about making another trip to Nevada, she hadn't anticipated crossing paths with Caleb in such a crowded city so far from Haven. Now she was sharing wine and conversation with him, remembering how much they'd once shared—and how much she'd missed him when he was no longer a part of her life.

She shook off the memories and melancholy and turned her attention back to her menu as Caleb set his aside.

"You know what you want already?" she asked, surprised that he'd decided when she'd barely skimmed through the appetizers.

"I've always known what I wanted," he said.

She felt his gaze on her and wondered—for a brief moment—if he was referring to something other than food.

"Steak," he said, when she peered cautiously at him over the top of the leather folder, and added a wink for good measure.

"Oh, right." She quickly skimmed the rest of the menu offerings, then closed the cover as the server returned to their table.

Brie ordered the prime rib with garlic mashed potatoes and pan-seared broccolini; Caleb opted for the porterhouse steak with a loaded baked potato and sautéed green beans and mushrooms.

When Eric disappeared again, Caleb buttered a slice of bread and offered it to her.

As she started to shake her head, her stomach growled in protest.

He grinned and moved the bread closer to her lips. She instinctively opened her mouth and took a bite. She didn't think about the intimacy of eating from his hand until her bottom lip caught on the pad of his thumb.

She abruptly pulled away, her lip tingling at the point of contact. Caleb's gaze dropped to her mouth, lingered as she carefully chewed the bread.

"Maybe it's not all in my head," he mused quietly.

She didn't ask.

She didn't want to know—or try to put into words whatever was still between them. Because she could deny it until the cows came home, but it was obvious that something still was.

Thankfully, Caleb didn't seem to expect a response. Instead, he set the bread on her plate and drew another slice out of the basket.

"Tell me how you know Grace and Lily," he suggested, as he dipped the knife into the butter.

She latched onto the neutral topic gratefully and spent the next several minutes telling him about her first weeks at Columbia and the development of her friendship with the other two women.

When the waiter returned with their meals, they stopped talking to focus on their food. After dinner, they lingered over coffee and warm apple cobbler with vanilla bean ice cream drizzled with brandy caramel sauce. Though Brie had insisted that she couldn't eat another bite, Eric brought two forks with the dessert and Caleb urged her to try a bite, and somehow one little nibble turned into more.

She didn't know what time it was when they finally got back to their hotel. She wasn't thinking about the clock as they made their way, still hand in hand, through the lobby where enormous chandeliers hung from the ceiling, casting glittery light over everything below. They skirted around the towering fountain, its basin filled with coins of various shapes and sizes, to the bank of elevators.

Caleb punched the call button, and while they waited for the doors to open, Brie realized that she wasn't quite ready to walk away from him again.

She'd agreed to see him tonight because Grace and Lily had insisted that it would give her a sense of closure, but now that it was nearing the time to say goodbye, she knew she couldn't bring herself to utter the words. Not yet.

Instead, she kissed him.

Chapter Four

Caleb didn't waste any time being surprised, because it felt too damn good to hold Brie in his arms again, to breathe in the scent of her skin and taste the sweetness of her kiss. Her lips were soft and full; her flavor was tempting and seductive—and somehow, even after so many years, achingly familiar.

The first time he'd kissed her, she'd been both shy and inexperienced. But what she'd lacked in finesse she'd more than made up for with enthusiasm, a quick and eager student. And while he'd patiently tutored her in the discovery and sharing of physical pleasure, she'd taught him something, too: that as enjoyable as sex could be, the experience was further heightened by emotion.

He traced the seam of her lips with the tip of his tongue now, and she sighed, opening for him. He hadn't forgotten what it was like to kiss her, but this present reality was so much richer and sharper than the memories imprinted on his mind and in his heart.

He wrapped his arms around her and drew her closer, so that the soft curves of her body yielded to the hard planes of his. Or maybe it was the heat generated by their proximity that caused her to melt against him as their tongues moved together in a slow, sensual rhythm.

His hand slid up her spine to the back of her neck, his fingers sifting through the soft strands of hair to cup her head as his mouth continued to move over hers. He didn't ever want to stop—except maybe to strip that sexy dress away from her sexier body so that he could kiss her all over.

He would start with her eyelids, then the tip of her nose, then her mouth again, her chin, her throat, her breasts. Maybe he'd linger there for a moment, listening to her sigh and gasp as he licked and suckled her nipples before trailing kisses down her belly, and lower still. And then, when she was breathless and quivering, when she was as desperate for him as he was for her, he would—

Brie pulled back, breaking the connection between them. "I just realized—"

"That we're in a very public place?" he guessed.

"That, too," she acknowledged, her cheeks turning pink. "But also, I never asked if you're involved with anyone."

"A few seconds ago, I was very involved," he assured her.

The color in her cheeks deepened. "I meant back in Haven…do you have a girlfriend?"

"I wouldn't have kissed you if I had a girlfriend," he said.

"Except that *I* kissed *you*," she pointed out. "You only kissed me back."

"That's true," he acknowledged.

And then *he* kissed *her*.

This was crazy.

Brie knew it, but she couldn't stop it.

She didn't want to stop it.

Because kissing Caleb—and being kissed by Caleb—made her feel more alive than she'd felt in a very long time. Want things she hadn't wanted in a very long time.

And right now, she wanted him.

He tasted sweet, like the dessert they'd shared, and a

little bit spicy, like the wine they'd drunk. But mostly, he tasted like Caleb. Even after so many years, there was something familiar about his flavor, and that familiarity was both comforting and arousing.

She'd missed this.

Missed *him*.

His tongue explored the inside of her mouth, stoking the fire that already burned inside her. Desire spread through her veins, hot and fast, so that nothing seemed to matter but how much she wanted this.

Wanted *him*.

Was it reckless to succumb to the heat of passion when they were both likely to get burned again?

She didn't know the answer to that question, but she knew it would be foolish to turn away from the pleasure she would find in his arms.

Maybe this was part of their healing. As a result of everything that had happened seven years earlier, they'd both been angry and hurt when they parted ways. Maybe they needed this time together now, a chance to finally put the past behind them and move forward, even if that was on separate paths.

He eased his mouth from hers. "My room isn't as fancy as yours, but I can promise there won't be anyone else in it tonight."

She hesitated for only a split second before need pushed aside logic. "Lead the way," she said.

He punched the button for the elevator again.

The doors whooshed open right away this time, and he gestured for her to enter. Her knees felt wobbly and weak as she stepped inside, grateful that she didn't have a chance to think about what she was doing, to question the wisdom of her actions or analyze her motives.

And yet, when she entered his room, she turned to him and said, "You do realize that this might be a mistake."

"It wouldn't be our first," he noted, reaching for her. "I

want you, Brie." His hands stroked over her torso, tracing her curves. "Right now, that's the one thing of which I have no doubt. But if you're not sure—"

She touched her fingertips to his lips, halting his words.

"I'm sure," she told him.

For the past seven years, she'd tried to atone for the mistakes she'd made, and she was tired of feeling sad and sorry. Tired of being plagued by remorse and regrets.

Tonight, she was going to take what she wanted.

And tonight, she wanted Caleb.

She realized he'd found the zipper at the back of her dress when she felt the cool air on her bare skin as he inched it downward. When the narrow straps slipped off her shoulders, he hooked his fingers in them and dragged them lower, exposing the swell of her breasts.

He dipped his head then and feathered his lips lightly over her skin, a caress more than a kiss. Her eyes closed on a sigh. His mouth moved lower, brushing over an already peaked nipple. He paused there, to lick and suckle through the delicate lace bra she wore, making her gasp as arrows of exquisite sensation speared toward her core.

Eager to touch him as he was touching her, she pushed his jacket over his shoulders, yanked his shirt out of his pants and made quick work of the buttons. He had a rancher's body. Tough and lean. His skin was warm and stretched taut over tight muscles.

When they were both naked, he lifted her easily into his arms and carried her the short distance to the bed, depositing her gently on top of the covers. She drew him down with her, wanting to feel his skin against hers, his weight pressing her into the mattress, his body merging and mating with her own.

His mouth skimmed along her jaw, down her throat. Nipping and nibbling. He took his time exploring her skin with his lips and tongue and teeth. Tempting and teasing her. Letting her know how much he wanted her; making her want just as much. More.

He nuzzled the hollow between her breasts, the scrape of stubble on his cheeks abrading her tender skin. The delicious friction raised goose bumps on her flesh.

"Cold?" he asked.

She moved her head from side to side on the pillow. "No, I'm not cold."

In fact, she was so hot for him she felt as if she was burning up inside.

Still, he rolled her gently to the side so that he could yank the top cover down, then he drew it up over her naked body and disappeared beneath it to embark on a leisurely and intimate exploration of her most sensitive places.

She felt a familiar tension coiling in the pit of her belly as he used his hands and his lips and his tongue and—

She cried out when her release came, hot and fast, leaving her gasping and breathless.

He groaned, a sound of pure male satisfaction, as he lapped up her juices and her body continued to shudder.

"Caleb." His name was a desperate plea from her lips. Because as good as he'd made her feel, it wasn't enough. She wanted the fulfillment that would come only from feeling him buried deep inside her.

He rose up over her then, answering her plea, pinning her to the mattress. She gloried in the sensation of his naked body pressed against hers and instinctively rocked against him, creating a delicious and dangerous friction.

He groaned again as he positioned himself at the apex of her thighs.

Yes, she thought. *Now.*

And then she remembered. "Condom."

He swore and immediately pulled away from her. "I don't—" He swore again, more fiercely this time. "I'm sorry. I didn't plan for anything like this to happen."

"I didn't, either," she said. "But Grace believes one

should always be prepared, and she tucked a couple in my purse—just in case."

"Thank you, Grace," he said, and sprinted to retrieve her purse from where she'd dropped it on the chair beside the door.

She found a little square packet and tore it open eagerly.

When he was finally sheathed, ensuring their mutual protection, she pulled him down onto the bed with her again.

He brushed his lips over hers—a brief and tender kiss. "I missed you, Brie."

The confession, simple and sincere, filled her heart and made her yearn. Because she'd missed him, too, and being with him now felt so good, so right. But she didn't—couldn't—say the words aloud. Instead, she gave him her body, fully and completely.

As always, there was tenderness underlying the passion. Even when they'd been hormonally driven teenagers, Caleb had been careful with her, not just patient but protective. Showing her with every brush of his lips and touch of his hands that he cared about her.

Was it any wonder she'd fallen in love with him then?

Or that her heart yearned to open up for him now?

But she couldn't go down that path again.

She wouldn't.

Because the same obstacles that had stood in the way of their relationship seven years earlier were even more insurmountable now.

But she could and would have this one last night with him.

To say goodbye.

There was a bird outside her window, chirping.

The sound pulled back the curtain of her slumber, forcing her to acknowledge the arrival of a new day.

Not a bird, she realized, but her cell phone. Tucked inside her handbag, which would explain why it sounded as if it was coming from a distance.

She shifted to reach for it, but the sheet was caught on something and refused to move with her.

Not some*thing*. Some*one*.

Caleb.

Which meant that the incredibly vivid and erotic dream she'd had the previous night hadn't been a dream after all.

She forgot about her phone as the memories flooded her mind, teased her body.

He'd been her first love, her first lover and, for a very short while, her husband. She'd loved him with an intensity that she suspected only a teenage girl could feel, and when their relationship had ended, she'd been certain that her heart was truly and forever shattered.

Of course, with time and maturity came perspective and healing. But she'd been wrong to assume that her feelings for Caleb were completely gone, because just seeing him again had churned up so many emotions.

When she'd lost their baby, she'd felt as if she'd died inside. She was convinced that was the reason she'd never fallen in love—or even into bed—with another man. Certainly it was a more reasonable explanation than that she'd never gotten over her first love.

She had a great job, a fabulous home and terrific friends, but she'd never given her heart to another man. She'd dated—not frequently, though more than her friends had implied—but no one else had ever made her feel the way she felt when she was with Caleb.

For the past seven years, there had been an emptiness inside her that no one and nothing else had ever been able to fill. Until last night.

Last night had proved that her memories hadn't been exaggerated. Making love with Caleb for the first time in so many years almost felt like their first time all over again, only so much better. But somehow the second time had topped even that. And the third—

She turned to the man sleeping in the bed beside her and put a hand on his shoulder. His skin was warm and taut over hard muscle. She nudged him gently.

He didn't stir.

"Caleb, wake up." A harder shove accompanied her command this time.

"What?" His eyes were immediately open, though clouded with sleep. Then they settled on her and cleared, as his lips curved. "Hey."

The warm timbre in his voice and obvious appreciation in his gaze might have made her belly quiver if it hadn't been so tied up in knots. "We had unprotected sex, Caleb."

Not the first time.

The first time, they'd used one of the condoms that Grace had tucked into her purse. Then they'd used the second. And then they'd awakened in the night and turned to one another, forgetting—or maybe not caring—that there were no more condoms.

He closed his eyes again and swore softly.

She nodded, wordlessly confirming his assessment of their reckless behavior.

Fully awake now, he pushed himself up into a seated position. The sheet dropped to his waist, exposing the upper part of his torso, marked by faint lines where her nails had scored his skin, a visible reminder of their passionate lovemaking.

She looked away and spotted her dress in a heap on the floor. Slipping out of bed, she began gathering up her clothes.

"Are you on any other form of birth control?" he asked her.

Brie shook her head as she fastened her bra.

"And now you're worried that you might get pregnant," he guessed.

Actually, the possibility that their actions might result in a baby hadn't crossed her mind until that very moment. And thinking about it now—

No, she couldn't think about it now.

"My more immediate concern—" she wriggled into her panties "—is that I have no idea who else has shared your bed in the past seven years."

"Are you looking for names or numbers?" he asked.

"Neither," she immediately replied.

Because she absolutely did *not* want to think about him with any other women. She knew there had been other women, she just didn't want to think about them. She definitely didn't want to know their names, because if she ever ran into any of them in Haven, she'd be stuck with the knowledge that they'd seen him naked.

She tugged her dress over her head. "I just want to know that you're not in the habit of having unprotected sex," she told him.

"I'm not," he promised. "In fact, the only time I've ever forgotten about protection is with you."

"Is that true? Or are you just trying to make me feel better?"

He crossed a finger over his heart.

She exhaled, an obviously relieved sigh, and reached behind her for the zipper of her dress.

"How about you?" he asked.

She shook her head. "Never."

His brows rose.

"Except with you, too, obviously," she clarified.

"Okay then, so that brings us back to the possibility that you could get pregnant," he said.

She swallowed and picked up her handbag then, to retrieve her phone and read the message she'd almost forgotten about. "I have to believe we couldn't be that unlucky again."

He leaned back against the headboard, his gaze fixed on hers. "Did you really think it was unlucky the first time?"

"It certainly wasn't what either of us planned," she reminded him.

"Not at that time, anyway," he agreed. "But I liked the idea of spending my life with you, raising a family with you."

Simple dreams from a simpler time.

She slipped her feet into her shoes. "That same idea put my grandfather in the hospital."

"I don't believe there was a connection between our wedding and your grandfather's heart attack," he said, pulling on his boxer briefs. "Though I have no doubt he took advantage of the timing—and your vulnerability—to drive a wedge between us."

"He wasn't the only one," she remarked. "*Everyone* thought our marriage was a mistake."

"Not everyone," he said quietly, and stepped up behind her to zip her dress the rest of the way.

"I really have to go," she said. "Already this morning I've had half a dozen messages from Grace and Lily, both eager to know how and why I spent the night with my ex-husband."

"Actually, that's what I've been wanting to clear up since I ran into you at the pool yesterday," he told her. "When I said that you were my wife, I didn't forget the 'ex' part. The truth is, we're still married."

Chapter Five

Still married?

Brie immediately shook her head in response to the ridiculous suggestion. "That's not possible."

"It's not only possible, it's true," Caleb assured her.

"It can't be," she protested.

"Did you ever get a certificate of divorce from the court?" he asked now.

"No," she admitted. "I mean, I don't think so."

But she hadn't worried about it, because she'd assumed the final paperwork had been sent to her address in Haven and her parents had put it away somewhere.

"Because there wasn't one," he said. "Because I never signed the papers."

She sank down onto the edge of the chair beside the door and stared at him. "Are you freaking kidding me?"

He took a tentative step back, as if to distance himself from the shock and fury that underscored her words. "I wouldn't joke about something like that."

His assurance did nothing to appease her. "Why didn't you sign the papers?" And then, without pausing long enough for him to answer, she said, "All you had to do was scribble your name on the line. There was even a little sticky note that indicated 'sign here' with an arrow."

He remained silent, as if giving her a chance to finish her rant.

And dammit, she *was* ranting. She couldn't seem to help herself. Because she was stunned and angry and hurt and, underneath all of that, there was a whole other layer of emotions that she wasn't ready to acknowledge never mind attempt to decipher. "Dammit, Caleb—why?"

"Because I didn't want a divorce," he admitted. "Because I wanted to give our marriage a chance."

"A chance for what?" she demanded.

"And I thought you'd come back for Christmas, after a few months away, having realized that you wanted the same thing," he continued, not actually answering her question.

"And when I didn't come back for Christmas?" she prompted.

"Yeah, that was a tough blow to my theory," he acknowledged. "But still…if not Christmas, I was sure you'd be home for the summer."

But she hadn't gone home for the summer—or the next Christmas or the summer after that. In fact, four years had passed before she'd returned to Haven, and even then, her return had not been by choice.

"I'd loved you for so long, I couldn't believe that it was over," he confided to her now.

"I didn't want it to be over, either," she said quietly. "But I knew that if we stayed together, after everything that had happened, it would tear our families apart."

"Instead, you let them tear us apart."

"I didn't *let* anything happen," she denied. "But when we lost our baby…"

"I was heartbroken, too," he told her.

"I *was* heartbroken," she agreed. "But…there was also a part of me that was relieved." She looked at him then, desperate for him to understand. "I was only eighteen, Caleb. Too young to be a wife and a mother. And then I felt so guilty about feeling relieved, and there wasn't anyone I could talk to—"

"You could have talked to me," he said. "We always promised we could talk to each other about anything."

"That was before I lost our baby."

"It wasn't your fault, Brie."

The logical part of her brain knew he was right, but the emotional part still struggled with both grief and guilt. She'd wanted a family with Caleb, and she'd loved their baby, but at eighteen, she'd been unprepared for everything that marriage and motherhood entailed.

But she wasn't eighteen anymore, and rehashing their history wasn't going to serve any purpose. "I think we've gotten a little off topic," she said.

"Have we?" he challenged.

"We need to put the past in the past."

Caleb remained stubbornly silent.

"Do you still have the divorce papers?" she asked.

He responded with a slow nod.

"Then when you get back to Haven, you can sign and file them," she told him.

"But last night—"

She shook her head, her heart heavy. "I don't want to hurt you anymore, Caleb. And that's what's going to happen if we try to make this into something more than what it was."

"Just a tawdry one-night stand during a girls' weekend in Vegas?" he challenged, in a bitter tone.

Though she suspected he was lashing out because he was hurt by her response, she winced as his words hit their mark. "It wasn't tawdry," she said. "And you know that what happened between us last night wouldn't have happened with anyone but you."

"So why do you still want me to sign the divorce papers?"

"Because you should have signed them seven years ago," she said. "And if you had no intention of signing them, you should have told me why."

"You're right," he acknowledged.

"But you never came to New York to see me—or even called to talk to me about it."

"I was waiting for you to come home," he said again.

The sincere admission tugged at her heart—but only for a moment, until she reminded herself that he'd lied to her. Or at least misled her. Because for the past seven years, she'd believed that their divorce was final.

Discovering that they were still married—well, that revelation had admittedly thrown her for a loop. But now that she'd had a (very) few minutes to wrap her head around it, she knew it didn't change anything.

Their marriage had effectively ended when she left Haven. That they were still husband and wife on paper was just a legal technicality—nothing more.

"It's what I want," she said. "For both of us."

"Okay, then," he agreed. "I'll sign the papers—"

"Thank you," she said, sincerely grateful.

"You didn't let me finish," he chided. "I'll sign the papers *after* we know for sure that there are no repercussions from last night."

The possibility that their lovemaking might have created a baby filled her with a sweet and intense longing. But she immediately quashed the feeling, unwilling to go down that road again.

"You don't have to worry about repercussions," she assured him.

"We had unprotected sex. And since you're not on any other form of birth control, a baby isn't outside the realm of possibility."

She could alleviate that concern by asking for the morning-after pill at her local pharmacy, but she knew that she wouldn't. Because as unlikely as it was that one night with her cowboy might result in another unplanned pregnancy, she couldn't bring herself to eliminate the possibility.

"It's not the right time of the month for me to get pregnant." Though she had no idea if that was really true, she didn't want him to worry—or hope.

"Don't you remember the joke that went around in high school? The one that asked, 'What do you call a woman who uses the rhythm method of birth control?'"

She nodded and responded with the punch line: "'Mommy.'"

"So you should understand why I want you to call me—one way or the other."

"You want to know when I get my period?" she asked, her tone dubious.

"Or if you don't," he confirmed.

"Okay," she agreed, because it wasn't an unreasonable request and she didn't believe lightning would strike them twice. "I'll call you."

He held out his hand. "Give me your phone."

"Why?"

"Because you can't call me if you don't have my number," he said reasonably.

She tapped to add a new contact, typed in his name and handed him the phone.

Caleb added his number and returned the phone to her.

She lifted a brow when she heard his cell ping, and she knew that he'd sent a message to himself from her phone so that he'd have her number, too.

"I said I would call."

He nodded. "But now if you forget, I can call you."

Caleb returned to the Circle G late Sunday afternoon and found the manila envelope where he knew it would be—locked in the bottom drawer of the desk he'd brought from the main house when he'd moved into his own a few months earlier. He opened the flap of the envelope now and dumped out the contents: one petition for divorce, signed and dated by Brielle Channing, "the petitioner," and a narrow platinum band that had nestled on the third finger of her left hand for all of three weeks.

Considering that she'd given him the papers seven years earlier, it was hardly a surprise to hear her say that she wanted to end their marriage. But still, it hurt.

Because when he saw her by the pool in Las Vegas, those seven years had faded away. And when she'd kissed him, he'd felt vindicated, as if this evidence of the attraction between them confirmed that he'd done the right thing in not signing the papers.

That illusion had lasted throughout the night, only to be shattered by her dismissive words in the light of day.

A sharp rap of knuckles on the back door interrupted his musing, immediately followed by Liam's voice. "Caleb? You here?"

"In the den." He shoved the papers in the envelope again and stuffed it in the open drawer. "What's up?" he asked when his brother appeared.

Liam propped a shoulder against the doorjamb, because there was nowhere else to sit in the sparsely furnished room. "Did she show up?"

Caleb blinked, startled by the question. "Who?"

"The girl Joe Bishop went to Vegas to meet," his brother clarified.

"Delia. And yeah—" he held out his hand "—she did."

Liam sighed as he reached into his back pocket for his wallet, pulling out a ten-dollar bill and offering it to his brother.

"You owe me twenty," Caleb said.

"The bet was ten."

"Ten that she would show and another ten if he put a ring on her finger," he reminded his brother.

"Joe really asked her to marry him?"

"They really got married," Caleb said. "I was a witness to their vows."

"Damn," Liam said, but he took back the ten and pulled out a twenty. "Maybe we should go double or nothing."

Caleb snatched the bill from his hand. "I'm not betting on the success or failure of my friend's marriage."

"You can't honestly believe it's going to last," Liam chided.

Caleb shrugged. "They seem well suited for each other—why wouldn't it last?"

"Because fifty percent of all marriages end in divorce."

"That's an inflated statistic—and a surprising one from a man who just got engaged."

"I'm not worried," Liam assured him. "Because I know that me and Macy, together, can beat any odds."

That's what Caleb had thought about him and Brie, too, when he'd put his ring on her finger. It hadn't mattered that they were young or that their families were opposed to them being together. It only mattered that they were in love.

At least, he'd believed it until she'd handed him divorce papers and moved across the country. And the only reason they hadn't contributed to the divorce statistic was that he had yet to sign the papers.

"Is everything okay?" Liam asked, his question cutting through Caleb's reverie.

"Yeah. Why?"

His brother cocked his head. "Your mind seems to be a thousand miles away."

More like twenty-five hundred, but Caleb knew better than to say anything to his brother about his encounter with Brielle in Vegas.

"Have you and Macy set a date?" he asked instead.

"She's thinking a spring wedding would be nice."

"What do you think?"

"I'm happy to let her take care of all the details," Liam said. "I just want her to be my wife, and Ava, Max and Sam to be my kids."

"You're going to adopt them?"

"As soon as I can," Liam confirmed.

"Triplets." Caleb shook his head. "You're a brave man."

"And a lucky one," his brother asserted.

Caleb knew it was true. And though he pretended to be surprised by his brother's willingness to take on a single mom and her three toddlers, the truth was, he was a little envious of the ready-made family his brother had found with Macy.

Way back when he and Brielle had first talked about their hopes and dreams, she'd suggested that his longing for a wife and kids was rooted in a desire to recreate the family unit he'd lost when his mother died. He didn't know if there was any truth to that—he only knew that whenever he'd thought about his future, he'd thought that Brie would be part of it.

He'd been gutted when she left for New York City. And yet, at the same time, he hadn't believed she'd stay away for long. He didn't think she could. Because they loved one another and had proved it by exchanging vows that promised "till death do us part."

As for the divorce papers, well, he'd been certain they were executed under pressure from her parents—pressure she'd succumbed to only because she was hurting over the loss of their baby. When that hurt started to fade, she'd be glad that he hadn't signed the papers—that they'd have a second chance to make their marriage work.

But now he knew the truth: he'd been a fool to believe that a first love could last forever, and it was time to move on, as she'd already done.

When Brielle first moved away, she'd been in communication with her parents every day. Margaret or Ben—and sometimes both—would send a text message to check in, and she'd respond to reassure them that she hadn't been mugged or murdered, as they'd worried might happen in the big, bad city. Eventually she'd managed to convince them to check in every other day, so her mom texted on Mondays, Wednesdays and Fridays and her dad on Tuesdays, Thursdays and Saturdays, and she FaceTimed with them on Sunday nights.

Yes, she was twenty-five years old, and yes, she wished they'd trust her to live her own life, but the few seconds it took to respond to a text message required a lot less effort than arguing with them about their overprotectiveness. And although the scheduled weekly check-in wasn't always convenient, she enjoyed hearing about what was going on at home, especially with her siblings and their families.

It was after midnight by the time she got home on Sunday, which meant that Brie had missed their scheduled call by more than an hour. And when she took her phone out of airplane mode, she found five text messages from her mother.

Being two hours earlier in Haven, it was reasonable to assume that her parents were still awake—especially if they were as worried as the messages suggested. But if she called now, they'd undoubtedly ask about her weekend getaway, and she was trying very hard not to think about Caleb and what had happened in his hotel room—including his bombshell announcement about their marital status.

Still married.

Yeah, she was still reeling from the aftershocks of that one while various thoughts and feelings battled for dominance in her head and her heart.

She was shocked, of course. And angry that he'd refused to do the one thing she'd asked of him before she'd left Haven. And maybe just a little bit flattered that he hadn't wanted to abandon the vows they'd made to one another. But mostly she was confused, because for seven years she'd managed to convince herself that what they'd shared was in the past. Now, after one night, she knew that she'd been kidding herself.

She also knew that there was no way she could hide her raw emotions from her parents. So instead of calling, she sent a quick text message:

Sorry I missed your calls. Got in late from Grace's birthday weekend getaway and heading straight to bed. Talk to you soon. xo

Then she went to bed and dreamed about making love with the man who was still her husband.

Staring death in the eye had a way of making a man take stock of his life and evaluate the choices he'd made.

Six months after his heart attack, David Gilmore knew this to be true, because he'd done exactly that when he'd been staring at the ceiling of his hospital room, wondering if he was going to live or die.

"You'll live," the doctor had said. He'd then proceeded to suggest some lifestyle changes that would ensure Dave saw his fifty-ninth birthday.

Lifestyle changes might impact his future, but they couldn't fix the mistakes in his past. And Dave had made more than his share of mistakes—done some things he'd regretted, and regretted not doing some others.

At twenty-seven, he'd met and fallen in love with Theresa Wheeler. Ten months later, they'd married. Two years after that, they'd welcomed their first child. Over the next four years, three more babies had followed, filling their home and their hearts.

Despite the sleepless nights and dirty diapers, those had been good years. Some of the best. Every year with Theresa had been one of the best. Not that everything had always been peaches and cream—his wife's favorite summertime dessert—but with Theresa by his side, he'd felt confident that they could triumph over any challenge.

But during an early morning ride only a few weeks before what would have been their fifteenth anniversary, she'd been thrown from the back of her horse and broken her neck.

I'm sorry...nothing we could do...already gone.

That had created a challenge he was ill-equipped to face alone.

He'd been devastated, not knowing how he'd survive without her. Not sure he wanted to. He'd been mired in grief and loneliness, so overwhelmed by his own sense of loss that he'd failed to see his children were grieving, too.

He hadn't always been the best father to Katelyn, Liam, Skylar and Caleb. In fact, he'd been emotionally AWOL after the death of his wife, abdicating responsibility to his own mother to fill the enormous, gaping hole left in their lives.

But over the years, with the love and support of his parents, they'd managed to put most of the pieces back together again. Now, suddenly, another piece had been thrown into the mix and he didn't know how to make it fit—or even if he should try.

His hands were steady as he folded the lab report and tucked it back inside the envelope.

Obviously his blood pressure medication was doing its job—or maybe, in the three months that had passed between the test being done and the results delivered to his door, he'd been preparing himself for this moment.

"So what happens now?" he asked the woman seated on the opposite side of his desk. "What do you want from me?"

Her gaze was steady, and he noted—not for the first time—that she had pretty eyes. An intriguing shade somewhere between gray and blue and fringed with thick lashes. She had a sweetly shaped mouth, too, though it was compressed in a thin line now.

"I don't want anything," she denied. "But your daughter needs a father."

The daughter he hadn't known about until her mother showed up at the hospital in Elko, the day after his heart attack.

She'd come to him, this woman with whom he'd spent a single night thirteen years earlier, because she feared it might be her last chance to tell him that he had another child.

He remembered the night: the fifth anniversary of his wife's death. He'd wanted some privacy to grieve—or maybe a few drinks to help him forget. So he'd gone into town and tossed back a few shots at Diggers'. The alcohol had created a pleasant buzz inside his head, but everything else still felt empty.

Valerie had been waiting tables at the bar that night. Apparently a falling-out with her father had compelled her to give up a cushy office job and respond to the Help Wanted sign in Diggers' window. It wasn't the first time Dave had seen her there, but she usually gave him a wide berth. He must have looked as lost and alone as he felt that night, or maybe she really wanted to piss off her father, because she detoured to his table and asked if he was okay.

Being a Monday night, the bar was mostly empty, and when she brought his next drink, she sat down across from him. He didn't talk to her about Theresa—he didn't ever talk to anyone about his wife. Truthfully, he couldn't remember what he and Valerie talked about, but he remembered that she stayed with him until the bar closed.

And then they went back to her place.

In the morning, they both agreed that it had been a mistake—and one that neither of them would ever speak of again.

Still, Dave felt guilty, as if he'd cheated on his wife, though she'd been gone for five years. And every time he saw Valerie in town, he couldn't help but remember that night, and the weight of the guilt would stagger him again. A few weeks later, when he heard that she'd taken a job in Washington State, he'd felt no regret, only relief.

And then, ten years later, she'd returned with a nine-year-old child in tow. There were whispers around town about a cheating husband and an acrimonious divorce that led to her coming home to raise her daughter with the support of her family. Dave didn't put much stock in rumors, but the reasoning made sense to him. Certainly, in the three years that had passed since her return, he'd never suspected that the truth was anything different.

Until she somehow got word that he was in the hospital and came to see him, to tearfully confide that everything he'd heard about her marriage were lies deliberately fabricated to eliminate speculation about her child's paternity. Because the truth was, her daughter, Ashley, was his daughter, too.

He'd been too stunned to respond to her claim. He hadn't believed it. Hadn't wanted it to be true.

He'd promised himself that the night they'd spent together was a secret he'd take to the grave.

Now there was a child—*his* child, according to the results of the DNA test, proof of his indiscretion.

Not just an affair, but an affair with a Blake.

Chapter Six

From the first moment that Valerie Blake knew she was finally going to have the baby she'd always wanted, everything she'd done was for Ashley. In the beginning, she'd been certain that the best thing for her unborn child would be to start her life far away from Haven, Nevada, where the news of Valerie's surprise pregnancy would be the cause of much scrutiny and speculation.

She'd been on her way to Seattle, to lose herself in the anonymity of a big city, when she stopped in a little town for a bite to eat at Wanda's Diner. She'd ordered a bacon cheeseburger with a side of onion rings, because she'd been on the road for hours and she was starving. And she'd washed down the meal with a glass of milk, because calcium was good for the baby.

She was counting out the money to pay her check when the baby decided she didn't want the meal that had been ordered and sent it back again.

Valerie had made it to the restroom—*just*—and when she returned to her table, she discovered that her dishes had been cleared away and, in their place, several packages of saltine crackers and a glass of ginger ale.

Wanda slid into the booth across from Valerie as she tore open a package of crackers. "How far along are you?"

She didn't see any reason to deny her condition, and

Wanda didn't look like she'd believe her if she tried. "About eight weeks."

"Got a husband?"

"Not anymore," she said. Because she'd caught the other woman looking at her ringless left hand, and because the truth was part of the narrative she'd decided upon for her new life. "After three years of trying to have a baby, he suddenly changed his mind about wanting to be a father."

It was a slight tweaking of the truth, which was that her ex-husband had only told her, three years after their exchange of vows, that he'd never wanted kids and had, in fact, undergone a vasectomy before their wedding. But somehow, according to her father, she'd given up on her marriage—just like she'd given up on so many other things.

"So you're on your own?" Wanda guessed.

Valerie nodded.

"Going where?"

"Seattle."

"You got family there?"

She shook her head.

"A job?"

She answered with another shake of her head.

"You ever waited tables?"

This time, she nodded.

"I could use some help around here for the early shift— how bad's your morning sickness?"

"So far, it's been late afternoon and evening sickness."

"Graze throughout the day rather than eating big meals and stay hydrated," Wanda suggested.

"I'll try that."

"The job's minimum wage," the other woman said, almost apologetically. "But tips are usually good and there's an apartment upstairs that you can have cheap."

"Is it furnished?"

Wanda shook her head. "Gord over at the thrift shop can help you out with whatever you need, though. Delivery and setup, too."

And that was how Valerie ended up settling in Serenity, Washington, working for Wanda and living above the diner. Because here, where nobody knew her or her family, she wasn't Jesse Blake's screwup daughter who'd dropped out of college to get married—and then divorced. Here she was simply an expectant mother who, despite only having a handful of accounting courses and waitressing experience on her résumé, was willing to work hard to provide for her unborn child.

Only a few weeks later, she found the owner scowling over her books and offered to help her figure out why her deposits weren't matching her daily receipts. Two days after that, Wanda fired Joanne for skimming from the till and added bookkeeping hours to Valerie's paycheck. Wanda also told her friend Ruth, who owned the local flower shop, that Valerie was a whiz with numbers, and soon she was doing Ruth's books, too. Within a few months, she'd added the bookstore and bowling alley to a list of clients that was growing not quite as rapidly as her belly. Still, by the time her middle had expanded so that she could no longer see her swollen ankles, she was able to give up waiting tables. But she continued to live above the diner and hang out with Wanda.

Throughout this time, Valerie kept in regular contact with her mother and her sisters. They knew where she was and that she was expecting a child—though they believed she'd met the baby's father after leaving Nevada, because she was determined that no one would ever know his true identity.

She'd been happy in Serenity. Of course, there were times that she'd missed her family, but whenever that missing became too much to bear, she'd make a quick trip home. She never stayed more than a few days—long enough for her family to fuss over Ashley but not so long that the awkwardness that lingered between Valerie and her father was evident to the rest of the family.

Then her mother died—a stark warning to Valerie of how quickly things could change. Although she was estranged from her dad, she still had family in Haven. More important, Ashley had family in Haven, and if anything ever happened to Valerie, she knew her little girl would benefit from being around her grandfather and aunts and uncles and cousins.

The move back to Haven was part of a carefully thought-out plan that had nothing to do with Ashley's father. Of course, as her daughter got older, she began to ask more questions about the man who had contributed to her DNA. Then she came home one day with a history-slash-art project: to create a family tree. And Ashley had cried, because her branches would be missing some pretty significant leaves.

Only a few days later, Valerie had been picking up pizza from Jo's when she heard about Dave Gilmore's heart attack. She'd realized then that she was the one who'd deprived her daughter of the opportunity to know her father. And when she'd gone to the hospital, she'd been acting purely on impulse—just like the night she'd invited Dave back to her apartment.

She didn't blame him for demanding proof, and so she'd said nothing to anyone else until the test results were in. When she'd finally told Ashley, she'd thought her daughter would be pleased to have the opportunity to know her father.

"Gilmore?" Ashley had echoed, not only shocked but devastated by the revelation of her father's identity. "But the Blakes and the Gilmores hate each other."

"That's ancient history," she'd said, in an effort to appease her daughter.

But Ashley wouldn't be placated. "How could you do

this to me? Don't you realize that this is worse than not having a father at all?"

"It's not," Valerie told her. "And when you've had a chance to get to know him, you'll discover that he's a good man."

Except that Ashley was no longer listening to her.

Or talking to her.

So now they were on a plane headed to the Big Apple, because Ashley had watched the movie *Enchanted* at least a hundred times and frequently expressed a desire to visit New York—and especially Central Park. And Valerie, desperate to reconnect with her daughter, had suggested a quick weekend getaway "just for fun," though she recognized that it was also a bribe. And maybe a plea to her daughter to forgive her. Or at least start talking to her again.

But just in case, she'd invited Ashley's best friend, Chloe, to come along.

Brie was on her way to The Met to check out the *Art of Native America* exhibit when she felt her phone vibrate inside her pocket.

In the two weeks that had passed since Grace's birthday, she'd kept herself busy so that she wouldn't think about Caleb. Of course, being busy didn't prevent thoughts of him from sneaking into her mind—and into her dreams. One night together after seven years apart, and she missed him as much now as when she'd said goodbye to him at the old cabin.

It was beyond frustrating to realize that, even after so much time had passed, her heart still wasn't her own. That the biggest part of it continued to belong to Caleb Gilmore—and probably always would. Even more frustrating was that she hadn't heard a single word from him since they'd said goodbye in Vegas.

"I can call you," he'd said, explaining why he wanted her number.

But he hadn't called, and she was admittedly a little disappointed.

And how screwed up was that?

She'd asked him to sign the divorce papers, clearly indicating to him that their relationship was truly and completely over, yet she was upset because he hadn't called.

Maybe Lily was right. Maybe Brie had deeper feelings for Caleb than she was willing to acknowledge. Grace seemed to have arrived at that same conclusion when Brielle made it back to their suite in Vegas the morning after.

"I'm not sure what my feelings are," she'd hedged, when pressed to explain why she'd spent the night in Caleb's bed.

"How many guys have you had sex with in the last year?" Grace challenged.

She frowned. "What does that have to do with anything?"

"How many?" her friend asked again.

Brie sighed. "One."

Lily nodded. "Caleb."

"And the year before that?" Grace pressed.

None.

Which they undoubtedly knew but which she had no intention of admitting aloud.

"So? Just because I don't sleep around doesn't mean I'm in love with my ex-boyfriend."

"He might be your ex-boyfriend, but he's also your current husband," Lily pointed out.

Because of course Brie had immediately told them about Caleb's revelation and their marital status.

And two weeks later, Brie was still reeling from the discovery that their marriage had never been dissolved. Still angry that he'd refused to sign the papers—and angrier yet that he'd never sought her out to tell her that they were still married.

So when her phone rang now, she wondered if it might be Caleb calling—and then pretended she wasn't disappointed when she saw her aunt's name and number on the screen instead.

"Help me!"

Despite the desperate tone of the words, Brie was more amused than alarmed by the plea.

Valerie was her mother's youngest sister, who'd moved to Washington State before Brielle started high school and only returned to Haven after she was gone. But Brie had a lot of wonderful memories of her aunt from when she was younger. In many ways, Valerie had been more like an older sister than an aunt to both herself and Regan.

"How can I help?" she offered.

"I'm in desperate need of some adult company and you're the only person I know in New York," Valerie said.

"First choice of one? I'm flattered." Then the rest of her aunt's words registered. "Wait! What? You're in New York?"

"Standing outside one of those tacky tourist shops on Broadway, waiting for Ashley and Chloe."

"Who's Chloe?" Brie asked.

"Ashley's best friend," Valerie said. "I thought it would be exciting for them to visit the big city."

"You couldn't find a big city closer to Nevada?" Brie wondered.

Her aunt sighed. "I wasn't sure that New York was far enough, but at least it would give me a chance to see you."

"As it turns out, I'm in Manhattan right now."

"Do you already have plans for today?" Valerie asked.

"None that can't be changed," Brie assured her.

"No," her aunt protested. "I don't want to be responsible for you standing up a handsome young man."

"My plans were solo," she said, already retracing her

steps to the subway. "And I'd love to see you. Can you give me more details about the souvenir shop you're at?"

"The one that sells the 'I Heart NY' T-shirts," Valerie said dryly.

Brie chuckled. "Let's try this—do you know where M&M's World is, near Times Square?"

"Yeah, it's where I spent almost two hours and two hundred dollars last night," her aunt confided.

"I'll meet you outside the main entrance in twenty minutes."

Thirty minutes later, they were seated inside Starbucks while Ashley and Chloe browsed the Sephora next door. Valerie was drinking a Black and White Mocha Frappuccino, and Brie was indulging her sweet tooth with a Double Chocolaty Chip Crème Frappuccino.

"Now are you going to tell me why you decided to bring Ashley and Chloe to New York?" she asked her aunt.

Valerie sighed. "I was hoping the trip might help Ashley forget that she's mad at me."

"I got mad at my mom a few times while I was growing up—she never brought me to New York," Brie mused.

"Ashley found out that I lied about who her father is," Valerie admitted.

She sipped her Frappuccino, waiting for the big reveal.

"He's…Dave Gilmore."

Brie's jaw dropped. *"Caleb's father?"*

Valerie nodded. "Is also Ashley's father."

"That's…a surprise." After she'd mulled it over for another moment, she added, "And it probably explains why, when everyone else was freaking out over the news that Caleb and I had eloped and were going to have a baby, you didn't."

"We don't always get to choose the people we fall in love with," Valerie pointed out.

"Are you saying that you're in love with—" Brie

couldn't call him Dave; it didn't feel right "—Caleb's father?"

Her aunt shook her head. "No. Me and Dave… Truthfully, there was no 'me and Dave.' I was still hurting over the failure of my marriage. He was mourning the death of his wife." She shrugged. "We were just two lonely people wanting not to be lonely, at least for one night."

"Lonely doesn't lead to naked without attraction," Brie pointed out. "Or at least alcohol."

Valerie laughed at that. "You're right. And there was some of both. He was a great-looking guy. Of course, being a rancher, he was also in good physical shape. And when he took off—"

"Don't need to know," she hastily interjected.

Valerie grinned. "Anyway, that's why Ashley's mad at me. After listening to her grandfather gripe and grumble about 'those thievin' Gilmores' for most of her life, she wasn't happy to learn that her father was one of them."

"And how did Gramps take the news?" Brie asked. "Because I assume it was also a surprise to him."

"He's pretty much giving me the silent treatment, too. Although that's really not new."

"Well, that's better than you giving him a heart attack."

"Oh, honey." Valerie touched a hand to her arm. "You don't honestly still believe what happened had anything to do with you and Caleb getting married, do you?"

"No," she said, because it was mostly true.

It was also true that she'd never forget the words her grandfather had spoken to her when he learned of the miscarriage.

"It's for the best," he'd said, not seeing—or maybe not caring—that her heart had been shattered by the loss of her baby.

Brie's parents had expressed a similar sentiment. Only her grandmother had mourned with them, lamenting the loss of the baby who would have been not only her first great-grandchild but also the best chance to end "the ridiculous Blake-Gilmore feud."

Brie pushed aside the painful memories to refocus on her conversation with Valerie. "And anyway," she said now, "we were talking about Ashley."

Who chose that moment to walk into the coffee shop, bringing their conversation to an abrupt halt.

Valerie offered her daughter a smile. "Did you get everything you wanted?" Her smile slipped when she realized that her daughter was alone. "Where's Chloe?"

"I need more money," Ashley said, responding to her mother's first question. "Chloe's trying to decide between Ultra Violet and Plum Fiction lip gloss."

Valerie pulled her wallet out of her purse and handed over a credit card. Her generosity was rewarded with a fleeting smile and quick wave, then Ashley disappeared again.

"You know she's totally exploiting your guilt," Brie mused.

"I know," Valerie confirmed. "But I do feel guilty. I turned her whole world upside down."

"She seems pretty steady on her feet."

"She doesn't let a lot of people see what's inside—similar to someone else I know," Valerie said, with a pointed look at her niece. "And since I dropped the bombshell about her dad, she isn't eager to confide in me anymore. That's why I brought Chloe along."

"So you can eavesdrop on their conversations?"

"No," Valerie immediately denied. "So that she'd have someone to talk to." Then she sipped her drink again, considering. "But I think I like your idea better."

Brie chuckled as she pushed her chair away from the table. "Come on," she said. "While we're here, I might as well get new lip gloss, too."

Three weeks after his return from Vegas, Caleb was shopping for groceries at The Trading Post and trying not to obsess over the fact that he hadn't heard a single word from Brie.

He shouldn't have been surprised by the lack of communication. She'd made it clear that the night they'd spent together hadn't been a "hello" but a "goodbye," and he was trying to accept that their relationship was over. Bracing himself for the call that would confirm it was time to sign the papers and move on. Because after all the hurt and heartache he'd caused, he knew it was the least he could do.

But what if—

"Excuse me," a female voice murmured.

He automatically stepped back as the woman reached into the freezer case beside him.

"Kenzie?"

Her gaze shifted to his face, her expression changing from surprise to recognition. "Caleb, hi." The greeting was followed by a smile—sincere and warm. "I don't think I've ever seen you here before."

"I moved into my own house a few months ago, so I have to do my own shopping now," he explained.

"And your own cooking?" she guessed, with a pointed look at the selection of microwaveable meals in his cart.

He nodded as she dropped the carton of ice cream she'd selected in her own cart.

"Not that one, Mommy." The protest came from an adorable little girl with blond pigtails. "I want strawberry."

"But your little brother or sister wants chocolate," Kenzie told her.

"Sister," the child said firmly.

"I can't make any promises on that, Dani," her mother reminded her, reaching into the freezer again for a tub of strawberry ice cream.

"I'd heard you were adding to your family," Caleb said, trying not to stare at her rounded belly. "Congratulations."

"Thanks." Kenzie smiled again.

Her daughter looked at him through narrowed eyes. "I don't know you," she said. "You're a stranger."

"I'm Caleb," he said. "And I know your mom from way back."

"I didn't live here way back," Dani told him. "I only came here with my daddy when my mommy died. But I've gotta new mommy now and I'm gonna get a new sister, too."

"Or brother," Kenzie interjected.

The little girl scowled at the reminder.

Caleb fought against a smile.

"You probably want to get that ice cream home before it melts," he noted, offering Kenzie a convenient escape.

"We do," she confirmed, but graciously added, "It was good to see you, Caleb."

"You, too," he said.

"Bye, Mister Caleb," Dani said, as they started to move away.

"Bye, Miss Dani."

She giggled and waved as she skipped along beside the cart her mother pushed toward the checkout.

The sound of the child's laugh was pure joy, and he felt a tug in the vicinity of his heart as he watched them go: the woman who had been Brielle's best friend all through high school and the little girl with deep blue eyes that made her instantly recognizable as a Channing.

The tug became a pang as he wondered if the baby he and Brie had lost would have had the same blue eyes, and what other characteristics of each of them might have been evident in their child. Of course that led him to again consider the possibility that they might have made another baby together, but he didn't let his thoughts wander too far down that path.

Because he knew it wasn't fair to hope that she might be carrying his child if it wasn't what she wanted, too.

And she'd made it pretty clear that it wasn't. He was her past and she was looking to the future.

Still, he had no regrets about the night they'd spent together in Vegas, except that he'd been careless with her. Not on purpose, of course. But he hadn't been thinking about potential repercussions when he woke up in the night, with her naked body pressed against him. He hadn't been thinking at all.

And now…

He frowned, because he had no idea how to finish that thought. It was quite possible that what followed the "now" was "nothing." After all, she'd assured him it wasn't the right time for her to get pregnant.

But what if she was wrong?

He was mostly ignorant about the internal workings of a woman's body, so he'd turned to the all-seeing, all-knowing Google and discovered that most women's bodies operated on a twenty-eight-day schedule, with ovulation happening around day fourteen, in the middle of the cycle.

So if they'd been together at the beginning of her cycle, then she was right and it was unlikely that there would be any repercussions from their night together.

But why hadn't she called?

…if you forget, I can call you.

He picked up his phone and scrolled through his list of contacts, his finger hovering over her name.

Chapter Seven

What happened in Vegas stayed in Vegas—except when what happened was a hookup with a not-quite-ex-husband who, more than three weeks later, Brielle still couldn't stop thinking about.

Of course, she'd always had trouble getting Caleb out of her mind. Everything she'd thought she remembered about him had been true, but her memories had been pale and weak in comparison to the reality of the man.

Being with him again, making love with him again, she'd finally accepted that it was unlikely she'd ever love anyone else the way she'd loved him—but she was going to try. When she came back from Nevada, she vowed to move forward with her life—to meet new people and welcome new experiences.

The start of a new school year was the perfect time for a new beginning. Brie had hit the ground running upon her return from Nevada, busy preparing her classroom and meeting her new students. The first weeks could be a challenge. Some little ones were eager to start school and fairly skipped into the classroom on the first day. Others were more hesitant about the unknown and clung desperately to the hands of their equally wary parents or caregivers.

The surprise visit of her aunt and cousin had been a nice distraction, too. Because being distracted meant that she didn't have a lot of time to think about what had happened in Caleb's hotel room—or dwell on the fact that her period was late.

Four days late.

She was usually pretty regular, but it wouldn't be the first time her cycle had been affected by external events or stresses. In fact, she'd been three days late when she'd gone back to Haven in the spring, after the birth of her sister's twin babies. The excitement and anticipation—and yes, uneasiness, because she was always a little bit uneasy about returning to the town where she might run into Caleb—had thrown off her system.

Of course, she hadn't worried at all about being late then, because there'd been absolutely no possibility that she was pregnant. And on day four, she'd awakened with telltale cramps that proved her cycle was back on track again.

When she woke up on the fourth day after her period was due in September, she felt nothing aside from a growing apprehension—because this time there *was* the possibility of something.

But was it really apprehension she was feeling?

Or was it anticipation?

Because while the idea of yet another unplanned pregnancy probably wasn't a cause for celebration, there was no denying that she wanted a baby. A family.

Of course, in the naivete of her youth, she'd believed that she would follow the traditional path of falling in love, getting married and planning to have a child. Even when the little plus sign showed up in the window of the pregnancy test she'd bought in Elko—because Battle Mountain wasn't far enough to ensure she wouldn't be seen by someone who knew her parents—she'd trusted that her dreams would come true. Because Caleb loved her and they were going to get married and be a family.

And they did get married. But then everything had fallen

apart, and the hurt had been so huge and all-encompassing, she hadn't known how to cope with it.

So she ran.

And he let her go.

She'd run again, the morning after the night they'd spent together in Vegas.

And again, he'd let her go.

And there had been no communication between them since.

Was he giving her space? Or had he already forgotten about the potential repercussions he'd seemed so concerned about three weeks earlier?

Had he forgotten about her?

Grace actually laughed when Brie ventured to ask that question aloud.

"He hasn't forgotten you," she promised her friend.

"How do you know?" Brie challenged.

"Because he looks at you the way Mr. Darcy looks at Elizabeth Bennet in *Pride & Prejudice*."

"I've never seen the movie," she confided.

"Well, there's a fabulous scene at the end when the hero walks across the field—"

"And Matthew Macfadyen is *so* hunky as Mr. Darcy," Lily filled in.

"—to confess his feelings to the heroine—"

"Played by Keira Knightley," Lily supplied again.

"—and you can tell, just by the way he's looking at her, how much he loves her. I actually said to Lily, 'That's what I want—a man who looks at me the way he looks at her.'"

"She did," Lily confirmed.

"You want a man to look at you the way an actor looked at the actress cast as his romantic interest in a movie?"

"You really have to see the movie," Grace said, unfazed by Brie's dubious tone. "Because that's the way Caleb looks at you." Then she sighed, a little wistfully.

"Even after seven years apart, he looks at you as if there's no other woman in the world."

She ignored the rush of warmth through her veins, refusing to let her heart be swayed by her friend's fanciful imagery. "You've been editing romance novels at work, haven't you?"

Grace waved a hand dismissively. "That's beside the point."

"No, I think that *is* the point," she said.

"And I think, if you're thinking about him, you should call him," Lily chimed in.

Brie had promised that she would, but she had no intention of doing so until she had some news to share. So it was both frustrating and inconvenient that her period had chosen this particular month to be late.

But as soon as her cycle was back on track, she'd call him and reassure him that there were no repercussions from their night together. Then he could sign the divorce papers and finally end their ill-fated union, returning her life to the familiar status quo.

So why did the idea of divorcing a husband she'd believed that she was already divorced from fill her with sadness?

Or was it just that seeing him again in Vegas had brought back so many memories of the happy times they'd spent together that she was saddened again to think about everything they'd once shared and how much they'd lost?

Ancient history, she reminded herself, as she turned the corner onto Provost Street on her way home from Briarwood Academy. As if there weren't enough reasons to love her job teaching at the prestigious private school, its walking distance from the home she shared with her best friends was another.

As she drew nearer to her destination, she saw someone sitting on the steps leading up to the front door of the town house.

A broad-shouldered and very familiar someone in well-worn jeans, a plaid shirt, cowboy hat and boots.

Caleb.

Her steps faltered even as her heart started to race. She deliberately resumed walking at the same steady pace, refusing to give any hint of the emotions churning inside her.

He rose to his feet when she reached the steps. "Hello, Brielle."

The low timbre of his voice skimmed over her like a caress, raising goose bumps on her flesh and making a mockery of her recent claim that her feelings for him were ancient history.

"Did you come all this way just to say hi?"

"No," he acknowledged. "But I thought we could at least start with the usual pleasantries."

"Hello, Caleb," she said. "What brings you to town?"

His lips curved in a slow, sexy smile that made her toes curl inside her shoes. *Dammit.*

"An airplane," he said, but tempered his flip response with a wink.

She resisted the urge to roll her eyes. "Apparently I should have asked '*why* are you here?'"

Though she could probably guess, it seemed a little extreme to show up at her door rather than picking up the phone.

"I wanted to see where you lived," he said.

"I could have texted you a picture, if you'd asked."

"You could have," he agreed, turning to look at the classic four-story bayfront brownstone behind him. "But I'm not sure a snapshot would have done it justice."

"Grace's parents own it," she said. "And they charge us a ridiculously discounted rent, which is the only reason any of us can afford to live in this neighborhood."

"You're a Blake," he noted.

"I'm a Channing," she clarified. "And I pay my own way."

He inclined his head. "Are you going to let me see inside?"

She started up the stairs; he shouldered his duffel bag and followed.

"Are you going to tell me why you're in town—aside from wanting to see where I live?" she countered.

"I wanted to see *you*," he admitted.

She slid her key into the lock, opened the door and stepped inside to enter the code and disarm the security system.

"And now that you have—" she turned in the narrow hallway "—how long are you planning to stay?"

He dropped his bag beside the ornately carved newel post at the bottom of a staircase leading to the upper levels. "I've got a return flight late Sunday afternoon."

Her low-heeled shoes clicked on the parquet floor as she led the way to the kitchen at the back of the house.

She couldn't blame him for peeking in the open doorways as they passed first the living room at the front of the house, then the dining room. Built sometime before the turn of the twentieth century, the house boasted gorgeous Victorian details, including eleven-foot plaster ceilings, hardwood paneling and moldings, marble mantels on each of the four fireplaces and beautifully etched glass doors.

But while so many original details had been immaculately preserved, the kitchen and baths had been updated to include all the modern conveniences—and a few luxuries. The brightly lit kitchen boasted custom cabinets, quartz countertops, stainless steel appliances and double doors leading to a covered deck and terraced garden.

"What do Grace's parents do?" he wondered.

"A lot of traveling," she said. "But if you're asking what they did that they could afford to buy this place in addition to owning another home in Gramercy Park—her dad previously worked as a hedge fund manager and her mom sold real estate, and they made some very lucrative investments over the years."

"I'd guess so," he agreed.

"They weren't overjoyed when Grace told them she wanted to pursue an arts degree, but they came around— probably because she's an only child and, if they cut her off, they wouldn't know what to do with all their money."

"What does she do with her arts degree?"

"She's an editorial assistant at Bane & Bloom Books in Manhattan. She works insane hours, but she loves it."

"And Lily?"

"Lily's still trying to find her calling. In the meantime, she works part-time as a curator at the Brooklyn Museum, part-time as a barista at a little café down the street and part-time as a dog walker for several couples in the neighborhood."

She dropped her bag on a chair in the kitchen. "Can I get you something to drink?"

"What have you got?"

She poked her head inside the fridge. "Cola, juice, milk, water and a couple of premixed vodka coolers."

"Cola sounds good," he said.

"Do you want a glass?"

"No, the can's fine."

She handed him the can, then retrieved a glass for herself, added ice from the dispenser in the door of the fridge and then filled it with water. It was, Caleb noted, the same fridge he'd put in his kitchen when he'd finished construction on his house in the spring.

He popped the tab on his drink, then lifted the can to his lips. After traveling all day, the sugar and caffeine provided a welcome jolt to his groggy system—and reminded him of the real purpose of this visit.

"Are you pregnant?" he asked bluntly.

"I guess we're finished with the exchange of pleasantries," she noted, lowering herself into a chair at the small table.

He straddled a seat across from her. "You're not answering the question."

She lifted the glass to her lips, sipped. "I don't know."

"You haven't taken a test?" he guessed.

She shook her head. "No."

"But your period's late."

She frowned. "You can't know that."

"No," he acknowledged. "But I figured, if you'd got your period, you would have called right away to tell me."

"And because I didn't, you hopped on a plane?"

"I wanted to have this conversation face-to-face, so that we could make whatever decisions need to be made together."

"There's nothing to decide," she said.

"Your period's late," he said again.

"Only four days—which doesn't prove anything."

"So why haven't you taken a test?"

She dropped her gaze and rubbed her thumb through the condensation that had formed on the outside of her glass. "Because I'm scared," she finally confided.

He shifted his chair closer, then tipped her chin up so he could see her eyes. "Scared to think that you might actually be pregnant?" he asked, his tone gentle. "Or scared that you might not be?"

"Both," she admitted.

Caleb knew what she meant, because he felt exactly the same way. If she was pregnant, a baby could be a second chance for them. If she wasn't, she'd expect him to sign the divorce papers—no more excuses.

And even if she was pregnant, he knew a baby wasn't any guarantee of a happily-ever-after for them. A baby wasn't a guarantee of anything, especially when there were so many unresolved issues between them.

"Why don't we go out to grab a bite to eat?" he suggested, because his brain functioned better when his stomach wasn't empty.

She glanced at the clock. "It's a little early for dinner."

"But very late for lunch," he countered.

"You're still on Pacific time," she realized.

"And I missed lunch."

She was immediately up from her chair. "Do you want me to make you a sandwich or something?"

"I don't want you to go to any trouble," he protested.

"You might find this hard to believe, but I've learned my way around a kitchen over the past seven years."

"I don't find it hard to believe. And while I appreciate your willingness to prove your wifely qualifications—" He held up his hands in mock surrender—and caught the apple that she'd grabbed out of a basket on the counter to throw at him. "I'm kidding," he assured her. "You know I have a grandmother and two sisters who would strenuously object to a gender division of labor."

"Lucky for you, I do know that."

He polished the fruit on his shirt then bit into it.

She opened the cupboard, frowning when she discovered a single slice of bread in the bag. "I was supposed to pick up a few things on my way home."

"Then let's go get them now," he suggested.

"Because you came all the way to New York to peruse the aisle of a Whole Foods?"

He shrugged as he chewed on another bite of apple. "We don't have a Whole Foods in Haven. And since I came all this way, I might as well see something of the city."

"I have a better idea," she said. "Let's go get a hot dog."

Caleb assumed they would take a short walk to a local park area and find a street vendor.

Instead, they took a short walk to a local subway. He dropped his apple core into a garbage bin as they entered the station, where Brie swiped a card and gestured for him to proceed through the turnstile, then swiped it again and followed.

"Good timing," she noted, taking his hand and tugging him toward the platform as a train pulled into the station.

They merged with the crowd that surged through the doors—not unlike cattle being herded into a pasture, he thought. There were a few vacant seats in the car but no two together, so Brie grabbed hold of a strap hanging overhead—obviously having done the same thing hundreds, or maybe even thousands, of times before. But this was Caleb's first trip to the Big Apple and his first subway ride, and he had no doubt that he looked like what he was: a small-town cowboy out of place in the city.

As the train lurched forward again, he reached up and wrapped his hand around the bar, holding on.

"Where are we going?" he asked, trying to decipher the colorful and convoluted subway map posted above the doors.

"To get what is arguably the best hot dog in New York," she told him.

"We couldn't get the second- or third-best hot dog somewhere closer to your place?"

She gasped at the suggestion. "Bite your tongue."

"Since I don't have anything else to bite right now, I guess I'll have to," he remarked.

"It will be worth the trip, I promise," she said, turning toward the doors as the train pulled into the next station.

His rumbling stomach was relieved that they were finally at their destination—until it realized they weren't. Instead, they transferred to another line and resumed their journey.

He wasn't claustrophobic. At least, he didn't think he was. But he wasn't entirely comfortable being trapped in a subway car speeding through an underground tunnel with no real idea of where he was or where he was going. Maybe it was a quick and efficient way for city folk to travel, but Caleb would rather be on the back of a horse under open sky any day.

Every day.

Brie seemed completely in her element, though. Steady on her feet despite the lurching stops and starts of the trains, unbothered by the bumping and jostling of other riders entering and exiting the car. He moved closer to her as more people packed onto the train, so that her back was aligned with his front.

She looked up at him then, amusement dancing in her pretty blue eyes. "You can hold on to me if you're afraid of falling."

They both knew he wasn't in danger of losing his balance, but he decided to take advantage of the offer, wrapping his free arm around her middle and anchoring her close to his body. Because it felt good to hold her, and because when he was breathing in the scent of her shampoo, he could stop speculating on the origin of all the unfamiliar and less pleasant smells around him.

He didn't think he'd ever been in a crowd with so many people. Well, possibly in Vegas. But in Haven, a community event was lucky to draw a crowd of a few hundred people, and even then many of them would be familiar faces—people he'd known his whole life or, if he didn't know them personally, who knew his father or his grandparents. Either way, no one was really a stranger.

He wondered if that was one of the things that had appealed to Brie when she decided to move to New York, the ability to be anonymous in a big city where no one knew her family or her personal history. Where she could wipe the slate clean. Where there was no chance of bumping into him at The Trading Post or The Daily Grind. And though he'd eventually come to understand that she'd needed a fresh start, that understanding hadn't helped him miss her any less.

The train emerged from underground and the car

was flooded with light. He watched the blur of scenery through the window and, after several more minutes had passed, glimpsed the top of a Ferris wheel in the distance.

"Coney Island?" he guessed, because even someone who'd never been to New York would recognize the attraction that had been depicted in iconic photographs and numerous movies.

Brie pouted. "I should have made you wear a blindfold."

"I'd be happy to act out your fantasies in the bedroom," he teased. "But no way would I venture out in public—especially in a strange city—with my eyes covered."

She rolled hers, even as her cheeks flushed with color. "New York isn't strange," she said, a little defensively. "It's just unfamiliar to you."

He glanced around the car, his gaze shifting from a fiftyish woman wearing a red leather miniskirt with fishnet stockings the same electric blue color as her hair, to a bald guy in a torn muscle shirt, his bulging biceps tattooed with the entire Looney Tunes cast, to a couple of teens with so many piercings on their faces he thought their lips might literally be locked together. And those were just some of the people in his direct line of sight.

"Unfamiliar *and* a little strange," he whispered in her ear.

"Says the guy in the cowboy hat," she replied dryly.

The next time the train screeched to a halt, there was a mass exodus of passengers.

"This is our stop." She took his hand again and led him off the train, merging with the flow of pedestrians making their way down the stairs to the street.

Brie led Caleb directly to the original Nathan's restaurant at the corner of Surf and Stillwell Avenues.

They walked right up to the counter—which she assured him was possible only because it was the off-season and between meal times. Few visitors to the area could resist the lure of Nathan's, even during the height of the season and in the face of daunting lineups.

While Caleb was still scanning the offerings on the menu boards, she ordered for him: a bacon cheese dog with a side of fries and a Coke. For herself, cheese fries and a lemonade.

The smell of grilled meat and onions made his mouth water and stomach growl as he pulled out his wallet to pay the cashier. The kid took his money and gave him change, then moved away from the counter to fill their order.

A few minutes later, Caleb was carrying a cardboard box toward one of the outdoor tables with an umbrella tilted to offer shade against the late afternoon sun.

Brie sat down across from him and reached for her drink, taking a long pull through the straw.

He went straight for the dog. It was possible that his opinion was influenced by his ravenous hunger, but as he chewed the first bite, he acknowledged that it could very well be the best hot dog in New York—or anywhere else.

"Is it good?" she asked, her pretty blue eyes sparkling with amusement as she watched him take another big bite.

"It's good," he agreed, around a mouthful of meat and bun.

"Worth the trip? From my place, I mean," she clarified, as she picked up a plastic fork and poked it into the mound of cheese-covered crinkle-cut fries.

He nodded and reached for his Coke.

A gull, circling overhead, swooped down to land on an empty table beside them. The bird cocked its head to the side, a wordless plea. Caleb pulled a French fry out of the paper sleeve and popped it into his mouth.

The bird squawked, as if in protest, and flapped its wings.

A couple of friends, drawn by the cry, joined it at the table.

"Don't you dare," Brie warned.

"I'm not going to feed the birds," he promised.

A couple of kids sat down nearby. One of them tossed a fry onto the ground and snickered as the birds attacked it—and one another—in their efforts to win the prize.

Caleb shifted his attention back to his companion as he sipped his drink.

An impartial observer might describe Brielle as a classically beautiful blue-eyed blonde, but the generic description failed to note the fineness of her features and the flawlessness of her creamy skin. Aside from the tiny lines that creased the corners of her gorgeous eyes, she didn't look much older than she'd been when she'd said goodbye to him seven years earlier.

But she did look different, he realized now. Stronger and more confident than the girl who'd left Haven. And though she had a delicate bone structure, the stubborn tilt of her chin ensured that no one would ever think her fragile. This wasn't a girl or a woman who needed a man to take care of her, and he found her new strength and independence incredibly appealing.

"You're staring at me," she remarked.

"I can't help it," he said. "You're still the most beautiful girl I've ever known."

"Look around," she suggested, as she poked her fork into her fries. "This city is full of beautiful girls."

"I've got the best view right here," he assured her.

"And I thought these fries were cheesy."

He laid his hand over his heart. "Ouch."

Brie chuckled softly. "Sorry, but I'm not seventeen years old anymore. If you want to make my heart flutter, you'll have to do better than telling me that my eyes are as clear and blue as the sky behind the Silver Ridge Mountains on a perfect summer day."

"I'm not sure there is anything better, because it's the

truth," he told her. "But I see just a hint of dark shadows beneath your eyes today."

"Which proves that I'm an idiot for spending forty dollars on a stick of concealer that obviously doesn't work any better than a ten-dollar one," she said lightly.

"Have you been sleeping okay?" he asked. "Or have memories of our night together in Vegas been keeping you awake?"

She licked a drop of cheese sauce off the side of her thumb to avoid answering his question. Because the truth was, erotic dreams aside, she'd been sleeping just fine. In fact, she'd been falling into bed by ten o'clock every night, unable to keep her eyes open any longer. When she'd suspected that she was pregnant, seven years earlier, exhaustion had been one of the first signs.

"Any other symptoms?" he asked. "Nausea?"

"Being tired isn't a symptom of anything except the start of a new school year," she said. "There's always a lot of extra prep required in the early days."

He held her gaze for a long moment, as if he suspected there was more going on than she was admitting. "And you really believe that's all it is?" he asked.

"There's no reason to think it's anything more."

"Aside from the fact that you're late," he reminded her.

Chapter Eight

Brie stabbed her fork into her cheesy fries. "Only a few days."

If it sounded as though she was repeating herself, it was only because he kept arguing the same point. And if her words gave the impression of a woman in denial, well, that was her happy place right now.

Caleb nodded as he nibbled on another one of his own fries, and she breathed a silent sigh of relief that he seemed willing to let the subject drop—at least for the moment.

Affecting a deliberately casual tone, he asked, "Do you come here often?"

"A couple times a year," she answered. "Early fall is my favorite time, though—when the summer crowds are gone but the weather's still warm enough to take off your shoes and walk barefoot in the sand."

He glanced at the motionless Wonder Wheel. "I guess the rides and games shut down for the season."

"They do, although they run on Saturdays and Sundays until the last weekend in October. After that, it gets really quiet along the boardwalk, but some of the shops and restaurants stay open year-round."

He looked at her for a long moment, as if trying to reconcile his memories of the country girl he'd known with the city girl sitting across from him now. "You really like living here, don't you?"

"I wouldn't still be here if I didn't," she told him.

"No regrets about the choices you made?"

"I don't imagine anyone goes through life without some regrets," she said lightly. "But if you're asking if I'm sorry that I left Haven, then the answer is no, because I know I did what was best for both of us."

"I think maybe we should agree to disagree about that," he suggested.

"Just because I chose to leave Haven doesn't mean it was an easy choice to make," she told him.

"I know."

She pushed aside the remnants of her fries and picked up her lemonade again. "Leaving you was harder," she confessed.

"And letting you go was the hardest thing I've ever done."

She lifted her gaze to his then. "Yet you never asked me to stay."

He shrugged. "You never gave me a chance."

"I guess that's true," she acknowledged.

"I only ever wanted you to be happy, Brie."

"I am," she told him.

"That's good then," he said, and gestured to the forgotten fries covered in congealed cheese sauce in front of her. "Are you finished?"

She sucked the last of her lemonade through the straw, then nodded. "I am now."

He collected the garbage and dropped it into a nearby bin. "You want to take your shoes off and walk on the beach?" he asked.

She did, except that the beach had always been *her* escape—the place she came to for peace and quiet reflection. And she worried that if she shared that space with Caleb, she wouldn't ever be able to come here again without thinking of him. And since thinking about Caleb was inexorably linked to missing Caleb, the beach would offer her no solace when he was gone.

"Let's stick to the boardwalk today," she suggested instead.

They walked down Surf Avenue toward the Thunderbolt, then turned and followed the path of its orange serpentine track toward the famed boardwalk.

Along the way, she recounted the history of the ride, explaining that the original Thunderbolt had been a wooden coaster and a favorite attraction at Coney Island for decades. The current rendition, made of steel, opened for business in 2014. And yes, she admitted, she and Grace had stood in line that opening weekend to experience it.

Though the rides were still and the games shuttered, there were plenty of food stands and shops open. There were also a fair number of people around— couples holding hands, moms pushing strollers, joggers kicking up sand, sunbathers soaking up rays. He noticed a few street artists hawking their wares and transient vendors peddling counterfeit designer goods to tourists who either didn't know better or didn't care.

A few blocks down the boardwalk was the Cyclone, a traditional—and rickety—wood coaster ride that had been an area landmark, although not continuously in operation, since 1927. In between were numerous other rides and attractions, including the iconic Wonder Wheel.

"Lily threw up on that one once," Brie told him. "Because her date insisted they experience the ride in a swinging car. It was their first and last date."

He chuckled at that as she paused to watch an old woman sketching near the aquarium.

"Some people head straight to Times Square, as if that's all New York has to offer," she said. "Don't get me wrong—you definitely have to see it before you go back— but there's a lot more to the city than Manhattan. And since

Grace first introduced Lily and me to Coney Island, it's been one of our favorite places to bring visitors."

"I'm a little surprised, considering how close the three of you are, that you never told them what happened with us."

"Well, they know the whole story now—including our marital status. And speaking of friends," she said, as her cell phone played a clip from the theme song of the popular television show, "that will be one of them now."

He took a few steps away, to give her privacy as she answered the call. He glanced back at the Wonder Wheel and, recalling the story about Lily's unfortunate date, wondered if Brie had ever been to the park with a man.

Of course, she'd lived in the city for seven years—it was possible she'd been here with several different men over that period of time. Not that he was going to ask.

"Is everything okay?" he said instead, when she tucked her phone away again.

"Yeah. That was just Lily checking in to see if I wanted to meet her and Grace for dinner."

"What did you say?"

"That I had other plans."

"Do you?" he asked, only now considering that his unexpected appearance on her doorstep might have disrupted her usual routines.

"I do," she confirmed. "I'm going to show an old friend around town."

They hopped on the subway again and took the train into Manhattan, exiting at Rockefeller Center where they wandered through the Channel Gardens, browsed some of the shops, admired the Prometheus statue, then journeyed to Top of the Rock just in time to watch the sunset.

From the seventieth-floor open-air roof deck, there was an incredible 360-degree view of the city. But the breeze felt much cooler here than at street level, 850 feet below, and when Brie shivered, Caleb moved closer to shield her from the wind.

"I'd give you a coat, if I had one," he told her.

She smiled up at him. "Always the gentleman."

"If that was true, we wouldn't be where we are right now," he noted.

She tipped her head back against his shoulder. "Why do I get the feeling you don't mean on Top of the Rock?"

"I'm not trying to push you," he said. "I just want to know if you're going to spend the whole weekend dodging the issue."

"Probably not," she said, though not very convincingly.

"Because I'm not leaving New York until we have an answer to the question I asked earlier today."

"I didn't expect you would," she acknowledged.

He nodded. "Now that we're clear on that, why don't you lead the way to the infamous Times Square?"

She did so, grateful for the temporary reprieve.

"Look at that," Caleb said, pointing toward a crowd that had gathered. "I'm not the only tourist wearing a cowboy hat."

"He's not a tourist," she told him. "And he's not wearing much more than the hat."

"Huh?"

Rather than try to explain, she guided him closer so he could see the mostly-naked cowboy posing with his guitar for photos.

Caleb's brows lifted. "Is he some kind of celebrity?"

"He's famous for being famous," she told him, laughing at his expression.

They moved on, continuing to sightsee in and around Times Square until his stomach was growling again. Brie then led the way to an old church with stained-glass windows which was actually a restaurant, where they enjoyed a thin crust pepperoni pizza from a coal-fired brick oven.

"I know New York is supposed to be the city that doesn't sleep," he remarked as they left the eatery. "But I was on a plane at six this morning, so if you could direct me to a hotel near your place, I wouldn't mind heading back and hitting the sack soon."

"You're asking me now—" she glanced at the time displayed on her Fitbit "—at 11:27 p.m.—to help you find a hotel?"

"I looked online while I was at the airport, but there were so many choices that I decided to wait and ask you for a recommendation."

"At this time of night, I'd recommend you crash on a friend's sofa."

"You don't think Grace and Lily will mind?"

She knew they wouldn't.

But they'd be intrigued to discover that the handsome cowboy from Vegas had suddenly made an appearance in New York. They'd probably also wonder why, after spending the night with him in Sin City, Brie hadn't invited him to share her bed again.

That was something she wondered about herself—especially considering that his proximity stirred her hormones in ways she'd forgotten they could be stirred. For a lot of years, she'd thought there was something wrong with her that she didn't miss sex. It was only after making love with Caleb in Vegas that she realized she did miss sex—*with him*.

And that was why she knew it would be dangerous to let him into her bed. Because she didn't know how to share her body without opening her heart, and she had no intention of letting him into her heart again.

"They won't mind," she responded to his question now.

"Because I don't want to impose—and I definitely don't want you to be uncomfortable," he told her.

"You should be more worried about your own comfort," she said lightly. "It's not a very big sofa."

On their way back to the subway, Caleb stopped outside a Walgreens. Clearly, despite their conversation on Top of the Rock, he didn't trust her not to dodge the issue all weekend.

Brie halted beside him. "Do we really have to do this now?" she asked warily.

"I only want to buy the test tonight."

"That's all?"

"Baby steps," he promised, then winced.

"Freudian slip?" she guessed.

He nodded.

"Okay," she said. "Let's go buy the test."

He squeezed her hand reassuringly as they walked into the pharmacy together. In the family planning section, he randomly selected a box from the shelf and turned it around to read the instructions.

Brie took the test out of his hand and exchanged it for a different brand.

He glanced from one to the other, noting the nearly identical promises of "Fast & Accurate Results!"

"Aren't they all pretty much the same?" he asked.

"Probably," she acknowledged. "But that's the same kind I bought last time."

It took him a moment to realize she meant the last time they'd been in this situation together—and another to understand the deeper meaning of her words. "You think if we get a different test this time, we'll get a different result?"

"I know it's silly and superstitious, but I don't want things to end the same way," she confided.

Aware that she was referring to the loss of their baby, he didn't think it was either silly or superstitious. "We'll get that one," he agreed.

* * *

Back at the brownstone, Brie easily located an extra pillow and blanket in the linen closet. It was going to be much more difficult, she suspected, for Caleb to squeeze his six-foot-plus frame onto the five-foot sofa. When she made her way back down the stairs, she discovered that he'd changed into a pair of sleep pants that rode low on his hips—and nothing else.

The rest of him was naked.

Gloriously temptingly naked.

She stopped in midstride, her heart pounding hard and fast inside her chest as her gaze moved over his bronzed torso, from his broad shoulders and sculpted pecs to the rippling abs dissected by a thin line of dark hair that arrowed into his waistband.

She managed to unstick her tongue from the roof of her mouth to say: "You should put on a T-shirt or something. It gets cold down here at night."

A smile teased the corners of his mouth. "How cold does it get in New York in September?"

Not cold enough, apparently, as her cheeks filled with guilty heat when he called her out on the obvious fabrication.

"Well, the sofa's leather," she pointed out.

"I'll be fine," he assured her.

She wondered again about offering to let him share her bed. She knew he wouldn't ever take advantage of the proximity, or even make a move without her explicit consent, so the problem wasn't that she didn't trust him but that she didn't trust herself if he was under the covers with her.

"Brie?"

She blinked. "Sorry?"

He tugged the pillow out of her grasp and dropped it onto the arm of the sofa.

"Oh." She tucked her now empty hands into the front pockets of her jeans.

"Are you okay?" he asked.

"Yeah," she said. "I was just thinking…maybe I should sleep on the sofa."

"I'm not letting you give up your bed for me," he said. Then his eyes took on a speculative gleam. "Of course, I wouldn't object to *sharing*."

"Been there, done that, bought the T-shirt," she reminded him.

Although if she really had bought the T-shirt, she might have insisted he wear it to cover up those mouthwatering muscles.

"As I recall, it was pretty spectacular," he noted.

Unable to dispute his recollection, she only said, "Good night, Caleb."

"No good-night kiss?" he asked.

All too aware that one kiss could easily lead to more, she took a step back, away from temptation.

"Lily will be up early," she told him. "She works at the café on Saturday mornings."

"I'm accustomed to waking up early, too," he said.

"Except that morning shows up here three hours earlier than in Nevada. And you'll probably be jet-lagged."

"Good point." He stretched out on the sofa, his head on the pillow at one end, his feet overhanging the other. "And my cue to get some shut-eye."

She retreated to her bed to do the same, but she tossed and turned for a long time. When she finally did drift off, she dreamed of him—and the future and family she'd once imagined they'd have together.

Brie slapped a hand on her alarm to silence the annoying buzz.

Just ten more minutes, she promised herself.

But as she rolled over again, her stomach churned. That's what she got for eating pizza so close to bedtime. With a resigned sigh, she pushed back the covers and slid out of bed. After showering and brushing her teeth, she wrapped herself in her robe again and headed downstairs for her morning cup of java.

If she was pregnant, she'd have to cut back on the caffeine, but that wasn't going to happen today. It might not need to happen at all, though there were no signs from her body that her period was imminent—and she was now five days late.

She peeked into the living room and found Caleb was still sprawled over the sofa, oblivious to the world. She continued down the hall, past the dining room to the kitchen, where her roommates were seated at the little table.

Brie lifted a hand in greeting as she made her way to the Keurig. Moving on autopilot, she selected a pod of her favorite French roast and dropped it into the machine.

"So tell us why there's a hunky cowboy asleep on the sofa in our living room," Grace said, when Brie had her coffee in hand.

She feigned surprise. "What? There's a man in our house?"

"And not in Grace's bed for a change," Lily teased.

"Hey!" their friend protested, though not too vigorously.

"Do you think he's naked beneath that blanket?" Lily asked, her attention preoccupied by their guest.

"I think I wouldn't mind if the cover slipped a little bit—or fell off completely—so we could find out," Grace chimed in.

"He's only half-naked," Brie told them.

"That's a shame," Lily said.

"The bigger shame is that he's on the sofa and not in your bed," Grace remarked.

"You know I'm not that kind of girl," she said demurely.

Lily snorted. "Says the woman who did the walk of shame our very first morning in—"

"What happens in Vegas, stays in Vegas," Grace interjected.

"I didn't think we were still bound by that rule when what happened in Vegas is now sleeping on our sofa," Lily remarked.

"An interesting point," Grace acknowledged. Then she turned to Brie. "Anything you want to say?"

She nodded slowly. "When we were in Vegas, I had unprotected sex with Caleb."

Grace's eyes went wide, but she recovered quickly and shook her head in obvious disapproval. "Why would you do something so careless?" she demanded.

"I didn't do it on purpose," Brie protested.

"There were condoms in your purse," Grace reminded her. "I know because I put them there."

"But only two," Brie pointed out.

Grace and Lily exchanged surprised looks before shifting their attention back to Brie.

"Are you saying that you used both of them?" Grace asked.

She nodded.

"And then there was a third time?" her friend prompted.

She nodded again, her cheeks flushing.

"Wow," Lily said, then her expression turned speculative. "Does your sexy cowboy have any brothers?"

"One," Brie said. "Recently engaged."

"Damn."

"Focus," Grace chided.

Lily nodded. "Right."

"Wait a minute," Brie said, as the flow of caffeine through her system finally kick-started her brain. "Aren't you supposed to be working this morning?"

"Marlene asked me to switch shifts so that she could go to some family thing this afternoon—and you're trying to distract us from the real issue at hand."

"I'm not," she denied, though not very convincingly.

"Is that why he's here?" Grace asked. "Are you pregnant?"

"I don't know," she admitted.

"You need to find out," Lily said gently.

"I know. I will."

"Today?" her friend prompted.

She nodded as Caleb shuffled into the kitchen.

His hair was sexily tousled, his jaw shadowed with stubble, and though he was still wearing his pajama bottoms, he'd pulled a T-shirt over his head. Of course, the thin cotton was stretched taut over his muscles so that the overall effect was no less appealing.

"Good morning." Lily's murmured words sounded more like a prayer than a greeting.

"Mornin'," he replied. Then, in a more hopeful tone, "Do I smell coffee?"

Brie retrieved another mug from the cupboard and selected a new pod for the Keurig. It took only half a minute to brew the coffee, but to Brie, it was an eternity as both her roommates stared at Caleb with unabashed curiosity for the duration.

"Thanks," he said, when she handed him the cup.

"There's a shower in the bathroom at the top of the stairs," she said. "I put a couple of towels on the counter for you."

"Thanks," he said again, and—taking the hint along with his coffee—headed out of the kitchen again.

"Subtle," Grace remarked dryly, when he'd gone.

"I wasn't worried about subtlety, I was worried about getting him out of here before you and Lily hit him with a tag-team interrogation."

"We don't do that," Lily protested.

"Yeah, we do," Grace countered. "Because we look out for our friends."

And for that, Brie was grateful.

* * *

Dave had been expecting to hear from Valerie, so he wasn't really surprised when he looked out the window of his office and saw her little red car zipping up the drive. He pushed his chair away from the desk and headed to the door, to spare his housekeeper a confrontation with the uninvited guest.

He pulled open the door before Valerie could ring the bell.

"You're a long way from town," he noted.

"I hoped the drive might help me get over some of my anger," she told him.

"Did it work?"

"No." She slapped a piece of paper against his chest.

"What's this?" Having left his reading glasses on his desk in the office, Dave had to hold the page at arm's length to read it. "And why are you giving me an itemized receipt from Serenity Spa?"

"Because you owe me three hundred dollars."

"I'm not paying for your—" his gaze shifted to the page again "—manicure, pedicure and teen facial."

"Not mine," she told him. "Ashley's and Chloe's."

"Who the hell is Chloe?"

"Your daughter's best friend. I booked the spa appointments for them to distract Ashley from the fact that she was uninvited for dinner last night."

"I didn't uninvite her—I told her I had to reschedule."

"You told her at the last minute," Valerie railed. "And after she'd been looking forward to it all week."

"The short notice was unfortunate," he acknowledged. "But I didn't realize myself until yesterday morning that Caleb wasn't going to be here."

"So?"

"So the purpose of the family meal was for Ashley to meet the family."

"Whether or not your youngest son was available, *you* are her family. *Her father,*" Valerie pointed out. "She wants to get to know *you*."

"Well, maybe you should have thought of that thirteen years ago when you decided to keep your pregnancy a secret from me," he shot back.

"And what would you have done if I'd told you thirteen years ago?" she demanded.

He huffed out a breath, frustrated and angry that he didn't have a ready response to her perfectly reasonable question. "I don't know," he finally admitted.

"Well, I do," she told him. "You would have reminded me that the night we spent together was a mistake, that you were still in love with and grieving for your wife, and that the last thing you wanted or needed was to further upset the lives of your children—who were still mourning the loss of their mother—by adding another child into the mix. Especially one who was nothing more than the product of an ill-advised one-night stand with Jesse Blake's daughter."

Dave scrubbed a hand over his face, unable to deny that everything she'd said was probably true. He wanted to believe that he would have responded differently, but the truth was, he never would have offered to marry her. There was no way he could have put a ring on her finger, even to ensure the legitimacy of their child, because he had still been in love with his wife. And he'd been swamped by guilt that he'd let himself find even a small measure of comfort in the arms of another woman, however temporarily.

"I'll reschedule," he told Valerie now.

"When?" she demanded, obviously unwilling to let him off the hook with nothing more than a vague promise.

"Next Saturday. I really can't do it any sooner," he said,

before she had a chance to object. "I'm out of town at a cattle auction the beginning of the week."

"Fine," she relented. "But this is your only warning—if you cancel again, you're buying her a pony."

Chapter Nine

"**A**re Grace and Lily gone?" Caleb asked, venturing downstairs again after he'd showered and dressed.

"Yes, they went to the local farmers market," Brie confirmed.

He noticed that she'd used the time that he was in the shower to dry her hair and change her clothes, and she was dressed now in a pair of slim-fitting capri pants with a sleeveless top with layers of ruffles. Apparently she'd been telling the truth about leaving the denim and flannel in Haven, and though he missed the girl from his past, he was equally enamored of this sexy city slicker.

"Good." He pulled out the pregnancy test that he'd stuffed into his back pocket and offered it to her.

"You want to get right to it, huh? No conversation? No foreplay?"

"No more stalling," he told her. "We need to know what the situation is so we can decide what we want to do."

"You're right." She took the box and disappeared into the powder room.

While Brie was figuring out the test, Caleb paced in the hall, waiting and wondering.

Hoping.

Was it selfish to want a child with the woman he loved?

Was it foolish to think that a baby could somehow fix whatever was broken between them?

Were they any more prepared to be parents now than they'd been seven years earlier?

Sure, they were both older—and already married, but they were also living separate lives in two different states. And part of the reason he'd decided to fly to New York rather than making a phone call was his desire to get a glimpse of her life here. To know what he was competing against.

Based on what he'd seen of the Big Apple so far, he could acknowledge that it had a certain appeal. But he still believed, in his heart, that the biggest draw for Brie hadn't been the university or the conveniences of city living but the distance from Haven. Now he just needed to find a way to bridge that distance—and convince her that she wanted to, too.

That their relationship was worth it.

When she finally came out of the bathroom again, he guided her into the living room. The pillow and blanket he'd used the night before were neatly folded at one end of the sofa, and they sat side by side in the middle. She'd put the test stick back in the box, probably so that neither of them would be tempted or able to peek until the requisite time had elapsed, and set the box on the coffee table now.

"How long do we have to wait?" he asked.

"Three minutes," she said, opening the timer app on her phone to begin the countdown.

Three minutes didn't seem like very long, but after the first ten seconds, he was desperate to break the silence.

"So…how about those Yankees?" he said.

"You really want to talk about baseball now?" she asked dubiously.

"I figured we should talk about something rather than watching the seconds tick off the clock."

She nodded. "Okay. I like the Yankees. I was even at their home opener this year."

"How'd that happen?"

"The dad of one of my students works for a company with a luxury suite. On Jersey Day at school, he saw me wearing a Rodriguez shirt and invited me to the game."

"You're a Rodriguez fan?"

"No," she admitted, a sheepish smile curving her lips. "It was Lily's jersey."

He chuckled. "I guess there must have been a whole group of you in a luxury suite?"

"Just seven," she said. "Me, Marcus, his son MJ, two business associates and their spouses."

"Marcus's wife wasn't there?"

She shook her head. "They're divorced."

"So…it was a date?"

"No," she said, sounding amused. "It was a baseball game."

"I bet he thought it was a date," Caleb grumbled. And though he wasn't sure he wanted to know, he heard himself ask, "Did he make a move?"

She tapped a finger against her chin as if trying to remember. "Well, he did pass me the mustard for my hot dog."

"Was it a Nathan's?"

"As a matter of fact, it was," she confirmed. "But he never made a move—I promise. Although, in the interest of full disclosure, I have occasionally gone out with other guys over the years."

"I didn't expect that you stayed home every night pining for the husband you left behind in Nevada," he said.

"By the time I was ready to start dating again, I assumed you were my ex-husband," she reminded him.

"Any serious relationships?"

She shook her head. "How about you?"

"No."

An awkward moment passed before she asked, "Does it seem strange to be talking about other people we've dated while waiting to find out if we're going to have a baby together?"

"A little," he admitted.

"We probably should have had this conversation before we fell into bed together. Or maybe we shouldn't have fallen into bed together."

"Whatever the test says, I don't regret that night for a second," he told her.

Before she could respond, her phone chimed to indicate that the three minutes were up.

She drew a deep breath, no doubt bracing herself for the results. His own heart was beating so hard and fast, he wondered if she could hear it.

"Are you ready?" she asked.

He touched his lips to her—a tender and hopefully reassuring kiss. "I'm ready."

Her hand trembled as she reached for the box and withdrew the stick.

He shifted closer, so that he could see the result at the same time she did. Of course, he hadn't read the instructions, so he wasn't sure what the two lines in the little window meant. So he looked at Brie, trying to decipher the result from her expression.

She exhaled an unsteady breath. "It's positive."

Positive.

He wanted to whoop for joy, but he wasn't sure that she was as thrilled with the result as he was. Instead, he attempted to ease the tension by asking, "Do the two lines mean you're pregnant with twins?"

"Ohgod—no," she responded immediately. Vehemently.

"I just wondered, because I've heard that twins run in families."

"Regan's the first in our family to have a multiple birth," she told him. "And it's only fraternal twins that are linked to a genetic predisposition, anyway. Identical twins are a completely random occurrence, which, now that I'm saying it out loud, is not reassuring."

But he didn't think that was why she was still clutching the stick in a white-knuckled grip. "So…are you happy? Sad?"

"Happy," she said.

And then she started to cry.

He immediately slid an arm across her shoulders and hugged her to his side. "I'm getting some mixed signals here."

Brie managed a watery laugh. "These are happy tears. Mostly."

"I'm happy, too," he said. Of course, mixed in with the happy was more than a little bit of "what the hell do we do now?" but he decided to focus on the happy.

So he continued to hold her, trying to be strong and reassuring, until her tears subsided.

"It's going to be okay." He murmured the words soothingly as he gently brushed the lingering traces of moisture from her cheeks. "No, it's going to be *amazing*. We're going to have a baby, Brie."

"A baby," she echoed softly, reverently, her hand automatically moving to cover her still flat belly. "When I think about it, it just seems so unlikely… I mean, what are the odds that we would both have been in Las Vegas on the same weekend, staying in the same hotel, then ending up in bed together? And now we're going to have a baby."

"Maybe it wasn't a string of coincidences," he suggested. "Maybe it was destiny."

"I think destiny is an excuse used by people who want to abdicate responsibility for their choices."

"And I think living in New York has made you cynical," he chided.

"I guess, if we're going to have a baby together, we

should postpone the divorce," she ventured, looking at him to gauge his reaction to her words.

"Postpone?" he echoed.

"I know I asked you to sign the papers, but under the circumstances, it might make sense to wait until after the baby's born."

"I tore up the papers, Brie."

"What? When?"

"When I booked my flight to New York."

Her brows drew together as she tried to make sense of what he was telling her. "What if the test had been negative?"

"I didn't tear them up because I believed you were pregnant—although I did consider the possibility," he confided. "I tore them up because I want to make our marriage work and this trip was about convincing you to give us another chance, regardless of the test results."

"A bold move, cowboy."

He grinned. "I thought you liked that about me."

"There were a lot of things I liked about you," she said. "But I don't know you anymore. And you don't know me."

"So we'll take some time to get to know one another again," he suggested reasonably.

"That's a good idea," she agreed. "Maybe we could plan regular Saturday night dates—oh wait, that won't work, because I live in New York and you live in Nevada."

"Regular Saturday night dates could prove a challenge," he acknowledged. "But I'm here now."

So they took the subway into Manhattan again, this time exiting at the Museum of Natural History, then cutting through Central Park to Fifth Avenue and the Metropolitan Museum of Art.

"Oh, you said The Met," he said, as they climbed the wide stone steps to the entrance.

"What did you think I said?"

"The Mets."

A smile tugged at her lips as she shook her head. "You did not. You know I'd only ever go see the Mets lose against the Yankees."

He chuckled at that as they entered the building. "Where do we begin?" he asked, looking around The Great Hall.

"That depends on what you want to see," she told him. "It's easy to lose a whole day in here."

"We can spend as much time as you want," he promised. "I don't have to be anywhere until the airport tomorrow."

"A tempting offer, but it's too nice a day to spend all of it indoors," she said. "And what I really want to see is the *Art of Native America* before it's gone."

So she led him to The American Wing, and after they'd finished perusing the temporary exhibit, they went back to the park. The half-mile wide by two-and-a-half-mile long green space in the middle of the city was pretty impressive—even to a man accustomed to the wide-open spaces of northern Nevada.

"This is one of my favorite places in the city, whatever the season," she confided, nibbling on a soft-serve ice-cream cone as they made their way along the paved path flanked by huge elm trees and dotted with statues of famous literary figures.

"It's beautiful," he told her.

"And not a cow in sight," she teased.

"Speaking of cows, I built a house."

The awkward segue made her smile. "That was always your plan—to have your own place on your family's ranch."

"*Our* plan," he reminded her.

She nodded.

"Anyway, I just thought I'd mention that there's a bedroom adjacent to the master suite that would make a terrific nursery."

"You're jumping the gun a little bit," she told him, both tempted and terrified by his suggestion.

She knew that moving back to Haven, to live with her husband and raise their child together, was the obvious answer. The easy answer. But that didn't mean it was the right one for her. And she had no intention of making any relocation decisions mere hours after taking a pregnancy test.

"I'm trying to make plans," he said, as he drew her toward one of the benches under the shade of the trees.

He'd always sensed when she needed to talk, and he'd always been a good listener. Maybe that was why, like so many times in the past, she found herself opening up to him. "I've wanted to be a mom for so long," she confided. "But now that it could finally happen, I'm afraid to think too far ahead."

The first time they'd been in this situation, she'd been overwhelmed by the implications of having a baby so young and the course it would set for her life. She wouldn't have gone to college then. Maybe she could have taken some courses online and eventually earned enough credits for a degree, but she might have lost the opportunity to pursue a teaching career.

Having grown up with two career-driven parents, she'd promised herself that when she had kids, she'd never let them feel as if they were in the way. Their questions wouldn't be interruptions; their activities wouldn't be distractions. They would know, every minute of every single day, that they were the most precious gifts she'd ever been given.

But at eighteen, an unplanned pregnancy hadn't seemed like a gift. Certainly not one that she'd wanted.

"When we were pregnant before, when we lost our baby…"

Caleb nodded, silently encouraging her to continue.

"I felt as if it was my fault," she confessed to him now.

"Why would you ever think that?" he asked.

"Because my first thought, when I saw the plus sign, was that maybe it was wrong. I *hoped* it was wrong. I actually prayed not to be pregnant—" her tears spilled over "—and then, only a few weeks later, I wasn't."

"Then it was my fault, too. Because I had the same thoughts," he admitted. "But it wasn't because we didn't love our baby. We were just young and scared and overwhelmed."

She wanted to believe it was true. But she still felt guilty—and worried. "What if—"

He must have known what she was going to say, because he cut her off before she could finish her thought. "Let's not go there," he urged. "No one ever wins the 'what if' game."

She nodded. "You're right."

"Let's just focus on doing all of the right things to take care of you and our baby," he suggested.

"Such as eating healthy?" she asked, popping the last bite of cone into her mouth.

"Calcium is necessary for strong bones," he said.

She smiled then, grateful for his willingness to support her ice cream addiction.

Of course, she'd always been able to count on Caleb to stand by her side...until she walked away.

The house was dark and quiet when Caleb slipped out early Sunday morning after a restless and sleepless night. By the time he returned, it was neither. He followed the sound of voices to the kitchen, where Grace and Lily were seated at the little table.

"I thought I'd be back before you made your coffee," he noted, setting the carryout tray on the table.

"We're always grateful for more," Grace said. "And is that a bag of Bergen Bagels?"

He nodded. "Brie mentioned that they were a favorite."

"And now you are, too," Lily said.

"When you weren't on the sofa this morning, we thought maybe you'd gone back to Nevada," Grace told him.

"I was awake early and didn't want to disturb anyone else, so I went for a walk then stopped at that little café down the street on the way back."

"That was thoughtful," Lily said, as he handed out the paper cups.

"I didn't know how you liked it, so they're all black, but creamers and sugars are in the bag."

"Black works for me," Grace said, prying the lid off her cup. "Thanks."

"I'm light and sweet," Lily said, tearing open three packages of sugar and dumping them into her cup.

"And that's how she takes her coffee, too," Grace remarked.

Caleb smiled as he lifted his own cup to his lips.

Lily emptied the same number of creamers into her cup, stirred.

"So...are you going to be a daddy?" Grace asked.

The unexpected question made him gulp, and he winced as the hot coffee burned his throat.

"You couldn't let me finish my coffee before the interrogation?" he grumbled.

"We just want to know what's going on," Lily told him.

"Isn't that for me and Brie to figure out?"

"We want her to be happy," Grace said.

"And you don't think I can make her happy?" he guessed.

"She didn't move to New York because she was happy in Nevada," Lily pointed out.

"She moved to New York to go to Columbia," he reminded them.

"There are some pretty good schools a lot closer to Nevada," Grace noted.

"You're right," he acknowledged. Because it was the same thing he'd said, when he confronted Brie about her decision. "But everything is different now."

"Then she *is* pregnant," Grace concluded.

"She wanted to be the one to tell you."

"You didn't reveal any big secrets," Lily assured him. "We'd pretty much figured it out."

"So what happens now?" Grace asked. "Do you expect her to move back to Haven?"

"I'd like her to come home," he said. "Every day of these past seven years, it's felt as if the biggest part of my heart was missing."

"And yet, this is the first trip you've ever made to New York to see her," Lily noted.

"I wanted her to come back because it was what she wanted, not because I begged. But now I'm willing to do whatever is necessary to be with her."

"Including beg?" Grace challenged.

"If that's what it takes to convince her to give our marriage a second chance—and to give our baby a real family."

The two women exchanged a glance.

"It has to be her decision," Lily said.

"But we won't stand in your way," Grace promised.

"Thank you," Caleb said sincerely. "I'm glad to know that Brie has such good friends here."

"And because we're such good friends, we feel compelled to warn you that if you break her heart again, you'll answer to us," Grace said.

He nodded. "Duly noted."

"Hey, sleepyhead."

Brie pushed herself up into a sitting position in bed. "What's that?" she asked, eyeing the tray Caleb carried.

"Breakfast."

"You made me breakfast?"

"Sadly, I can only take credit for the delivery," he said. "Grace was in charge of the stove."

She surveyed the contents of the tray he set across her lap. "Is she upset about something?"

"Why would you think that?" he asked cautiously.

"Because she doesn't cook very often," Brie explained. "And when she breaks eggs, it's usually a form of therapy."

"She did more than break eggs. She chopped onions and peppers, fried ham and grated cheese."

"This is a really nice treat," she said. "But I thought we were going to the Milk + Honey Cafe for brunch today."

"That was the plan," he confirmed. "But when you slept through your alarm, we decided you probably needed sleep more than you needed crème brûlée French toast."

"*You* decided?" She frowned, her fork in the eggs. "You, Grace and Lily are making decisions for me now?"

He held up his hands in mock surrender. "We only decided to let you sleep."

"You woke me up now," she pointed out.

"Because it's almost noon, and I didn't want to leave without saying goodbye."

"What?" She twisted her head to look at the clock beside the bed. "Ohmygod, it's almost noon."

"That's what I said," he agreed, his tone tinged with amusement.

She chewed on a bite of omelet, swallowed. "What time's your flight?"

"Four."

"As soon as I finish eating, I'll hit the shower so I can go with you to the airport," she said.

"You don't have to do that," he protested.

"I want to be sure you make it to JFK in time."

"That eager to get rid of me?"

"I only meant that you seem to have a little bit of trouble with our public transportation system."

"That's why I was thinking about calling an Uber," he admitted.

"Or you could save fifty bucks and have the pleasure of my company a little longer."

"In that case, eat up and get moving."

They didn't talk much on the way to the airport, but they sat close together on the train—their hips and shoulders touching, their hands joined.

Though she'd lived without him for seven years, Brie knew she was going to miss Caleb when he was gone. Because he was no longer just the boy she'd loved and impulsively married—he was the father of the child they were going to have together. And this time, despite the circumstances of conception, she had no doubts about her readiness to be a mother, and she already loved their baby more than she could have imagined.

Sure, she had some questions and concerns, but those were mostly focused on her relationship with her husband. And okay, there was some residual anger that he'd kept that status a secret from her for so many years. But the fact that he'd flown halfway across the country to be with her when she took the pregnancy test proved to Brie that he was committed to being a father to their baby.

And now he had to fly back again.

She got off the train and walked beside him through the airport. He was already checked into his flight and his only bag was carry-on, allowing them to linger for a few minutes outside the TSA checkpoint.

"I had a really great weekend," he said.

"Me, too."

"So maybe you wouldn't mind if I came back again sometime?" he asked hopefully.

"Anytime," she said.

"How about next weekend?"

She chuckled, because she knew he was only kidding. As much as she'd enjoyed the time they'd spent together, the journey was too time-consuming to expect him to make it again anytime soon. "I'm going to be in Haven for Thanksgiving this year, so I'll see you then if not before," she promised.

"Thanksgiving is more than two months away," he pointed out.

"We can keep in touch in other ways between now and then."

"You're right. I'll call you every day. And text you between calls."

"That might be a little much," she cautioned.

"Maybe," he acknowledged. "But I want to know how you're doing. And I want to make sure you don't forget about me."

"If I didn't forget about you in seven years, I don't think I'm going to forget about you in a couple months. Especially not with a constant reminder growing in my belly."

He pressed something into her palm and folded her fingers over it. "Here's another reminder."

She turned her hand over and opened her fist to reveal the simple circle of platinum that had, for a very brief while, adorned the third finger of her left hand. She'd given the ring back to him before she left Haven, because she hadn't wanted any reminders of what they'd once had and lost. Because she'd wanted only to forget the hurt and heartache.

Looking at it now—a tangible symbol of the promises they'd made to one another—she wondered: What did it mean that he'd held on to it all these years? And why had he torn up the divorce petition without even knowing if she was carrying his child?

Though these questions swirled around in her mind,

she didn't ask because she wasn't sure she was prepared for his answers.

The cold metal bit into her palm as she instinctively curled her fingers around the ring again, holding on tight. "I can't—"

"I don't expect you to put it on," he said. "Not yet, anyway. I just wanted you to have it."

Then he dipped his head to brush a quick kiss over her lips before joining the passengers making their way toward security screening, leaving her alone with her head spinning and her heart aching.

Chapter Ten

Brielle always felt a little apprehensive before her weekly FaceTime conversations with her mother and father. She loved them dearly, but she didn't feel particularly close to either of her parents and sometimes wondered if she was to blame—if her decision to move away from Haven was responsible for the disconnect. But the distance was more than physical, and the fact that her sister and each of her brothers felt the same way reassured her that she wasn't the cause of the problem.

Still, she wished their relationship could be different, that she could share her thoughts and feelings with them. But it wasn't and she couldn't, so she was doubly grateful for the closeness she enjoyed with her sister, both her sisters-in-law and Grace and Lily.

"Sorry I'm late calling," Margaret said, when Brie connected. "Jason and Alyssa were here for dinner tonight and they just left."

"On a Sunday?" She was understandably surprised, because Sunday was the cook's usual night off and her mother had been known to burn water if left unattended in the kitchen.

"Your dad barbecued steaks," Margaret explained.

"How are Jason and Alyssa?" Brie asked, more interested in her brother and sister-in-law than the menu. Although she kept in regular contact with her siblings, she always worried that she was missing out on something because she was so far away.

"Alyssa is six-and-a-half months and *finally* starting to look like she's pregnant. And she's having some strange cravings, too, because she insisted on having her strip-loin cooked until it was gray inside." Margaret shuddered delicately.

"The well-done steak is more likely a recommendation than a craving," Brie said. "Expectant mothers aren't supposed to eat undercooked meat."

Her mother frowned. "I've never heard such a thing, but I suppose that makes sense considering how worried Alyssa is about every little thing. Did you know they even had some special test done on the baby's heart?"

"Is the baby okay?" she asked, feeling an empathetic ache in her own heart for Alyssa. Jason's wife was so healthy and active that Brie sometimes forgot her sister-in-law had been born with an atrial septal defect that had required three surgeries in the first five years of her life.

"Oh, yes. Everything's fine," Margaret said. "And before they went for the test, I reminded Alyssa that she has a lot of childbearing years left, if it turned out that something was seriously wrong."

"Please tell me you didn't actually say that to her."

"I was being supportive." Margaret's tone was indignant. "And you, of all people, should understand—look at how you bounced back."

"Like a rubber ball," she said dryly.

"I'm not sure what to make of your tone, so I'm going to ignore it," her mother said, though the comment itself proved otherwise. "Now tell me what's new with you."

"Since you asked," she began.

Margaret waited expectantly for her to continue.

I saw Caleb in Vegas and discovered that we're still married, but only after I'd slept with him and now we're going to have a baby together.

But of course Brie didn't say any of that aloud, because she couldn't count on her mother to be happy for her.

And it was too early to be sharing the news, anyway.

"I finally got to The Met to see the Native America art exhibit," she said instead.

And spent another half an hour talking to her mother—and her father, when Ben joined the conversation—about absolutely nothing of importance.

Dave braked behind the yellow bus that stopped at the Happy Harts Ranch next door to his own. He knew the Hartwell family had two school-age boys, because he remembered Martina making and delivering a casserole after each birth so the new parents would have one less meal to worry about. It was what folks did in this part of the country when there was a birth or a death or other life-changing event.

The boys—about twelve and ten now, he guessed—exited the bus and headed down the lane. Then a third kid got off. A girl with a blond ponytail and purple backpack. She followed the boys across the street, but instead of continuing down the long, winding drive, she turned toward the Circle G.

At least, he assumed that was her destination, although his driveway was another quarter mile up the way.

After checking to ensure the road was clear, he steered into the oncoming lane and slowed to a crawl beside her. She moved away from the truck as he lowered the window, and he tipped the brim of his hat back so that she could see his face.

"You look lost," he said, though he suspected she knew exactly where she was—just as he knew who she was though they'd never met.

She shook her head. "I'm going to the Circle G." Then her gaze narrowed. "You're Dave Gilmore."

He nodded.

"I'm Ashley Blake," she told him. "My mom says that you're my dad."

"She told me the same thing," he acknowledged.

"I know she wanted to arrange a formal introduction, but I'm impatient."

"A Gilmore trait," he noted, impressed by both her self-awareness and her honesty.

She frowned, clearly less impressed by his remark.

"You going to walk the rest of the way or you want a ride?"

"I guess I'll take a ride," she said. "I mean, technically you're not a stranger, right?"

"Technically," he agreed.

She walked around the front of the cab, then opened the passenger side door and climbed in. He waited until she'd buckled her seat belt before resuming his journey—and their conversation.

"Does your mom know where you are?" he asked.

"No, but she won't be worried," Ashley hastened to assure him. "She works late on Wednesdays."

"Where does she think you are?"

"Doing homework with my friend Chloe."

He took his cell phone out of his jacket pocket and offered it to her. "Call her and tell her about your change of plans."

"I've got my own phone," she told him. "I'll call her when we're done."

"Done what?" he asked.

"Getting to know one another."

"Call her now," he suggested. "Then when we get to the house, we can continue this conversation with cookies and milk."

She considered his offer. "What kind of cookies?"

"Oatmeal raisin."

"I like oatmeal raisin," she said. "But oatmeal chocolate chip are better."

"I'll let you debate that with Martina another time. She's at the dentist this afternoon."

"Who's Martina? Your girlfriend?"

"My housekeeper."

"Do you have a girlfriend?" she pressed.

"Call your mother," he said again. "And tell her I'll give you a ride home in a little while."

Ashley reached into the side pocket of her backpack and pulled out a slim phone in a pink case covered with sparkly stones.

Though she spoke quietly, in the close confines of the cab he didn't have any trouble hearing both sides of the conversation. As he pulled into the driveway, she disconnected the call.

"She's pretty mad," Ashley confided, tucking her phone away again.

He parked the truck and turned off the ignition. "I would be, too, if I thought you were at one place and found out you'd gone to another."

"But I'm with my...you," she decided, unwilling to paste the "father" label on a man she'd just met.

And he suspected the fact that Ashley was with him was the biggest reason for Valerie's anger. She'd confided that her daughter had shut down since she'd learned the truth about her paternity, refusing to talk to her mother about what she was thinking or feeling. That Ashley had now sought out her father would undoubtedly seem like a slap in the face to the woman who'd raised this child on her own for twelve years.

"Nice place," she said, kicking off her shoes at the back door before following him down the hall.

"Thanks." He washed his hands at the kitchen sink, dried them on the towel hanging over the oven door, then reached for the cookie jar—restocked by Martina earlier that day.

He started to carry the jar to the table, then, picturing

his housekeeper's frown of disapproval, he took a plate out of the cupboard instead. He put a handful of cookies on the plate and set the plate on the table.

Ashley had dumped her backpack on the floor beside her chair and hung her coat over the back of it.

"You want to wash up?" he asked, more a suggestion than a question.

"Sure," she said.

Before he could direct her to the powder room, she went to the sink, using dish soap as he'd done, then drying her hands on the same towel.

He poured two glasses of milk and set them on the table.

She helped herself to a cookie, broke it in half. "My mom said you had a heart attack."

Of all the things he'd anticipated she might say, that wasn't one of them.

"I did," he confirmed. "Just about five months ago."

She nibbled on her cookie. "Are you okay now?"

"Fit as a fiddle."

"How can you tell if a fiddle's fit?" she wondered.

"I have no idea," he admitted.

"That's not very reassuring."

"Are you looking for reassurance?"

"I don't want to get attached if you're going to die," she told him.

"Well, we're all going to die eventually," he pointed out.

"There's a big difference between eventually and imminently," she said, in a matter-of-fact tone that made her sound much older than her twelve years.

"True enough," he acknowledged. "All I can tell you is that my doctor doesn't seem to think I'm in any imminent danger."

"That's good then," she decided.

He exhaled a quiet sigh that she seemed satisfied by

his response. But his relief was short-lived, as she moved on to another and even tougher question.

"Did you love my mom?"

"Do you always jump into the deep end when you go swimming?" he wondered aloud.

"Yeah, but what does that have to do with anything?" she asked, baffled by his question.

"It proves you're a Gilmore," he remarked.

Her chin lifted. "I'm a Blake."

"You're also a Gilmore."

"You didn't answer the question about my mom," she pointed out.

Not just brave but bullheaded, he noted.

Definitely a Gilmore.

"Did you ask your mom that question?"

"How is she supposed to know your feelings?" Ashley challenged.

He rephrased. "Did you ask her about our relationship?"

"Of course."

No doubt this was some kind of test, to see if he would tell her the truth. Assuming her mother had told her the truth. But why wouldn't she? It didn't paint Valerie in a negative light.

"Don't lie to her," Valerie had advised him.

"Why would I lie to her?"

"I don't know what kind of questions she's going to ask you. I'm just telling you to be honest. She's heard enough lies from me over the year—she doesn't need to hear any more."

"Truthfully, I didn't know your mother well enough to love her, but she was there for me when I needed someone."

"So you used her? For sex," she added, as if the meaning of her question had been at all unclear.

He winced inwardly. Because the last thing he wanted

to talk to his twelve-year-old daughter about was sex, especially in regard to the relationship between her parents. As if a few hours together could be considered a relationship.

"We each had our own reasons for being together," he hedged.

She rolled her eyes at his response.

He pushed away from the table to clear their dishes. Looking out the window above the sink, he could see Sky's mare and her chestnut foal in the near pasture.

"Do you like horses?" he asked.

"You're trying to change the subject."

Desperately, he acknowledged to himself.

Aloud he said, "I thought you might like to meet Enigma."

"Who's that?" she asked.

"Mystery's eight-month-old foal," he told her.

And that, thank God, was mission accomplished.

"What brings you into town?" Skylar asked, as Caleb settled onto a vacant stool at the bar side of Diggers' Bar & Grill.

"I'm meeting Joe for a drink," he told his sister.

She tipped a mug under a tap and pulled the lever. "How are the newlyweds?"

"Still married, in case you made a bet with Liam."

"I would not," she protested indignantly. "I was only asking because I like Joe. He was usually the least annoying of your friends, and I'm happy that he found someone to make him happy."

"I'll be sure to pass along your best wishes," he said, nodding his thanks for the beer she set on the paper coaster in front of him.

"Now if only *you* could find someone to make you happy," Sky remarked.

"And if only *you* could focus on your own life rather than worrying about everyone else," he countered.

She shrugged. "It's what I do best."

"Well, you don't have to worry about me," he told her.

"Then tell me why you've been even more preoccupied than usual since you got back from New York," she said.

He frowned. "What makes you think I went to New York?"

"When I stopped by your place to drop off the leftover steak pie, as Martina requested, the boarding pass from your return flight was sticking out of the end pocket of your duffel bag," Sky told him.

"Oh."

"So why were you there?" she pressed.

"I went to see Brielle."

His sister sighed. "I love you, Caleb, but you are one screwed-up dude."

"Why? Because I've been in love with the same woman for ten years?"

"And you're not even trying to deny it," she said.

"Why would I deny it?" he challenged.

"Because she dumped you and moved twenty-five hundred miles away," she reminded him, though not unkindly.

"She went away to school."

"And never came back."

"There's Joe now," he said, as his friend walked through the door, saving him from rehashing old arguments yet again.

"We're not finished this conversation," Sky warned.

Caleb ignored her as he picked up his beer and gestured his friend toward a table far away from the bar and his interfering and opinionated sister.

Caleb and Joe ordered a platter of nachos with their second round of drinks, but before the food was delivered, Joe's phone beeped.

He opened the screen and checked the message, then abruptly decided: "I've gotta go."

"Is everything okay?" Caleb asked him.

"Yeah. It's just, uh—" the tips of Joe's ears turned red as he dropped his voice and confided "—Delia's order from Victoria's Secret came today."

"Go." Caleb waved him away. "Have fun."

His friend grinned as he tossed money on the table to cover his beer. "Oh, I will."

A few minutes later, the waitress delivered his nachos. "Can I get you another drink?" she offered.

"A Coke," he decided, because it was a long drive back to the ranch.

"Coming right up," she promised.

He picked up a chip laden with spicy ground beef and melted cheese, and popped it into his mouth.

"I thought that was your truck outside," his father said, taking the seat Joe had recently vacated.

"What are you doing in town?" Caleb asked.

"I had something to deliver."

He pondered the deliberately vague response as he nudged the platter of nachos toward his father.

Dave shook his head. "I don't want to spoil my dinner."

"This is my dinner," Caleb said, munching on another chip.

"Are you going to be around this weekend or are you planning to jet off to New York City again?"

"Does everyone know that's where I went last weekend?"

"Not because you told anyone you were going—or why," his father remarked.

"I'm twenty-seven years old," Caleb reminded him. "I didn't think I needed your permission to take a weekend trip—or that you'd be interested in my reasons."

"Because you went to see that Blake girl?" his father guessed.

"If you mean Brielle, then yes. And she's a Channing."

Dave shook his head. "Don't kid yourself, son. Channings and Blakes are one and the same in this town. And I thought—*I hoped*—your relationship with her was in the past."

"Do you really want to get into this now?" Caleb challenged.

"No," his father decided. "I only wanted to make sure you were available to come for dinner on Saturday."

"Is it a special occasion?" he asked, wondering if he might have forgotten someone's birthday. Between his siblings and cousins and all the recent additions to the family, it was getting hard to keep track of them.

"Not a special occasion, really. I just thought we should have a family dinner." Dave cleared his throat. "The whole family."

"You've invited Ashley," Caleb realized.

"I have," his father confirmed. "And her mother."

He couldn't resist the opportunity to get in a dig of his own. "Oh, you mean the other Blake girl?"

His father flushed. "I'm not asking for your approval or your forgiveness."

"That's good. Because I don't think I could offer either."

"I'm sure you think me being with another woman was somehow disloyal to your mom—"

"Actually, my irritation has nothing to do with mom and everything to do with the fact that you went ballistic when you found out that I'd married Brielle."

"Because you got her pregnant."

Caleb pointed a finger at his dad and said, "Pot." Then he turned his hand to gesture to himself. "Kettle. And interesting note," he added. "Only one of us did the right thing."

"Valerie never told me that she was pregnant," Dave said in his defense. "And anyway, that's in the past."

"Did I hit a little too close to home?" Caleb taunted.

"I'm not proud of what I did," his father acknowledged. "But I don't want Ashley to pay the price for my mistakes."

"What do you want?"

"Only for you to show up for the meal and be polite to your half sister and her mother."

"I can do that," Caleb said, because he'd never take his conflict with his father out on Ashley or Valerie. And because he was admittedly curious to get to know the sister he'd only recently learned was his.

"Thank you." Dave rose to his feet then. "Now I'd better get home before I'm late for dinner."

On his way out, he passed his other son coming in.

"What is this? Family night at the bar and grill?" Caleb asked as Liam joined him.

"So it would seem," his brother agreed. "What was Dad doing here?"

"He saw my truck and stopped by to invite me to the big family dinner on Saturday."

"I still can't believe, after everything he's said about the Blake family over the years, that the first woman he bangs after Mom dies is a Blake," Liam remarked.

Caleb winced. "Please. I don't want that image in my head."

"I'm just saying—it's more than a little hypocritical."

He nodded his agreement.

Liam stole a nacho and dipped it into the cup of salsa. "You don't think he's in love with her? Valerie, I mean."

This time Caleb shook his head. "I don't think he would have let her disappear from his life if he'd been in love with her."

"You let Brielle go," his brother noted.

"That was a completely different situation," he said.

"Was it?"

Because he didn't want to do an autopsy on a relationship he was hoping to revive, he turned back to the topic of the family dinner. "Are you bringing the soon-to-be wife and kids on Saturday?"

"Of course," Liam said. "Macy will be a neutral buffer and the triplets are always a great icebreaker.

"And I checked with Kate to make sure Reid was coming, too," his brother continued. "I figured it can't hurt to have the sheriff on hand."

"How was the family dinner?" Brielle asked, when Caleb called her the day after the big event.

"You mean the family disaster?"

She winced sympathetically. "That bad?"

"The only good thing was Martina's fried chicken with mashed potatoes and creamed corn."

"Yum," she said.

"Everyone agreed it was delicious," he said. "Except for Ashley who, it turns out, is a vegetarian."

"Oh, no."

"Oh, yes," he said. "As the food was being passed around the table, Valerie reminded my dad that Ashley doesn't eat meat—to which he replied that chicken isn't meat, it's poultry."

"So he tried to be accommodating," she noted, willing to give him credit for the effort.

"And failed miserably," Caleb said. "Ashley pushed her potatoes and corn around on her plate but barely ate anything."

"The whole situation must have been overwhelming for her."

"And it wasn't even the whole family," he said. "Macy stayed home with Ava, who had a snuffly nose. And Reid didn't make it because he was called out to the scene of a collision on the highway."

Still, Brie had always been a little intimidated by Caleb's father, so she imagined her young cousin had probably felt as if she was in the midst of a lions' den. Knowing that the king of the beasts was her father wasn't likely to have eased her apprehension.

"But you could tell Ashley was eager for the meal to be over, because as soon as the dishes were cleared away, she asked if she could see Mystery's foal."

"And I bet you were the first to offer to take her out to the barn," Brie guessed.

"I think we all wanted an excuse to escape the tension-filled dining room," he confided. "But I was closest to the door."

She chuckled. "I'm sure that wasn't an accident."

"It wasn't," he agreed. "And anyway, I'm glad I got some one-on-one time with her. Ashley's a bright and interesting kid."

"Of course she is—she's a Blake," Brie teased, tongue-in-cheek.

"She's also a Gilmore," he reminded her. "Though I get the impression she isn't exactly thrilled about that."

"Can you blame her for feeling conflicted?"

"No," he acknowledged. "I guess I was just hoping it would be easier for her, because then I could believe it will be easier for our child."

"It will be easier for our child, because we'll both be in his or her corner from day one," she pointed out to him.

"Speaking of…how are you feeling?" he asked.

"Pregnant," she said brightly.

"How does pregnant feel?"

"Tired all the time, with sore breasts and occasional bouts of nausea."

"So why do you sound so happy?" he wondered aloud.

"Because I am happy," she said. "Because every time I want to throw up, I'm reminded that there's a baby growing inside me. *Our baby.*"

And more than three weeks after she'd taken the test,

it still gave Brie a thrill every time she thought about the tiny life in her womb.

But the thrill was almost always followed by a twinge, as she remembered that she'd been down this road once before—and it had not ended happily. She was taking care of herself: eating healthy (most of the time) and exercising moderately. But it was still early days, and she didn't want to make too many plans or look too far ahead, just in case.

Was it her fault, then, she wondered, that there was blood on her panties when she got home after school on Wednesday afternoon?

Chapter Eleven

Brie surveyed the contents of her refrigerator, contemplating her options. Did she want leftover pasta from the previous night, half a bowl of sad-looking salad, a single slice of pizza or some kind of Chinese food of indeterminate age and origin?

She'd decided on the pizza and salad when the doorbell rang. Closing the door of the fridge with her hip, she set the food on the counter and went to check the security camera.

"Caleb?" She immediately yanked open the door to let him in. "Ohmygod—what are you doing here?"

"Lily called me from the hospital last night."

Though the revelation was news to Brie, it probably shouldn't have surprised her. "I wish she hadn't done that."

"I'm glad she did," he told her. "Especially since you didn't let me know what was going on."

"Because *I* didn't know what was going on," she explained. "And I didn't want you to worry when there was probably nothing to worry about and nothing you could do, anyway."

"I wish I could have been there with you," he said. "I was on my way to the airport when she called the second time to tell me that you were being released."

"And you still flew twenty-five hundred miles," she noted. "Why? To hold my hand?"

He linked their fingers together now, then lifted her hand and touched his lips to the back of it. "Worth the trip."

She managed a smiled. "I'm okay," she assured him. "The baby's okay. It was just a little bit of spotting that the doctor said isn't anything to worry about in the early stages of pregnancy."

But there had been a moment—not of worry but of sheer and complete panic—when she saw the blood and thought it was happening again. That she was going to lose another baby.

The fear had been so strong and real, she'd barely been able to breathe. She'd wanted him then, wished he could be there with her, because she knew he would understand everything she was feeling without having to say a word.

Instead, she'd called Lily, because her friend was at work at the museum, only an eight-minute subway ride away.

Lily had rushed home and then summoned an Uber to take them to Kings County Hospital. She'd stayed with Brie the whole time while she waited to see a doctor, had another test to confirm her pregnancy, then a physical exam. Brie didn't know when her friend would have found the time to call Caleb—unless it was when she'd left the room to call Grace. And though she thought jumping on a plane was an overreaction to the situation, she appreciated that he wanted to be there for her.

Still, she felt compelled to protest. "If your instinct is to fly halfway across the country every time I freak out, you could spend a lot of time in the air over the next seven-and-a-half months."

"Then I guess I better start collecting frequent flyer points."

She tried to smile, but her lips trembled rather than curved and her eyes filled with tears.

He pulled her into his arms, tucking her head against his chest. "It's going to be okay."

"I was so scared," she admitted.

"And I wasn't here."

"Talking to you might have helped," she said. "I should have called you—I'm sorry I didn't."

"This long-distance thing really sucks," he grumbled.

She could only nod.

And then, realizing that they were still standing in the entranceway, she extricated herself from his embrace and closed the door.

"I was just thinking about my options for dinner," Brie said, leading the way to the kitchen.

He glanced at the salad and single slice of pizza on the counter. "I hope you were thinking about something better than that."

"I didn't feel up to cooking," she admitted.

"Do you feel up to going out?"

"I'm a little tired but even more hungry, so yes, we can go out."

"Last time I was here, you mentioned there was an Italian place close by."

She put the pizza and salad back in the fridge. "It's as if you read my mind."

"Should we ask Grace and Lily to join us?" he asked, as they were on their way to Nonna's Kitchen.

She shook her head. "It's Thursday."

"They don't eat dinner on Thursday?"

"Lily is at the museum until ten on Thursdays and Grace usually stays in Manhattan to have dinner with her parents."

"Then I guess we only need a table for two."

* * *

"How long are you planning to stay this time?" Brie asked, when they were seated inside the restaurant.

"I was in such a hurry to get here, I booked a one-way ticket," he told her.

"So you can hang out for a few days?" she asked hopefully.

"Do you want me to?"

"Well, it doesn't make sense to come all this way just to turn around and go back again," she pointed out.

"You want me to stay," he realized, unable to hold back the smile that curved his lips. "You missed me."

"I've thought about you some," she acknowledged. "But I don't know that I'd say I missed you."

"Well, I missed you," he said.

She seemed surprised by his admission. "You did?"

"I know it's crazy. We've spent a total of four days together over the past two months, but I think about you all the time and wish we could be together every day."

And when Lily had called, when he'd thought that Brielle might lose their baby, he'd felt as if he'd been cut off at the knees. Having been through that emotional trauma once before, he knew how scared she'd been—because he'd felt the same way.

He'd got the second call, assuring him that it was a false alarm and that both Brie and their baby were fine, when he was on his way to the airport. He could have turned around and gone home, but the need to see her, to hold her, to reassure both of them, was stronger than everything else.

Because as much as he hoped and believed this pregnancy was a second chance for them together, he knew that losing their baby would end all of their hopes and dreams.

By the time they left the restaurant, he could tell that Brie was wiped out. In addition to the physical toll the pregnancy was taking on her body, he guessed that she was mentally and emotionally exhausted.

"Did you want to watch a movie or something?" she asked, when they got back to the house.

"You don't have to entertain me," he told her. "Just give me a pillow and blanket so I can crash, then you can do the same."

"I can get you a pillow and blanket...or you can share my bed tonight, if you want.

"I'm not suggesting anything other than sleeping," she hastened to add. "But my mattress is probably more comfortable than the sofa, and you won't be awakened by Grace and Lily when they head out to work in the morning."

"I guess you have to work tomorrow, too."

"I was planning to go in," she said. "But my plans changed when a handsome cowboy showed up at my door."

His brows lifted. "You're going to play hooky?"

"I'm taking a personal day."

"Is that what teachers call it when they play hooky?"

She nudged him with her elbow. "I already emailed my principal so that she could call in a sub to cover my class."

"So what are our plans for tomorrow?" he asked.

"For starters, sleeping in."

They did sleep in.

And then they went into Manhattan because Brielle wanted to show Caleb the trees in Central Park in all the glory of their fall colors.

This time, they got off the subway on Fifth Avenue to approach the park from a different direction. It was, he realized, a major shopping hub. Not touristy shops, like on Broadway, but high-end retail outlets—including Tiffany's.

"I never did get you a diamond," he remarked.

She followed his gaze to the iconic store across the street. "We had other things to worry about."

"Plus, I was broke."

"You were barely twenty years old."

"I'm not twenty years old—or broke—anymore," he said, and then he wondered. "If I'd taken you to pick out a ring, what kind would you have chosen?"

"I did pick out a ring," she reminded him.

And though he didn't know it, since he'd returned that ring to her at the end of his last visit, she'd been wearing it on a chain around her neck.

"I mean, what kind of engagement ring?" he prompted.

She shook her head. "It doesn't matter. You're not buying me an engagement ring."

"What kind of wife objects to her husband buying her jewelry?" he teased.

"The kind of wife who expected her husband to sign the divorce papers she gave him," she retorted.

"Papers that no longer exist," he reminded her. "And since we're having a baby together, I want my ring on your finger."

"Possessive, much?" she asked, unwilling to admit that his fierce protectiveness made her belly quiver. Because she was far too enlightened to be turned on by a man beating on his chest. Even if it was a spectacular chest.

"Yes," he said, without hesitation or apology.

"Putting a ring on my finger isn't going to solve all our problems," she pointed out to him.

"What are all these problems that you're so concerned about?" he asked.

"The biggest and most obvious one is the previously noted distance between your place and mine."

"That's one problem," he agreed. "And I'm working on it."

"What does that mean?" she asked. "Do you think

you can somehow rearrange the geography of our country so that Nevada and New York are closer together?"

"Not likely."

"So what you mean is that you're working to convince me to move back to Haven," she guessed.

"Right now, I just thought we could look at some engagement rings."

"But we're not engaged."

"No, we're married," he reminded her. "And skipping the engagement part is an oversight I'd like to fix."

"Not necessary," she said coolly, resuming her journey toward the park.

"Hey." Caleb caught her arm and turned her to face him. "What's wrong? Why are you upset that I wanted to buy you a gift?"

"A teddy bear is a gift," she said. "A diamond—especially in the form of an engagement ring—is a bribe."

"There's that cynicism again," he remarked. "Most people would think of it as a promise."

"I'm not asking for any promises."

"Maybe I want to make one to you, anyway."

She shook her head. "We did that once before," she reminded him. "And then we broke those promises."

"We were young. Scared. Heartbroken."

"I'm still scared."

"I am, too," he admitted. "But maybe it's time we stop worrying about all the things that could go wrong and focus on the things that are right.

"Our baby is one of those things—our second chance to finally be the family we were always meant to be."

"That all sounds tempting and wonderful," she acknowledged. "But there's a major snag in your plan—I live here and you live in Nevada."

"So you'll move back to Nevada," he said, as if it were a given.

"Excuse me?"

"It makes the most sense," he remarked, in a reasonable tone.

"So all that stuff you said last time you were here, about how you could appreciate the life I've made for myself, et cetera—did you mean any of it?" she challenged.

"I meant every word," he promised. "But that was before we knew you were pregnant."

"And now, just because of two little lines on a pregnancy test, I'm supposed to give up everything I've worked for to be your wife?"

"Not just because of two little lines," he argued. "Because those lines represent *our baby*."

And okay, thinking of their baby did fill her heart with so much joy she felt as if it was overflowing.

But moving back to Haven where there was so much history? Where she'd loved him and lost him? Where they'd faced opposition and conflict with their families at every turn?

Thinking about *that* made her stomach cramp.

"I don't want to move back to Haven," she said.

He looked sincerely baffled by her statement. "Why not?"

"My job is here. My friends. My life."

He scowled. "You have friends in Haven. Family there. *Me*."

"Haven hasn't been my home in seven years," she reminded him. "And I'm not going to be bullied into moving back to the place where no one ever supported our relationship."

"Forget about our parents," Caleb urged. "Let's focus on you and me—what *we* want."

"I don't want to be bullied into moving back to Haven," she said again.

He sighed but seemed to relent. "And I don't want

to fight with you, so why don't we drop the subject for now?"

"Okay," she agreed. "But there is another possibility that you're overlooking."

"What's that?"

"You could move here."

"To New York?" he asked dubiously.

"You should at least consider it."

"I can't imagine there are many job openings for ranchers in Brooklyn."

"There aren't many job openings for kindergarten teachers in Haven, either."

"You always said you'd like to spend the first couple of years at home with a baby," he said. "By then, Mrs. Enbridge might finally be ready to retire."

"And if she isn't?"

"There's a day care in town now, where you could work with preschoolers. Or you could look at teaching one of the primary grades."

"You make it sound so easy," she said. "As if it's not a big deal for me to uproot my life, give up all the things I've worked for and move twenty-five hundred miles away."

"I know it's a big deal," he said. "I just think that being together so that we can give our child a real family is a bigger deal."

Valerie poured sauce over the spinach and cheese enchiladas, then sprinkled them with more cheese, set the baking pan in the oven and turned on the timer. The day after the family dinner disaster—as she'd overheard Caleb refer to it—Dave had called asking for a do-over, and she'd suggested that a more intimate gathering in a familiar setting might help put Ashley at ease. Somehow that had translated into Valerie cooking their daughter's favorite meal.

But she didn't really mind, and Ashley was so pleased that her dad was coming for dinner, she'd set the table without having to be asked. She also chattered nonstop while she completed the task, seeming to forget—at least for the moment—that she wasn't talking to her mother.

She even followed her into the master bedroom, perching on the edge of the mattress as Valerie began to unbutton her blouse.

"Are you going to put on something sexy?" Ashley asked, in a tone that was more curious than judgmental.

"What? No," Valerie immediately denied.

"So why are you changing?"

"Because I got sauce on my shirt."

"Would you bother changing if Dave wasn't coming for dinner?"

She frowned. "I really wish you wouldn't call him Dave."

"It's his name, isn't it?"

"And Jesse is my father's name, but I call him Dad."

"When you bother to speak to him at all," her daughter remarked.

"I don't have a great relationship with my father," Valerie acknowledged. "I hope that you'll have a better one with yours, and that's why I invited him to come here for dinner."

She rummaged through the basket of laundry she hadn't yet had a chance to put away, looking for a top to replace the blouse she'd tossed aside.

"The red sweater," Ashley suggested.

She pulled the sweater out of the pile, then looked at her daughter. "You think?"

Ashley nodded. "It looks good on you."

A compliment? She was surprised. And flattered. And of course Valerie wasn't going to ignore her daughter's advice, even if she did worry that the soft fabric hugged her curves enough that it might be considered sexy.

"And even better with jeans," Ashley added.

"What's wrong with these pants?"

"Nothing's wrong with them, but this is supposed to be a family dinner not a business meeting, right?"

"Right," Valerie agreed, and unhooked the button of her pants.

Ashley picked up her discarded shirt. "I'll take this down to the laundry room to spray it."

"Thanks." She pulled on her jeans, then turned to check her reflection in the full-length mirror on the back of her door, chiding herself as she did so.

This dinner was an opportunity for Ashley to spend some time with her father—it wasn't a date. So it didn't matter what she was wearing or even if she had enchilada sauce on her shirt.

Still, she took another minute to run a brush through her hair and add a touch of gloss to her lips, because she wanted to look good. Not because Dave was coming over but because she was a woman who took pride in her appearance.

And maybe it was true, but that justification didn't explain the flutter in her belly when she looked out the window and saw his truck pull into the drive.

It wasn't fair that the rancher was as handsome now as he'd always been. Sure, he was older—they both were—but the years sat comfortably on the lines of his face and in the silver threads of his hair. She, on the other hand, spent far too much money on creams to hide the crow's-feet at the corners of her eyes and hair dyes to pretend her shoulder-length tresses were the same natural honey-blond color they'd been twenty years earlier.

One thing that hadn't changed, though, was the way her heart still pounded hard and fast whenever she saw him, but she was determined to ignore the inconvenient attraction—for the sake of their daughter.

And maybe the protection of her own heart.

* * *

"Did you like the enchiladas?" Ashley asked after Dave had cleaned his plate.

"I really did," he said, surprised to discover it was true and, even more, that the meal—including a side of Mexican rice—had satisfied his hearty appetite.

"Mom's a really good cook," she said.

"I'm not going to argue with that," he assured her, as Valerie pushed away from the table and began to stack the empty dishes.

He'd never been particularly adept at reading a woman's moods or signals, but he sensed that she was on edge about something—though he had no idea what that something might be. Conversation throughout the meal had flowed smoothly, with a lot of help and direction from their daughter. The little girl who'd barely said a dozen words at his table the week before had been a veritable chatterbox tonight.

"We've got key lime tarts for dessert," Ashley said now.

"Did your mom make those, too?" he asked.

She shook her head. "No, we got them from Sweet Caroline's."

"Can't go wrong with anything from Sweet Caroline's," he said.

Valerie put the plate of tarts on the table. "Do you want coffee with dessert?"

"I don't want you to go to any more trouble," he said.

"It's no trouble," she assured him. "All I have to do is stick a pod in the Keurig and press a button."

"In that case—do you have decaf?" he asked.

She nodded and turned away to make his coffee.

Ashley got up to refill her glass of milk.

"Help yourself," Valerie said, gesturing to the tarts as she set a steaming mug in front of him.

"Aren't you going to sit and have dessert with us?" he asked.

"No, I want to get started on the dishes."

"I'll help you—after dessert," he said, snagging her wrist to draw her back to the table.

Mistake.

He immediately dropped his hand away but continued to feel the sizzle of the contact all the way up his arm.

The widening of Valerie's eyes assured him that she wasn't unaffected by the touch, but she sat back down at the table and reached for a tart.

When there were only crumbs left on her plate, Ashley excused herself to work on a science project and Valerie left the table to resume clearing up.

Dave carried his empty mug and plate to the dishwasher. "Did I do something wrong?"

"No. Of course not," Valerie said, not meeting his gaze.

"Are you sure? Because you're holding that pan in a white-knuckled grip."

She set the pan in the sink, squirted dish soap in it and filled it with hot water.

He tried again. "I thought dinner went well."

She nodded. "Very well."

"So why do you look worried?"

She sighed. "Because a few weeks ago, Ashley was so furious that I'd lied about her father, she wasn't even talking to me."

"She seems to have gotten over that," he remarked.

"You really are clueless, aren't you?"

"So it would seem," he acknowledged. "Do you want to tell me what I'm missing?"

"Our daughter's playing matchmaker."

He frowned.

"Now that she finally has a father, she's trying to maneuver us together in the hope that we can be a real family."

Valerie was right; he was clueless. Because now that she'd brought it to his attention, he saw his daughter's pointed comments and compliments about her mother in a different light.

"And when she realizes that her plan isn't going to succeed, somehow that's going to be my fault again," she said unhappily.

He took a step closer. "But what if her plan did succeed?"

"As if."

But though her words expressed derision, her gaze lingered on his mouth.

Testing her—and maybe himself—he settled his hands on her denim-clad hips.

Her breath caught in her throat.

"Maybe it *was* more than grief and alcohol that drew us together that night," he suggested.

And then he kissed her.

Chapter Twelve

There was a definite bite of winter in the air when Caleb rode out to check the fence around the perimeter of the east pasture Monday morning. On his way home from the airport the night before, he'd spotted what looked like a post toppled over. He could have stopped his truck and got out to check it then and there, but another flight delay had left him in no mood to do anything but hit his mattress for the three hours before he had to be up with the sun again.

He'd ridden out at first light, secured the post and returned to the barn to take care of his horse. Only then had he gone to the little office in the back, confident that someone would have been there before him to put on a pot of coffee. He nearly whimpered with gratitude and desperation when he saw the half-full carafe on the warmer.

In fact, he was so focused on his need for caffeine that Caleb didn't see his father standing by the window until he spoke.

"Where the hell have you been for the past four days?"

Caleb took a moment to swallow a mouthful of coffee before he responded. "I told you—I had something to do."

"You didn't tell me that you'd be gone four days and neglect all the things you're supposed to take care of here," his father pointed out.

"It couldn't be helped," he said.

"Dammit, Caleb. You have responsibilities that don't just go away when you want to."

"I know, and I'm sorry but—"

"*Sorry* doesn't it cut it. We were vaccinating the stock and needed every pair of hands."

Having already apologized—and had the apology thrown back in his face, Caleb remained silent.

"Were you in New York?" His father wanted to know.

He nodded.

Dave shook his head. "You couldn't find a girlfriend a little closer to home?"

Irritated by his father's dismissive tone, Caleb shot back: "She's not my girlfriend. She's the woman I love and the mother of my unborn child."

The shouted words hung heavy in the room for a long minute before Dave responded. "You're telling me that Brielle's pregnant again?"

Caleb winced. "Damn—I promised her that I wouldn't say anything to anyone until she was past the first trimester."

His father's brows drew together. "It's your baby?"

"Yes, it's my baby," he confirmed.

"When? How?"

"We ran into each other in Vegas at the end of the summer," he explained.

"It must have been more than a run-in if she's pregnant," Dave remarked dryly.

Thinking back on that weekend, Caleb couldn't prevent the smile that curved his lips. "Well, it started with a run-in," he said. "And led to something more."

"*Something more* being unprotected sex?" his father guessed, frowning his disapproval.

"Are you really going to go there with me?"

"Yes, because I'm still your father," Dave said.

"And she's still my wife," Caleb told him.

His father frowned. "What are you talking about?"

"We never got a divorce. I never wanted a divorce."

"Things were a lot simpler when Gilmores and Blakes stayed on opposite sides of Crooked Creek," Dave grumbled.

"I love Brielle," Caleb said. "I've always loved her. And we both want this baby."

His father's sigh was more resigned than unhappy. "Then I'll say congratulations, Daddy."

Hearing the word aloud made his heart swell inside his chest. "Just say it quietly, Grandpa," he cautioned. "Brie will have my head if her parents hear about the baby at The Daily Grind."

When her sister called Tuesday night, Brie was grateful for the distraction. Since she'd said goodbye to Caleb two days earlier, she'd spent far too much time thinking about him, twenty-five hundred miles away, and wondering if they were fooling themselves by imagining there was a way to bridge what was more than a physical distance between them.

"What's up?" she asked, when her sister's face appeared on the screen.

Happiness radiated from Regan's smile. "Poppy rolled over," she said proudly.

"That's great," Brie replied, because the excitement in her sister's voice suggested the news was cause for celebration. "But wasn't she doing that last week?"

"Front to back," her sister confirmed. "But now she's also rolling back to front."

"Oh."

"She was on her baby quilt on the floor and rolled from one side all the way to the other—where she bumped into her sister. Piper was not impressed."

Brie laughed. "What are they doing now?"

"Sleeping," Regan said. "It's the only time I can take my eyes off them for a second."

"I want to see them," she said. "I bet they're getting so big."

"Still small for five months, but that's not unusual with twins."

Brie could tell that her sister was moving now, taking her phone into the girls' room to accede to their aunt's request. Regan passed the camera over one crib, then the next.

"Oh, they are *so* sweet. And I miss them *so* much," Brie whispered to ensure she didn't wake her adorable nieces.

"We miss you, too," Regan whispered back, as she tiptoed out of the room again.

"So other than the girls' honing their motor skills, what's going on?" Brie wanted to know.

"Well, since you asked… When I was at The Daily Grind yesterday, I heard that Caleb Gilmore recently returned from a trip to New York City."

"That's…interesting," she said. And surprising, because for the past seven years, her sister had mostly honored Brie's unspoken request not to hear his name mentioned. "But since when do you pay any attention to gossip at The Daily Grind?"

"When I think it might have something to do with you," her sister said.

"You think Caleb came to New York to see me?"

"Did he?" Regan asked, knowing Brie would have trouble skirting a direct question.

"Okay, yes," she finally said. "He was here to see me."

"Out of the blue, after seven years?"

"Not exactly out of the blue."

"I need more than that," her sister told her.

"Do you remember me telling you that I was in Vegas for Grace's birthday at the end of August?" Brie asked.

"Of course. And I remember giving you a hard time about being so close and not coming to see me," Regan said.

"Well, as it turns out, Caleb was in Vegas that weekend, too, and we…reconnected."

"You mean you slept with him," her sister guessed.

"We had a drink together, and then dinner and…yes," Brie admitted.

Regan looked worried. "And now you two are trying to make a long-distance relationship work?"

"We've got some things to figure out."

"Let me save you some time—long-distance relationships don't work," her sister said.

"I probably shouldn't have said anything," Brie acknowledged. "But I actually thought my sister might be supportive."

"I want you to be happy," Regan said. "I just don't know that Caleb Gilmore can make you happy."

"I've never been happy with anyone else," she confided.

Her sister sighed. "I stand by my concerns about long-distance relationships. So if you really want things to work with Caleb this time, you should come home and give it your best shot."

"You just want me to come home so I'm close enough to help with Piper and Poppy," she teased.

"I want you to come home because I've missed you," Regan said. "Because we've all missed you."

It was only after they'd said their goodbyes and ended the call that Brie realized she hadn't corrected her sister when Regan referred to Haven as "home." Usually Brie was quick to remind her friends and family that she lived in New York now, but maybe it was true that home is where the heart is…

And maybe her heart had always been with Caleb.

"There's still more than a week before Halloween and the kids are already bouncing off the walls," Brie complained to Caleb during one of their late-night conversations two weeks after his impulsive visit to New York.

He chuckled. "I imagine it's even worse after the thirty-first, when they're on a sugar high from eating all the candy they got trick-or-treating."

"You'd be right," she confirmed.

"How are things otherwise?" he asked.

"I had an appointment with my doctor yesterday."

Though her tone was casual, the mention of "doctor" was enough to bring back memories of Lily's frantic call and his own worry and panic. "Is everything okay?"

"It was just a routine checkup," she was quick to reassure him. "And yes, so far so good."

The knotted muscles in his stomach began to loosen. "That's great."

"The doctor scheduled an ultrasound—also routine," she hastened to add. "And maybe it's crazy to even mention this to you but, since it will be a first look at our baby, I thought I'd let you know in case you wanted to be there."

He didn't remind her that he was twenty-five hundred miles away or reference the cost of a flight halfway across the country or even point out that he'd already made the trip twice in the past six weeks, because of course he wanted to be there. Instead he asked, "When?"

"November sixth."

"I'll be there," he promised.

"Look at you," Grace teased, watching Brie turn chicken in a pan on the stove. "The doting wife preparing dinner for her husband."

"There are four chicken breasts here," Brie pointed out to her friend. "If you can refrain from making any more snarky comments, I might feed you and Lily, too."

Grace surveyed the ingredients on the counter. "Chicken Parisienne?" she guessed.

Brie nodded.

"I can refrain from snarky comments," her friend promised. "I can even slice the mushrooms, if you want."

"That would be great, thanks."

"What time is Caleb's flight getting in?"

"It was scheduled to arrive at 4:49," Brie told her. "But there was some kind of delay in Phoenix and now his plane isn't supposed to land until 8:16."

And although she knew the flight delay was completely out of his control, she was still disappointed. She'd been looking forward to this visit since he'd agreed to come to New York for the ultrasound and practically counting the hours since he'd sent her the original flight info.

"So why are you making dinner now?" Grace wondered.

"Because I'd already started before I thought to check the flight status. And because I didn't want you and Lily to starve waiting for him to get here."

"You don't need to worry about us," her friend said.

"I know. But it's rare for you to actually be home in time for dinner and I wanted to make a nice meal for all of us, to thank you guys for being so supportive about the baby."

"Are you kidding? We're thrilled to be honorary aunts—and secretly competing for the role of godmother."

"Yeah, covert ops are not really your strong suit," Brie noted dryly.

"But I'll be a kickass godmother," Grace promised.

Brie laughed as she mixed the wine into the chicken broth.

"I'm sorry I'm late," Caleb said, when he finally showed up at nearly eleven o'clock.

"It's not your fault your flight was delayed."

For more than five hours.

"Did they say what the problem was?" she asked.

"There was some vague mention of a mechanical issue that they promised would be a quick fix, but apparently it wasn't, because they ended up bringing in another plane."

"You must be starving," she said.

But he shook his head. "I ate at the airport, since I didn't have anything else to do."

Which made sense, and she shouldn't be disappointed because he wasn't hungry for the meal she'd cooked. The chicken was probably dry now, anyway.

"Tired?" she asked.

He nodded.

"Let's go to bed."

The words were music to Caleb's ears.

Because more than he wanted to collapse on top of a mattress, he wanted to hold her in his arms. Yes, the delays at the airport had been frustrating, because there was nothing he hated more than sitting around and twiddling his thumbs.

Several other passengers, informed of the delay, had pulled out their electronic devices to carry on with business as usual. A rancher couldn't fix fence with his smartphone or water his cows remotely, but there were enough other hands at the Circle G to ensure all the chores were covered in his absence.

His bigger concern and focus had been Brielle. Because every hour that he was stuck on the ground in Phoenix was another hour that he wasn't with her.

But now, finally, he was here.

And she was in his arms.

And the five-hour delay was forgotten.

Brie woke up before her alarm and reached out to shut it off so it wouldn't disturb Caleb.

They'd snuck around often enough when they were younger, but the night in Vegas was the first that they'd actually slept together. Well, aside from the one time they'd fallen asleep after making love in the cabin—then awakened in a panic when they realized they'd fallen asleep. Thankfully, their nap had been of short duration, and they'd hastily dressed and returned to their respective homes before anyone discovered they were missing or suspected they were together.

So when he shared her bed on his last visit, Brie had been happy to discover that while he tended to gravitate toward the center of the mattress, he didn't shove her out of the way but held her close. An added bonus was that she didn't need any covers, because his body gave off so much heat she would never feel cold.

Snuggled in his arms now, she realized how empty her life had been without him in it. So why wasn't she already making plans to move back to Haven? Did her job and her friends in New York really mean more to her than the opportunity to share the joys and responsibilities of parenthood with her baby's father? Or was it fear of loving him again—and risking her heart again— that made her wary of leaving the comforting embrace of the friends who'd helped her put the broken pieces back together?

Because lingering in bed wasn't giving her the answers to any of these questions, she pushed her worries aside and slid out of bed.

Since the ultrasound wasn't scheduled until the afternoon and Brie had already taken several personal days, she went to school in the morning, promising Caleb that she'd be back by noon. And since that was lunch time, he decided to surprise her by preparing the meal. Not that he planned anything fancy, but he figured he could throw some sandwiches together—so long as there was more than one slice of bread in the cupboard.

After confirming there was half a loaf, he looked in the fridge to see what other ingredients he might have to work with—and found a baking pan with two chicken breasts in some kind of mushroom sauce. A much more appealing option than sandwiches, he decided. And crossing his fingers that he wouldn't be stealing anyone's dinner, he put the pan in the oven.

"You found the chicken," she noted as he dished it up alongside the leftover rice.

"You cooked this for me," he realized. "For dinner last night."

"You were coming all this way—I figured the least I could do was feed you."

"And then I wasn't hungry."

"You had a long, crappy day," she acknowledged.

"And crappy airport food for dinner," he told her. "This is much better."

"I'm glad you like it."

"So I guess you really have learned to cook," he teased, when they were on their way to the prenatal clinic.

"Well enough that I don't starve," she told him.

"I think you're being modest."

"Not really," she said. "The chicken Parisienne is one of my favorite recipes because it always turns out well. Even overcooked, the sauce prevents it from tasting too dry."

"What else do you make?"

"Penne with sausage and peppers, and a pretty decent maple-glazed pork roast."

"Mmm, they all sound good," he said. "Although as a cattle rancher, I couldn't help but notice that none of those meals was beef."

She laughed softly. "I like a nice juicy steak as much as the next person. I just prefer to order it off a menu in a restaurant."

"We'll have to try to sneak away to The Home Station when you're in Haven at Thanksgiving," he said.

"The Circle G is the exclusive supplier of beef for their menu."

"If we're serious about having Thanksgiving with both my family and yours, that's probably more food than I want to eat over one weekend."

"But you're eating for two," he reminded her.

"My doctor said that's a fallacy," she admitted, pouting just a little. "She also said that while the occasional bowl of ice cream is okay, what I really need to be eating more of is fruits and vegetables."

"Clearly, your doctor's a spoilsport," he noted, as they entered the clinic.

She smiled at his response and handed her insurance card to the receptionist.

"Are you nervous?" he asked, as she sat down beside him in the waiting area.

"A little," she said. "More excited, though, to finally see our baby."

"Do you really think we're going to be able to see much today?"

"That's why we're here," she reminded him. "Why do you sound so skeptical?"

"Because nobody looking at you would even suspect you're pregnant," he pointed out.

"They'd suspect it if they heard me throwing up."

"You've had morning sickness?" He recalled her mentioning some nausea, but feeling sick wasn't the same thing as being sick.

"Occasionally," she said. "And not always in the morning."

"Why am I only hearing about this now?"

"There was no reason for you to know. Nothing you could do."

Unfortunately, that was true. He couldn't even be there to offer her saltine crackers or flat ginger ale, or to hold her hair back while she leaned over the toilet.

"I hate that you're going through this on your own," he told her.

"Are you kidding? I'm hardly ever alone—Grace and Lily are driving me insane with their hovering."

"But it should be me," he insisted. "I'm the father."

"You can hover till your heart's content over the next few days," she promised.

Her teasing remark was no consolation to him, because a few days here and there couldn't begin to make up for the weeks and months that they were apart.

"We really need to figure out this distance thing," he said.

"What's to figure out?" she asked, a little defensively.

He didn't want to upset her, but they needed to face facts. "We can't raise this baby together if we're living twenty-five hundred miles apart."

"We've still got more than six months until the baby's due."

"Which seems like a long time now," he noted. "But we can't keep putting off these conversations."

Her silence suggested otherwise.

"Do you realize that it took three connections and fourteen hours for me to get here yesterday?"

"I know it's not a quick or easy trip," she acknowledged. "That's why I told you that you didn't have to come."

"I wanted to be here with you," he said. "But the delays made me realize that if I'm in Nevada and you're in New York when you go into labor, I won't get here in time for the birth."

"Do you want me to promise to wait for you? Because I'm not sure that's a promise I'd be able to keep."

"I know," he admitted. "So I guess I'd better not be twenty-five hundred miles away when you go into labor."

Chapter Thirteen

They didn't wait much longer before Brielle was called into an exam room. As instructed by the technician, she climbed onto the table, pushed the waistband of her leggings down to her hips and pulled her shirt up to the bottom of her ribcage. Caleb took a seat on the stool behind her as the tech squirted warm gel on the expectant mom's belly and spread it around with a transducer that would send out and receive sound waves, translating them into an image on the screen.

Brie clung to Caleb's hand, but her gaze remained fixed on the monitor.

"There's your baby," the tech said, as the image came into focus.

"Wow," Caleb said, his tone reverent as he leaned forward for a closer look.

Brie remained silent, her throat clogged with emotion.

The tech moved the mouse around, taking measurements of their baby. Then she tapped a few more times, and suddenly the rhythm of the baby's heartbeat was displayed on the bottom of the screen, with each spike that indicated a beat accompanied by deep 'woop' sound.

Brie turned her head to look at Caleb then, and through the tears that filled her eyes, she saw that his were wet, too.

They'd never had a chance to see their first baby. She'd

made a doctor's appointment as soon as they got back from Vegas, but she'd miscarried before the scheduled visit. She never even knew if the baby she'd lost was a boy or a girl.

Of course, at just under ten weeks, it was still too early to tell the sex of this one, but at least they could be sure their baby was real. There was no longer any doubt that a tiny person was growing inside her womb—a new life that she and Caleb had created together.

They left the clinic half an hour later not only with that sense of awe and wonder but photographic evidence of their baby.

And snuggled in Caleb's arms later that night, Brie knew that nothing mattered as much as sharing every joy of parenthood with the father of her child—the only man she'd ever loved.

Caleb fell asleep to the soft, even sounds of Brielle's breathing—and woke up to the blaring of a guitar riff.

"What the—" He jolted upright, his brain scrambling to decipher what he was hearing.

Then the music cut off, and he heard Brie say, "Hello?"

Obviously what he'd heard was another customized ringtone on her cell phone.

He dropped his head back onto the pillow and squinted at the glowing numbers on the clock beside the bed.

4:17.

"Who the hell is calling at four o'clock in the morning?" he grumbled.

She touched her fingertips to his lips, silencing him.

"Oh, Spencer, that's wonderful news," she said, answering his question. "How are they?"

Caleb closed his eyes as she continued to talk quietly. He slid an arm around her, tucking her close to his body, and nearly fell asleep again while she finished up her conversation.

"Boy or girl?" he asked, when she'd set her phone aside.

"An almost ten-pound baby boy they're calling Owen. Spencer has yet to break the news to Dani."

"She wanted a sister," he noted, recalling his brief conversation with the little girl at the grocery store.

"Well, of course." Brie rolled over so that she was facing him, and even in the darkness he could see the smile playing at the corners of her mouth. "Because boys are yucky."

He raised his brows. "Do you think so?"

"Not anymore," she said, and brushed a soft kiss on his lips. "But when I was a five-year-old girl, I probably did."

"So if we had a boy…you'd be okay with that?"

"I'd be thrilled," she told him. "I know it's cliché, but I really don't care if we have a boy or a girl—I just want our baby to be healthy."

That was his number one concern as well.

Number two was figuring out how to give their baby a real family when his or her parents were living twenty-five hundred miles apart.

Caleb was already in the kitchen with a cup of coffee by his elbow and his phone in hand when Brie made her way downstairs the following morning.

"Going somewhere?" she asked, noting the open map app.

"I'm figuring out the best route to the east end of Long Island," he told her.

She selected a coffee pod and positioned her mug under the spout. "Why do you want to go all the way out there?"

"Because I have a job interview this afternoon."

"What kind of job?" she asked, surprised.

"Working as a ranch hand at a cooperative cattle operation."

She sipped her coffee as she considered this information.

"I did a lot of thinking about what you said the last time I was here, and I realized you were right. I never should have assumed that you'd want to come back to Haven just because you're having my baby. If we're going to make our marriage work, we need to be willing to compromise."

"You'd really move to New York?"

"Well, setting up house halfway between Brooklyn and Haven doesn't seem to be a viable solution," he pointed out.

"But you love working at the Circle G."

"And I'd hate being a long-distance dad that my son or daughter only sees a couple times a year," he said.

Brie didn't want that, either, but she couldn't imagine that he'd ever be happy so far away from his family or working on a ranch that wasn't his own. The fact that he was even contemplating such a scenario made her wonder if she wasn't being a little bit unfair, asking him to leave everything that was comfortable and familiar just because she'd chosen to do so seven years earlier.

And yes, she felt a little bit guilty that he seemed willing to make such a sacrifice for their future together. *For her.* Because she'd talked about wanting to work things out and then dug in her heels when he'd mentioned the possibility of her moving back to Haven.

Uncomfortable with the introspection, she dragged her attention back to the present to ask, "What time's your interview?"

"Two o'clock."

"You do realize it can take more than three hours to get to Long Island using public transportation?"

"I do now," he said. "I was trying to put together all the schedules and connections when Grace dropped a set of keys on the table and told me to take her car."

Because mass transit was so easy and efficient for her

daily travels, Brie sometimes forgot that her friend owned
a vehicle—and paid four hundred dollars a month to keep
it in a parking garage two streets over. "But did she tell
you where to find her car?"

"She gave me the address of the garage, the number of
her parking space and her license plate," he confirmed.

"Then I guess you're all set."

He nodded. "But I probably won't be here when you
get home today."

"Actually, I'm going to be late tonight," she told him.
"It's our fall open house, so I'll be at the school until six.
You're welcome to come by, when you get back."

"I'll do that," he promised.

He made it, but not with a lot of time to spare.

By the time he'd finished his interview and toured
the facilities, he was heading back to Brooklyn in rush
hour. Not that the earlier drive had been without delays,
but the midday traffic hadn't prepared him for the snarl
and congestion he encountered on the same route a few
hours later.

He tried to focus on the positive as he parked Grace's
car in its designated spot. He was confident that the interview had gone well, and he'd enjoyed the tour of the
facility. But it was a hell of a commute from Brooklyn
to Long Island and not one he could imagine looking
forward to every day. On the other hand, ninety minutes of driving added to each morning and night so that
he could spend those nights with Brie and their child?
Totally worth it.

Of course, that assumed they'd find a place they liked
and could afford in Brooklyn. Or maybe Brie would be
willing to move a little farther away from her job to lessen
his commute. But then they'd both be spending more time
away from home and their child.

And until he had a job offer, all those questions and

concerns were moot. So he pushed them to the back of his mind and walked the short distance to Briarwood Academy.

It had been a long time since he was in kindergarten, but he didn't think his classroom had looked anything like this bright and spacious room with the students' artwork prominently displayed on the walls. His teacher had definitely not looked anything like Miss Brie, as she was identified on the nameplate on the door.

Venturing into the room, he saw that there were bins of toys and building blocks and musical instruments on shelving units below the windows, a "Reading Corner" with colorful pillows on the carpet, and a "Discovery Center" with water and sand, rocks and shells. Folders were set out on a round table, each neatly labeled with a child's name: Jayden, Bayleigh, Aeryn, Kalvyn and Peyton, making him wonder if there'd been a sale on the letter *y* the year all these kids were born.

There were several people—adults and kids—milling around in the classroom, so it took him a minute to find her. She spotted him at the same time, and her smile widened as she waved him over.

"I was beginning to think you might not make it," she said.

"Traffic."

The man she'd been talking to nodded his understanding. Of course, anyone who'd ever driven in the city could probably commiserate on the subject.

She quickly made the introductions, then excused herself as a little girl with red pigtails dragged her away to meet her parents.

"Do you have a student in Brie's class?" Caleb asked the man who'd been introduced as Marcus Crawford.

"Not this year," the parent replied. "But she taught my son MJ last year."

"You took her to the Yankees game," Caleb realized.

"She told you about that?"

"Of course. We don't have any secrets from one another."

Comprehension slowly dawned in the other man's eyes. "You and Brie are...dating?"

"Actually, we're married," Caleb said, as his wife rejoined them.

"I hadn't heard the news," Marcus said, directing his comment to Brie. "When did this happen?"

She sent Caleb a look that warned he would answer to her later but curved her lips into a smile. "It was a quick trip to Vegas."

"Well, congratulations to both of you."

"Thank you," Caleb said.

Brie managed another smile and a nod.

The few lingering visitors made their way to the door a short while later, and Brie and Caleb exited with them. But she waited until they were out of earshot of her colleagues before she turned to him and said, "You can't go around telling people that we're married."

"Why not? It's the truth."

"Because it could get back to my principal," she said. "Although it would probably be better for her to find out that I'm married before she hears I'm going to have a baby, so I'm not in violation of the morals clause in my contract."

"Are you suggesting that she could fire you for being pregnant?" he asked incredulously.

"It's a private school," she reminded him. "As role models for the students, teachers are expected to uphold certain standards of behavior. An unmarried teacher having a baby would not meet that standard."

"Then I guess it's good that I made an honest woman of you," he said.

Brie responded to that with a roll of her eyes.

"Of course, your principal might not believe you're married if you don't have a ring on your finger."

"You don't have one on yours, either," she pointed out.

"She can't fire me."

"Speaking of firing—or hiring," she said. "Tell me about your day. How did the interview go?"

"I think it went well. So long as they don't call anyone at the Circle G for a reference."

"I guess you didn't tell your father you were looking for a job in New York?"

"I didn't realize that I was until I saw the posting," he admitted. "I also didn't realize how long the commute would be from Brooklyn to Long Island."

"Are you seriously considering a move to New York?" she asked, not convinced his search for a job wasn't anything more than an elaborate attempt to manipulate her.

He turned to face her, his gaze steady and true. "I'd move to Timbuktu, if you were there."

She sighed. "I know that should make me happy, but I want you to be happy, too, and I can't imagine that happening here."

"Being with you makes me happy," he assured her.

"What if you only *think* being with me makes you happy?" she asked worriedly.

"I'm not sure I understand the question," he admitted.

"We don't know each other half as well now as we did seven years ago," she pointed out to him.

He slid his arms around her and pulled her close. "Do you really think we've changed that much?"

"I know we have." Though the way her body responded to his nearness was one thing that hadn't changed.

"I can't speak for you," he said. "But I know I still want the same thing I've always wanted."

"A wife and a home on the Circle G?" she guessed.

He shook his head. "You."

It was Tuesday night and Caleb's cupboard was pretty close to being bare. His freezer, too. Of course, he'd missed his usual shopping day when he was out of town, but the lack of food was a price he was willing to pay for the pleasure of spending the weekend in New York with Brielle—and being there for her ultrasound.

Now he had a picture of their baby in his wallet and was chomping at the bit to shout the news of her pregnancy far and wide. But they'd agreed to wait until she was home for Thanksgiving—and into her second trimester—so they could make the announcement to their families together.

Of course, he'd slipped up already and told his father, but Dave had promised to keep the news a secret until the expectant parents were ready to share. Caleb was grateful for his discretion and optimistic that his father's experience with Valerie and Ashley meant he'd be supportive of whatever choices Caleb and Brielle made for their future together.

But for now, he was on his own and without anything for dinner, so he made a quick trip into town to pick up some groceries and a pizza.

While his pie was cooking, he watched Jo roll out dough, spread sauce, sprinkle cheese and add toppings. But the tinkle of the bell over the door had him automatically turning to see who'd entered the restaurant—and brought him face-to-face with Spencer Channing.

Brielle's brother nodded, an acknowledgement more than a greeting.

"I hear congratulations are in order," Caleb said.

"Thanks." The proud father's grin confirmed that his happiness exceeded his hostility toward anyone named Gilmore.

But only temporarily, Caleb realized, when the grin faded and Spencer said: "You must have good ears to have heard the news when you were out of town all weekend."

"Keeping tabs on me?" he asked, amused.

"Looking out for my little sister," the other man clarified.

"Your little sister's a big girl."

The former rodeo star drew himself to his full height and squared his shoulders, as if to prove that he was bigger.

Bigger, but still about an inch shorter than Caleb, though he didn't straighten to prove it. He had no intention of getting into a contest with Brie's brother because he knew that even if he won, he'd lose.

"How's that half-cheese and half-pepperoni?"

Though Jo called out the question to the teenager working the ovens, she pinned her customers with a narrow-eyed stare that warned she wouldn't tolerate any trouble in her place of business.

"Coming out now," the teen replied, sliding the wooden paddle under the hot pie, then dropping it into an open box.

Jo picked up a cutter and quickly sliced the round into eight pieces, then folded the top of the box into the bottom.

Spencer reached into his back pocket for his wallet, but Jo waved him away. "Congrats on the new baby."

"Thanks," he said again, and exited without another word to Caleb.

"Friendly guy," he remarked dryly.

Jo shook her head as she sliced Caleb's bacon, mushroom and pepperoni pie that had just come out of the oven. "Always stirring the pot, aren't you?"

"I was trying to play nice," he said.

"You've been playing with his sister," Jo pointed out.

"And you've been listening to gossip," he chided.

"Not much else to do in this town," she reminded him.

Brie was counting down the days to Thanksgiving and her trip to Haven when she and Caleb would finally share their joyful news. The expectant parents knew a baby wouldn't magically erase the conflict between the

Blakes and the Gilmores, but they hoped their friends and relatives could at least be happy for them.

"Have you arranged for someone to pick you up from the airport?" Margaret asked, during their usual Sunday night FaceTime call before the holiday.

"I have," Brie confirmed. She'd also decided to take another personal day and leave New York on Wednesday to ensure that any delays wouldn't make her late for the midday meal at Miners' Pass.

After much discussion, she and Caleb had agreed that he'd go with her to her parents' house for lunch, after which they'd head over to his dad's place for dinner. Though Thanksgiving was generally a feast shared with family and friends, there was a possibility their announcement would generate more fireworks than a Fourth of July celebration.

"I'll make sure Greta has your room ready," Margaret told her daughter.

"That isn't necessary," Brie said.

"Don't be silly—it's her job."

"I mean it's not necessary because I won't be staying at Miners' Pass."

"Why not?" Her mother wanted to know. "We have a lot more space than Regan and Connor—especially now that the twins have moved into their own room."

"I'm not staying with Regan, either."

Margaret frowned. "You're not planning on being all the way out at Crooked Creek with Kenzie and Spencer?"

"No," she agreed. "I'm planning to be all the way out at the Circle G. With Caleb."

"Oh, Brie." Her mother shook her head despairingly. "You haven't hooked up with him again, have you?"

"As it turns out, we've always been hooked up," Brie said. "Caleb and I are still married."

"I don't understand… You signed the divorce papers before you went to New York."

"I did," Brie confirmed. "But Caleb never did."

"Ben!" Margaret called out, summoning her husband.

"What is it?" he asked. "Oh, Brie," he said, when he saw her face on the screen. "How are you, honey?"

"She's *married,*" Margaret interjected in response to his question.

"What? You eloped again?"

"No," Brie spoke up. "Of course not."

"Apparently she's still married to Caleb Gilmore," Margaret explained. "Because he didn't sign the divorce papers."

"Is he demanding some kind of financial settlement?" Ben asked. "Does he want money?"

"No," she said again, rolling her eyes. "Caleb's not after my money."

"Maybe she can get an annulment," Margaret suggested, speaking to her husband as if their daughter's wishes weren't a factor to be taken into consideration. Because Brie's wishes had never been of any concern.

She responded anyway, determined to be heard this time. "I don't want an annulment."

"Well, you can't want to be married to him," her mother insisted.

"Actually, I can and I do," she said. "And before you say anything else, you should know that I'm only coming for dinner on Thanksgiving if my husband is invited, too."

Chapter Fourteen

"I can't believe you gave them an ultimatum," Caleb said, when Brie recounted the conversation to him later that night.

"I realized that if I wanted them to respect me as an adult, dammit—I had to show them that I was willing to stand by my choices."

"You might have asked if I was willing to stand by your choices." His teasing remark earned him a small smile, but he could tell that she was still upset about the friction with her parents.

"You can sit beside me at the table," she said. "And be happy that Celeste is doing the cooking."

"Did you confirm what time the meal will be served?"

"It's always at one o'clock."

"So we'll have lunch with your family and dinner with mine and run screaming into the night afterward," he said. "Although you won't be the only Blake at the Gilmore table this year."

"Ashley's going to be there?" she guessed.

"And Valerie."

"It's still weird to think that my cousin is your half sister."

"That doesn't mean that we're related," he assured her. "Except by marriage, I mean."

"Lucky for us," she noted.

"And our baby."

She smiled again, as she always did when thinking about their child. And because she was happy at the thought of seeing her baby's daddy in person very soon.

"You're getting an early start on your packing," Lily noted, when she walked by Brie's room a short while later and saw the suitcase on her bed.

She gestured to the laundry basket on her bed. "It doesn't make sense to put my clothes in a dresser today only to take them out again two days later."

Lily nodded. "I understand. It's all about efficiency and has nothing to do with the fact that you're excited to spend the holiday with your sexy cowboy."

"Well, I didn't say I wasn't looking forward to seeing Caleb," she pointed out.

Her friend was chuckling as Grace entered the room with a pair of jeans in her hands. "You left these hanging in the laundry room, and I thought you might want them for your trip."

Brie added them to her suitcase, then took them out again. "I can barely do the button up now. There's no way they'll stay fastened after a turkey dinner."

"Or two turkey dinners," her friend teased.

"Yeah," she sighed, silently acknowledging that wardrobe options were the least of her worries.

"Having second thoughts about a meal with his family?" Lily guessed.

"More about my family," she admitted. "Because if that doesn't go well, we might not make it back to the Circle G."

"It's going to be fine," Lily said soothingly.

"Easy for you to say—you're going to be in Connecticut for the holiday."

"And you're going to be cuddling Spencer and Kenzie's new baby," Grace said, because she knew that image would soothe her friend's worries.

"And Jason and Alyssa's baby, too," Lily added, naming Brie's other brother and sister-in-law.

"What? When did that happen?" Grace asked.

"Just a few hours ago," Brie said.

"And I'm only hearing about this now?"

"You only got home a short while ago."

"A little girl. Seven pounds ten ounces." Lily, who had been home when Brie got the call, filled in the details for their roommate. "After only four hours of labor."

Grace looked at Brie. "Is that true?"

She nodded. "Jason said her water broke at 12:35, just after they finished having lunch, and Lucy was born at 4:38."

"Impressive," Grace said. "But you do know that's not normal, right?"

"I know," she confirmed. "Regan was in labor twenty-two hours with the twins and Kenzie for fifteen with Owen." Then she frowned.

"What's wrong?" Lily asked.

"Nothing, really. I was just thinking about something Caleb said when he came to New York for the ultrasound.

"I mean, I don't want to be one of those women who suffers with contractions for days before giving birth, but even fifteen hours probably isn't long enough for Caleb to get here in time for our baby to be born. Anything less is definitely not."

"Do you really think you'll still be living here in May?" Grace asked gently.

Her brow furrowed as she glanced from one friend to the other. "Are you planning on kicking me out?"

"Of course not," Lily assured her.

"Unless we have to," Grace said.

"I don't understand. What happened to turning the upstairs office into a nursery?"

"What happened is that we realized we were being selfish," Lily said.

"I thought you were being supportive," she said, as she folded her favorite pink sweater into her suitcase.

"I know you're afraid of risking your heart again," Grace said. "But Caleb loves you. I don't think he ever stopped loving you."

"Then why, in the more than seven years that we were apart, did he never once come to New York to see me? To tell me how he felt? To fight for our relationship?"

"Stupid male pride," Grace guessed.

"Or maybe he did try to get in touch with you," Lily suggested. "But he didn't know where you were living or how to reach you."

Brie couldn't deny that was a valid point. "But if it had been important to him, he could have asked my sister to relay a message or forward a letter," she argued.

"And what if we hadn't connected in Las Vegas that weekend?" she wondered. "What if Joe had decided to get married a week earlier or a week later? Even a day earlier or later and our paths might never have crossed. How much longer would he have waited to tell me that we were still married?"

"Does that matter now?" Grace asked.

"I think it does," she said stubbornly.

"But you're the one who left," Lily pointed out. "Why would he chase after you?"

"To let me know that I was worth chasing after." She swiped at the tear that spilled onto her cheek.

"Oh, honey. You were eighteen years old. He was barely twenty," Grace reminded her. "You were both young and stupid—don't let those mistakes get in the way of your future together now."

"He loves you," Lily said, taking up the cause again. "After everything he's done over the past few months, you can't honestly doubt that."

Brie sighed. "I don't doubt that he loves me, I just don't

know that love is enough to overcome the animosity between our families."

"Love is everything," Lily insisted. "And just as important as the fact that he loves you is that you obviously love him, too.

"And you can say whatever you want about your life being here, but everyone in this room knows that your heart is in Haven."

She closed the lid of her suitcase and zipped it up.

"You've always been meticulous about details," Grace noted. "You check and double-check to ensure you've crossed every t and dotted every i."

"Are we on a new topic now?" Brie wondered aloud.

"No," Grace said. "We're pointing out that you left the divorce papers with Caleb but never followed up to make sure he signed them."

"And in all of the seven years that came after, you never once checked to be sure that the thread you'd left dangling had been tied off," Lily added.

"Your point?" Brie asked wearily.

"Maybe you never really wanted the divorce," Grace suggested.

"Because you never stopped loving him," Lily said again.

As promised, Caleb was at the airport to pick Brie up when she arrived. And although it was barely two o'clock in the afternoon, she struggled to keep her eyes open as the Jeep turned onto the highway to begin the hour-long journey to Haven. When she lifted a hand to stifle yet another yawn after they'd been on the road only a few minutes, she silently cursed her friends and the echo of their words that had caused her to toss and turn during the past few nights.

Maybe you never really wanted the divorce.
Because you never stopped loving him.

She yawned again, and Caleb assured her that he didn't mind if she closed her eyes. So she did, and she was asleep before they were ten miles outside Elko. She didn't wake up again until she heard a click when Caleb released the clasp of her seat belt.

He helped her out of the Jeep, then went to retrieve her suitcase from the back. And she stood for a long moment, just staring at the gorgeous two-story stone-and-timber house with a wide porch wrapped around three sides and huge windows that afforded sweeping views of the gorgeous landscape.

"Caleb, this is...wow."

He grinned, obviously pleased with her reaction. "I'd hoped you'd like it."

She followed him to the door, eager and a little apprehensive, too. Because she knew this was what he'd always wanted—his own house on the Circle G. And now that he finally had it, was he really willing to leave it all to be with her?

The front door opened into a wide foyer with natural stone tiles on the floor and textured walls. She kicked off her shoes to explore the rest of the house. The kitchen did not disappoint. The maple cabinets, granite counters and high-end appliances created a space that would entice even the most reluctant cook. The living room boasted a leather sectional facing the enormous flat-screen TV over a river rock fireplace flanked by floor-to-ceiling windows that looked out toward the Silver Ridge Mountains in the distance. Off the living room was an office, sparsely decorated with a desk and chair and one short bookcase. There was also what she assumed was a dining room, because it had a ceiling-mounted fixture that seemed designed to cast light over a long table, though the room was currently devoid of furniture.

"Did somebody come in and steal half your stuff while you were out?" she asked.

"Ha ha," he said. "I've got everything I need for right now."

"Unless you want to host a dinner party."

"Upstairs is the master bedroom and bath," he said, choosing to ignore her teasing comment as he carried her suitcase up the second level. "Plus a second bathroom and three more bedrooms. However, as those are currently empty, you're going to have to bunk with me."

She sighed, feigning disappointment. "If I must."

Then she followed him into the master bedroom, and her jaw dropped as she realized he might have blown his entire furniture budget on this room. Possibly on the king-size mission-style platform bed alone.

"Can I go to bed now?" she asked. And without waiting for a response, she fell face-first onto the luxuriously thick slate-blue comforter and let out a blissful sigh.

Caleb chuckled and swatted her gently on the butt. "Get up."

"But I'm tired," she protested.

"You shouldn't be—you slept the whole way from the airport."

"Not the whole way," she denied, still refusing to move.

"Okay," he relented. "You stay here and rest. I'm going to get myself a bowl of ice cream."

She lifted her head. "Ice cream?"

"You can have a nap now and ice cream later—if there's any left."

She pushed herself up off the bed. "I'm not taking any chances."

She needn't have worried. There were four different flavors in his freezer. She opted for a scoop of each of cherry chocolate chunk, chocolate chip and rocky road. He had two scoops of chocolate.

She teased him about eating dessert before dinner, but he insisted the ice cream was a pre-dinner snack, because dessert was, by definition, served at the end of a meal. They'd just finished their snack/dessert when a brisk knock sounded on the front door.

While Caleb went to see who was there, Brie put their bowls and spoons in the dishwasher. Then, drawn by the sound of voices in the foyer as much as her own curiosity, she peeked down the hall.

And immediately recognized Caleb's grandfather.

Born and raised on the Circle G, Jack Gilmore looked every one of his eighty-four years, with deep lines etched into his tanned face and slightly bowed legs that attested to a lifetime in the saddle. But his body was still trim, his hair thick beneath the brim of his Resistol and his mind as sharp as a tack.

"Company?" The old man snorted, obviously in response to something his grandson had said. "You're too ornery for anyone to come all the way out here to visit with you."

Brie decided that was the perfect cue to announce her presence. "Hello, Mr. Gilmore."

Jack snatched his hat off his head. "Brielle. When did you get back into town?"

She glanced at her watch. "About an hour ago."

The old man's bushy eyebrows lifted. "Your parents know you're here?"

"They do," she confirmed.

Jack's gaze shifted to Caleb again, his expression worried. "Well, your grandmother wanted me to invite you to dinner tonight, so I'm extending the invitation to both of you."

"Thanks," Caleb said. "But we planned a quiet evening to brace ourselves for the chaos tomorrow."

"You've still gotta eat," his grandfather pointed out. "And it's pot roast on the menu tonight."

Caleb looked at Brie.

"Sounds good to me," she said.

Jack smiled. "I'll tell Evelyn to set the table for four. Dinner will be ready at six."

"We'll be there," Brie said. "Thank you."

"Are you sure you want to do this?" Caleb asked, as they drove along the access road that bordered the north pasture toward his grandparents' house.

"How could I resist the pot roast that you've told me, a dozen times, is the best thing ever?"

He reached across the console to take her hand and link their fingers together. "Tonight was supposed to be our time," he reminded her.

"The calm before the storm?"

"Something like that," he admitted.

"Maybe everyone will be happy for us," she said, though the hopeful words were contradicted by her doubtful tone.

"And if they're not, who cares? All that matters is that we're happy."

Brie knew he was right. And that as long as she was with Caleb, she would be happy.

She wasn't even really nervous about sharing a meal with his grandparents. Because although she wasn't well acquainted with Jack and Evelyn Gilmore, they'd always been pleasant to her. Even before their encounter at the movies when she and Caleb were both still in high school.

Fast Five had finally come to town and Caleb had convinced her that a dark movie theater was the perfect place for their first official date, because they wanted to be together but not be seen together. So they'd snuggled close in the back row, their hands dipping into the same box of popcorn, their mouths sipping from a shared straw. And for the two-and-a-half hours that started with previews of what was "coming soon" and ended with the final credits, Brie had felt as if everything was perfect in her world.

Then they'd walked out of the theater, hand in hand,

and almost literally bumped into his grandparents. She'd tried to untangle her fingers from his—because while most people knew that Brie and Caleb were friends, they'd been careful to hide their blossoming romance from their respective and disapproving families, which meant hiding it from everyone else in town for fear that word would get back to their them. But Caleb had held firm as he exchanged pleasantries with his grandparents, who happened to be there for the late showing of the same movie.

For the next several weeks, she'd been on tenterhooks, waiting for the day that her parents found out that she'd been at the theater with Caleb. But as far as she knew, Jack and Evelyn had kept their secret.

Still, she didn't know how they'd feel to discover that their grandson had taken up with "that Blake girl" again. But if Evelyn thought it strange that her grandson had invited Brielle to visit him at the ranch, she didn't say so. In fact, she wasn't anything but warm and welcoming when she greeted them at the door, and conversation flowed easily around the table during the shared meal.

"Everything was delicious," Brie said, as she began to load plates into the dishwasher.

"My pot roast has always been one of Caleb's favorites," Evelyn told her. "I'd be happy to share the recipe, if you want it."

"Thank you," she said. "And for letting me come to dinner tonight."

"You're welcome anytime," the other woman said.

Brie felt herself unexpectedly fighting back tears. "That's very kind…considering."

"Considering what?" Evelyn asked.

"The history between our families. And between me and Caleb."

"One of the most important lessons we can learn from history is not to repeat the mistakes of the past."

Brie felt her stomach tighten as she dropped the cutlery into the basket. "You don't think Caleb and I should be together?"

"That's not what I meant at all," Evelyn immediately assured her. "The mistake I was referring to was letting other people interfere in your relationship."

"Oh." She quietly exhaled a deep breath.

"And at the risk of sticking my nose in where it doesn't belong, I have to ask—when's the baby due?"

She bobbled the plate in her hands. "Caleb told you?"

His grandmother shook her head. "He didn't have to. I had three babies of my own. Five pregnancies…but only three babies."

Brie was surprised not only by the confession but by Evelyn's willingness to share it with her. "You had two miscarriages?"

"One between each of my babies."

"I'm sorry," Brie said sincerely.

"My doctor assured me it wasn't anything I'd done or didn't do, that sometimes babies aren't meant to be born. Of course, that didn't stop me from worrying, with each successive pregnancy, that something might go wrong again."

Brie nodded in understanding.

"It's a natural fear, especially for a woman who's been through it before," Evelyn said sympathetically. "But hopefully the joy and wonder of a new life are stronger than the fear."

"A little more so now that I've passed the first trimester," she said. "The baby's due the end of May."

"I guess that gives you some time, then, to work out the logistics of co-parenting twenty-five hundred miles apart."

Again, the older woman had surprised her. "You're not going to tell me that I should move back to Haven?"

"I'm trying not to interfere," Evelyn reminded her.

Which Brie appreciated. But Caleb's grandmother was

the first person who hadn't immediately tried to tell her what to do, as if Brie wasn't capable of making up her own mind. Except that with so many people expressing differing opinions, she was having trouble sorting through all the noise to know what was in her mind and her heart.

"What if I asked for your advice?"

"In that case, I'd find it hard to bite my tongue," Evelyn admitted. "But I really think this is something you and Caleb need to determine for yourselves."

Chapter Fifteen

Ben and Margaret's cook had prepared a feast for the midday Thanksgiving meal at Miners' Pass, and four leaves had been added to the dining room table to comfortably seat all the guests, including two high chairs for Piper and Poppy. Of course, Owen and Lucy were too young to sit up at the table, so they stayed in their respective baby carriers—within view of their doting parents.

Seven months earlier, at a slightly smaller family gathering, Kenzie and Spencer had announced they were expanding their family. That had been followed by Alyssa and Jason sharing the news that they were expecting, too—then hugs and tears and congratulations all around the table. Brie wasn't anticipating the same fanfare when she and Caleb revealed that they were going to have a baby, so she wasn't disappointed.

Her parents didn't call for champagne, perhaps because they remembered that pregnant women shouldn't have alcohol. But Ben did lift his wine glass in a toast to the expectant parents. He even sounded sincere when he said he was looking forward to future celebrations with more grandchildren around the table. True, that was a rather generic remark, but at least the sentiment was positive. And Margaret managed to curve her lips into some semblance of a smile before she downed the contents of her glass before quickly refilling it.

But Brie's sister and sisters-in-law offered warm and heartfelt congratulations—and teasingly promised to inundate her with all kinds of unwelcome advice and birthing horror stories over the next several months. Her brothers and brother-in-law took their cues from their wives, and though their best wishes were admittedly low-key, she was relieved that they didn't want to discuss the situation outside with Caleb.

Gramps said nothing at all, which was probably for the best. Because Brie knew she wouldn't ever forgive him if he again suggested her baby was a mistake.

They skipped out before dessert and coffee to be at the Circle G when dinner was served. Their news received a slightly warmer response at the Gilmore table. Dave seemed pleased that he had another grandchild on the way, Jack and Evelyn were sincerely thrilled, and Caleb's siblings said all the right things.

When Brie and Caleb finally got back to his place at the end of the day, she was relieved the big reveal was over—and exhausted. Of course, she knew it wasn't really over. The news of her pregnancy would spread like wildfire, and anyone and everyone she crossed paths with in town would have an opinion—and not hesitate to express it.

Thankfully, she had no need to go into town. Although on Friday, she borrowed Caleb's Jeep and drove over to Crooked Creek to visit with her friend/sister-in-law and steal some cuddles with Kenzie and Spencer's new baby. She'd been introduced to her nephew at Miners' Pass the day before, but there had been so many people around, she hadn't had much time to fuss over the new addition or catch up with her friend.

As soon as Kenzie finished nursing and burping the infant, she passed him to his aunt. Brie snuggled him close and breathed in the sweet scent of baby shampoo.

"He's absolutely perfect," she said, blinking away the moisture that filled her eyes.

"I think so," the new mom agreed proudly. "But I'm not exactly unbiased."

He was also a perfect blend of each of his parents, which made Brie wonder what her child would look like when he or she was born, what features he would inherit from Caleb's DNA and which would reflect her own. And though she knew the baby in her womb was still only the size of a peach, she was eager to hold him or her in her arms as she was holding Owen right now.

"He's got your mouth and chin and Spencer's eyes," she remarked.

"And Dani's nose," Kenzie added, as the little girl skipped into the room.

"He is almost as adorable as his big sister," Brie said, with a wink for her niece as Dani climbed up onto the sofa.

"You mean the big sister who's already tried to trade her baby brother away?" Kenzie asked.

Brie fought against the smile that tugged at her lips and turned to the little girl who'd snuggled up on her other side. "Did you try to swap babies with Aunt Alyssa?"

"I wanted a sister," Dani reminded the adults present.

"And you got a brother instead," Kenzie acknowledged.

Her daughter folded her arms over her chest and thrust her lower lip forward in a pout. "And Daddy said 'Suck it up, buttercup.'"

"That sounds like something my brother would say," Brie admitted.

The little girl tilted her head to gaze quizzically at Brie. "Who's your brother?" she asked, obviously struggling to wrap her head around the sibling relationships of the adults in her world.

"I have two brothers—your daddy and your uncle Jason, and one sister—Aunt Regan."

Dani took another minute to think about this revelation, then turned to her mom. "So I can still get a sister someday?" she asked hopefully.

"Maybe," Kenzie said cautiously. "Let's see how we make out with this baby before we think about another one."

Brie winked at her niece again. "I'm sure Dani will be such an awesome big sister to Owen that you'll definitely want another one. Or two."

Kenzie slid her friend a look that warned she wasn't amused. "But right now, I want Dani to get ready for her riding lesson," she said, eager to move away from the topic of future babies.

"Okay." Always happy for the opportunity to ride Daisy—the pony that had been a birthday gift from her grandparents—Dani hopped down off the sofa. But before she went to do her mother's bidding, she turned around and touched her lips to the sleeping baby's cheek.

The gesture was spontaneous and sweet, and Brie's eyes went misty again. "See? She's already an awesome big sister," she pointed out to her friend.

"She tried to trade her little brother away," Kenzie said again.

"I'm sure she's not the first sister to do so. Although I can understand why, after working so hard to bring this beautiful little guy into the world, you might not see the humor in the situation."

"Suffice it to say, I understand why they call it labor."

"Alyssa said something similar yesterday," Brie remarked, tongue-in-cheek.

"I can only imagine how much she suffered during those four hours of labor," Kenzie replied dryly. "Honestly, if I didn't love her so much, I'd hate her."

Brie laughed at that.

"And I know I said it yesterday, but congratulations," Kenzie said again. "I'm really happy for you and Caleb."

"Thanks," Brie replied, grateful not just for the words but also her friend's sincerity.

"So…does this mean you're back together?"

"The only thing I know for sure right now is that we're having a baby together."

"Together but twenty-five hundred miles apart?" her friend asked skeptically.

Brie sighed, but was saved from answering when Dani bounced into the room wearing adorable pink cowboy boots on her feet and a matching pink cowboy hat on her head.

"I'm ready!" she announced.

"Coat?" her mother prompted.

The little girl bounced out of the room again.

Since she knew that her grandfather would be in the barn preparing for Dani's riding lesson, Brie decided it was the perfect opportunity to corner him for a long-overdue conversation. So she returned the sleeping baby to his mother and went to find the cranky old man.

The barn door slid smoothly, making no sound as it opened and closed. But Gramps must have felt the change in temperature as a blast of cold air came in with her, because he turned to the door.

His brows knitted together in a frown. "What are you doin' here?"

"Mom thinks we should talk," she told him.

"Your mom has a lot of opinions," he remarked, as he guided Dani's pony out of its stall.

"Maybe she's right about this."

He shrugged. "You wanna talk? I'm listening."

"I want to have a conversation," she said. "That requires each of us to talk, and each of us to listen."

He finished saddling Daisy before turning around. "And then are you gonna forgive me?"

"If you want forgiveness, you might try apologizing," she suggested.

"You want me to apologize for havin' a heart attack?"

"No, I want you to apologize for using your heart attack to manipulate me when I was in a fragile emotional state."

"I only ever wanted what's best for you."

"That doesn't sound like an apology to me," she noted.

He sighed heavily. "I don't like the way things have been—this distance between us."

She heard the weariness in his tone, and the sincerity, but she refused to be manipulated again. "Still not an apology."

He huffed out a breath. "I'm not gonna apologize for believin' you could do better than a thievin' Gilmore."

Not that Caleb had ever stolen anything—other than her heart—but to her grandfather, all the Gilmores were thieves because they'd taken the best land for their cattle, leaving the Blakes to struggle before gold and silver were discovered in their hills.

"I was in love with Caleb," she told him now.

"You were eighteen," he said dismissively. "You didn't know what love was."

"Yes, we were young," she agreed. "And yes, getting pregnant was irresponsible and rushing off to Vegas to get married was impulsive, but our feelings for one another were real."

"If that's true, why'd you run off to New York only a few weeks later?" he challenged.

"Because it hurt too much to stay," she confided.

"Because *he* hurt you," Gramps said accusingly.

"Because *everything* hurt. But leaving didn't mean I stopped loving him. And I still love him," she said, imploring him to understand. "And despite the nasty things you said when you found out I'd married him, Gramps, I still love you, too."

He opened his mouth, as if there was something he wanted to say, then closed it again and turned away.

* * *

"Wake up, sleepyhead."

Brie snuggled deeper under the covers of Caleb's enormous bed. "Can't I stay here all day today? Please."

"Sorry," he said. "We've got other plans."

"This is payback, isn't it? I dragged you all over Manhattan when you came to visit me, so you're not going to let me have a moment of peace while I'm here."

"Actually, I'm dragging you away from here to guarantee that we'll have some peace."

She pulled the covers away from her face. "Tell me more."

"I'll tell you anything you want to know—after you get your butt out of bed and get dressed."

So she did, then followed the smell of coffee down the stairs and into the kitchen, where Caleb was packing containers and drinks into an insulated bag.

"You made lunch?"

"Actually, my grandmother made it for us. Leftover turkey sandwiches, coleslaw and pumpkin pie."

"Yum." She immediately reached for a container of pie—and had her hand slapped away. "Hey."

"It's for lunch," he reminded her.

"But I'm hungry now," she protested.

"Have a muffin."

Pouting just a little, she reached into the basket on the counter. "They're still warm."

"Fresh out of the oven," he told her.

"Your grandmother again?" she guessed.

He nodded.

She bit into the muffin, sighed with pleasure. He half filled a travel mug with coffee for her, then topped it up with a generous splash of milk. Per the doctor's suggestion, she'd cut down on her caffeine consumption but still indulged in a single cup in the morning.

"Are you ready?" he asked.

She nodded and grabbed a second muffin.

"So where are we going?" she asked, when Caleb had stored the food in the backseat of the Jeep and slid behind the wheel.

"To the cabin."

"At Crooked Creek?"

He nodded.

"You're going to trespass on Blake property?"

"It's only trespassing if you get caught."

"I'm not sure that's true," she cautioned. "You should probably check with your sister about the legal definition of that—preferably *before* my grandfather shows up with a shotgun."

"I don't think your grandfather ventures that far out anymore."

"I hope not," she said.

It took them fifteen minutes to drive to the fence that marked the boundary between the properties, and another five minutes, after they'd climbed over the barrier, to hike to the cabin.

The frigid air felt even colder with the wind that blew across the open field, and they were almost at their destination when Caleb realized he'd forgotten their lunch. He sent Brie on ahead to the shelter while he went back for it.

She found the key where it had always been kept—tucked in a slot under the window by the front door. After unlocking the cabin, she stomped her feet on the mat to knock the snow off her boots and stuffed her mittens into the pockets of her jacket.

The simple box-like structure wasn't just rustic but primitive, without any electricity or heat, so she unzipped her coat but kept it on for now. The overcast day didn't provide much light to illuminate the interior of the cabin, but she knew there would be a kerosene lamp on the counter with a box of matches beside it. She quickly found both and lit the lamp.

She'd been a little apprehensive when Caleb had mentioned the cabin, unable to predict how she'd feel to return to the place where they'd spent so much time together in the past. And she braced herself for the assault of memories as she looked around the room.

The wood table, scarred from years of use, had been built by her great-great-grandfather as a wedding gift for his bride. Years later, when they'd replaced the set with something fancier and more expensive, his table and chairs—there had been four that matched it—were moved into the cabin.

Rumor had it that a couple of ranch hands, stranded for nearly a week by a raging blizzard, had broken down three of the chairs for firewood when their supply had run out. The single ladder-back that remained was flanked now by a paint-splattered Windsor style chair on one side and one that looked like a reject from a '50s diner on the other.

She'd lost track of the number of times she'd shared a makeshift meal with Caleb at that table with its trio of mismatched chairs. But she had a very clear memory of the time he'd snuck up to the cabin in advance of their arrival to set a romantic scene for her. There had been place mats and napkins and slender candles in fancy holders that he'd snuck out of Evelyn's china cabinet. They'd nibbled on cheese and crackers and sipped fruit punch out of crystal glasses—also borrowed from his grandmother.

And then they'd made love on the narrow and rickety cot tucked against the wall. The thin mattress hadn't been comfortable enough that anyone would want to sleep on it, but it served the purpose for a cowboy stranded overnight—or a couple of teenagers who cared only about being together.

At some point during the past seven years, that cot had been replaced by an actual twin-size bed covered by a rail-fence quilt, while the old woolen blankets that she remembered were tossed over the back of the ancient sofa in the middle of the room. An equally ancient chair and wobbly end table completed the small clustering of furniture that faced the stone fireplace.

A narrow door on the adjacent wall opened to a tiny bathroom—a late addition to the construction of the cabin and useless during the winter months, when the water was shut off and the pipes emptied to ensure they wouldn't burst in the frigid temperatures.

She peeked into the pantry, noted at least half a dozen jugs of water, various canned goods and other nonperishable food items stored securely in sealed plastic containers. Gramps had always kept the cabin stocked for emergencies, though she suspected it was her brother Spencer who saw to the supplies now. She moved some cans around and finally found what she was looking for: a jar of homemade sweet pickles with a neatly marked label in familiar handwriting.

She brushed the dust off the lid, remembering the kind and loving woman who'd prepared the cucumbers in brine before slicing and packing them into jars, adding the vinegar solution and sealing the containers in a boiling water bath. Anna Blake would be so disappointed to know that hard feelings lingered between her husband and his granddaughter as a result of things that had been said seven-and-a-half years earlier, but Brie didn't know how to break the distance that had grown between them and her grandfather had given no indication that he wanted to.

She set the jar back on the shelf, tucking it behind the cans of beans and chili, and closed the pantry.

A blast of wind announced Caleb's arrival. He muscled the door shut and stomped his feet as Brie had done, then set the bag of food on the table before shrugging out of his jacket and hanging it on a hook by the door.

"It's chilly in here," she warned.

"Not for long," he promised, making his way to the stockpile of wood beside the fireplace.

"What do you want me to do?" she asked, as he picked through the logs.

"Sit down and relax," he suggested.

"I'm not helpless, you know."

"I know, but I promised you a lazy day, so that's what you're going to have."

She had no objection to that plan, but she moved the lamp closer, to provide additional light for Caleb while he completed his task.

He topped the stack of logs with paper and twigs. After opening the damper, he struck a match. True to his word, it wasn't long at all before flames were crackling and dancing.

With the fire providing sufficient light and heat now, she lowered the wick in the lamp to extinguish it and returned it to its usual place on the counter. When she moved closer to the fire again, Caleb tugged off the hat she'd forgotten she was still wearing and helped remove her jacket, then hung both items by the door.

"It looks different in here," he noted.

She nodded. "The curtains on the windows are new. And the quilt on the bed. Both Kenzie's doing, I'd bet."

"I never considered that your brother and sister-in-law might use this place," he admitted.

"I don't think we need to worry about them coming out here only a few weeks after the birth of their baby."

"Thank goodness for that," he said.

"Why? He was civil at Thanksgiving dinner, wasn't he?"

"Yeah, but I figured that was only because there were too many witnesses to kill me then and there."

"Kenzie wouldn't let him kill you," she promised. "She grew up without a father and wouldn't want our child to do the same."

"I feel so much better now," he said dryly.

She nudged him with her shoulder. "They'll come around."

"It might have helped if you'd told them we were married before you told them that we were going to have a baby."

"They know now," she pointed out. "And so does your family. Though Sky looked more worried than happy to hear that she was going to be an aunt again. And her questions about my career plans weren't exactly subtle."

"She thinks you're going to break my heart again," he confided.

"Should I remind her that you broke mine, too?"

"No." He shook his head. "Because that's the past and we need to focus on our future."

"You do know that if I ever decided to move back to Haven, every major holiday would be like Thanksgiving."

He nodded. "It's too bad you didn't really enjoy cuddling with your nieces and brand-new nephew."

"Too much cuteness crammed into one room," she remarked.

"Far too much," he agreed.

Of course, they were both joking.

And while Brie had been helping with the babies, she'd listened to her sister and sisters-in-law talk about how excited they were to have children close in age who would grow up together. And how lucky their babies were that they'd have so many cousins to play with—when they were big enough to actually play.

They *were* lucky, Brie realized.

She'd also realized that she wanted her child to benefit from the same close family connections. Which would be impossible if they were living twenty-five hundred miles away.

"So you'll move back to Nevada."

Caleb's words from weeks earlier echoed in her mind now.

"Not just because of two little lines," he'd argued. "Because those lines represent our baby."

She'd dismissed his suggestion out of hand, because she wasn't going to let anyone else—even the father of her child—make decisions about her future.

But she wanted to be with Caleb. She wanted to live with him in his house on the Circle G—and help him pick out furniture to transform that house into a home where they would live and laugh and love together. She wanted to turn the spare bedroom closest to the master into a nursery for their baby. And then fill the other rooms with more children. Because more than anything, she wanted a family and a future with him.

But before she could share this realization with him, he said, "I got a call from the ranching co-op on Long Island yesterday. They offered me a job."

Chapter Sixteen

Though only three weeks had passed since his interview, Brie had almost forgotten that he'd applied for another job. Because she'd been certain that even if they offered it to him, he'd never take it. Because he'd never want to leave the Circle G.

Now she didn't know what to think, what to say. But he was obviously waiting of her to say *something*.

"They told me that I had forty-eight hours to give them an answer," he said, when she remained silent. "But of course, I'm going to take it."

"You are?"

He frowned, no doubt confused by her lackluster response. "It's what you wanted, isn't it? To stay in New York?"

She couldn't blame him for thinking so when she'd told him exactly that countless times over the past two months. But in the past two days, everything had changed.

"Actually, I want to have our baby here."

"Here?" He looked around. "In the cabin?"

She laughed then. "No. I definitely want to be in a hospital with access to pharmaceutical pain management—just in case. I meant here in Haven," she clarified. "Well, Battle Mountain, probably, since that's the nearest hospital."

"But…your doctor's in New York," he reminded her.

"Obviously I'm going to have to find a doctor a little closer," she acknowledged.

His only response was a slow nod.

"I thought you'd be happier about this."

"I am happy," he said, his tone cautious. "I'm also a little worried that this might be an impulsive decision, and I don't want you to have any regrets later."

"The truth is, I've been thinking about it since those two lines appeared in the window of the pregnancy test, but I was afraid to admit it was what I wanted.

"I was barely eighteen when we got married," she reminded him. "And pregnant and terrified. I didn't object when you said we were going to Vegas, because I wanted to marry you. Just…maybe not so soon. I didn't protest when you said we had to keep our plans a secret from our families, because I knew they wouldn't approve.

"Then we lost the baby, and I didn't argue when my parents told me that there was a way to undo all the mistakes I'd made. Because I knew I'd made mistakes—I'd been reckless and irresponsible, and it only seemed right to try to fix things.

"Moving to New York was the first decision *I'd* made. And when you suggested that I should come back to Haven, I think I was afraid such a move would somehow undo that decision and undermine my independence.

"It took me a while to put all of that aside and think about what I really wanted—for you and me and our baby. But now the answer is obvious. I want to have our baby here, with you by my side. I want us to live together as husband and wife, right next door to both of our crazy feuding families."

"It sounds like you've given this some thought," he acknowledged.

"I'm sorry it took me so long to figure it out."

He touched his fingertips to her lips. "Didn't we agree to forget about the past and look to the future?"

She nodded. "I want my future to be with you—every day, for the rest of our lives together."

"I want that, too."

"Of course, I'll have to go back to New York to give notice to my principal and pack up my stuff," she pointed out to him.

"And tell Grace and Lily," he said, his tone indicating he didn't envy her *that* task.

But she wasn't concerned. "I think they already know."

"How can they already know if you only made up your mind right now?"

"Because they know my heart," she said. "It was my head that needed some time to catch up."

"You all caught up now?" he wondered.

She smiled and leaned forward to touch her lips to his. "Almost," she said, and began unbuttoning his shirt.

"Um, Brie?"

"Hmm?" she asked, her attention focused on her task.

"I brought you here because I wanted some time alone with you where we weren't likely to be interrupted by one of my sisters or your brothers or anyone else," he told her. "I didn't bring you up here to seduce you."

"I know." She pushed his shirt over his shoulders, then yanked his thermal undershirt out of his jeans and slid her hands beneath it. "That's why *I* decided to seduce *you*."

"Are you sure about this, darlin'?"

"I'm sure."

"And it's…safe?"

"Well, I'm already pregnant, so I don't think we need to worry about birth control," she teased.

"I meant safe for the baby," he clarified.

"I know what you meant," she said. "And yes, it's safe."

"In that case," he said, and whisked her sweater up and over her head.

She chuckled softly. "I love that you're so easy."

"I love *you*," he said, and kissed her again.

She wanted to respond, to tell him that she loved him, too, but her mouth was too busy kissing him back to worry about words.

When he had her stripped down to her undergarments, he paused and touched a finger to the ring that dangled from the chain around her neck. "I wondered what you'd done with it."

"I wasn't ready to put it back on my finger," she admitted. "But I wanted it close to my heart." Then she drew his mouth down to hers again. "And now I want you."

He yanked the quilt off the bed and spread it out on the floor by the fire. Then he lifted her into his arms and lowered her gently onto the cover.

"Okay?" he asked.

"Very okay," she responded.

He eased away, just far enough so that he could look at her. His gaze skimmed from the top of her head to the tips of her toes, a leisurely and thorough perusal.

Suddenly aware of her nakedness and growing belly, she reached for the edge of the cover to pull it over herself. But he caught her wrist, thwarting her effort.

"You are so beautiful," he said, the reverence in his tone assuring her of his sincerity.

"I'm going to get fat," she warned.

"I can't wait."

She smiled. "You're a strange man, Caleb Gilmore."

"Because I want the world to see my baby growing inside you?"

"There's plenty of evidence of our baby already," she told him.

He splayed his palms over the slight curve of her belly, so that they covered the baby in her womb. "Are you still having nausea?"

"Hardly ever now."

"That's not a *no*," he noted.

"I'm not feeling nauseated now," she assured him.

He smiled at that. "Your breasts are bigger."

"I didn't think that would escape your notice."

He moved his hands now and lightly traced the edge of her bra, his fingertips skimming delicate lace and silky skin. "Are they more sensitive?"

She nodded.

He dipped his head to touch his lips to the creamy flesh, then nuzzled the hollow between her breasts, making her shiver.

He released the clasp at the front of her bra and slowly peeled back one of the cups, exposing her flesh a fraction of an inch at a time. His lips followed the same path, skimming over her skin. She closed her eyes on a sigh as his mouth closed around the taut peak of her nipple, suckling gently. She threaded her fingers through his hair, holding his head close to her breast as heat began to build low in her belly, flickering like the flames in the hearth.

He shifted his focus to her other breast, giving it the same care and attention, then hooked his fingers in her panties and tugged them over her hips, down her legs, before finally tossing them aside. Then he worked his way back up again, brushing his lips over her ankle, skimming her calf, the inside of her thigh. Higher.

Their first time together had been here, in this cabin. But unlike that first time, when everything was new and unfamiliar, she had a good idea about what to expect this time. She knew how he could make her feel, all the ways he could please her—and she knew how to please him, too.

She marveled at the contrast of smooth skin and hard muscle as she explored the contours of his body with her hands and her mouth, pleasing him as he'd pleased her. She swirled her tongue around his hard, velvety length, licking from base to tip, then parted her lips to take him in her mouth. A low growl sounded deep in his throat and he wrapped his hand in her hair and tugged gently, to draw her away. "Brie. Please. You have to stop."

She recognized the desperation in his voice, knew he was close to the edge. And though she was tempted to ignore his plea, glorying in the knowledge that she had to power to push him over, she acceded to his request—and her own desire.

She straddled his hips with her knees. She was already wet, more than ready, and her thigh muscles quivered as she pushed her hips forward to take him inside. Though she was on top and he was letting her set the pace, she knew better than to assume she was in control. As he proved when he reached down to where their bodies were joined and brushed a callused thumb over the ultrasensitive nub at her center. She gasped as pleasure jolted through her.

She bent forward to brush her mouth against his, and he surged upward, burying himself even deeper. She grasped his shoulders, holding on to him as their bodies merged and mated, seeking and finding a rhythm that drove them toward their mutual pleasure and beyond.

"I've missed this," she said, after she'd collapsed on top of him and managed to catch her breath again.

"Sex?" he queried.

She smiled as his hand stroked lazily down her spine. "That, too," she agreed. "But even more, I've missed just being with you."

"Me, too," he said. "That's probably why there hasn't been anyone since you."

"You mean, since Las Vegas?" she guessed.

"I mean since our first time together," he clarified.

She tipped her head back to look at him. "But... I've been gone for seven years."

"I'm not saying I didn't date. And it wasn't unusual for a date to end with a good-night kiss. But anytime there was a possibility of it going any further—I just couldn't," he confided. "We were still married, whether you knew it or not, and I couldn't break the vows I'd made to you."

"I didn't know we were still married," she reminded him gently.

"I know. And that's okay. I don't expect—"

"But even without knowing, even without a ring on my finger, my heart always belonged to you," she interjected. "It always has. It always will. And that's why there's never been anyone but you."

"I love you, Brie."

"Last night, when we were snuggled up in bed, I didn't ever want this weekend to be over," she confessed. "Now I can't wait to go back to New York."

His brows lifted. "I just told you I loved you and you responded by telling me that you're leaving."

She smiled. "I love you, too. But I'm eager to get back to pack up and prepare for our life together here."

"You're sure about this? You're not going to change your mind again when you're in New York?"

"I'm not going to change my mind," she promised. "When you assumed I'd move back to Haven so that we could raise our baby together, I dug in my heels to prove that I was in charge of making my own decisions.

"But just because me moving back to Haven is what you want doesn't mean it's not my decision, too. Because it is what I want, more than anything."

"That makes my next decision easier," he said.

He eased away from her then and reached for his jeans. After pulling them on, he walked over to the table and reached into the bag he'd packed with their lunch.

"Did you decide that we can have pie before sandwiches?" she asked hopefully.

But when he turned back around, she saw that it wasn't a food container in his hand but a plush toy.

"You once told me that a teddy bear was a gift," he reminded her.

"I remember." She accepted the offering, her fingers sinking into the shaggy, soft fur. "Oh, Caleb. He's adorable."

"He?" he asked, amused.

"Well, his name is Teddy," she pointed out.

"Well, he's a gift for you. And this—" he tugged on the end of the blue satin ribbon around the bear's neck, releasing the bow and the stunning two-carat diamond solitaire ring it had secured in place "—is a promise."

She swallowed. "That's a heckuva promise."

"I want you to be my wife, Brie. I want you to live with me and raise a family with me, and for us to spend every day of the rest of our lives together."

For a man of few words, he'd somehow managed to put all the right ones together. As happiness filled her heart to overflowing, she felt compelled to remind him: "We're already married."

"But, as you pointed out a few weeks back, I never actually proposed," he said, and dropped to one knee. "So I'm asking you now, Brielle Channing—will you stay married to me, for today and all the rest of our tomorrows?"

"It's Brielle Gilmore," she said, smiling. "And yes, I will stay married to you, Caleb Gilmore. Forever."

And they sealed their promises with a kiss.

Epilogue

Brielle gave her notice to the principal of Briarwood Academy when she returned to New York after Thanksgiving. Her resignation was effective in the New Year, allowing her to move back to Haven at the start of the Christmas break. Five months later, she didn't have any regrets.

Sure, there were some aspects of life in the big city that she missed—including the variety of restaurants that allowed her to eat any kind of food she wanted without having to cook it. But under the patient tutelage of Caleb's grandmother, she was trying different recipes and learning to cook new things—including Evelyn's famous pot roast. And she sometimes missed her friends, though she kept in regular contact with Grace and Lily.

She was a little disappointed that, despite her incessant pleas, her former roommates had yet to make the trip west. She understood that they both had busy lives, especially now that Grace had been promoted from editorial assistant to assistant editor and Lily had added volunteering at a local retirement community to her schedule, and she tried to be satisfied with frequent, if irregular, FaceTime communications.

But her life with Caleb was everything she'd always imagined it would be, only better because it was real. She fell asleep in his arms every night and woke up with him every morning.

It was only in the past few weeks that she'd started to feel bored and restless. The baby's room was ready: the walls and trim freshly painted, the furniture delivered and set in place. The change table was stocked with all the essentials, and the dresser contained a modest selection of tiny onesies and footed sleepers.

They hadn't gone overboard buying a lot of stuff because they still didn't know the sex of their baby, having decided—after much debate—to wait and find out in the delivery room. Of course, everyone in town had an opinion one way or the other. Frieda Zimmerman said she could tell by the way Brielle was carrying that it was going to be a boy. Judy Talon argued that the roundness of her belly suggested a girl. Jo Landry said boy; Sheila Enbridge said girl. Sky and Macy both voted boy; Regan and Alyssa put tallies in the girl column.

Caleb chimed in only to suggest that he wouldn't mind if the Gilmores added a boy to the roster, just to even things out a little—especially since his sister Kate had recently confirmed that she and the sheriff were expecting their second child and already knew Tessa was going to get a little sister.

Brie just hoped the question would be answered soon. Though there were still five days until her due date, she felt as if she'd been pregnant forever and was eager for their baby to be born.

"Where are you going?" she asked, when Caleb scooped his keys off the counter one Saturday morning late in May.

"Out," he told her.

She frowned at the uncharacteristically vague response. "Out where?"

"I've got an errand to run."

"Can I come with you?"

"Not this time," he said.

She pouted. "Why not?"

"Because I'm picking up a surprise for you."

Her mood immediately lifted. "What kind of surprise?"

He shook his head. "If I told you, it wouldn't be a surprise, would it?"

"I guess not," she admitted. Then, "How long are you going to be gone?"

"Why?"

"Because we're supposed to be at The Stagecoach Inn by four o'clock for the surprise baby shower."

He winked. "Just remember to act surprised."

"I've been practicing for weeks," she said.

Her sister was the one who'd slipped and told her about the shower, though Regan argued that it wasn't really a slip because no one had told her that the event, cohosted by the grandparents on both sides in an effort to prove to the expectant parents that they could—and would—get along, was supposed to be a surprise.

"Good." He bent to brush a quick kiss over her lips. "I'll be back by three."

"Back from where?" she asked.

His only response was a chuckle as he made his way to the door.

She'd thought she would have to pretend to be surprised, but when Brielle walked into the restaurant and saw Grace and Lily were there, her surprise was real. As were her tears of joy when she hugged them—as best she could around her enormous belly.

She wanted to spend hours catching up with her friends, but this was a baby shower, which meant there was food to be eaten and gifts to be opened. One of the leather wing chairs from the hotel lobby had been brought into the room for the expectant mother, and Brie happily sank into it, then wondered if she would ever be able to get out again.

While she chatted with various guests, her gaze skimmed around the room and her heart filled with happiness to see so many of her family and friends gathered together. Even Gramps was in attendance, and currently in conversation with Dave Gilmore—who had recently gotten engaged to Valerie Blake.

"How are you holding up?" Caleb asked, setting a plate of finger sandwiches on the table beside her chair.

"I'm doing okay," she said. "Just trying to anticipate who's going to draw first blood."

He chuckled. "I don't think you need to worry—everyone seems to be on their best behavior."

"That's what's making me nervous." But she turned her attention to the plate he'd brought for her and frowned as she perused the offerings. "I don't see any of the little cupcakes."

"Dinner before dessert," he reminded her.

"Are you going to be this strict with our baby?"

"I guess we'll see."

She smiled, excited to know that it wouldn't be too much longer before they'd have a chance to do exactly that. "Yes, we will," she agreed.

"Are you sure you're okay?"

"Yeah." She picked up a peanut butter and banana pinwheel sandwich and took a bite. "Why do you ask?"

"Because you're holding your back."

"Am I?" She dropped her hand away. "I didn't realize I was, but I guess I have been having some twinges."

His brows lifted. "Contractions?"

"Twinges," she said again.

"Maybe we should call your doctor."

"I'm fine," she said. "But maybe…"

"What? Tell me what you need. Anything."

"One of those little chocolate cupcakes would be nice."

His gaze narrowed. "Did you just play me?"

She smiled sweetly. "And one—no, two—of your grandmother's pineapple squares."

And after her sweet tooth was satisfied, at least for the moment, they turned their attention to the mountain of presents.

There were practical gifts—an infant carrier, a baby swing, an exersaucer, a portable play yard; fun gifts—a soft elephant that rattled, floating bathtub toys, a musical night-light; and keepsake gifts—a silver spoon, a picture frame, a set of Bunnykins.

There was also a quilt from Kate and Reid, handmade by a deputy in the sheriff's office, and a coupon for five hours of free babysitting services from Ashley—who promised she'd babysit whenever they wanted but was clear that, after the first five hours, it would cost them.

Grace and Lily gave an adorable onesie with a graphic depicting the New York City skyline and a trio of yellow baby carriages in lieu of the city's infamous yellow cabs, along with a gift certificate for Pink Olive—Brie's favorite shop for unique baby gifts in Brooklyn—with the stipulation that she had to bring the baby to New York for a visit so they could all go shopping in Park Slope together.

When all the gifts had been unwrapped, Caleb helped her to her feet—because standing up wasn't an easy task when she was carrying an extra twenty-two pounds in the shape of a beach ball at her middle—so that they could thank their guests.

"Wait—there's one more present," Margaret said, gesturing for Spencer and Jason to bring it forward.

Her brothers approached with the last and very cumbersome gift. Although a blanket had been draped over it, Brie could tell, by its shape and size, that it was a cradle.

"Who's it from?" she asked, because there was no card attached.

Her mother's soft smile surprised Brie as much as Margaret's response: "Your grandfather."

She searched the room until she found him, standing at the back, looking as if he wanted to be anywhere but there. So she turned her attention back to his gift, pulling away the blanket to reveal elegant lines and a glossy finish.

A long time ago, before the birth of his first child, Jesse Blake made a cradle. And each of his children—including Brie's mother—slept in that infant bed. Years later, it was tucked away in the attic at Crooked Creek Ranch, where it remained until Dani found it while exploring the dusty storage area.

To Brie's knowledge, her grandfather had never made another cradle. He'd occasionally puttered around with other things—bookcases, coffee tables, storage units—until his arthritis got so bad that it was painful to hold his tools.

And yet, he'd created this for her baby.

No, not just her baby—hers and *Caleb's* baby.

The same frustratingly stubborn man who'd refused to apologize for interfering in her relationship with Caleb nearly eight years earlier had gifted them with this beautiful heirloom. Was the cradle a way of saying he was sorry without using the words? Was it proof that he was willing to not only accept their relationship but celebrate their child?

"Gramps, this is incredible." She stroked a hand over the side rail, painstakingly sanded to a satin-smooth finish. "When did you find the time to do this?"

"Here and there," he said, with a shrug that suggested it was no big deal.

But Brie knew it was a big deal, even before Kenzie said, "He's been working on it, almost nonstop, since Thanksgiving."

"Tattletale," Gramps grumbled.

Caleb's hand tightened on hers when Jason pulled the

cover all the way off to reveal the name that had been carved in the headboard: GILMORE.

She shifted her gaze and saw the same surprise and pleasure she felt reflected in her husband's expression. The tears that she'd made such a valiant effort to hold in check refused to be held any longer as she breached the distance to her grandfather.

"Thank you." The whispered words were wholly inadequate, but they were the most she could manage through a throat tight with emotion.

He responded by hugging her with a fierce strength that belied his years and attested to the love in his heart.

"You're welcome," he said, and when he finally released her, his eyes were a little misty, too.

He turned then, and Jesse Blake offered his hand to his granddaughter's husband, and Brie knew the day couldn't be any more perfect.

Then her water broke.

Ten hours later, Colton Jesse Gilmore entered the world with an indignant squall. His exhausted parents cried right along with him, overjoyed that finally they were a family.

* * * * *

COMING SOON!

We really hope you enjoyed reading this book. If you're looking for more romance, be sure to head to the shops when new books are available on

Thursday 8th August

To see which titles are coming soon, please visit

millsandboon.co.uk/nextmonth

MILLS & BOON

Coming next month

A SECRET, A SAFARI, A SECOND CHANCE
Liz Fielding

'Oh, look,' one of the women said, looking at the pinboard with photographs of all the pupils in the class. 'They have a photograph of you when you were here, Eve.'

Maria took a closer look.

'That's not Eve. She has green eyes. This is her little girl. Peter said you'd given a picture of her to the children yesterday,' she said. 'She is very like you as a child.'

'It's just the hair.'

The scent of the sea had warned her of his presence a split second before Kit spoke. Before he reached over her head and took the picture down to look at it more closely.

'This child is the image of my sister at the same age.'

She turned, her mouth working, but no words coming out. She didn't have to say anything. One look and he'd known.

'What is her name?' he asked.

Her tongue was stuck to the roof of her mouth and it took a moment before she could say, 'Hannah Rose Merchant Bliss.'

He glanced at her, a nod acknowledging the inclusion of Merchant. 'She's beautiful.'

'Yes.'

'When were you going to tell me?' he asked, those blue eyes unreadable, his voice even, unemotional. 'Were you ever going to tell me?'

The others, at a signal from Maria, had melted away, leaving them alone.

'No,' she admitted.

'Why, Eve? Why would you do this? Why didn't you tell me?'

'Why do you think?' she demanded. 'You meet a girl on a beach, have a one-night stand, then disappear.'

'I told you my name. All you had to do was pick up a phone.'

'And what? Ask for the money to take care of it?'

He took a step back as if she'd slapped him.

'You weren't hitting on me, remember? I jumped you and I chose to take responsibility for my own actions.'

'There were two of us in the room.'

'And then you left.'

He lifted a hand in a gesture at once helpless and exasperated. 'You know why!'

'Now I know. Then...' She shook her head, willing him to understand.

'Then you thought I'd had a good time and walked out on you.' She didn't want to tell him everything she'd thought. That was enough. 'Despite that, you chose to keep her,' he said, his voice softer.

'There was never any question about that, Kit. Hannah is my joy.'

'What about my joy?' he demanded. 'I have a child, a daughter, and you chose to keep her from me.'

Continue reading
A SECRET, A SAFARI, A SECOND CHANCE
Liz Fielding

Available next month
www.millsandboon.co.uk

LET'S TALK
Romance

For exclusive extracts, competitions
and special offers, find us online:

f facebook.com/millsandboon

𝕏 @MillsandBoon

◉ @MillsandBoonUK

Get in touch on 01413 063232

For all the latest titles coming soon, visit
millsandboon.co.uk/nextmonth

MILLS & BOON

THE HEART OF ROMANCE

A ROMANCE FOR EVERY KIND OF READER

MODERN

Prepare to be swept off your feet by sophisticated, sexy and seductive heroes, in some of the world's most glamourous and romantic locations, where power and passion collide.
8 stories per month.

HISTORICAL

Escape with historical heroes from time gone by. Whether your passion is for wicked Regency Rakes, muscled Vikings or rugged Highlanders, awaken the romance of the past.
6 stories per month.

MEDICAL

Set your pulse racing with dedicated, delectable doctors in the high-pressure world of medicine, where emotions run high and passion, comfort and love are the best medicine.
6 stories per month.

True Love

Celebrate true love with tender stories of heartfelt romance, from the rush of falling in love to the joy a new baby can bring, and a focus on the emotional heart of a relationship.
8 stories per month.

Desire

Indulge in secrets and scandal, intense drama and plenty of sizzling hot action with powerful and passionate heroes who have it all: wealth, status, good looks…everything but the right woman.
6 stories per month.

HEROES

Experience all the excitement of a gripping thriller, with an intense romance at its heart. Resourceful, true-to-life women and strong, fearless men face danger and desire - a killer combination!
8 stories per month.

DARE

Sensual love stories featuring smart, sassy heroines you'd want as a best friend, and compelling intense heroes who are worthy of them.
4 stories per month.

To see which titles are coming soon, please visit

millsandboon.co.uk/nextmonth

JOIN US ON SOCIAL MEDIA!

Stay up to date with our latest releases, author news and gossip, special offers and discounts, and all the behind-the-scenes action from Mills & Boon...

 millsandboon

 millsandboonuk

 millsandboon

It might just be true love...